THE EDICT

Book I of The She Trilogy

Works by P. J. Keyworth

HISTORICAL ROMANCE NOVELS

The Widow's Redeemer
The Unexpected Earl
Fool Me Twice

HISTORICAL ANTHOLOGY

Castle, Customs, and Kings: True Tales by English Historical Fiction Authors

THE EDICT

Book I of The She Trilogy

By

P. J. KEYWORTH

For Him who saved me

The Kingdom of Emrilion

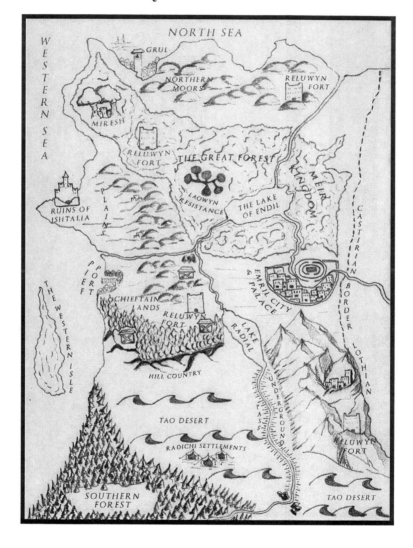

Prologue

B efore the guttering fire was allowed to flicker into oblivion, a small servant scurried over to bank it with fresh logs. Smoke billowed out from the irritated fire but did little to cover the stench of fever, and now in these late stages, of putrefaction.

Thick tapestries showing great battle scenes hung on the walls of the chamber. Rich fabrics covered the furnishings, whilst deer furs were piled high upon the bed. All of them filthy. Weeks without fresh air had seen to that. Servants, fearful of causing the King's sickness to worsen, had stopped up the windows and any other opening that might cause a draft. Death was present. Everything smelt of it.

Every servant who ran in and out with remedies demanded by healers feared what was coming. Every courtier who came to see how soon they could expect the King to die and their position solidified or rendered obsolete by a new regime. All of them wore fear on their faces.

The King's gnarled fingers gripped at the fur covers with what little strength they had left, his lined face creasing, his thoughts drifting between consciousness and other realms. The healer had not left his side, and in all honesty Garesh found the man an utter fool. His ridiculous ceremonial costumes fashioned from the skins and heads of wildcats were of no help to a feverish King. Then again, perhaps the King's second-in-command should be happy. As High Councillor to King Emril, so close to absolute power, Garesh didn't want his superior to recover. He wanted him to die.

King Emril had reigned with power, raising the Reluwyn from an independent kingdom of settled nomads. Now they ruled an empire that spanned half the known world hubristically named Emrilion. He had been a ruthless king, his cruelty furthered his domination and his single-mindedness was never questioned by his subjects; but now that time was over and Garesh had waited long for this. He was ready to rise up, all that was needed was the King's signature scrawled upon the Regency document Garesh had already drawn up. After all, Emrilion had no Queen. Emril's wife had been deemed by him a threat to his power, and so he had dealt with her accordingly. Her Alakvalto blood, which drew from an ancient shape-shifting magic, had been her undoing. No King of the Reluwyn could allow himself to be seen as second to his Queen. The marriage had served a purpose. Then it had not. The King had signed an Edict condemning all Shifters to death, supressing their kind and accusing them of being influenced by dark spirits. Queen Anis had been burned alive, cleansed of her dark spirits, and her own husband had watched. Now an entire ancient magic was left in the realms of silence.

For Garesh, such a move had unwittingly cleared the way for ascension to power as regent upon Emril's death. No one had expected the tenacious King to catch fever with the rest of the crowded Emril city, but he had. Despite the lack of a mature heir to call upon, Emril was ever wilful, until now refusing to hand over any of the power he had spilt rivers of blood to build. The only hope left was to bring the young Prince Trevisian to the dying King, and hope that the boy's presence would persuade him to sign the document in the pocket of Garesh's silk robe. As regent, Garesh would rule in the boy's stead until his taking of a wife as Reluwyn custom dictated. Then the Prince would be elevated to Kingship. When that time came Garesh would make the decision on what to do next. Until then, he needed to secure his power.

The High Councillor was going for the boy now. He strode through the palace with all the purposefulness that had once led him out of the courtier's muck heap and up to the King's right hand. The robe he wore flared out behind him and his leather shoes thudded on the tiled floors. He passed walls with frescoes depicting the ascent of the Reluwyn, from a tribe in the Tao desert into a mighty nation. The quickest way to get to Prince Trevisian's chambers was to pass through a fountain courtyard made of sandstone, the chambers off it containing the King's numerous concubines. Since the King's illness, Garesh had taken to passing by those rooms more often.

This time, however, he did not stop but went on. He passed the fountain which had frozen on the first day of true winter, its icy shards suspended, waiting for the first day of spring to release them. He entered the Hall of Banners where all the bloodlines of the Reluwyn - apart from that of the Alakvalto - were represented. Courtiers and council members milled about, waiting for news of the King, forming factions and fighting amongst themselves.

Garesh, usually taking his time to flatter and persuade the most influential courtiers, instead skirted the main throngs and headed to the left of the great stone columns. He had no time to waste: the healer had said the King would die any day, and without that document signed Garesh's plan would surely fail. No amount of flattery would be able to unite the courtiers and council members under his authority without the King's signature.

He took a side door from the hall and headed to the north of the palace. The Prince's rooms were soon reached and Garesh strode into the brightly painted seating chamber that looked out onto the heart of the palace: a jewelled courtyard.

Trevisian's dark head was bent over the stick he was carving, while in the corner his tutor sheathed a pair of swords, no doubt from a recent training session. The boy started at Garesh's entrance. His eyes widened but quickly relaxed when they saw who it was.

"Out." Garesh's voice brooked no argument. In spite of the turmoil at court, he still held the highest sway. The tutor needed no second bidding, and obeyed the High Councillor without pause.

Garesh didn't even bother to watch the man leave, as his eyes were already focused on the Prince and, once the door had closed, he strode forward. The rapid movement caused the boy to drop the stick, which rattled to the floor, and hastily retreat to the window in the far wall.

"My Prince, do not be startled, I am come to take you to your father."

Trevisian said nothing. He took another step back, his eyes widening again.

"Your father is dying." Garesh didn't expect sorrow from the boy. The yellowing bruises visible on the Prince's neck when he had been bent over carving were reason enough for lack of tears. Garesh knew exactly what beatings felt like, but his thrashings had ceased with his mother's last breath. His pity for the boy was short-lived. After all, this pathetic creature was heir to an entire Kingdom, a position Garesh would kill for. Right now he needed the Prince to come to his father. "*You* are to be the new ruler."

"Ruler?" came the small boy's voice. He was not more than twelve. "Father is King," he said, as though nothing else made sense.

"For now, but you are his heir Trevisian. Do not be frightened. I know you fear the responsibility, but that is why I am here. We are to go to your father and ask that I may help you rule. Would you like that? Or would you like to do it all alone and make mistakes? Would you like to disappoint your father?"

This was the closest the young Prince had looked to crying. He stood very still, but did not answer. Garesh's impatience grew: they had to get back to the King.

"I can help you. But if you do not help me now, you will be alone, and there is no telling what could happen to you…" Garesh let his ominous words work on the child's imagination. "We wouldn't want what happened to your

Shifter mother to happen to you, would we? Isn't that why I told you to do as I said the other day? Now, will you come and do as you're told again?"

Whatever images the boy conjured in his mind, it was enough to make him nod his head. Without waiting for a change of mind, Garesh's hand reached out and grabbed the boy with his vice-like grip. He dragged the Prince after him, the child having to skip and run to keep up with the legs of the tall, thin man.

They entered the festering room where the King lay prone. His eyes were open now, their bright green irises a startling contrast to his white skin. He looked almost lucid, but his breathing remained shallow.

"My lord High Councillor," The healer bowed, "The King grows weak…" he trailed off, his eyes completing the sentence.

Garesh threw him a look of derision but said nothing. He had work to do.

"My Lord King," he said, kneeling beside the bed, taking the coarse, gnarled hands that had once wielded blades and sent armies on to victory. "I have brought your son." Garesh turned, keeping one hand on the King's, reaching the other to Trevisian who stood at the threshold. "Come," commanded Garesh. The boy flinched, instinctively making himself smaller, but he came. The little Prince knelt beside the bed and Garesh placed one of the boy's shaking hands on the King's.

King Emril turned his head. His eyes took in both faces – that of his councillor, sharp and lined; and that of his son, dark and young. His breathing became louder.

"I have been speaking with your son, Lord King. You may well get better… but if not, your time may be soon, and you have made no provision. Your son's young years make him ignorant, so he has asked that I guide him in his ruling, that the glorious Kingdom you created might endure."

"Weak…" wheezed the King. "Weak." His green eyes were hard upon his son's face.

"Young, my Lord King, only in need of guidance," Garesh continued doggedly. "I put myself forward to be his regent, Lord King. It is his wish, and best for your Kingdom. Will you sign the document, my Lord King?" The question was out and the King was angry. Now all Garesh could do was hope the King would die, for if he recovered, Garesh would lose far more than his position.

"No…" whispered the King. The slightest of movements indicated he wished to shake his head.

Garesh tightened his hand over the Prince's and the King's, his fingers claw-like. He glanced at Trevisian. Had the boy heard?

The King shuddered, his breathing harsh and ragged. The healer approached but Garesh swung around like a wild animal, cursing him away. This would not be the end, he could not let the King go peacefully without signing that document. He flung Trevisian's hand away and rose up, obscuring the Prince's view.

Garesh snatched up the quill from its inkstand beside the bed. The King still shook, his body spasming. Garesh wrenched the document from his own pocket, spreading it across the King's chest. The King's green eyes dulled, his breathing stopped, he finally lay still.

Behind him, Garesh could hear the voices of mourners, summoned by the healer. Had he been wailing like that this whole time? Garesh hardly knew. He felt the Prince's hand on his back. Did he know his father had died?

Garesh couldn't let this power slip away, not when it was so close. He seized the King's hand, placing the quill between dead fingers, marking the paper with the signature he had witnessed a thousand times. The ink glistened in the lamplight, a simple series of lines that slowly dried to an indelible mark, and the future of the Kingdom was set.

CHAPTER 1

10 Years Later

K iara drew the short sword from the sheath on her belt and worked quickly on the rope that bound the child's hands. She felt the bonds give way and moved onto the next child.

"Run, Talia," she called to the first. "Quietly. Keep to the shadows."

The little girl leapt up and darted to the cover of the nearest porch. There was a gathering of Imperial Guards further down the earthen street. They stood together muttering to each other, a good day's work done. As the two suns were setting, Kiara had come. She wouldn't let the Laowyn children be taken away from their mothers for palace slaves, no matter what her uncle said about obeying the ruling authorities. Damn the Reluwyn!

Another set of ropes broke under the stone-sharpened sword, and another child ran after Talia, darting in and out of the shadows of doorways before being lost in the alleys of Miresh.

"Rue, you must send a message to your parents to tell the others: the Reluwyn's are taking children for slaves; people must hide their children. Do you hear me?" Kiara whispered urgently. The young boy nodded and ran.

Kiara went to the last of the children, a boy, whimpering, younger than the others. When she took the ropes between her two hands the boy yelped and she froze, praying that the guards had not heard. Seconds ticked by. The murmur of voices had stopped.

Hearing nothing, but not daring to turn and look, Kiara began again on the ropes, but the movement of her arms gave her away.

"You! Stop! Stop in the name of the Prince!" The harsh command rang out against the wooden forest buildings.

"Run!" Kiara yanked the boy to his feet by the bonds she hadn't managed to cut yet, thrusting her sword into her belt. She pulled him into an alley to the left, not sure if the boy was even running or if she was simply dragging him. Her muscles burned with his weight. She turned left then right along another passage way.

The guards' legs were long and they were gaining on her. She heard something whistling through the air and a lancing, hot pain pierced her thigh. She stumbled, cursed and freed an arm from the boy to steady herself. She knew what they did to Laowyn woman, what their Prince permitted, she would not be taken alive. She caught sight of the dagger sticking out of her thigh. If she kept running she'd bleed to death before they took her, and she might just get the boy to safety.

A surge of adrenaline pulsed through her as she lunged sideways, her free hand finding the rim of a water jar and yanking it over. It crashed across the path behind her, the clay smashing and water flushing out. She stumbled forward, not looking back as her pursuer fell.

She made it to another junction in the maze of alleys, and as she desperately turned a corner a hand dragged her through a doorway. The door shut quickly behind her and the boy, leaving them both sprawled across the floor.

Immediately, hands were jammed over mouths to muffle their moans of pain. The kidnappers and kidnapped waited together in darkness.

Footsteps thudded past the door and Reluwyn shouts could be heard. Kiara's breathing was ragged. She felt the seep of warm blood run down her leg, but she still clutched at the boy.

After some time there was movement in the dark house.

"Will you be silent?"

Kiara nodded and knew the boy did so too. As she

rolled over onto her back, the dagger cut further in. She covered her face and groaned into her coat sleeve.

"And who is this young man, Kiara?" came the voice again. A familiar voice.

She hadn't realised just how close she had been to getting home.

"This is Raffy," she replied, between heavy breaths to control the pain.

"Raffy," repeated her uncle, suddenly illuminated.

Kiara's eyes ached but began to adjust as Djeck, her uncle's servant, walked towards them with the bright oil lamp. Uncle Zephenesh helped Raffy to his feet, though the boy still cried and attempted to collapse again.

Now unable to speak for the pain, Kiara pulled out her knife and threw it to Zephenesh, who swiftly cut the boy's bonds.

"Djeck, leave the light and take Raffy home. The Imperial Guards should be lost in the maze of alleys by now, but you must be careful."

Djeck obeyed without objection. He covered Raffy with his cloak before slipping out with the boy's hand firmly in his.

Zephenesh turned to his niece, and without a word began to tend her leg. He tied his own belt around her leg above the embedded dagger, tightening it without warning. Kiara wrenched upwards in pain.

"This will hurt." Her uncle took hold of the dagger's handle. Even the pressure of a hand felt like burning inside her thigh.

"No, no, no," gasped Kiara. She kept murmuring it, even when Zephenesh counted down from three, and another scream came when he pulled it out on two.

She felt the blood flow, but the belt did much to stem it. And then her uncle was up, gathering strips of fabric from the box of medicinal herbs and bandages that sat beside his bed in the adjoining room. He took a cup of water from a jar beside a bowl and poured it across the wound. By the time he was bandaging Kiara's leg she had passed completely out of consciousness.

❂❂❂

Over the North Sea, the two suns following the train of dusk, finally dropped their red heads down. Darkness descended unbidden over moorlands that stretched for miles beside the rolling waves, and crickets sang out their evening ballad from under the purple heather.

The Reluwyn thief, rising as darkness fell, stood halfway down one of the moorland hills listening to the sounds from the dirt track below. The parched earth of that ground was a perfect medium for carrying every sound. The heather-heads trembled as though they feared what was coming, the crickets were silenced.

Drawing back the wide cuff of his coat, he pulled an old friend from a leather holder on his forearm. In the moonlight, the small dagger reflected his sharp nose and dark eyes as he stabbed it into the stony hillside.

A three-day-old beard he had no intention of shaving blunted the hard lines of his square jaw. Dropping to his knees, he crouched until his ear was very close to the knife. His raven locks fell across his temple as he blocked out other noise with both hands.

Thud. Thud. Thud. One, no wait... a two-horse carriage. A heavy one judging by the vibrations, although it travelled at speed. He raised his head from the knife, dark eyes taking in the road below. At that pace it would only be a short while before the carriage came round that corner, and the driver would surely slow his horses to avoid the risk of turning over the carriage. That worked well for the thief. That worked perfectly.

He closed his eyes in the evening breeze, smelling the brine on the air that came up from the sea. Taking a deep breath, he let out a long, low whistle. That done, he tugged his dagger free of the dirt and returned it to its holder, rising as he did so.

Thin drabs of clouds were strewn across the star-laden canopy, obscuring the brilliant burning diamonds in places. The moon, just escaping the veil, let down a soft silvery light, casting the landscape in an eerie grey. Through this metallic world Dainus moved with fluidity. His great smooth flanks tensed repeatedly through his grand stride. His thick-crested neck let wild an ebony mane like black fire. His lustrous hooves met the rough heathery ground assuredly, although he moved with such rapidity. He responded to his master's summons like the flash of dark lightning.

Reaching the head of the hill on which his master stood, the horse slid with practiced skill to a timely halt, hocks sliding beneath him, hooves digging into the soil, skin quivering in the night air as he surveyed the valley below. He was as a night phantom: a shadow on the skyline, a trick of the light.

The thief's broad shoulders were straight and unflinching, his feet firmly planted on the side of the slope. With his back turned, he would have appeared ignorant of Dainus' presence, but for his hand beckoning the horse closer. Dainus picked his way slowly down the slope, barely making a sound, until his muzzle touched his master's outstretched hand.

The track still stood empty, but he saw the moonlight glinting off a carriage window on a distant bend in the road. The black horse's ears pricked up, listening to the far-off sounds of the wheels. Master and beast waited, the only movement around them was the wind in the heather and the carriage on the road.

With an unexpected suddenness, the thief deftly grasped the reins and launched himself into the saddle. Without waiting he drew a blade from beneath the folds of his coat. It sliced through the air, its double edge ending in a viciously sharp point. He twirled it unconsciously, licking his lips, tightening his grip.

The shift in weight was imperceptible, but the horse knew his master's will, gathering his haunches and bounding forwards down the hill.

Before they reached the track, the carriage appeared at the bend of the road. Saliva flecked with blood foamed at the horses' mouths as they cantered around the corner, the carriage leaning over, the fat driver squealing in dismay.

The thief did not expect the speed. He cursed the driver and adjusted his course. Dainus' head swung sideways, shifting the weight to his left as he swerved. His master didn't take his eye from the goal, riding on despite the change.

For a moment, the carriage seemed as though it would topple down the hill, but the horses stayed true to their course. The lumbering vehicle threw itself back onto all four wheels, jolting and thudding before settling.

The moment had come. The thief held his sword high, and seconds before colliding with the vehicle, let out an almighty cry.

The astonished driver, who had been distracted by steering the carriage, faced the oncoming rider headlong. His eyes widened and his hands froze on the reins, before he sprang to life, urging his horses on in an attempt to outrun the highwayman.

But the thief had not misplaced his trust in Dainus. The fearless beast kept on course and swung in front of the carriage rearing as he did so. The carriage horses slid to a shocked halt, one rearing in response, the other trying to bolt. The harness that had born the strain of the carriage's two-wheeled trip around the hillside finally gave up. Leather cracked and snapped. One horse escaped as the other wheeled around in circles, his bridle caught in the wreckage. The carriage shafts were forced into the dirt by the momentum, as the driver flew from his seat onto the ground.

Dainus hop-skipped out of the broken carriage's way, the thief staying in the saddle as the vehicle came to a final halt. The highwayman could not afford to lose his advantage: if there were guards inside, they would use their first opportunity to attack. The minutes ticked by but no one came out.

Dainus pranced in agitation, impatient to charge again. The thief reined him in and then dismounted. If anyone *was* in the carriage, they were in no fit state to fight. He let Dainus go and continued on foot. He was stilled by a groan coming from the foot of the opposite hill. The highwayman turned, approaching the noise cautiously. There was a tangled heap showered in shards of wood from the carriage shafts. When he got close, the thief could see the twisted form of the carriage driver. He cast his eyes over the body, its legs bent at inhuman angles and its face bruised and bloody.

"Mercy…" whispered the man, "Mercy…"

The thief was an ominous shadow to the driver, perhaps death had come to take him. A muscle jerked in the thief's jaw, he moved the blade in his hand, the point coming up under the driver's chin. One push, and the man would be dead. Temptation lingered and then the thief moved swiftly, turning the blade, kneeling and knocking the driver out with its black handle.

Something creaked by the carriage. The highwayman was quick to swing round, his sharp eyes picking out a dazed figure clinging haphazardly to the carriage door, swinging back and forth, unable to steady himself. The thief advanced. Poles to which the horses had been lashed were shattered, shards of the wood strewn everywhere and several of them crackled under his heavy boots. The stranger glanced up in acknowledgement of the thief's presence, muttering something inaudible.

The highwayman came to a halt before the traveller,

his cloak falling in heavy folds around him. Dark eyes took in an elderly man crowned with a ring of straggly grey hair. With age, the missing hair must have long migrated to his chin, to form a very long beard.

But it wasn't the traveller's hair or face, no, it was his attire that made the highwayman take a step back. He glanced around now, to ensure that no one else was present, then looked back at the man. He took in the deep navy of the silk tunic, the silver length of cloth that hung from each shoulder, the gold emblem of Emrilion pinned to the chest. This man was from the palace in Emril city. This man was a Reluwyn courtier.

People in the Northern Moor villages had long spoken of Reluwyn officials moving in the Kingdom, travelling far, carrying messages. The tittle-tattle had grown increasingly louder since the noose had tightened around racial differences. All of Emrilion were interested to know exactly what their Prince and High Councillor were planning. And even with his current nomadic existence, the thief had heard whispers.

Anyway, it didn't matter who the stranger was. His rank had proved that there was precious cargo inside this vehicle.

"You shall never get away with this," the old man's voice scraped like metal on stone.

The thief's eyes flicked from the open door of the

carriage to the man's face. He said nothing.

"I ride under the protection of the Reluwyn High Council."

Still the thief remained silent.

"Under the High Councillor Garesh!" The man's voice rose higher, courage winning against fear. "Under the Prince himself – he shall not let you go unpunished."

The thief's body tensed. His fingers were tight on the handle of his sword and he no longer leaned back on one leg. He set his thin lips in an uncompromising line, and his eyes blackened. "The Prince does not concern me, old man. But your cargo does."

Harsh rasping laughter sounded out. The man looked pained but he chose defiance. The thief would have admired his spirit if there wasn't still work to do.

"We carry nothing but the Prince's laws. He shall punish you for this. Your body shall hang on the gates of Emril city for the vultures to peck at."

"I think not." With that the thief did to him as he had done to the driver. The old man crumpled readily, his hands released from the door, his frame falling in the dirt.

Leaving the man behind, the thief determinedly followed the point of his sword into the carriage. The silk curtains billowed fitfully in the evening breeze; the cushions all thrown about in disarray. The carriage lay empty of inhabitants, empty of the treasure he'd hoped to find.

He sheathed his sword and began picking up cushions, throwing them into a pile, searching for anything of worth. His hands hit the wooden seat, ran along it, until they felt something cold, colder than wood. He drew out a silver box. Returning to the moonlight to examine it, the thief recognized the royal crest: a desert wildcat, like the Alakvalto Shifters of old had favoured when protection had been needed in the Tao desert. Pausing only briefly to take this in, the thief turned to opening the box.

It was locked. Perhaps if he could manage to smash off the crest, at least the silver box might fetch a little. Instead, the thief placed it on the ground and went to rifle the dead man's pockets for a key. His guess was right and before long he found what he was looking for. He unlocked the box, lifting up the lid. He cursed loudly. There was nothing in it but a paper sealed with dark red wax, stamped with the same wildcat emblem.

He broke it open seeing large archaic scrawls in old nomadic Reluwyn threading their way across the pages:

Provinces of Emrilion,

By royal proclamation, from the court of the Lord Prince Trevisian Alakvalto of the Kingdom of Emrilion, under the charge of lord High Councillor Garesh, all Kingdoms loyal to Emrilion, the Reluwyn, Meir Elves, Chieftains and Radichi Warriors, are to cease all trade and communication with the Laowyn.

A group of Laowyn, claiming to speak for their people, claiming they are a resistance against the Kingdom of Emrilion, are the root of insurrection within the Laowyn People. They are in direct conflict with Lord Prince Trevisian and the High Councillor Garesh and all free peoples of the Kingdom of Emrilion. No toleration shall be given to the Laowyn, no mercy shown, and no commercial interactions are henceforth permitted.

Any man, woman, or child found in contravention of this Edict, shall be found guilty of rebellion against the Lord High Crown Prince of Emrilion and sentenced to death by beheading.

This proclamation is being sent to every corner of Emrilion. All Laowyn who read this proclamation shall know that further insurrection will result in swift and crushing retribution with no further mercy shown. The Great Kingdom of Emrilion will not bow to rebellion.

By order of High Councillor Garesh.

Lord Prince Trevisian Alakvalto, Son of King Emril of the
Kingdom of Emrilion.

The thief crumpled the paper in his hands, dropping it in the dirt of the roadside. This was no concern of his.

CHAPTER 2

"Oh, you complete wretch!" Kiara's eyes flashed at her uncle who stood, sombrely watching the painful proceedings with a judgmental countenance.

"You're horrible! It's not as though I was the instigator - they were!" She drew in a gasp of air as Djeck ran another wet rag across the wound to clean it. "We're oppressed, when will you realise it uncle? You yourself have said the Reluwyn have been tightening the straps at our throats ever since we were conquered. We've been subsumed into an empire that is not our own."

"You speak as if you were there twenty years ago." Zephenesh was teasing her, Kiara could see the left side of his mouth twitching.

"Amuse yourself at my expense, why not? In this house at least one Laowyn won't bow to the Reluwyn's cruelty."

Zephenesh turned away, hiding his face from her. Curse him! Why did he not care? Why wouldn't he do something, anything, to stand against them?

"They were taking children, Uncle." Her voice became quiet with concern. "They were taking Laowyn children for their slaves. They say," she stumbled, half in pain, half in distress. "They say that when they take us they remove our mark, that which makes us Laowyn. They just cut it out."

"Dogs," Djeck muttered.

If Zephenesh heard, he made no indication. Instead he came forward and moved the shoulder of her tunic aside.

"Your Ensper is still blue, healthy."

"They don't understand us and so they persecute us. They don't trust us because we have a Great Spirit and they don't. But the Spirit has given me the ability to fight them, in whatever way I can, so don't judge me, Zephenesh! Don't judge me!"

She jerked away, causing the bandage to tighten around her leg far quicker than was desirable. "Be careful!" She winced a little as Djeck finished tying the linen.

"It's the price you pay for mischief," said the servant with typical elvish venom.

"So what happened to the dogs, the ones you curse?" hissed Kiara.

"I may curse them, but I will never condone a woman fighting. I'm no fool." Djeck was bustling around now, his rapid movements as sudden as flinching. Kiara was used to it. Djeck had been subjected to the Reluwyn's punishments when the Meir Elves were suppressed. How could beatings with willow rods be just, when all the Meir Elves had done was participate in their usual harvest fayre? And that was just for the common elven folk – the leaders had seen worse. Contravention of Reluwyn laws which suppressed local customs had always met with harsh reprisals. That's why Kiara hated the Reluwyn, hated the council, and hated the Prince.

"But you're foolish enough to doubt me. To doubt my hate, Djeck. Just because you do not stand in immediate danger doesn't mean you should do nothing, that we should do nothing!" Unlike those who didn't know her, the fierceness in those blue eyes did not daunt Djeck, not after this many years in Zephenesh's household.

"Neither is it clever to be completely reckless!" Zephenesh exploded. His usually calm demeanour fractured. "You were no match for one Imperial Guard, let alone more, no matter how many Laowyn they were harassing."

Now it was Zephenesh's turn to berate Kiara, Djeck resumed his normal chores.

"Our responsibility is to obey the rulers of this world, and to trust that the Great Spirit has control over them.

We must trust he will protect us."

"And maybe he gave me the ability to fight - to protect myself and others! What do you say to that, Uncle?"

"I only taught you how to use a blade because I thought it prudent." Zephenesh cast his hands up, although his face remained expressionless. "You are giving me cause to regret it!"

"Now you do not think it prudent? In the midst of this... this... suppression!" The sarcasm had quickly given in to fervour and Zephenesh had to give up. He had given up rather often lately.

Soon the noise in the small forest home was reduced to just the banging of pots, as Djeck heated meal and honey for breakfast. Zephenesh, having given in to silence, walked around the dwelling with his hands tucked in his sleeves, and every now and then turned to survey his glowering niece.

Breakfast, when served, was a silent and awkward affair. Kiara didn't lift her eyes from her plate, uncle and elf exchanged glances, and the meal was consumed quickly by all. Once it was over Kiara watched her uncle walk out the door. He would be going for one of his long walks no doubt. She would not see him again until the afternoon.

"A new proclamation reached Miresh yesterday," said Djeck, not looking up from scrubbing a saucepan. "I couldn't find you to tell you, and I didn't see you again until you came through the door with that knife stuck in you," he said accusingly. "All your people are considered to be in rebellion, although it's only the Laowyn Resistance that causes insurrection. All trade and commercial activity between the Laowyn and other races is prohibited. The Reluwyn plan to crush you through economic means."

The anger boiled up in Kiara again. Righteous indignation coursed through her and she wanted to rise up and cry out. Her injured leg prevented her, so instead she slammed a fist down onto the reclining table making a spoon jump and rattle.

"How long before we are starving do you think, Djeck?"

"A while yet, Kiara, a while yet."

"And yet my uncle is content to do nothing."

Djeck made a face at that but said nothing, carrying on his vigorous scrubbing in sullen silence. With a stab of sympathy Kiara realised that in choosing to continue his service here, Djeck was most likely choosing the same fate as the Laowyn.

She sighed in frustration at his silence. "It will get worse, I am sure of it. I just wish more of us would rise up against it before we are all condemned to die!"

"Oh, stop your sour talk!" snapped Djeck.

"It's not sour if it's true. I would give anything to join the Laowyn Resistance. At least they fight for what is right."

"They are defending, not seeking violence." He put down the pot he had finished and picked up the dirty spoon. "Besides, your uncle would die before he allowed you to follow your parents footsteps into the Resistance. He seeks the Great Spirit and peace above all else." Djeck eyed her over the handle of the spoon.

"There is no use in seeking peace when your enemy seeks war." Kiara ignored his mention of the more peaceful endeavours.

"Dramatic, considering all that's happened so far is a trade embargo."

Kiara rolled her eyes at Djeck's pragmatism. The Laowyn Resistance was all that what was left of the old Laowyn army that had fought King Emril in the wars that had seen the Laowyn conquered.

Rumours had been spreading since the Resistance had helped many of the Meir Elves escape punishment for their harvest fayre. They had protected many others from Reluwyn cruelty and they were increasingly all that made sense to Kiara. Zephenesh could argue for peace all he wanted, but violence in Emrilion was escalating and no amount of pacifism would stop the wave of aggression yet to come.

○○○

Garesh threaded his way like a fine needle between the courtiers that thronged the Hall of Banners. A gentle hum of voices filled the cavernous room as news was passed on, allegiances were established and enemies were flattered.

The High Councillor remembered the days when he had been the news bearer, the persuader, the flatterer, but those days were behind him now. He had dragged himself up from being the nobody son of a courtesan to the most powerful man in the empire next to the Prince. What would his mother say now if she were alive? He'd make her eat the cruel words cursing his birth and her prediction of his pitiful future. Look at him now. No more fear of factions, no chance of losing power. The regency document was written in indelible ink and signed by Emril, King of the Reluwyn, the Elves, the Laowyn, the Radichi and the Chieftains. No more pandering to courtiers, for now they pandered to him. Garesh had never been easily persuaded to do another man's bidding, and now he had a tight grip on the reins.

He skirted the throne at the end of the columns and disappeared through a door in the back of the hall. This led him to the chambers once used by Emril for Imperial business, which were now Garesh's primary place of work. Mishka and Sameedos awaited him in the principal chamber.

Mishka was a small, round man, with dark Reluwyn colouring and a terrible squint. He squinted even now, as he bobbed respectfully in front of Garesh.

Sameedos, though quite as portly as his fellow Councillor around his middle, was much taller, with strangely gaunt facial features. He rose from a chair he had taken by the window and bowed gracefully.

"High Councillor, how pleasing it is to see you. We are assembled to do your bidding as you asked. What would you have us do?"

Sameedos was useful to Garesh. He too had risen through the ranks, except his penchant for palace concubines had placed him firmly in Garesh's hand. After all, the Prince's absence hardly negated the royal law which made all concubines his and his alone. It would not do to be found partaking of the Prince's fruits, and Garesh had made that clear to the courtier. Apparently fear bred sycophantic talk as well as a biddable attitude. The former Garesh could do without.

"What would I have you do?" Garesh picked at a bunch of grapes that lay in a bronze dish upon the desk. He popped the first between his front teeth, splitting the skin and then sucking it back into his mouth. "I would have you, as I have already asked you to do countless times before, find my Prince." The question had been uttered sweetly but the accusation was unmistakable.

"We have covered the main settlements in the north of the empire and are now looking to the south, my Lord," replied Mishka, eager to please his master. "If he is in the north he must be avoiding larger settlements."

"Yes, that does seem to be the case, doesn't it?" Garesh strode over to the window and split another grape with his teeth, sucking the flesh from it mercilessly. His councillors couldn't help wondering if that was how he would devour them if they failed him.

"It's not good enough!" Garesh banged a fist against a glass window pane whose broad expanse showed a splendid view of the jewelled courtyard, gems shining in the midday suns. "I have already made plans for a bride to be selected for the Prince. All he need do is bed one of these maidens and if she please him, as nomadic tradition dictates, he may declare her his wife there and then. A simple deed. But how am I to keep him busy with a new wife and babies when I cannot even find the damned man?" Garesh, in spite of his excellent planning, knew what it would mean if the other courtiers found out that he had lost the Reluwyn ruler. A Regency document could only come into effect when there was a Prince to be

Regent on behalf of. Without Trevisian, Garesh was nowhere, his carefully laid plans would be ruined.

Further, his pursuit of a wife for the Prince would establish him as first councillor to the King of Emrilion even after the Regency ended. Trevisian would gain his majority and become King the moment he took a wife and if Garesh could have a hand in engineering the Prince's ascent to full power, he could maintain his premier position within the Reluwyn government. His influence would continue and the Prince's disinterest in ruling would leave Garesh the sole wielder of power.

Before the Prince had gone, he had encouraged him to marry. It had all been working according to Garesh's original plan. Then the Prince had disappeared, a nasty habit he had indulged in in his youth which Garesh had thought cured. Apparently not.

As a child, Prince Trevisian had gone to live like an urchin on the streets of Emril City - until palace guards had found him skinny and dirty, and brought him back to the palace. It was easily explained away when he was just a boy, but as a man it was a different matter entirely. Garesh had his suspicions. The Prince had his mother's shape-shifting blood, so it stood to reason the magic may have been passed down to her son. But Garesh had warned Trevisian years ago never to think of his mother, never to follow in her footsteps. Over the years the Prince's repeated disappearances had only grown Garesh's suspicions. The law King Emril had passed against the Shifters still stood, therefore Garesh's suspicions were hardly something he could share with his advisors. He would never jeopardise his power in such a manner. As it was, the Prince's most recent disappearance, if it got out, would make him look like a fool. How he loathed looking like a fool.

"Are we not to select a bride from Castir? We could easily annex our eastern neighbour with such a diplomatic match. The child-Queen's deposition has left the throne with multiple female claimants," said Mishka, his small black eyes creasing at the corners, an obvious sign of pleasure at his own cleverness.

"No." replied Garesh. "We have an Empire to keep united, and how is that done?"

"By ensuring uniformity among the races," supplied Sameedos, in a tone which suggested he had been asked to repeat that answer before.

"Exactly! We are the Reluwyn, the ruling race, why should we give in to cultural differences when we have conquered those weaker nations? We should not! No customs and traditional differences. If our Prince were to marry into a neighbouring country, they would expect their traditions to be accepted here. What kind of message would that send? How are we to enforce order and keep control? We must ensure uniformity among all the peoples and provinces. Difference breeds contempt and contempt breeds rebellion.

"We shall take Castir by force when we are ready. Until then I have scribes copying out the Edict of Maidens for circulation within the five provinces. When the eligible women pour into the Prince's harem, one should no doubt tempt his eye. The prettier the better, and whatever race she is will only strengthen our inner unity. We shall be closer to a stable Reluwyn Kingdom." The High Councillor failed to mention his unwritten disqualification of Laowyn women from the throne. Let the Prince use them for a night of pleasure but not one drop of Laowyn blood would ever sit upon the throne of Emrilion.

Neither of Garesh's fellow councillors pointed this out. Garesh's tolerance for the race that defied his power had run out weeks ago. Any mention saw furious eruptions.

"But this is all to no purpose if we do not know where the Prince is!" Garesh snapped again, turning away and running a hand through his black beard flecked as it was with grey now. "I leave for the western forest fort tomorrow. The Laowyn Resistance is becoming more of a problem there but, unlike the Laowyn, we do not have the weakness of mercy when it comes to killing our enemies.

When I get my hands on the rebels I will rip out their Enspers myself!" He was spitting and hissing like a snake. Taking a deep breath, he looked to his fellow councillors again. "I expect updates on the search."

"The Laowyn Resistance have been operating in that whole area. To be so close to their old capital of Ishtalia, is that really wise, my lord?" asked Sameedos, rubbing his hands together jerkily.

"Silence!" Garesh roared. "I have a rebellion to put down and no Prince to place at the head of the suppression! There is work to be done: the overseeing of the Edict of Maidens, and my presence to quell any thought of rebellion. Did the thought not enter that thick skull of yours, Sameedos?"

The councillor bowed sycophantically and offered his profoundest apologies.

"I don't need your honeyed words, I need progress." Garesh was pacing now, his fellow councillors watching nervously for his next actions.

"Just find him!" he barked and then, without waiting for any obsequious replies, he turned on his heel and left.

○○○

"I refuse to do it!" shouted Kiara, throwing her plate down and flying away from Zephenesh who reclined opposite her.

"It's not whether you wish to do it, Kiara," he replied calmly, "the Edict reached us yesterday, and the guards will come up from the southern forest fort to enforce it." His tone softened, "You may not even be chosen." He watched her flinch slightly. "All you have to do is stand for inspection in the market square. The guards will probably pass you by." Even as he said it he wasn't quite sure he believed it.

Kiara was beautiful. Even in her anger, as she was in this moment, her golden curls were framing her face, her lips were full and her eyes a piercing blue. She had grown into her female figure, a figure that men now desired - that now perhaps a Prince would desire.

"And what if they wish to see more, uncle? Surely the Prince needs any harlot of his own to be inspected thoroughly. What if they see my marking, my Ensper? I'm sure that would end well for me." Sarcasm dripped from her voice like honey from a spoon.

"It's not a harlot he's looking for, Kiara, it's a wife. He's picking one out of all the empire that is matchless in beauty. Unless you are arrogant enough to believe yourself more beautiful than the thousands of other maidens in this Kingdom, you really should not be worrying."

Zephenesh pinched the bridge of his nose, and wearily spread his fingers over his eyes. He carried on, "As for your mark, you will not show it."

Every Laowyn was born with the mark. A single large gem, known as the Ensper, growing from their scapula, with a unique surrounding tattoo given to every child at a week old.

"Am I supposed to hide who I am now?"

Zephenesh's words were not meant to provoke, but merely to ground his niece. Evidently, they were doing the former rather than the latter. If she showed her mark she might be chosen merely for the humiliation of losing her honour to a Reluwyn. They knew the Laowyn customs, that they did not marry outside of their race, that they held the marriage bed as a pure space. An opportunity to disrespect them would be too tempting to pass up. Zephenesh might want to obey the rulers, as the Great Spirit demanded, but he was not a fool. If Kiara hid her mark she had a greater chance of not being chosen.

She was facing the window now, shaking in indignation, her body taut with distress. He rose slowly and came to her, placing a hand on each of her shoulders.

"Your mother and father gave charge over you to me when they died, Kiara, and I have raised you like my own daughter. All I ask is your obedience in this. Our calling as a people is to peace, and to respect the rulers over us. Do you think I would ask you to do something that would put you in danger?"

"Even if they are not our own people?"

"Yes. And I cannot see you disobey them, or me."

It was the only thing he could think of to protect her. If she stood for inspection, as any other maiden in the Kingdom between fourteen and twenty would, she might remain unchosen. Zephenesh was sure she would. No one would pick his little Kiara. She was still so young in his eyes. Of course he saw she was beautiful, but his paternal love for her overshadowed that. If he tried to hide her from the authorities and they found out, she would be taken, regardless of whether she was chosen.

She made no reply to his plea for obedience.

"The Great Spirit protects you. We must trust him that you will not be chosen."

"And if I am? If they found out my race they would execute me - as they have executed so many others. If they so much as suspect that I have hidden who I am, I will surely be imprisoned."

Zephenesh turned her to face him and saw the fragility in her eyes. It was not often she admitted fear or any other weakness. She was strong. But he was sure of this: that she would obey the law as the Spirit demanded, saying nothing of declaring her race, and she would not be picked. She would be saved from further scrutiny, and that's all that mattered.

"This is the best way Kiara. If you hide your race you are less likely to be chosen for nefarious purposes. Besides, your features are fair, and they are likely looking for a dark-haired beauty." He ran a hand over the crown of her head, the curls soft and golden beneath his fingers.

He left her then. She must come to terms with this alone, and besides he needed to pray. Things were getting worse for all races, not just his own. Not only were the Reluwyn suppressing racial customs, now they were taking daughters and sisters for the pleasure of their Prince.

Kiara was right in a way - only the one chosen would be the new Queen. Every other maid would be used for the night and then consigned to life in the harem. The very thought saddened Zephenesh, but fighting against the authorities to hide Kiara could only lead to more trouble. Besides, surely she would not be chosen?

⊙⊙⊙

The following day Kiara was told to wash and dress herself for the choosing. Zephenesh had suggested she wear a plain woollen dress. She obeyed him silently, and soon they were walking together to the market square. Other girls from Miresh joined them from side streets, walking with their parents. Some smiled, as though they were in a competition they wished to win; others were barely old enough to be called women, terrified of what could happen if they were chosen.

There were a lot of Laowyn women, but other cultures were represented too. There were many Reluwyn and several Southerners from around the meadowlands and near the Tao desert. There were even some Meir Elves present. Some Laowyn bore their marks proudly, others covered themselves from the stares of Reluwyn women. One woman Kiara and Zephenesh knew to be of their own people glanced sideways when she saw Kiara's mark was hidden. Although modest, the traditional Laowyn dress had a neckline designed to reveal the wearer's Ensper.

Kiara fixed her gaze on the path ahead, not wavering to the left or right. Her shoulders were drawn back and she clenched her fists a little. If they chose her she would strike the guard. Yes, that's what she would do, she would cause a riot and run away. Zephenesh seemed so confident, and had told her calmly that she was to obey the authorities without question. Perhaps he would be happy to send her to the Prince, it didn't seem like he cared.

They rounded the corner and came to the square at the centre of Miresh. Hundreds of feet stood together on the clay tiles. Shops whose produce usually hung out of windows and lay in baskets outside were shuttered up. Was that because the Laowyn had no trade after the last proclamation? Or had the guards who had come for the choosing forced the owners to do it? As she looked upon the small contingent up ahead, no clue was given. The Reluwyn stood in rows, and amongst the ones wearing military dress were some wearing dark blue robes with silver sashes. She could see their badges winking at her in the morning sun.

They were surrounded by the many women who had already arrived in the square. A low murmur of voices sounded, but was suddenly cut across by a piercing scream. All heads turned towards its origin. A guard was yanking at the arm of a woman, dragging her from the shop on the other side of the open area. Another pulled along a girl of about fourteen, her face tear-stained and red.

Kiara wasn't even conscious she had started toward them until Zephenesh put a stern hand upon her shoulder.

"Don't." he commanded in an undertone.

Kiara watched as shackles were put on the mother's wrists and she was hauled away down a side street. The young girl was forced into the crowd with the rest of the women waiting.

"Now I see why you weren't willing to hide me," accused Kiara, turning merciless eyes upon her uncle. "You were afraid of being arrested." She felt a twinge of shame at dealing so harshly with the man who had raised her, but she stifled it. He was doing nothing in the face of this injustice.

The young girl was still stifling sobs. No one dared to comfort her. Kiara pulled against her uncle's restraining hand. She felt it tighten around her arm.

Her eyes flashed at him, "You would not let me stop the guards but I *will* comfort that girl." She yanked her arm away and strode off through the crowd. Many eyes watched her, but she ignored them.

Upon reaching the child, Kiara immediately put an arm around the smaller girl's shoulders and took one hand warmly in her own.

"Now child, you must stop crying," she said in a firm whisper. "They will only take her away until she calms down, and you are drawing attention to yourself until you do the same." The words seemed harsh, but the girl wiped the tears from her face and stopped sobbing. She straightened but did not let go of Kiara's hand.

"I am Kiara."

"I know," the girl's voice was barely audible, still shaking with tears. "Mama says you buy from her."

"So I do, the best salted fish…"

"Silence!" One of the official's voices rang out across the courtyard and every whisper was immediately hushed.

Kiara looked up, jumping slightly when she locked eyes with the official. Both he and the official to his right stared at her. She wanted to look away, but she cursed herself for jumping in the first place and instead levelled her chin, meeting them stare for stare.

"I am here," he carried on, his eyes finally leaving Kiara's and roving over the crowd, "In order that the Edict of Maidens be carried out. Maidens from every part of the Kingdom shall be inspected, the fairest selected and taken to Emril, where one of them shall be chosen by the Prince himself to become his future Queen." The official turned and handed whatever he had been reading from to his colleague. He turned his dispassionate eyes upon the female crowd once more. "The inspection shall begin."

No one moved. Even Kiara failed to breathe for the next minute. Her dress had a high neckline, there was no chance the Reluwyn could see her markings or the Ensper they surrounded, but she felt that they shone out, showing who she really was for all to see. Her grip tightened on the girl's hand.

Every young woman stood still, the guards and officials coming to stand before each one in turn. They stared at faces, poked at teeth, pulled at hair and raised arms to examine the width of waists. The mildest head shake from the officials meant not good enough, too ugly, too fat. Kiara felt the indignation swelling in her chest as maiden after maiden was passed by.

Finally, one was chosen, a woman Kiara recognised as a neighbour's daughter. She was indeed beautiful, and was commanded to return the following morning to the market place where the caravan to Emril city would await.

More inspections passed, and only two more women were chosen before they came to stand before Kiara. Her bright blue eyes stared stonily ahead, while her fingers itched to slap away the first hand that came to tug at her hair.

"Yes, it is attached to my head," she muttered. She felt a thump in the back, probably Zephenesh. Too late.

"What's that you say woman?"

Finally her eyes focused. She saw the sharp, small features of the official, and the height and muscle of the guard who stood by him, his eyes boring into her. Suddenly she realised they had no colour - they were bright white, two tiny black dots at their centres. Her resolve shook a little.

"Nothing, my lord," she answered, her head bowing and courage failing her yet again. Was this who she was? Able to talk confidently in private but cower at the first sign of danger elsewhere?

"You have very striking eyes." The official grasped at her chin and pulled it harshly upwards to look into them again. He stared for several minutes until Kiara could not help heat rising up her neck. "A blush, how very... maiden-like." The official was smiling as a cat would at a mouse.

Before she could pull away, he had relinquished his grip.

"She is chosen."

And then he moved on, as if nothing had happened, as if he hadn't decided her fate, as if her life had not been irrevocably changed.

CHAPTER 3

A clay oil lamp flickered as the air around its long flame moved. Kiara tugged at the strings of her trousers, tying them about her waist and doing up the buckles down the length of her legs. She'd stolen them from Djeck's wardrobe, along with a large linen shirt. Both garments were dark, suiting her purposes. With the trousers on, she took up the length of material she had torn from her bed sheet. It had been jaggedly cut with the short blue sword that had once been her father's, the very weapon she had freed the children with only a few days before.

She placed the first section of the white cotton over her chest and drew it around herself, keeping it flat and pulling it tightly back on itself. She continued to wind it around her body, watching it change her shape from woman to boy. Deftly ripping the last part in half, she twisted the material and tied it behind.

Reaching up to a shelf hewn into the wood of the house, she picked up the scissors she had taken from the kitchen. Her blue eyes were apprehensive as she surveyed the two blades. It was necessary, that's what she told herself, all of this was necessary. The lies she'd told about going to bed early in order to rest, the stealing of the clothes, and her planned escape. That's what she was doing after all, escaping the cruel choices that others had made to destroy her last hope.

Her eyes narrowed, her teeth clenched together, and her breath came harder. She would not be anyone's victim, certainly not of the Reluwyn. Stilling the quaking of her hand, she took a lock of fair hair and wedged it between the shears. She squeezed her fingers together, gently at first, then more ruthlessly as her breath came faster. One heavy lock fell, and then another, and another. They piled silently upon each other at her feet, along with the tears she couldn't stop from falling. Damn them! Damn all of them!

When the locks had become lengths, and the lengths had become spikes of hair upon the crown of her head, she sat back exhausted. The longer hair left at the front was all the better to hide her face from others. She couldn't look in the mirror anymore, not as she dragged on the man's shirt, nor when she put on the cloak that obscured her frame from scrutiny, nor when she slung the sword belt around her waist. It wasn't until she was tying the mask she'd cut from old leather that she finally stared at herself, or rather, stared at the crystal blue eyes, scornful mouth, and uneven short hair – of a boy.

She would have stayed there a long time, perhaps until morning, if she had not heard movement beyond her door, in the living room and kitchen of her home. The home she was leaving. Surely Zephenesh would have handed her over to the greedy Prince, destroying her virtue. Kiara's hands gripped the pack she'd filled with food even harder. She picked up the last part of her attire - the only thing she felt bad for stealing.

It was a curved blade, shining silver-blue in the lamplight. Down its sharp length were beautiful engravings, markings she remembered being mesmerised by as a child. Her father had carried this blade when he stood in the Laowyn army, and he had left it to his brother Zephenesh. Now Kiara was taking it, the hate Zephenesh had stirred in her by his betrayal made it right in her mind. Her knuckles whitened about the handle; she had no more time, the sounds in the next room were not abating and at any moment Zephenesh might come in to her room, wishing to speak to her about tomorrow.

She would not be spoken to. Throwing the pack over her shoulder, she sheathed the blade beneath her cloak, and made for the window.

Once she was outside the cold night air bit at her through her clothing. She would need to keep moving if she wanted to keep warm. She progressed through the passageways and alleys she'd played in as a girl, and wondered if she would ever see them again. Probably not.

But tonight, tonight she was on her own, and she was angry. There was work to be done, girls to be saved from the clutches of a corrupt Prince, edicts to be burned!

⚫⚫⚫

Burning stars gazed down from the heavens, ready to observe the villainy that was to be enacted below. A thundering of carriage wheels and horses' hooves on the track sounded out. A thief, blade held high, headed hell-for-leather at the Reluwyn carriage.

He'd waited on the hillside near the forest for some time and this was the first vehicle that had come his way. He hoped for more than the worthless proclamation he'd picked up almost a month ago.

His manoeuvres were well-practiced, and soon the carriage had shuddered unsteadily to a halt. The coachman jolted forwards, falling between his horses, caught by the leather of the harness like a fly in a spider's web.

He would be some time in extricating himself, so the thief needed only to disarm him, leaving him to his struggles, tossing the knife aside. There was nothing more irksome than thinking a man disarmed, only to find yourself skewered a moment later. The thief wrapped his fingers around the gilt handle and, drawing breath, flung open the crested door of the carriage.

What happened next was something the thief could never have expected. Moonlight fell into the carriage's interior, just as the opposite door was wrenched open. Both doors smacked back on their hinges and the thief's dark eyes took in the shadow of a small man on the other side of the carriage.

"What in the name of?!" He was already half way in, the blade tickling the chin of two passengers. But the sight of another highwayman made him wrench back, his leather hat hitting the door frame and falling off into the carriage.

"Damn!" Without thinking he reached forward to snatch it up just as he heard a gurgle of laughter from the opposite doorway. He snapped upright, coming to himself and resuming the customary snarl. He turned from the boy, whom he'd misjudged as an amateur. He'd deal with him later.

"Hand over what cargo you bear!" he barked, eyes hard and blade ready.

The guard inclined his head slightly, and at this signal, the official drew a silver box from beneath the folds of his cloak, handing it over. The thief dropped his hat and took the treasure, missing a barely perceptible movement on the other side of the carriage.

Making use of the moonlight, the thief examined his prize, and cursed loudly. Staring back at him was a box almost identical to that which he'd finally managed to sell a week ago from the last robbery. When would High Councillor Garesh tire of sending his proclamations and edicts?

He didn't have long to think. His guard was down. Glancing back up through the carriage to check on his unwelcome nocturnal kin, he was confronted only by the moon and stars visible through an empty doorway.

"What the...?" He didn't need to finish, the cold steel of a sword tickling at his ear was all the answer he needed. He obeyed its beckon and stepped away from the carriage.

His opponent kept him at arm's length, forcing him to face the carriage. The boy-thief commanded the carriage occupants to lock the doors.

He was careful, thought the thief, but still young. And youth may still betray him. The thief's swordsmanship was a match for the best in the Empire, and he knew it. But he would use it only to get away unseen. He had no desire to draw attention to himself.

Now he could get a better idea of his opponent, standing at least a foot smaller than the thief, and wearing baggy clothes. He knew smallness did not mean inability, experience proved many a small warrior made up with agility and speed what they might lack in stature or strength.

Any thoughts of fighting were dashed when his captor commanded him to drop his sword. The thief did so, but did not throw it far, deciding he would bide his time.

The thief's dark eyes took in the length of the elegant blade pointed at his jugular. The light set off a silver-blue blaze between the two cloaked figures. The smaller highwayman turned to the driver, who had finally extricated himself from the leather harness-straps, and manage to sit again on his high perch.

"Get on with you," came a gruff command from the small figure, whose face remained obscured by the shadows of his hood.

The taller thief watched in disbelief as the carriage moved off. He pushed forward. "Wait!" He hadn't checked the rest of the vehicle. There may be valuables still wrapped in the folds of that official's cloak. Worse than that, he'd lost the shadows cast by his hat, and they might have seen his face. The cutting of the sword-point through his coat persuaded the thief to halt.

He turned eyes filled with fury upon his rival. "What did you do that for? You idiot!" He kicked the dust with his boot, suddenly uncaring of the blade pointed directly at him.

When he looked back, he was pleased to see the small man shift uncomfortably. The taller thief smiled. Yes, the amateur couldn't handle his opponent stepping slightly out of his control.

"You want this?" He held up the silver box tauntingly, chin rising and smile twisting into a sneer. He levelled the young man with a gaze. "Come and get it."

"Give me the contents and you may have the silver," came the reply.

The taller thief's brow rose a little. What did this man want with the contents? Did he know of something the thief did not?

"Gemstones is it? Why would I settle for a box if there is a greater treasure?"

The stranger shifted his feet again. "I only want the Edict it contains."

The thief casually lounged back, as though considering his options. Then, with a swiftness that caught his opponent off guard, he flung the box, dropped to the floor and rolled to reach his weapon. He sprang up with sword in hand, ready to attack.

Although surprised, the stranger immediately jolted into action, taking on a crouching stance. The two circled each other, like carrion birds around a carcass. The smaller man leapt forwards, slashing downwards with sheer ferocity; the thief quick-stepped back, using the seconds gained to lunge forwards again. This sly move was parried, but the thief immediately lunged again, his blade stopping an inch from the man's abdomen.

The hood fell, and the thief saw he had been fighting a mere boy. He hefted a shoulder into his young opponent, using his considerable height and weight against him.

The small blond boy flew backwards, stumbling, as his heel caught on a tree root. He landed in a crumpled heap on the floor, crying out and clutching with both hands at his leg.

The thief took a step back. He knew he hadn't caused the wound. Snatching up the blade, the boy pulled himself to his feet and resumed his battle-ready stance.

"Not giving up?" asked the thief provokingly. He had no desire to kill the youth. He didn't need to draw that kind of attention to himself and he held no taste for blood. Now would be the time for him to run.

There was no response. The box still lay between them. Both looked at the box and then to each other again, but before either could make a move voices were heard, and lights appeared on the road. The thief felt the vibrations of many hooves on the path, and before he could even think of running, the riders were upon them.

●●●

Horses slid to a halt, stamping and snorting at the two in the centre of the path. Armour grated as the soldiers yanked reins, and blood-flecked foam dappled the horses chests.

Kiara flailed around herself with her blade causing horses to shy away. The soldiers forced their beasts back towards her, dropping their lethal spears inches from her face. Her heart raced. Her breathing was rapid. What had she done? The wound on her leg was throbbing and she could feel blood trickling from Djeck's stitches.

"Circle!"

The harsh command made Kiara jump. It came from the leader of the Imperial Cavalrymen. She saw him between spear points, his piercing white eyes glaring at the two on the ground.

With a lurch, Kiara recognised the guard from the choosing. What if he recognised her too? What if he took her back, or worse? Flanks banged against each other as horses and spears hemmed them into a barbed prison.

"Drop your weapons!" ordered the Captain, his gaze bright and terrible as he looked down at them. Kiara obeyed without a moment's hesitation; the thief took more time, carefully placing his sword on the ground before straightening.

"We crossed paths with an Imperial carriage not too

far from here who had a most interesting story about being attacked," he carried on, as if an interrogation on a deserted road in the middle of the night was perfectly normal. Kiara looked down, hoping in vain that doing so would make her invisible. "The culprits match your descriptions. Tell me, are you total fools to still be standing here?"

"Apparently," muttered the thief, too quietly for the Captain to hear but loud enough for Kiara.

Was the man insane? He had taunted her into fighting him and now he joked while they were surrounded by Imperial Guards. What was wrong with him? If it had been any other situation Kiara might have laughed at his levity. But it wasn't, and her life was hanging in the balance. She stepped away without thinking.

"You, remove the mask!"

Kiara froze.

"Shouldn't have moved," hissed the thief with some satisfaction.

She nodded dumbly but didn't touch the mask.

"Now!" shouted the Captain.

She pretended to recoil again, stumbling a little and falling purposefully. She grabbed handfuls of dust, rubbing dirt across her face as she removed the mask.

When she rose, she was just a scruffy looking youth.

"No more than a boy, a shame that tonight you shall

not be suckling on your mother's breast but lying cold in Grûl's jail."

"Captain Aktabad!" came a cry.

Taking full advantage of this new distraction, the thief leaned in closer, his voice still menacing. "You may be a boy, but you are not too young to die by my sword for getting me caught like this."

Kiara's skin prickled, hairs rising on the back of her neck. She stared straight in front of her, imagining a thousand appropriate curses, while good sense prevented her uttering a single one. She was caught, just as he was. Pushing the threat from her mind, she watched the soldier retrieve the silver box lying in the road and hand it over.

The Captain's white eyes took in the royal seal of the Reluwyn royal family. He smiled at his captives. "Your reservations at the jail are confirmed." He turned his huge horse and shouted back his orders. "Tie them up and move out!"

Rope was taken from the saddlebags of the horses and dropped over Kiara's wrists. The material was tightened abrasively against her skin. Her arms were tugged upwards and her shoulders burned as the rope was secured to a saddle.

She looked to her left, and saw that the same was happening to the man she had been fighting. She could see his face properly now that the lanterns hung above it.

His hair was dark, his features too. Reluwyn. She wished for a brief moment that she had killed him. Such fury licked like flames over her. How dare he say he would kill her. She would happily have taken a knife to *his* throat if it would rid the world of one more Reluwyn. Then, as quickly as it had come over her, her anger was snuffed out. The horses moved out and she was dragged forward into a stumbling run.

The pace was unforgiving. Half a mile was reached and she felt the blood soaking through her trouser leg. She was concentrating so hard on keeping going that she didn't notice the thief watching her. His dark eyes flicked over her struggling frame, taking in the increasing dark stain.

A moment later she faltered and knocked into the thief, and whatever sympathy he had been harbouring was eclipsed by a flash of rage.

"Watch it!" he spat, barely regaining his balance.

Kiara was oblivious. She staggered back over to the path of the horse she was tied to, but before long she stumbled again. This time she didn't have anything to land on but the ground.

Dirt and gravel cut into her face, the tug on her arms didn't give way and her body thudded between the horses, rolling her over. The pain seemed unbearable, and she could hear a ringing in her ears. She wasn't a fool, she knew she wouldn't survive this. The ringing grew louder, and all other sounds seemed far away. There was an excruciatingly deep click as one of her arms was wrenched from its socket, and then all at once everything went black.

Unconscious, she didn't hear the yell that stopped the cavalcade, nor did she notice when a soldier hoisted her onto the back of one of the horses. At least she was alive.

CHAPTER 4

It was another hour before the cavalrymen and their prisoners finally reached the Reluwyn stronghold in the northern coastal town of Grûl. Exhausted, the thief dragged his feet through the sewage that ran down the streets of the overcrowded settlement. The mingling stench of fish and waste was acrid in his nostrils, but just being allowed to walk felt like heaven to him, no matter the stink.

They had passed through the west of the Northern Moors where they had been caught, and were now at one of the northern settlements. The town of Grûl sprawled around the harbour's muddy banks serving as one of the main fishing ports of the North Sea.

It was buzzing when they arrived, in spite of the late hour. The streets were crowded with ruddy sailors, fat-looking merchants, and women of pleasure catcalling the passers-by. One of the prostitutes reached out to lay a hand on the thief's broad shoulders.

"Lonely night in the jail, friend? Just a wink and I'll keep you warm." He looked up to see a face that had once been beautiful, now stained with chalk paint and lined with hard years. He shrugged her off and carried on, ignoring the choice words she used in response. Reluwyn prisons allowed whores if the prisoner could pay, and perhaps that was where she found most of her business.

The troops wound down through cobbled streets toward the dockside, lanterns lighting darkened inns while ships rose and fell with the tide. A left-turn and they were climbing once again. The thief's legs ached and his feet tripped on the cobbles.

Grûl's jail could be seen rising up against the horizon. It sat amidst the houses but loomed above them, clearly outlined against ominous rain clouds. The doorway glowed in the heavy blackness, a welcome sight. The coming downpour would quickly make swamps out of the streets, forming a river of sewage that would invade the dwellings of those less wealthy.

The thief was led into the Watchtower behind the Captain. They stopped abruptly before a Lieutenant sat at his desk. The man looked up without pleasure, nodding curtly to the Captain, offering a standing salute before cocking his head inquiringly at the thief. His eyes flicked back to the Captain.

"And what's this then?"

"Two prisoners for a night in the jail and a formal trial. Charged with robbing an Imperial coach on the

Edict of Maidens dispatch."

The thief's brow furrowed but he maintained his silence. His time would come to speak. He looked between the Captain and the Lieutenant, but they said no more of the Edict. He hadn't known it had been released, and was thankful that his beard and rough clothing concealed his identity, for the time being at least.

"Captain, may I ask, where is your second prisoner?" The Lieutenant still stood rigidly to attention, his superior finding no impulse to let him stand at ease.

"Here." Aktabad didn't turn but the thief did. The fair-haired boy was still unconscious and slung over the shoulder of one of the dismounted riders.

The thief cast his dark eyes over the battered frame of the boy. Not even the dirt and blood on the youth's face could coerce pity from the frustrated thief at this moment. If it weren't for this boy he would still be on the Northern Moors, far away from any minions of the Imperial Court.

"Yes, Captain, very good Captain," the Lieutenant called to a colleague who was sat further down a corridor leading off the main entrance hall. The jangling of keys heralded his approach and the man's bulging stomach arrived around the corner before he did.

Orders were rapped out and the prisoners, one walking, one carried, were taken to a stone cell towards the back of the building. The thief was thrust in first, tripping down the steps and sent sprawling on the dirty floor. The blond-haired boy was thrown in after, almost landing on top of his cellmate. The guard cut their hands free and then left, the click of the locking door a sound of finality in the quiet that followed.

The thief rolled over, tempted to stay lying on the floor after his marathon this evening. He rubbed his face and ran his fingers through his damp hair, scraping it back from his face. It wouldn't be long now; his life would be forfeit when they found out who he was.

The groaning of the youth forced him up. Damned boy! He'd be dead within a week, perhaps he should be happy about that. The thief turned away and made his way to the wooden bed. He dropped down onto it with a heavy sigh, crossing his long legs in front of him. A quick nap before being hauled in and interrogated would not go amiss.

The boy continued to moan, and the rowdy yells of a twilight port-town could be heard. The thief's eyes were shut, but damn it all, he could not sleep! All he could think of was the rough sea wind over the Northern Moors, the stars that had once lit his nights, and the suns that had warmed his back by day. All gone. The freedom to be himself. No more robbing, no more wild, no more freedom.

His eyes sprang open. Curse that boy! He looked over

to the slowly moving heap - it seemed to be more clothing than boy. Perhaps he was an elf. A sharp cry rang out as the youth rolled over onto the arm he had dislocated. He jolted to full consciousness flying upright and immediately grasping his injured limb.

The thief felt a twinge of sympathy. He'd dislocated his arm once, during cavalry drills. Dainus had shied and bolted, leaving the thief in the dust. Except he hadn't simply fallen - one of his arms had been caught in the reins, and the long drag had dislocated his shoulder. There was only one way to fix a dislocated shoulder.

He walked across the cell. The dirt on the boy's face hid his exact features, but the thief could see they were delicate. Definitely an elf, though he couldn't see the ears beneath the mop of blond hair. Tears of pain cut clean tracks through the grime on the boy's cheeks.

The youth shuffled backwards and glanced nervously around himself.

"It's the prison of the Watchtower." The thief answered the unspoken question. He crouched so he could lock the boy's blue eyes in his. "Your fault. Thanks."

The youth flinched, before answering defiantly. "You didn't have to fight me. You could have given me what I wanted."

The thief raised an eyebrow. "And leave you with that

prize? I am not quite so young and stupid. I've been playing this game a while."

The boy leaned on the wall in surrender. "I only wanted the document."

"And what use does a boy have with royal documents?" said the thief, rising.

"As much use as they should have," the boy snapped, his anger distracting him from his predicament. "I would have burned it!" He met the thief's gaze squarely, blue eyes blazing with fury.

"Such hostility over a document that doesn't even affect you."

"A document demanding that every beautiful maiden in the Empire be taken to the Prince for inspection. A wife is to be chosen, but only after he has stolen their virtue. He makes whores of these women for his own pleasure - and what of them?"

The tall thief was taken aback, but in spite of this his taunting reply came quickly. "A lover of yours is to be taken by the Prince then?"

The boy dropped his gaze immediately.

"Ah, so that's it," the thief carried on, warming to his theme.

Fresh tears rolled down the boy's face. He clenched his jaw against the agony.

The thief's eyes hardened.

"Your arm is dislocated."

The boy said nothing.

"You aren't a good thief. Stealing paper not gold. Getting caught. You really should take up another profession." The thief paused. "Then again, you'll be dead soon."

The boy looked up shortly. "As will you be. But I will have fought for a cause; you fight simply for your own greed."

"Ha!" The thief's laugh was mirthless as he paced over to the window. "A cause? A cause you'll *die* for."

"Gladly," spat the boy, an involuntary groan coming soon after. He looked up to the ceiling as if in supplication.

This youth was odd. He was a robber stealing things of no value. He didn't care about death. Who was he? Turned away his narrow back was shaking with heavy breaths of pain.

The thief exhaled loudly. Why was he going to do this? He came up behind, before the boy even knew what was happening. Putting one strong hand on the small shoulder and the other on the wrist he took a firm hold of the dislocated arm.

The boy cried out half in pain, half in shock, but the thief ignored him. If he knew it was coming it would hurt all the more. He pulled back. Hard. The boy thrashed wildly, but the thief wouldn't let go. A boot caught the side of the thief's face hard. He cursed loudly, but the extra pull was all that was needed. The arm popped back into its rightful place with a satisfying click.

The boy gasped and then moaned pitifully. The thief fell back onto the wooden bed, rubbing his jaw and calling down such curses it would have made anyone wince. He was lucky he hadn't broken his jaw - and the boy was lucky he hadn't done so. The thief would have set to work undoing the shoulder if the boy had given him more than a bruise.

Busy nursing his own injury for some time, the thief ignored the boy who now lay on his side, clutching the arm and waiting for the pain to subside.

Why did he bother? The boy was as thin as a rake, he hardly felt like he could survive a cold night in this cell, let alone any longer. Besides he'd be hanging from the gallows by the end of the week. He couldn't afford to care about another now, he needed to watch out for his own future.

"Thanks."

The small word came from the boy. The thief paused in the massaging of his jaw long enough to catch eyes with the boy who was now sitting up. He did not reply.

The silence stretched out between them, the thief gazing into the middle distance and the boy staring at the opposite wall. The thief didn't want conversation, and apparently neither did the youth. Good. He'd be out of here soon enough, no point conversing with the Emrilion rebel in the meantime.

As the minutes stretched by, it was almost peaceful in the cell. Outside the rain eased, and on the hour the night watch tolled the bell, announcing to the residents that the bawdiness of the inhabitants hadn't resulted in any serious crimes yet.

Across this came a screech of wood against stone and the door was thrown open. Lights shone in, beams spotlighting the two prisoners. The boy held up his hands to shield his eyes but the thief didn't move from the bed. Let them take the boy first.

Unfortunately for his sleeping plans, the two guards walked straight over to the thief, kicking his lounging legs to rouse him to standing.

"Up!" shouted the first of the guards when the prisoner didn't immediately obey the brutal kicks. He stirred, rising slowly, provoking in his laziness and then, knowing that his deception was finally at an end, followed them out the door.

◉◉◉

"My lord," a small, wheedling voice sounded in the dimly lit bedchamber.

Oil lamps flickered beside crimson hangings, bathing the room in a warm glow.

"My lord." That irritating voice again.

Garesh stirred and rolled over, the silk sheets sliding over his skin and pulling across the naked woman who lay beside him.

"My lord?"

"Mishka?" snapped Garesh, dragging a hand across his lined brow, "What is so important that you must raise me from my bed? Are the Laowyn rebelling at our very gates?" There was no other reason to forgive this disturbance.

"No, no, my lord."

Then no mercy would be afforded to the spherical courtier. Garesh opened his eyes to see that Mishka had entered the room backwards, bowing moronically to the doorway. He and Sameedos had arrived only two days ago to report that the Prince had still not been found. Their very presence tried Garesh's patience. Perhaps if he had one of them flogged they would both improve their performance. For now words would have to do.

"Turn around you fool," Garesh growled, and then shoved the concubine who slept next to him. "And you can get up and get out."

The woman sat up, exposing herself to Mishka who shook his head vigorously and stuttered something incomprehensible.

"Yes, my lord."

Garesh noted the hint of irritation in her voice. He couldn't afford her bad graces. She had dark skills that could prove useful, skills that were hard to find in a race who had learned to fear the Spirit Realm.

Before she could reach for her discarded gown, Garesh grabbed her by the hair, twisting it as he kissed her. Let that satisfy her ego for now.

"Leave," he commanded, and then rose, donning an open-fronted tunic which he tied about himself.

"Give me a reason not to have you flogged, Mishka," he said benevolently.

The small councillor's round face, which he expected to show fear, was instead creased into what resembled a smile. "It is good news, my lord, we have news of him."

Garesh's sour face altered considerably. "The Prince? Where?" He pushed impatiently at a cloth strewn with Reluwyn runes upon the table.

His concubine, Nisa, had been working here, asking the dark spirits for assistance in destroying the Laowyn rebels. Garesh had thought it rubbish until things in the room had moved on their own. Now he realised that Nisa could be valuable.

"To the north, my lord, a messenger has just arrived."

Garesh saw Mishka avert his eyes from the runes. Spirit conjuring was forbidden among the Reluwyn. Most feared it, but some, like Nisa, still practiced it. Not that Mishka, or Sameedos for that matter, would admit to their leader's involvement in such a thing. It could bring them down as well as him. Even so Garesh pulled down a narrow embroidered length of material that hung by a pillar and threw it over the runes.

He turned back to Mishka. "The messenger, where is he?"

The arrival of a servant halted the conversation. Garesh ordered preparations for traveling to be made with a caravan ready to leave within the hour.

"You are going to him, my lord?"

"Of course, I am! He will not slip through my fingers at such a time as this. The maidens are flooding into the palace's harem; I can hardly hide his absence any longer. What providence that he is found." He had no doubt his spirit conjuror Nisa would lay the providence at the door of the dark spirits, and he had to admit, the timing was impeccable. "The messenger, Mishka?" Garesh barked impatiently.

"You wish to see the messenger, my lord?" asked Mishka confused, sure that there was no need.

"Yes, you fool! How am I to gather all the facts of the

Prince's absence if I do not speak to the man who has seen him?"

Mishka's face still held incomprehension, but Garesh expected no better. How was this imbecile to realise Garesh must know everything in order to concoct a story the courtiers would be satisfied with.

"The messenger says there is a man in Grûl claiming to be the Prince. So we think it is the Prince, or it may not be…" Mishka seemed intent on idiocy tonight.

To be fair to the councillor, the Prince was not necessarily recognisable outside Emril City. Despite ruling over the entire Empire under Garesh's Regency, he had been a mere boy when he had taken the throne. Garesh had always been his public sign of power.

Garesh drew his brows in sharply, "The man who told them that he was the Prince?"

"Yes, my lord." Mishka shifted from one foot to the other, dropping his eyes from Garesh's gaze.

"Told who, exactly?" asked the High Councillor, with a sudden inexplicable feeling that he was not going to like the answer.

✪✪✪

"My lord." Captain Aktabad bowed, his breastplate digging into the silk of his wide fitting trousers. He rose again, his white eyes taking in the High Councillor.

A long-flowing green tunic and a blue travelling cloak swathed about Garesh's frame, and a contingent of officials and Imperial Guards gathered around him. Under his arm was the leather document pouch he had brought with him.

"As much as I enjoy exchanging pleasantries," Garesh replied, his face full of displeasure and his words lacking sincerity. "I am here on pressing business."

"Yes, my lord." Aktabad bowed again, reverence for the High Councillor offsetting his usually fearsome countenance. He led Garesh away from his entourage towards the interrogation room.

"In here, my lord."

"Your presence will not be needed." Garesh waited for the Captain to shut the door before looking at the prisoner.

Prince Trevisian was in a chair on the other side of the table, feet up on the desk, eyes barely open. He almost smiled at Garesh's shocked expression. He must look filthy to this man who had taught him to rule from childhood. His hair had grown long in the few months he'd been gone, and the stubble on his chin was dark over the swelling on his jaw where that insolent youth had kicked him.

"Was that caused by the guards?" asked Garesh, his eyes looking at the bruise. "I could have them whipped?"

Trevisian opened his eyes. "No," he paused. "And yes."

Garesh looked as he always did: smart, clean, and in control. "Then why do you wish them to be whipped?" he replied calmly.

"I curse them for capturing me."

"You wish you were still... wherever you have been for the past few months?" queried Garesh, attempting to keep his voice level. "Tell me, just where was that?"

"Ah," replied Trevisian, bringing his legs down off the table and leaning forward in his chair. "Now that would be giving away secrets." Garesh might be the closest thing he had to a mentor but Trevisian's mother had been killed for her magic by the government the High Councillor served in. Trevisian was hardly going to admit that he ran away not only from responsibility but also from the law that made him hide his true nature.

"Stealing from your own carriages is what I heard."

Trevisian didn't respond. All he afforded Garesh was a quick upturn of the corner of his mouth.

"And receiving beatings." Garesh gestured at the bruise.

Trevisian touched his palm to it.

"You have had your fun, my Prince, and now you must return to Emril city." Garesh cut across his thoughts. "Women from all over the Empire are arriving at your harem, waiting for your inspection."

A faint flicker of annoyance stirred in Trevisian's mind. "I gave no permission for that." He didn't speak the words loudly, they were unfamiliar in sentiment.

"No," Garesh's voice turned soft, patronizing. "But you were absent. You decided to go off into the wilds and leave the governing of your country to someone else."

Was that not how it had always been? Trevisian didn't want to rule, and he didn't want a wife either.

"A wife will secure your dynasty and your own rule, not to mention strengthen your public image. We had already talked about your marrying had we not? I simply put the idea into action."

"To bring me every attractive maiden so that I may choose?" Trevisian had no intention of making a spectacle of himself where women were concerned. That was why he had a harem, as all Reluwyn rulers had before him. He could satisfy his needs without complication. He had no intention of obeying a formality in order to gain his crown and his majority. "Tempting," He stared at Garesh, intent on causing discomfort. "But I do not want a wife."

"You would not want the inheritance of your father to crumble, would you?"

Trevisian felt unable to reply.

"The Laowyn are forming a resistance to the west, and the Radichi warriors are stirring up trouble in the Chieftain Lands north of the Tao. The only people you may rely on now are your own. The rest must be suppressed, and how much stronger will your arm be if your enemies see you finally take your crown."

Again, Trevisian did not answer. Garesh stepped out of the room, aware he would get no more from the Prince. He returned a few moments later with Mishka, whose arms were filled with clothes made of silks and muslins. Such luxurious materials had not touched Trevisian's skin since he had slipped out of the palace in servant's clothes two months ago.

"No doubt you shall feel much better when you are washed and dressed. The Lieutenant of this stronghold has agreed for your use of his private quarters, and a bath has been drawn for you. We shall talk more later."

Trevisian rose, knowing that Garesh was dismissing him in all but words. He knew how to obey, how to do his High Councillor's bidding. After all, Garesh had helped him rule since he was a boy, faithfully, never failing in his duties. Perhaps Trevisian should be more thankful.

Garesh spoke again, making Trevisian pause by the door, "Your accomplice, my Prince – apparently, you were not alone in your thieving – you know that the punishment for attacking royal vehicles has increased in its severity. The youth you were with will be hanged."

Trevisian's hesitation only lasted a moment. When he had convinced himself that there was no point in his protest, that the boy's naivety would eventually get him executed for some other crime, and that Garesh knew best, he exited the room. A careless 'yes' was cast back over his shoulder.

CHAPTER 5

Kiara couldn't believe it. The thief had been asleep. They'd actually kicked him awake! How had he been able to rest in such circumstances? She only paused for a moment after he was taken, before scrambling over to sit on the edge of the bed.

Flexing her shoulder, she could still feel pain in the stiffening joint – but at least she could now use her arm. Why he had helped she had no idea. One minute he'd been threatening to kill her, the next coming to her rescue. Anyway, it hardly mattered now: he was gone, perhaps to another cell, and she was left alone.

Shadows that had not seemed too dark before suddenly loomed thicker, blacker. The cold sea breeze came in through the window and laced around her body where her clothes were loose or open. She shivered and then touched a hand to her thigh. She retracted it immediately, inhaling with the pain.

She needed to take a look at it though - she didn't even know if Djeck's bandage was still in place. She undid the buckles on her trouser leg and peeled back the blood-soaked fabric. She could see where the bandage had slipped and the wound had congealed. The blood was threaded in thick clots along the length of stitches.

Muttering to herself in an attempt to alleviate the pain, she began unwinding the bandage in order to retie it. Voices in the corridor outside the cell made her stop. She cocked her head to listen to the sound. Would they come in? Then, as quickly as they had risen they faded, carrying on past the door.

It took her some time but she managed to smooth and retie the bandage over her wound. She re-buckled her trouser leg and then rose and walked, limping slightly, over to the window.

As she looked over the dark silhouette of Grûl's dwellings, it suddenly dawned on her how fortunate she had been. No one had discovered she was a woman, not even that thief when he had fixed her shoulder. She stretched, still feeling his strong hands where they had pulled mercilessly on her arm. But her fortune could not last much longer. She had been in the dark most of the night, with only faint lanterns to show a face disguised with mud and blood. She could feel the grit and dirt under her fingertips even now. When they saw her by the daylight they might guess the truth.

Kiara drew a necklace out from beneath her shirt, running it between her fingers. A coin bounced on the end of the long chain, as her thoughts ran towards the future.

When they found out she was a woman what would they do? Would they send her to the palace for the Prince's inspection? Or would they discover she was Laowyn and kill her for stealing from the Royal carriage? The thief had said that she would die. Her hands trembled a little making the necklace tinkle.

Gazing up at the heavens, she hoped the stars that hung there might hold an escape plan, or any plan for that matter. But the stars were no use, they did not speak to her, no plan came. Dejected she removed her gaze from the sky and let it fall back down over Grûl. If they didn't discover she was Laowyn, just that she was a woman, would she go to the palace? Would she want to live if the cost was freedom?

"A curse on all this!" she screamed out into the night, pounding the stone windowsill and the movement inadvertently causing the clasp of her necklace to ping open. Before she could stop it, the heavy coin and chain flew through the bars and onto a ledge outside the window.

Her father and mother had given her that necklace. It was a Laowyn symbol, a coin from their abolished currency, from before the conquest. They'd given it to her when she was a child, before they'd died. She pressed her face against the bars and stretched her fingers out, desperate to catch hold of the chain. It was the closest she had come to tears this whole evening.

"Please, please, please," she whispered through the bars, but her fingers would not reach. She put her foot in a notch on the inside of the stone wall and hoisted herself higher. She could see the necklace on the ledge, only about four feet from the ground below. Then suddenly, she paused, drew herself backwards and looked at the width of the bars.

A small smile crept across her face. "This is good." And with that she bent forward and fit her head through the bars, her shoulders soon following. Apparently the Reluwyn built their jails for men, not women. She was about to cry out in exultation when her clothes caught, making her too wide.

She pulled herself back in, her mind racing. After all, they could come back for her at any minute. If they were questioning the thief, he would lay the blame at her door. She had no doubt - it was only a matter of time.

She knew what she must do, but still she hesitated. Then, remembering the seriousness of the situation she was in, she began pulling off her clothes. Fearing at any moment a guard might come for her and everything would be lost she worked quickly. Before long she stood in just the material bound around her breasts, the bandage on her leg and her linen underwear. If they came in now, they would not only see that she was a woman, but recognise her as Laowyn by her marking.

She pulled herself back up onto the window ledge and, looking around the path at the back of the Watchtower for any guards. Seeing none she pushed her trousers, shirt and cloak through the bars. They landed in fluttering piles below, and then it was her turn. With much wiggling, and some very unladylike words, she was balancing on the ledge. She scooped up her necklace and drew it over her head.

Dropping to the ground she collapsed on her wounded leg. Biting her lip hard to stop from crying she tasted the metallic flavour of blood. There was no time to waste however; she could hear soldier's voices around the front of the jail. She gathered up her clothing, not stopping to dress, and darted off into the cover of darkness.

❂❂❂

Trevisian looked like a new man. Gone was the unkempt stubble across his chin, a neatly trimmed beard, black as coal, lined his jaw. His hair, which had been tousled across his face and grim with dirt, was now clean, smelling of cinnamon powder and combed back off his face.

He stepped out of the Watchtower with far more dignity than he had entered it, robed in a silk tunic, loose fitting trousers and soft leather shoes. A light muslin undershirt peeked out from his collar adding an extra layer of warmth and covering any hint of the Alakvalto tattoo that covered most of his back. He paid no attention to the surprised stares of prisoners and guards alike inside the Watchtower, nor those lining the street for his passage outside. He strode past them and into the carriage before even one set of eyes could gain contact with his. He was not looking forward to this journey.

His assumptions were proven right: Garesh spent the majority of the three-day journey lecturing him on his foolishness. Did he not know that there was unrest in his Kingdom? That his council was suffering criticism? That his very person could have been in danger had anyone identified him? Trevisian allowed each speech to wash over him like dirty water, staring out of the carriage window, the High Councillor's words melding into one long drone. The final warning of Garesh's did not shock the Prince in the least. Instead he amused himself by remembering who would definitely have killed him if they'd known he was the Prince. Well, Trevisian gave himself some credit, the boy in Grûl's Watchtower would have at least *tried* to kill him.

Trevisian almost laughed. What would the boy have

done? Would he have had the resolve to take a man's life? Thoughts of the boy drifted intermittently through Trevisian's mind, mingled with the knowledge of his lost freedom. It was not until they reached the palace, after he had been shown to his chambers and his traveling gear was laid out on his bed, that he realised the boy would surely be dead by now. It was the short silver-blue sword that brought it to his mind. Handed over at the Watchtower along with Trevisian's possessions, Garesh's servants had thought it the Prince's.

Trevisian picked it up, drawing it out from its embroidered leather sheath. He ran a finger along the flat length of it, feeling the swirls and engraving running down it. This was perhaps the only remnant from the boy thief's rebellious existence.

"Trevisian!"

The Prince jolted out of his reverie and turned, sword in hand, to meet the intruder.

"Please!" cried the man at the door in mock surrender. He held up his hands and grinned. "Don't stab me."

The man could not have been more than thirty, although it was difficult to tell his age from his bright blond hair. He wore a leather covering which could only be described as a slightly fuller loin-cloth, and leather boots. An ensemble hardly suitable for a courtier, but most fitting for a Radichi warrior from the Tao desert.

"Johan!" Trevisian re-sheathed the sword and dropped it on the bed. He embraced his friend affectionately, slapping him on his tattooed back.

"Welcome back to the land of the living, for all I knew you could have passed into the Spirit Realm." The laughter on Johan's face did not quite match his pale eyes.

"I know, I should have sent you word I was fine. I just…" Trevisian struggled to explain his reasoning to his friend.

"Didn't think about it," Johan countered, suddenly taking up sparring with his friend. He bounced from one foot to the other with fists raised, chuckling away. "Having too much fun running about your Kingdom unknown, were you? I heard you were robbing carriages."

"Already? My, the gossip in court circles really isn't what it used to be if you've only *just* heard about it."

"Cynic." Johan winked at Trevisian, following his old friend to the large, plush cushions which were strewn around a low table in the adjoining chamber. A gentle breeze wafted in from the open balcony door.

"Ha! Oh, how I've missed this place." Trevisian grimaced.

"Yes, I can see it in your eyes," mocked his friend, leaning back and stretching his arms out on either side of him, showing the true size of the giant warrior. He surveyed his Prince. "Your own carriages?" He raised a brow questioningly.

"Oh, my noble friend!" Trevisian sat down opposite him. "Surely robbing from myself rather than others isn't something your moral compass can turn away from?"

"And the purpose was?"

"I merely needed money for food. Really, it would be no different if I walked down to the palace kitchens right now and took some bread to eat."

"Yes," murmured Johan. "No different. And what of Dainus? I bred that horse specially for you and now I find he has not returned with you."

"He's living free," said Trevisian, knowing his horse would be happy wandering the wilds for a while, although the saddle on his back and the bridle on his head would be an impediment. "At least for the moment."

They sat in silence for a while, the sound of the fountain in the courtyard below serenading them. Trevisian's mouth pulled up into the semblance of a smile as he looked at his old friend. Johan had been with him since he was a small boy. He had been kept as a companion and bodyguard for the Prince, after being captured during the conquest of the southern Tao desert. No matter his surroundings he always stayed true to his race and Trevisian admired him for it. He was the only man at court with whom he felt connected.

Trevisian's mind began to drift back to his time at court, watched by everyone. He wondered what Garesh would ask of him next.

"I am to be wed," He said suddenly, not knowing entirely why, and frowning as he did so.

"A beautiful woman to bed and bear you babies. A hard life you lead," said his friend, half a smile crossing the Radichi's customarily calm face.

Trevisian gave him a hard look, and Johan put up his hands in response, nodding his head in understanding.

"You do not wish it?" he asked, dropping his hands again.

"Others may not."

"What others? I believe the whole Council wishes you would wed and provide the Kingdom with an heir."

"Just others." Trevisian's mind drifted unintentionally back to the blue-eyed boy. He pushed the image away from him. The boy was dead and he had allowed it to happen. "And how has the court been?"

"Much the same. Garesh continues to flatter every group to keep them at his beck and call. Rumours filter in, of rebels causing disruption in the Great Forest. Garesh believes they are Laowyn. From what I hear they are taking no offensive actions, only defensive, in the face of hardship, but Garesh sees them as acts of aggression. With his interpretation, people in the court are beginning to hate them. Even the Radichi have better relations with your people - do you know I was greeted by no less than three of the twenty people I passed on the way to your rooms today?"

Trevisian smiled. His friend's humour over his race always surprised him. He hadn't noticed it much when he was young, but as he grew up he had seen how others shunned him. Discrimination against other races was simply accepted, but where Johan was concerned it irritated Trevisian. If he wasn't so obviously Radichi it would be easier, but the tattoo pattern which lay just beneath Johan's skin was a clear demarcation of his race. The faint swirling brown markings described what line he was descended from, but no one outside the Radichi had been taught to decipher the code. Even Trevisian knew very little of their people and culture. Perhaps that was why no one fully trusted the desert warriors.

Johan carried on, his deep voice so familiar to Trevisian, "And then there are the many beautiful women flooding your harem. They have caused a great deal of talk amongst the courtiers."

"Ugh!" Trevisian threw his hands up in the air before going out onto the balcony. He looked down to where men and women talked by the fountain, birds swooping and playing in the water.

He glanced above his head at the flight of a hawk

wheeling far over the high towers of the palace. It swooped back and forth, proud wings stretched out wide, riding the winds wherever it wished. Free as Trevisian had been, less than a fortnight ago.

"How can the thought of beautiful women upset you?" Johan leant his patterned arms alongside his friend's on the sculpted stone of the balcony edge.

"It's not just that. It's being here, with all of this, with Garesh breathing down my neck. I can..." Trevisian rubbed a hand along the back of his neck. "I can still see my father, everywhere here, and I... I can't be like him."

The bubbling of the fountain and the song of the birds took over the silence.

"You told me before," Johan interjected his thoughts, "how you were not ready to rule your Kingdom. You wished to go somewhere that you could be..." The Radichi avoided eye contact with his Prince. "Be yourself. If you have not done that yet, then why are you back here?"

"Trust me," Trevisian pushed back from the balcony in frustration. "I didn't choose to come back."

"No, that's true." Trevisian could hear the smile in Johan's voice. "You chose the much easier transportation option of being arrested and shipped back by Garesh."

"Shut up, Johan." Trevisian wanted to laugh.

"Trevisian," Johan took his friend by the shoulders.

"If you need to leave again, leave."

"Garesh won't let it happen twice."

"He won't be able to help it."

A spark of a smile passed between the two friends.

⊙⊙⊙

Kiara coughed, the sound crawling out of her lungs slowly, painfully, threatening to crack her chest in two. She blindly clutched at her cloak, keeping it close around her thin frame, trying to keep from stumbling.

She had left Grûl three days ago, but her wandering in the forest had gotten her nowhere. She couldn't go back to Miresh, not after she had run from the Edict and her uncle. One of two things would happen if she did: either she would be sent off to the palace harem, or she would bring down a battalion of guards upon her uncle when they came searching for their escaped prisoner.

She had been trying to find the lair of the Laowyn Resistance - it was they who had first inspired Kiara to fight back, for what was right and just. People had whispered about them in the market place back in Miresh, but she hadn't found them.

As soon as she had escaped Grûl she had headed south, but her leg was making her progress slow. At first it only impeded her running, then her walking, and now she could barely touch her foot to the ground. She collapsed beside a river, leaning down the bank to cup the water in her hands, the liquid stinging the cracks in her lips. It was the first drink she had found the whole day. The last was from a puddle gathered on one of the many tracks that threaded through the forest, connecting settlements through an otherwise wild and beast-infested wood.

The Reluwyn had no desire to enter the trees between which shadows moved unchecked and men went missing – and that was why the Laowyn Resistance were safe here, although they too kept out of certain areas.

Inhabiting the eastern half of the forest, it was the Northern Elves of the Meir Kingdom who really knew the beasts. They tracked them, tamed them, spoke to them as only the Meir elven folk could. It was their power over these beasts and their own secrecy that made them a target for the Council's oppression. Last year, during the elves annual autumn gatherings, they had been arrested, accused of inciting unrest with their revels, and sentenced to having their leaders' ears cut off. Paraded through the streets of Emril city, the leaders had carried their pride as elven folk in their hands, blood dripping between their fingers.

Kiara had avoided the forest tracks after that last puddle drink, as a band of merchants had almost discovered her. She couldn't risk getting caught now she was a fugitive as well as a Laowyn woman. She'd heard how Reluwyn soldiers treated Laowyn women during the conquest. Rape and murder. Kiara shut her eyes against those thoughts. When she opened them again, she saw an animal disappearing into the bushes further down the bank.

She pushed all thoughts of capture far from her mind and wiped her forehead. Her body temperature had been rising steadily over the last few days. Perspiration shimmered across her skin. Dropping her hand to the stab wound on her leg, she felt its tenderness through the layers of fabric. It wasn't healing. When she had pulled the shoulder of her shirt down and looked at the few coils of her Laowyn mark that were visible to her, she'd seen that the colour was turning. The spirals were leaching black in favour of red, the colour of illness, and her Ensper was dimming.

She lay back upon the bank, careful to avoid leaning on the arm that had been relocated by the thief. It was getting better, although still sore. She wondered what the thief's jaw was like now. Bruised? Swollen? Or was he dead?

Her mind wandered as far as it could before the pain dragged her back to the task at hand. She undid the leg of her trouser and tugged a little at the bandage, rhythmically breathing against the pain. It throbbed, it was always throbbing, but the tugging caused a sensation of red-hot wire being dragged beneath the surface of her skin.

All she could see were congealed ridges of blood, several ripped stitches, and the outbreak of white pus oozing its way along the black tracks. It should be healing, but her movement impeded it.

She heard the crack of a twig and looked up. Low lying ferns on the river's bank fluttered in the wind and the trees swayed above, birds and small creatures migrating between them. The hairs on her neck rose. Was it the animal she had glimpsed earlier?

She gave up watching after a time. If it was a person, surely they would have shown themselves by now. She turned back to her leg, covering up the wound. It may need rest to heal, but her life depended on not staying too long in one place.

Struggling to her feet she limped on. She didn't know where she was going, nor did she know what she was going to do when she got there. One thing she was sure of - she wouldn't be dying here.

CHAPTER 6

"They're all very beautiful."

"So they are, my Lord Prince," Johan responded. Moving onto the sparring platform, he hefted the Reluwyn scimitar in his left hand. It was unlucky, according to the Reluwyn, to be left-handed in battle, but it hadn't worked out so badly for him.

"Come, are we sparring or chatting like your harem concubines around the fountain?" Johan watched his friend come to life a little. The Prince picked up his sword and stepped up onto the platform.

Various personages of the court stood about the training room. The mirrored room with its huge barrel roof was part of the men's quarters, a place for them to return to their cultural roots and fight by strength and cunning.

The Reluwyn were not so different from the Radichi warriors, thought Johan. They craved the blood of battle and the bodies of women, but they had abandoned their nomadic roots in favour of settling. In doing so they had built the largest empire in a thousand years. They saw themselves as superior to the Radichi, and so had taken the desert warriors as mercenaries.

Johan did not mind much since he was favoured personally by the Prince. More than that, they were friends.

"I have to choose a wife."

"You mean to tell me you have made it through all the beautiful maidens your Kingdom has to offer in two days?"

"No, but Garesh is anxious for me to decide. I can tell by the way he hovers around me like an insect, commanding me to inspect them in various ways."

"Various ways?" Johan wiggled a brow, chuckling when the Prince responded in kind.

"The bedding does not begin for a fortnight. A shame, it's almost worth staying for."

"A shame indeed," Johan lunged forward, connecting his blade with Trevisian's and getting close enough to whisper, "for you are to be away this very night. It is all arranged."

Johan acknowledged the Prince's nod, backing away and allowing Trevisian to lunge forward and swoop low. Johan responded by feigning a stumble and Trevisian's blade was at his neck instantly.

"You have become quicker with your travels, Trevisian. I do wonder how that came about…"

"If I return you'll have to watch your back."

"If?"

Trevisian avoided Johan's enquiring eyes. The Radichi warrior was tempted to probe further, but from experience he knew the Prince would not share if he did not wish to. It was a symptom of a court with ears everywhere and few people to trust.

"Do you know," asked Johan, his voice as relaxed as if he told an amusing anecdote, "that tonight there is to be a banquet held in your honour. Who knows what lies Garesh had to tell to hide your absence and explain away the rumours. And with all the important persons arriving, your guards will be occupied with protecting them. The outer gates of the palace will be left rather thin of company."

Trevisian smiled. "Go on."

"Well, my Lord Prince." Johan returned his grin. "I've taken the liberty of placing garments in your chambers, under the covers of your bed, that are not quite the thing for a Prince to wear, and I've had words with the guards scheduled to be on the Western Gate."

Johan thrust Trevisian off then, his raw strength far outmatching the Prince's.

Trevisian landed back on his feet. "Good!" The Prince handed his scimitar to a waiting servant and was given a muslin towel which he dabbed across his brow.

Johan followed him but dispensed with the towel in favour of his forearm.

"All is set then?" Trevisian asked, though the question was rhetorical.

It was what the Prince had done last time. It was his way of saying goodbye without having to speak the words.

"You understand, Johan?" Trevisian didn't look him in the eye as they turned for the door of the hall.

"I understand that you cannot be here for the moment, my Lord Prince." Johan let the cryptic words fall and the Prince comprehend them. As far as the Radichi warrior was concerned, he believed Trevisian could be a great King one day, when the shackles of Regency were removed and the shadow of his father had passed, but that day would not be today.

"As the Radichi say, I wish you great victory in battle, and great women to fight for." He slapped Trevisian's back and they walked out together.

⚫⚫⚫

Kiara was curled up between the broad roots of a star tree, its yellow leaves adding brightness to the clear night sky. One by one the stars faded into the pale dawn light, leaving the pointed leaves to dance alone above the sleeping traveller.

She snuggled closer to the tree trying to keep warm, but was only rewarded, as she had been all night, with the scratch of bark against her cheek and the bony nobbles of distorted roots digging into her limbs.

She'd barely slept over the past week, which coupled with a lack of food meant she was on the brink of passing out. The constant throbbing in her thigh, and the knowledge of definite death if captured, meant that she cared less and less. Perhaps it didn't matter if she collapsed here. Zephenesh could believe she had escaped, even if he disliked it he would think she was alive. She wouldn't be known as a woman ruined by the Prince, or a hanged criminal who shamed her family.

She froze as she heard twigs cracking behind the oak tree. The sounds were sharp and getting louder. She rose as silently as she could. The dawn light was reaching through the trees, desperate to reveal her to whoever was making their way through the forest.

Moving away from the star tree, Kiara slipped through the surrounding saplings to the giant trees beyond. As the crackling increased around her, she glanced back, but no movement disturbed the ferns or dead leaves behind her.

Her heart beat faster. She tried to silence her breathing, but it just became more laboured as she ignored the pain and tried to limp forward. She would not be taken alive.

Ahead of her, the path between the trees widened. The leaf-covered floor expanded and fell into a downward slope. There was probably a river or lake down there. Perhaps she had finally made it to Endil, the lake that separated the old Laowyn Kingdom from the Meir.

She didn't have time to think: the sounds were growing louder. Was it a troop of Imperial Guards? She stumbled across the scattering of dead leaves, glancing down to drag her wounded leg over the roots. That's when she saw it - but it was too late. Ropes slithered like snakes in the grass as the net closed in around her, hoisting her into the trees.

The pressure of ropes tearing across her wound made her scream. Through the slits of her pain-ridden eyes she scanned the ground beneath her. No one there. Another shot of pain lanced through her thigh. She tried to cover the wound but the net stopped her. One finger managed to touch it and she felt the flow of warm, sticky blood. There was a loud rustle to her left, it seemed to be moving farther away as her head became heavy. Just before the darkness descended, she saw feet running across the forest floor below, lots of feet.

⚙⚙⚙

Trevisian shook the water from his hair, flinging droplets that caused Dainus to shake his own mane in irritation. The Prince had truly missed bathing in freshwater at dawn, and he'd made it to the lake of Endil in just two days.

He had arranged for his trusty stallion to be brought back from the moors after he had decided on escape again. Dainus had been less than impressed at being confined to the palace stables - in fact, when Trevisian unbolted the stable door, his horse had almost run him over in a bid for freedom.

Traversing the crowded streets of Emril city, where sand-coloured buildings rose up either side of the street and oil lamps could be seen flickering in arched windows, was easy for Trevisian. He'd spent so much of his youth escaping into the city, that the streets which rose and fell and twisted left and right made complete sense to him. It was in the dark of these very streets that he had been able to be himself, far away from what was expected of him as his father's son. When he was on his own and hidden, he could give in to the natural urges he knew came from the magic of his maternal line. No one could condemn him for it.

Night had been descending when he left the city two days ago and it reminded him of those times as a boy. He had left just before the banquet as Johan had suggested, and the Imperial Guards were concentrated around the jewelled courtyard just as he had predicted.

Now he stood here in the light of the two suns, alone and free. Early morning mist rose above the water making it take on a look of infinite depth. Trevisian stretched out on the grassy bank in a patch of sun, drying off as Dainus ate his well-deserved fill. Blades of grass tickled Trevisian's ears as his eyelids slowly closed, the rise of his bare chest falling into a rhythm as he finally relaxed. It was good to be out of the heavy garments, although he could still feel the blisters on the back of his heels from the boots. Johan had really been scraping the bottom of the barrel with this disguise, Trevisian wouldn't even have dressed his servants in that garb. It must have been from one of the palace urchins who entertained for a few coins in the outer courtyards.

An hour slipped by, barely heeded, as the Prince enjoyed the euphoria of freedom. His mind drifted over all he'd escaped for the second time, at least until Garesh's long arms caught him again. Perhaps it would be different this time. No more documents to sign, no courtly appearances, no feeling of weight when confronted by new laws which affected so many, and no expectation to be the hard ruler his father was.

Trevisian's only regret was leaving all those maidens behind. He didn't want the responsibility of a wife tying him to the palace, but the idea of women lining up, offering themselves to him? No man could resist that, especially no Reluwyn man. The race was known for their virility and had already managed to populate most areas of the Kingdom alongside the natural inhabitants. His father had married his mother to beget an heir, and Trevisian knew how that had turned out: he didn't have a mother, not anymore.

He remembered her smooth oval face looking down at him with kind eyes; her ebony hair braided to her waist, low enough to tickle his face. She had always encouraged him in his magic, in the blood that ran in his veins and the freedom it could offer him. Well, now he could have it.

Rising from the grass he walked over to Dainus. "I'm going for a run, boy, I'll be back." He dropped the trousers we wore and stood naked in the sunlight. It always started as tingling in his fingertips. Then it grew, sparks firing up and down his arms, his chest heating. Every inch of his body coming alive as if all the energy he would ever have was in him right at this moment bursting to get out.

He started running, first on two legs and then he fell onto all fours. It wasn't hands and feet that fell on the soft lakeside grass, but paws. Fur starting around his newly changed claws ran up his arms and legs like the speed of light. His body changed, becoming sleeker, lower to the ground. The last to change was his head and it always happened so quickly he was howling like the wildcat he had become before he realised.

He pounded the ground, enjoying the freedom of being the true self he was always forced to hide. He didn't know how long he ran for, or where he was going, but when he was like this he could trace his way back easily, his mother had taught him how. But for this moment in time he just enjoyed the freedom.

When he returned an hour later, Dainus was still grazing further down the bank. Arching his back, Trevisian reined in the fiery power that burned through his veins. It was always more difficult to shift back. Even now pain lanced through his body as it contracted back into his human form. He bore it because he must. He had been caught out before, and could not afford to be again.

After his shift was complete he picked up his things and took them to where Dainus now grazed. He pulled his trousers back on and lay down finally feeling calm. All the thoughts which had begun to plague him before the run had faded and now his stomach growled. Johan had been thoughtful enough to supply some food, but since this had been long finished, he'd have to use the bow. He sat up, pulling his shirt from the rock it lay on. It slipped easily over the tattoo that marked most of his back, a design of feathers shimmering in different colours with flames at the base, and a large eye that appeared to move.

He stroked the sleek neck of Dainus, his hand gliding along the lines of muscle and over the horse's shoulder. He would find food enough for several days ride in the forest, and then he'd turn south. Garesh knew Trevisian had been in the Northern Moors for the past few months and once the search parties came, they'd have to be long gone. He could live unknown in the Chieftain Lands above the Tao desert. It had good hunting, and plenty of wild spaces between the tribes where Trevisian could live undetected.

"How would that be, boy? Southern climes, warm sunshine and verdant hills?" Trevisian leant forward and rested his forehead against the horse's. The stallion's neck arched, his crest standing out proud and beautiful as Trevisian swung up into the saddle. They headed away from the lake and back into the forest.

They had been riding along slowly for less than an hour, hoof beats deadened by the mulch on the forest floor, before Trevisian heard any prey. The bow Johan had packed was clasped in his hands, and the shaft of the loaded arrow rested against his thigh as he silently scanned the woodland. Dainus pricked up his ears as a branch fell back into place, followed by the movement of shadows between the trees.

Dainus halted, tensing his muscles. Trevisian raised the bow, training it on the area of movement. He narrowed his eyes and took aim. A sudden glimpse of pale skin - not fur – surprised him. It was too late: he had already let the arrow fly.

A cry sounded far off in the woodland. Not an animal cry.

Trevisian reached for another arrow. He wouldn't get caught by Garesh, not yet.

A man staggered forward into plain sight, regaining his balance quickly. Trevisian could see the arrow sticking out of his left arm, immobilising it.

"You're lucky," said Trevisian roughly, "I was aiming for your neck." He sat up straighter, readying himself to trample this unwelcome intruder.

"Then you should better your aim," came the blunt reply. The man was dressed in what looked like the whole forest, with leaves covering his clothes and mud smeared across his face. Still, Trevisian could see from the way he didn't flinch at the arrow, and his great size, that he was not to be underestimated. Running him down was clearly the best course of action.

"I wouldn't do that if I were you," said the man, seeing him gather his reins. He reached up and snapped off the end of the arrow in his arm, wincing only slightly. "I never travel alone."

With that, five other men appeared from the undergrowth, from branches of trees and holes in the forest floor, all in similar camouflage. They moved in on Trevisian. He let loose a stream of Reluwyn curses that would have made any man cringe.

Dainus started prancing. At a nod from the man, Trevisian threw the bow down. It was useless at such close range anyway. He was quick to pull a curved, vicious-looking dagger from a sheath on his right arm. The men responded in kind, each pulling a mean-looking weapon out and training it on their prisoner.

Trevisian exhaled roughly in agitation. What did these men want? He dropped the dagger, and then stroked Dainus once, whispering into his ear. Finally, he dismounted in obedience to the leader's command.

He noticed their uniform, beneath the dirt: swathes of coloured camouflage cloth. With a small gold emblem. He recognised it as the sign of the Laowyn.

Ordinarily, Trevisian would have used his true identity to escape, but this time he thought better of it. The feuding between the Reluwyn and Laowyn was reaching a head, and these men didn't seem the peaceable type. There would be no easy escape this time.

CHAPTER 7

Kiara lay on a makeshift straw bed in the corner of the room. There was no natural light, only oil lamps that burned in the corners. The room was made of earth: earth floor, earth walls, earth ceiling. She had already guessed that she was underground when they had first brought her in blindfolded. The smell of damp soil had pinched at her nose not long after they had cut her down, placed material over her eyes and commanded her to walk, or rather limp.

That meant that the entrance could only be a short walk from where she had been captured. It also explained why there was a trap in which she could get caught. They were protecting their base, and as Laowyn Resistance, why wouldn't they?

Even now it seemed ridiculous to Kiara. *The* Laowyn Resistance. She was in the base of *the* Laowyn Resistance. Of course, it would be far more exciting if she wasn't a prisoner, but why pick at small details like that?

"Why are you smiling?"

She shifted her gaze from the ceiling, wincing as her turning set off fresh throbbing in her leg.

"You know we have offered to have a look at whatever it is you keep clutching beneath your trouser leg."

Kiara's eyes flashed at the elf who was half crouched, half sat, in what looked like an immeasurably uncomfortable and quite honestly, weird, position. He always sat like that.

"I'm fine."

"Alright." Her cell-mate crossed his arms in a way that suggested he didn't believe her.

"And my thoughts are my own."

Kiara instantly regretted her words. She had gotten quite friendly with Zeb, the elf she had shared her cell with for several days.

"I'm hungry."

"Finally!" said the elf, who was *always* hungry. "You know it really isn't good for you to wait for so long between meals."

Kiara smiled, getting to her feet awkwardly and limping over to a few overturned buckets where some bread, cheese and apples had been left by the guard this morning.

She broke off a crust and handed it to Zeb, who had come to stand beside her. Although shorter than most

men, he was just as tall as her and average height for his
race.

"Thank you." He took the offered food.

"What's the difference between Southern and
Northern Elves?" Kiara had never met his kind before.
Zeb looked different to Djeck who was from the north,
but the contrast was so subtle it was hard to notice at first.
Zeb had fair hair and looked darker in his skin. Apart
from that, it had taken two days of staring for Kiara to
realise that Zeb was a stockier, more muscular elf than any
of the slender Meir Elves, although still wiry compared to
other races. He also had larger more rounded ears with
less defined points, that were still unmistakably elvish. His
accent was more lilting and broad than that of the Meir
Elves. He said he had spoken a different language back
home in the Wild Southern Forest, but that's all he had
said about that place.

"We eat what we kill or find without leaving any to
waste. We believe in looking after the land and the people
in it. That's about it." He took a huge bite of bread,
sending cheese down after it a few seconds later.

"And," Kiara paused, not sure she should ask. "And
what lives in the Wild Southern Forest for you to kill?"

Zeb didn't answer. It was as if he hadn't heard, but
Kiara knew that he had. He hadn't answered her yet on

why he was in the northern part of the Great Forest, and why he was so far from his home.

"Tell me, why was a boy like you roaming alone in the Great Forest?" Zeb asked after a time. He was crouched in his funny position again. Kiara joined him, preferring to sit on a bucket. She kept her wounded leg straight out before her, bumping lightly on the bucket as she sat.

"I've told you, I lost my father on our way to the farms in the Chieftain Lands."

"Ah, yes," Zeb nodded, folding the arm that wasn't holding food across his taut stomach. He didn't believe her again. Kiara didn't much mind, as long as they didn't find out that she was a woman.

"And what does a Southern Elf have to do with the Laowyn Resistance?"

Zeb looked at her sharply.

"Oh, come on! I'm no fool. I've seen the emblems on the guards' tunics – you must have done too. An underground lair, secretive and in the centre of the old forest. I think I know exactly whose prison in which I sit."

The corner of Zeb's sharp mouth twitched up quickly before dropping again. "Clever."

Kiara couldn't help the smug look that came over her face.

"But you realise that if they find out that you are not who you say you are, and you know as much as you say, they'll have to kill you."

Kiara swallowed her mouthful of bread, the food suddenly feeling like hard stone.

"I have led no men here, nor have I sent out any communications, and besides, what about you? Is that why you say nothing of your homeland, or why you're here, even to me, a fellow prisoner?"

"Maybe. If you continue not to cause any trouble for them, they may release you." Zeb's voice had turned gentle.

"And you?"

"Don't worry yourself over me."

They sat in silence for a time, as Kiara handed out pieces of food and Zeb nodded his thanks. He appeared not much older than Kiara, but Elves lived longer than Laowyn by about fifty years, so he could well be her senior by a decade. Yet Kiara could see young lines of laughter on his face, and every now and then his eyes twinkled. Still, there was something in those pale eyes she couldn't quite put her finger on.

She didn't get a chance to muse much longer: the door was suddenly opened and a dark bundle was thrown roughly onto the cell floor.

The two inmates looked at each other, and then back at the groaning pile. There was a grunt, then a curse. An arm from underneath the pile pushed the body up a fraction.

Zeb went to the door to take a new tray of food from a guard who leant in and spoke. "Watch this one Zeb. Vicious! Got Captain Fidel in the arm with an arrow and then beat three of our men who tried to restrain him. Even his horse was a beast, refusing to be caught. Got *him* back here by clobbering him with sword butts. Been unconscious for the past hour." He gestured with a careless hand at the captive. "Looks like he's waking up." A sardonic smile was thrown at Zeb.

"Thanks," replied the elf with equal sarcasm.

The door shut and Zeb assessed the new prisoner. Kiara stood, hands on her cocked hips, a brow raised in warning.

"Watch this one?" she queried, "Haven't you already got one to *watch*?" She was an idiot to think that she had been making some kind of ally. He had been placed in the cell to find out if she was an enemy.

"It's not what you think," Zeb, for all his stalwartness, suddenly looked like a child who had done wrong. Without his usual solemnity he looked much younger. "I…" he hesitated. "I assess prisoners for…"

"The Laowyn Resistance?!" Kiara finished the sentence for him. "You lied to me!"

"Think of it more as an embellishment." Zeb's angular face attempted a smile. "I am technically a prisoner. It's just I can leave whenever I wish."

Kiara felt the corner of her mouth twitch. It begged to pull upwards but she wouldn't let it.

"I have certain abilities when it comes to assessing people. If it helps, I do not think you're a threat." He threw out the verdict without much care, turning back to the new prisoner who was still protesting on the floor.

Did that mean they would release her? Did she even want to be released? She was fed here, believed in their cause, wanted to join them. Scuffling drew her attention to where Zeb was already staring.

Kiara saw them then, those eyes flashing around the room and stopping on her and the elf for a moment. They moved on, but hers did not. She froze. All thoughts of Zeb and the Resistance disappeared. On the floor, locked in a cell with her, was the thief! Maybe he wouldn't recognise her.

The thought, or rather her fervent wish, wasn't granted by the Great Spirit. The dark eyes had left hers only for a moment, assessing the cell, the walls, the door, before they paused and darted back to her.

There was a trickle of dried blood at his temple and he looked different from the last time, but those eyes remained the same. The same intensity lay within them, the same ferociousness that had scared her before.

"You!" cried the thief, rising with disbelief and anger. When he reached his full height, he towered over both Kiara and the elf.

"You know him?" Zeb asked incredulously. He looked between the two of them but Kiara wouldn't speak. Couldn't speak.

"Still upset over that silver box I wouldn't let you have?" The thief's words were thrown out like knives trying to find their mark, his top lip pulling up into a sneer.

When the words did come, Kiara was surprised by them. Without wavering she matched the man malice for malice. "I thought you'd be hanged by now, feeding the gulls on Grûl's dockside."

The thief's smile increased. "And I you. Tell me, how does a boy escape an Imperial Watchtower?"

"What lies did *you* tell to get you out of that pit?" Kiara spat back, his reply only incensing her more. She couldn't give ground. He had not guessed she was a woman before, but now she stood in the bright light of the oil lamps, maybe he'd guess. His cross-examination might raise Zeb's suspicions too.

The thief brought his hand down, but Kiara caught it before it could hit her. Stepping back she realised that there was no force behind it.

"I see that shoulder's been healing nicely." He spoke smugly.

Kiara tried to move away from him but only managed a pathetic hobble.

"Not that leg though."

"That's enough!" Zeb shouted. "Although this little reunion is touching, you two need to separate before I call in the guard."

❍❍❍

Trevisian growled in response to the elf's reprimand, stepping back towards the straw bed and laying himself down on it. He touched the bruise on his jaw. Damn those Laowyn! And damn that boy! Was he part of the Resistance? Was that why he'd been hell-bent on keeping those Edicts from circulating? He couldn't be; why would he be sleeping in this prison if he was one of them? Trevisian didn't know the answers to any of his questions. What he did know was that no one must find out who he really was. There was no telling the danger he would be in if they did.

He glanced over at the boy who was sitting beside the elf on an upturned bucket. He would have to assess the situation, his fellow captives, and the room he was in if he wanted to escape. His combat training rose to the surface. The Laowyn must be short of space if this cell had to house three prisoners. He had heard the elf talking to the guard, maybe he was one of the Resistance.

He studied the face of the boy carefully for the first time. He had last seen him covered in mud and blood, and now he was clean. He was odd-looking, with small features and that huge mop of golden hair. There was something not quite right about his appearance. He wasn't elfin though, he was too...feminine. The dark lashes surrounding Trevisian's eyes closed in, narrowing on the boy.

The boy looked back at him then, his blue eyes locking with Trevisian's boldly, a gaze the Prince was not used to. Courtiers glanced at him before looking away in supposed reverence; Garesh occasionally gave him hard looks between lectures, but even these were short-lived. This creature stared at him openly. The size of them, that blue, the boy's eyes were... striking... Trevisian felt the pieces of the puzzle falling into place. How else could someone have escaped the jail at Grûl? Seducing the guards would have worked very well. The small stature, those features, the outrage at the Edict of Maidens.

Perhaps she had been chosen herself, although most maidens would have been thrilled to spend a night with the Prince.

No! This couldn't be true. How could a woman have fought him so well with her sword? How could a woman even possess such a sword? Trevisian's thoughts drifted back to the palace and the silver-blue blade that must still sit in his quarters. His unbroken stare had perhaps given too much away, because the object of his fascination suddenly looked away, a blush stealing up their cheeks.

It couldn't be.

"You're bleeding." The elf leant forward, looking at the fresh blood wetting the already stained trousers the prisoner wore. "You should have let us treat it."

The pain made the boy's body shudder, and the elf caught him just as he crumpled. The elf glanced over without friendliness to the Prince. "Give me a hand over to that pallet."

Thoughts of the boy's true identity were gone for a brief moment. Trevisian did as he was told, helping carry the unconscious youth, laying him carefully down on the bed.

"Get the guard," the elf commanded, not looking up from his patient. He unbuckled the trouser leg, peeling it back and revealing the infected wound that looked ready to burst its remaining stitches.

"You need to cut the rotten flesh out and burn the skin together to sterilize and seal it." Trevisian said, not moving. "Shall I ask for a knife?"

The elf gave him a condescending glare. "Not all of us are as barbaric as you Reluwyn when it comes to healing." He turned back to the fair-haired boy, raising his hands over the leg, hovering them in slow concentric circles.

Trevisian had no intention of moving until he had confirmed his suspicions. He leant in to get a closer look.

"Get the guard," snapped the elf.

The curtly repeated command set Trevisian's blood boiling. No one ordered him around. The boy suddenly moved and groaned but didn't quite regain consciousness. Trevisian exhaled in frustration before turning to the door. He hammered on the wood until a guard answered.

"The elf wants…" Trevisian paused.

"I want my healing satchel, they'll know where it is."

He relayed the commands through the door and then leaned against it, watching the drama being enacted across the room.

The guards weren't long in procuring the requested satchel, and Trevisian was left with no more time to think. He brought the bag over to the elf whose hands were still moving in strange patterns over the boy's leg.

"I've never seen an elf heal before," he mused, dropping the pack carelessly beside him. "I thought your giftings were in the taming of forest animals. Although if that creature dies, I won't be complaining."

The elf huffed, trying to concentrate. "I'm Southern."

Trevisian's brows rose at this. "A Southern Elf? I had it on good authority that your kind had exiled themselves across the Western Sea."

"They did." The elf offered him nothing more, and Trevisian gauged from the tension that probing could prove unhealthy. "And I would question whose authority you gained that information from."

Definitely unhealthy for him. Only the government was aware of the Southern Elves' exile, and they had tried to keep it quiet to prevent other economically important races from following suit. Garesh's approach to maintaining a firm rule depended upon uniformity.

The elf halted suddenly, leaning over the boy's face listening for breath. After a few moments he snatched up his satchel, he fishing through it until he found the tool he wanted. He drew out a dagger.

"Too civilised, eh?"

"His breathing's shallow," replied the elf, ignoring Trevisian's tone.

The Prince kept back. The last time he had been in a sick room had been with his father. He felt suffocated by the smell of the herbs that peeked out of the elf's bag. He shut his eyes against the flood of memories, only opening them when he felt calm.

The elf snatched at the loose shirt the boy wore. The knife went through it quick enough, but what it revealed the elf was at a loss to understand. Trevisian, however, was not. All thoughts of the past evaporated in an instant. He came closer to better see the tight binding on the prisoner's chest.

"She's a woman."

At these words, the stunned elf recovered his senses. "Stand back," he commanded.

"And miss all the fun?"

"She can't breathe with this on." The elf didn't bother asking Trevisian a second time. He took the knife, pulling up part of the binding and slipping it underneath. The linen tore apart under the pressure with which it had been bound. Zeb pulled up the shirt sides with his hand to cover the woman but it wasn't easy. As the last of the linen gave in to the blade, the woman heaved to life.

She gasped, inhaling all the air she had missed in the last few minutes. Her eyes flew open, fear evident. She flashed blue irises between the elf and the man and then down at her destroyed shirt. She snatched at the material, covering the smooth, bare skin that had been on display down the centre of her body.

"Oh please," Trevisian said, leaning casually against the wall, a smile licking his lips. "Don't worry on my account...*woman*."

She was frantically shuffling away from the elf and the Reluwyn until her back hit the cell wall.

"It's okay, it's okay," the elf tried in vain to soothe her.

"What are you doing? What happened?" Her voice was panicked and strained.

Seeing her as a woman for the first time, Trevisian could not help but acknowledge how beautiful she was. The eyes were what had struck him before, now he noticed the fuller lips, the perfectly formed nose, and that body...

●●●

"Your leg – the pain made you fall unconscious – and you couldn't breathe because of your..." Zeb apparently didn't know what to call it.

"Because you were trying so hard to hide your womanly attributes."

Kiara could see the Reluwyn's gaze running all over her body. She pulled the two torn halves of her shirt together more tightly. She had been near tears a moment ago, her voice strangled by the shock of waking up practically naked in front of a man and an elf. The latter's eyes were averted, but the Reluwyn's were filled with that look of... she didn't like to say what. Her fear was rapidly morphing into fury.

"You're even more attractive when you're angry."

He came closer then, leaning towards her, his breath against her cheek. She tried to swat him. Too slow. Zeb's movement was quick and hard, punching the Reluwyn's forearm away.

"Get off her!"

The Reluwyn put his hands up. "I've never met a female thief before."

"My lady," Zeb turned back to Kiara, his address coming out stilted and unfamiliar. "You must let me treat your leg."

"After you've torn off my clothes? Go to the Spirit Realm!" She wished them both to the darkest parts of that other world.

"So fiery," murmured the Reluwyn from a safe place by the far wall. He continued to stare at her in a way that made her skin crawl.

Zeb's voice softened and dropped too low for the Reluwyn to hear. "Let me treat it. I promise no harm will come to you. I won't let that man near you. As soon as I have the wound dressed I'll get the guard to move you, but for now you're bleeding and it must be stopped."

Kiara finally retracted her gaze from the Reluwyn and saw in Zeb's eyes real earnestness. He wasn't touching her anymore, nor did he do so until she gave him her permission. She'd spent several days with the elf, perhaps she could trust him. And anyway, what choice did she have?

He put the knife away in his bag and drew out various herbs and bandages. He pounded the plants together, forming a paste with some kind of elixir from one of his bottles, and then placed them on her leg and bound the poultice on with the bandages. She was biting her lip against the stinging and finally had to shut her eyes. When she opened them again she caught eyes with the Reluwyn. He still watched her.

"Zeb," she whispered, "I'm Laowyn. Please, get me out of here." She knew what Reluwyn men were capable of. They were a barbaric race, living on drink and women, worshipping nothing but pleasure and excess. She had not known someone look at her like he did, and she didn't want to find out what that look meant. It held such intensity that he either wanted to kill her or… she didn't want to know.

"Come to the door, I'll help you." Zeb put an arm under Kiara's shoulders, pulling her up and going to bang on the door. "Teo! Come now, it's an emergency!"

Kiara turned back to see that the Reluwyn had risen.

"What? Going so soon after such revelation?"

She flinched at his words, at his look, and the elf must have sensed it for he hammered on the door more vigorously.

The door was finally unlocked, and Zeb barked instructions at both guards. One came in to keep the Reluwyn in place, the other helped Kiara and Zeb out of the cell.

It wasn't until the door closed that Kiara relaxed. She rested heavily against Zeb, exhausted. Soon she'd be unconscious again, although hopefully she wouldn't wake up half naked this time.

Zeb nodded to one of the guards, who went over to a door across the way. As he opened it, oil lamps illuminated a store of barrels, dried fruit and bread.

"This is the only other place I can put you."

"But I'm Laowyn, I've already told you." Kiara's mind was tiring, along with her body. The small room before her was moving and dancing. The ringing from far off down the corridor was growing louder in her ears.

"I can't confirm that."

"Yes," Kiara, not fully realising what she was doing anymore, reached up and pulled at one side of the ripped shirt. "Yes, I'll show you."

"No." Zeb dragged her forcefully towards the room, grabbing her shirt at the neck to prevent her from opening it and sitting her down among the barrels. If Kiara had been fully aware of her surroundings, she would have seen the elf's discomfort, the way the muscles in his jaw jerked, his hands twitched, and the warring in his eyes.

"I'll get you a blanket." Zeb disappeared through the door. A guard took his place on the threshold, but Kiara wasn't going anywhere. Her head bobbed gently, finally falling back against one of the sacks of grain, her eyelids flickered and then shut.

She wasn't awake to see Zeb come and place a blanket over her. Nor did she see the conflicted look he gave her. He shook his head and walked away before he could think more. He needed to report to Captain Fidel; someone else needed to check for this woman's mark, it couldn't be him.

CHAPTER 8

"She's a woman." Fidel stood at a table on which a leather map and markers had been placed.

"Really?" Ikara, the Commander of the Laowyn Resistance couldn't hide her surprise. "How did we not know this?"

Fidel shrugged, there was no one else in the Commander's meeting room, he could be informal with his childhood friend in here. He looked over at her, catching ice-coloured eyes that matched the silver hair. It was an unusual combination, and Fidel had joked that it was this supernatural look that gave her the ability to command the masses.

"She was dressed as a boy, short hair, and she didn't say anything."

"She's been in a cell with a male elf for days. We should have realised this."

"There's no way we could have done."

"How did we find out then?"

Fidel cringed inwardly. He'd rather not tell the story to Ikara. The look from his Commander ordered him to do so however. When Fidel had finished recounting the events, he attempted to reassure his Commander. "She's already been moved to a cell opposite. Zeb expects her leg to be healed by tomorrow."

The distraction of Zeb's healing powers was enough for Ikara. "Tomorrow? That elf's abilities never cease to amaze me. Yet he still didn't guess - she must have made quite the impression." She sighed in frustration and straightened. When standing, she was as tall as Fidel. "Another room taken up with prisoners when our numbers grow daily. There isn't enough space for our people, let alone those we catch in the woods. Especially strange women."

Fidel would have expected Ikara to smile, but she didn't find amusement as easy these days. None of the Laowyn did and her lot was harder than most. So many lives depending on her decisions.

"Zeb wasn't keen on the looks the other prisoner was giving her. The Reluwyn is particularly vicious, but it isn't just that, from the way he speaks to her, he seems to know her."

"You mean they're involved?" Ikara did little to hide her distaste at the thought.

"Not necessarily. He was not exactly kind to her. Either way the Reluwyn's dangerous."

Ikara eyed the bandage on Fidel's arm. "Or perhaps age is catching up with you." A gleam appeared in her eye but no smile on her lips.

Fidel answered with a crooked grin. He was handsome and well built, a man, known for his honour - everything a Laowyn woman could want. "I can still take you in combat if you dare, Commander."

Sensing they were on dangerous ground, Ikara changed the subject. "Have we confirmed his identity?"

"He wears all the garb of a palace entertainer from Emril city. That and his dark colouring suggests he is of Reluwyn descent."

Ikara nodded. Though the Laowyn's colouring could differ, Reluwyn always had hair and eyes that varied from brown to black. "And is she from the palace too? Is that how she knows him? I was given to understand she claimed she was Laowyn."

"She did, but her colouring is fair. She could just as easily be from the southern parts of the Kingdom. Zeb was going to check for her mark but he wishes you to do so now her sex is known."

"So careful, and Zeb is usually the one to break all the rules."

"He's very particular about his treatment of women, even more so when it comes to this one," Fidel drifted in thought.

"One day I will have a long chat with that elf."

"I doubt he'd tell you anything more than he already has."

"We know so little of him."

"He's useful," replied Fidel, as though that were enough. He watched Ikara shut her eyes briefly, as if in weariness.

"Very well, I will check her mark, if she is one of us then she must be missing from somewhere. The sooner we can find that out, the quicker we can restore her to her kin." Ikara spoke with finality.

"I…"

"Yes?"

"If she's disguised as a boy, don't you think she would not wish to return? This isn't the first I've heard of Laowyn women disguising themselves to escape the Edict of Maidens."

"Yes, and the ones that have been caught have been executed." Ikara turned away and looked towards the fire that slumbered in the grate. It was always cold and damp in this place. Even in high summer fires were needed, but careful watch had to be kept over smoke generated above ground. "It's not our place to decide her fate, Fidel. Besides, as you say, there's no room for any other Laowyn at present, especially not women. We'll need fighters if war comes."

Fidel looked at her quizzically but she didn't take the bait. Everyone had doubted her ability at first, after her father, the first leader of the Resistance had died - nevertheless, she had risen to bear the mantle, refusing to pass it on to a man. The scepticism went hand-in-hand with the Laowyn attitude towards protecting women. Fidel couldn't imagine anyone trying to protect Ikara. And maybe she was right: for all they knew, this prisoner could be a risk to them all.

"How many replies have we had from the Laowyn Elders? We must meet soon if we are to plan the future of the Resistance. Our protection of those persecuted by Reluwyn radicals is all very well now, but not if the situation escalates. And High Councillor Garesh seems intent on upping his suppression of our people."

"We have had seven of the twelve. Zephenesh of Miresh replied yesterday that he travels already."

"Excellent - we should expect him in a few days. Great Spirit give us wisdom," Ikara prayed, looking towards the earthen ceiling. She then turned to Fidel. "What's more pressing is the twins scouting news. They've sent word that Reluwyn troops are mobilising all along the eastern border of the forest. They say they are preparing to enter the central area."

Fidel rubbed the back of his neck, the furrows in his broad brow increasing.

"We have no information on their purpose but we must be ready. Garesh may have decided to do an entire sweep of the Great Forest in order to smoke us out."

"We have been fortunate not to incur such a sanction already."

"Give thanks to the size of this forest and its beasts. The only thing that stopped him before was a lack of troops, but it seems he's not hesitating on that count anymore. If they are looking for our base we should not have much trouble picking them off." Ikara's eyes turned ominous along with her voice. "One by one if needs be."

"Hopefully not," Fidel decided to change the subject, "If the twins' scouting mission is done, are we expecting them back?"

"Presently." Ikara was no longer listening, her pale eyes refocusing on the map before her, her long-fingered hands moving pieces towards the east.

As she leant forward, the armour's carefully sculpted shoulder panel revealed her Ensper. A bold series of unique wide pointed slashes surrounded a large gem which was the same colour as her eyes.

The Ensper had caused the Reluwyn to admire the Laowyn at first, before it had become a desirable object. Fidel knew that the Reluwyn were removing this mark so they could add the gems to their royal treasury. Such barbarity was unspeakable. Soon their race would have no defining factor - they would be nameless among the masses - and if Garesh had his way, they'd be suppressed to the point of extinction.

Worse than all this; if they were without their Ensper, they were without knowledge of the Great Spirit's favour. For centuries the Laowyn had relied on their markings, and the inner light which guided them in matters concerning their people. They had not seen that light in many years, something which the Elders attributed to remaining in a conquered land, or even abandonment by the Spirit. Fidel had faith that the Spirit was still present, that soon he would speak and bestow favour upon them, and until that time came they must wait and trust. But what good would that be if the Ensper was taken from them?

Ikara reached across the table for another piece shaped like a Laowyn archer, her breastplate impeding her movement.

"You know, you don't need to wear your armour here."

"It's good for the men to see me in it." She had the Commander's position but that didn't stop some of the Resistance fighters from remembering she was a woman.

"Are there men here?"

Ikara sighed. "Help me out of it." She turned her back to Fidel who started working on the leather straps that suspended the breastplate from her shoulders. "It weighs heavily on me."

They were both caught off-guard when a knock sounded on the door, and then without waiting for a response two young men bowled into the room.

"No!" cried one, elbowing the other and leaping in front of him.

"You can't! I won't let you!" The second rubbed his ribs briefly before grabbing at the belt of his comrade. His fingers managed to slip beneath the top and he yanked his fellow spy back so hard he hit the wall.

"You idiot!" said the wall hugger, glancing up at the Captain and Commander. "Can't you see we're interrupting?"

Ikara brushed away Fidel's hands, turning to face the two intruders with her armour still very much in place.

"Calev, Jaik, what news?"

"Control yourselves!" Fidel rebuked the two before him. "Salute your Commander."

The men straightened themselves up and stood side by side obediently. They were identical, even down to the way their beards were clipped. Despite their Captain's disapproval, the twins couldn't stop nudging each other with their non-saluting elbows.

"Yes, yes!" Ikara waved down their hands. "The news?"

"Well…"

"No! I shall tell the Comm…"

"I was the one who overheard it."

Ikara's icy eyes, now robbed of patience, fell upon the Laowyn scout to the left. "I don't care who heard it. Jaik, speak."

He capitulated with little persuasion. "We were scouting the woods as commanded."

"And you saw the royal army mobilising to the east." Ikara corroborated, placing the pieces together in her mind.

"Yes, Commander. We reported back the army's presence - but we also have news as to why they are here, good news."

"How can it be good news?" Fidel asked. Despite their motley appearance, the twins' performance in the field was exemplary. Fidel had never met any warriors that were as given to stealth as these two; their scouting abilities were unparalleled. It was only in the underground caverns that they would become uncontrollable.

"Captain, we overheard the lieutenant of one of the contingents. He was commanding his troops to look for a runaway - from the palace in Emril city. That's why they aren't in full battle attire."

"They're not looking for us!" cried Calev, apparently unable to hold his tongue anymore. Jaik shot him an evil stare.

"Good." Ikara raised a dismissive hand. "Go feed yourselves."

They needed no second bidding. Three days without food, sitting in trees and moving silently on the ground really worked up a man's appetite. Coming to life, they barrelled out the door and down the hallway to the kitchen.

"I feel sorry for the cook." Fidel gave a crooked grin.

"Who can they be looking for?"

"A runaway servant?"

"He must be a valuable servant." Her sarcasm was without humour.

"We could send scouts out ahead of them. After all, we're far more at home in the forest any Reluwyn."

Ikara shook her head. "Our priority is the protection of those who have come to us. We would be jeopardising their safety. No, only the twins should go back out – their stealth I can rely on."

"What about the Reluwyn in our cell?" Fidel's voice was stronger, tones of realisation evident. "Perhaps he knows of this runaway. He appears to be some kind of beggar, he could have come from Emril city, maybe even the palace itself."

Ikara nodded quickly. "Interrogate him."

Fidel was halfway to the door when Ikara's voice stopped him.

"But before that, you can get this armour off me."

⊙⊙⊙

"More Laowyn have disappeared from the cities and towns, my lord." Sameedos cowered as he spoke the words.

"More? And where do they go? How do they run past my Imperial Guards so easily in the towns?" Garesh wasn't looking for an answer. He threw the goblet of red wine he had been drinking against a wall. The gold painted clay shattered against a mural of a naked woman, staining the image.

"The Prince is gone again, there are no reports back from the troops, and the Laowyn are plotting. How did I come to deserve such idiocy? They must be amassing some kind of force." Garesh rose up, his silk tunic swishing, forcing Nisa's hand to relinquish his neck.

"There is no evidence of violence as of yet, my lord."

"*Yet* being the operative word, Sameedos." Garesh raked his long fingers through his black hair. "We cannot trust them: they have refused to accept our customs since Emril conquered them; they don't intermarry with our race, treating us like underserving outsiders; they refuse to take up arms within the ranks of our army. They are a constant question to me." Garesh did not like questions.

"My lord," came the soft voice of Nisa. Garesh should have sent her away when Sameedos came. She had already spent the night and he had no need of her now. He was about to dismiss her when she continued to speak. "It is time to crush them, my lord. Your rule is all that holds this Empire together. Your wisdom has caused this Kingdom to remain even in a minority rule. Not even that much can be said of Castir when their Queen was a child."

Garesh resented the boldness of Nisa who was usually compliant and silent. That was how he liked his women. But what she said *was* interesting.

"And what does this whore have to say about my problems?" Garesh dragged a finger down her cheek. His hand fell to her throat, wrapping around the small circumference and tightening.

The temptation to snap her neck ran through Garesh's mind. How easy would it be? Perhaps it would calm him. His thin lips curled into a sneer.

"I propose," Nisa's breathing became pressured. "That you kill them. *All* of them." Her dark eyes held some kind of deviance that Garesh had never noticed before.

He released her then, turning away with laughter. "And how do you suppose the rest of the Kingdom shall react? How will I hold together an Empire of races when I am seen to be a murderous tyrant."

"As far as I am aware," Nisa swayed her hips and draped a hand across the back of a chair. "It is not you, but the Prince who sets the laws of this Kingdom. If the Kingdoms rise up, they can only blame him."

Garesh's sneer grew.

"But my lord, they will blame the Reluwyn." Sameedos, almost forgotten, spoke up.

Garesh stared through his fellow Councillor. "Exactly."

"My lord?"

Garesh turned back to Nisa and grabbed the dress she wore, pulling her towards him. "They cannot blame the Reluwyn if they are not the only ones involved." Nisa's face was close enough for his breath to fall upon it. Her defiance boiled his blood. "An Edict commanding all nations to protect the Empire by destroying the Laowyn."

"Nothing like that has even been done before, my lord."

Garesh did not look to Sameedos. "Get the experts of the law to look into constructing such a decree."

"Yes, my lord."

"And find that damned Prince. The maiden examinations are to start next week and we have no Prince to examine them!"

Garesh pointed to the door. "Get out!" he barked at Sameedos again, his eyes intently locked on Nisa. Sameedos retreated obediently.

"You have dark spirits in you, whore." Garesh smiled, his eyes taking in the curve of Nisa's mouth.

"You have only just noticed, my lord?"

"Why do you hate the Laowyn?" His hands sought her body. "I don't trust you."

"You should, my lord, for I have been watching you. I know who should be ruling this Kingdom. When the Laowyn are wiped out, the Prince will be blamed. You'll strengthen your position as his Regent and High Councillor when he marries – you'll be indispensable."

"And now you've told me? Why would I need you?"

"You know what I can do."

"Spirit Conjuror."

"You profess public disbelief, but I know you believe."

Garesh did. He knew better than anyone what Emril had been intent on hiding. He was the only one in the new government who had seen proof of the Spirit Realm and all the old legends. He had no intention of giving that leverage to anyone, let alone this whore - but to keep her onside was only wise.

"What do you want in return?"

A hand reached up and fingers entwined themselves in his hair. "Security."

"Nothing more?"

She shook her head.

Garesh did not trust her. But for now, he had an ally in his plan to kill that irksome race and consolidate his power.

He bent down, his mouth meeting her already open lips.

⊙⊙⊙

"Show me the mark," Ikara's voice was hard. She had learned to control her compassion, finding it unhelpful.

The woman, who claimed her name was Kiara, undid the scrap of material she had found to close her torn shirt. Ikara saw Zeb turn away in the corner of her eye.

The Commander could see she was young. She was also beautiful. It was no wonder that she had been chosen by the overseers of the Edict of Maidens. Ikara had listened to the story patiently, hardly believing that Kiara had escaped the Reluwyn unharmed and undiscovered.

Zeb was right to have moved her from the cell of the other prisoner. In his position Ikara herself would have wanted to hurt someone who had gotten her caught. Fidel would be interrogating him now, and Ikara was very interested to hear how he'd escaped the prison of Grûl with his life. But for now her concern was Kiara's identity.

As the dirty linen of the shirt fell from her shoulder. Kiara's gold hair grazed the smooth skin. The fair hair was growing longer, no doubt a by-product of Zeb's poultice. Whatever he used to heal wounds also caused other things, like hair, to mend and grow.

Ikara saw the thin spirals of black spreading in all directions across Kiara's shoulder blade, gathering around an ice blue Ensper.

Ikara nodded briskly once. "Cover yourself."

The woman did as she was bade and turned back to face the Commander.

Zeb re-joined them. He watched the proceedings silently.

"From where do you come? If you ran away as you said, your family will be looking for you." Ikara saw the sudden light of defiance in Kiara's eyes.

"My family was happy to send me to the Prince's harem, happy to allow me to be found out and executed. I don't come from anywhere anymore."

The look in her eyes had become defensive. Ikara understood, but as Commander there was a responsibility to uphold Laowyn law.

"You are under your family name and must honour their wishes until you are married. You know the law."

"As do you," Kiara shot back. "Obey the law of the land unless in direct contradiction to the Great Spirit's ways. There is nothing that condones your robbing of carriages or resisting royal governance."

Ikara admired her tenacity, but would not be cowed. Kiara did not know what was happening - perhaps she should. "We have been watching their movements; they are mounting forces in strategic places across the Empire."

"Meaning?" The prisoner's temper was clearly flaring but the Commander's words had the sobering effect she'd intended.

"Every one of our race is in danger."

Ikara saw the puckering of Kiara's brow, comprehension dawning in her mind as her blue eyes fell to the Commander's breastplate and then to the floor.

"I must return you to your family as the law dictates."

"You speak of law when you live outside of it!"

"If we do not obey even our own laws we become the criminals the government thinks we are. The criminals they tell other races across the Empire that we are. They stir up hate against us and paint us as rebels. You must return home."

"If I am to die let me do so here fighting for our people." Kiara pleaded.

"You will return home."

"Zeb?" Kiara's eyes were misted, though she forced herself to maintain a calm façade. She turned her gaze on the elf whose resolve shifted but did not falter.

"If I return to my hometown I shall be taken to Emril city and the royal harem. When they find out my race I will be killed for it. If they don't, I will be used." Kiara's shock turned into rage. Her eyes became blue fire and she came to within inches of the Commander's face, though she stood below it. "You know what the Reluwyn will do to me." The words were an accusation.

Ikara felt it between the plates of her armour but she remained resolute. She must command, as her father would have. She must not give in to ill-judged compassion.

"Tell us your home before nightfall and we will arrange safe passage. Do not, and we will leave you wherever we deem fit without protection." Ikara's words were cutting and she saw the pain they inflicted upon the prisoner. She turned away, catching Zeb looking straight at her, tormented, his mouth a hard line. She walked on.

Judgment was not needed, this was her burden. She would be hated as a leader as well as loved.

She commanded Zeb from the room, doubting that he would have left if she hadn't, and then nodded to the guard. The door was shut with a heavy thud.

CHAPTER 9

Dying oil lamps flickered against their oncoming demise, in a last attempt at warding off the darkness. Kiara was laid back against the sacks of grain that filled her new cell. Her leg was feeling much better, almost pain free, the best it had felt in days. She'd managed to sleep a little too before Ikara had come in to examine her mark.

How could she send her back to her death? How could the leader of the Laowyn Resistance condemn one of her own people? Kiara could not believe it. Her brow was puckered as she looked up at the earthen ceiling above, her emotions like a pendulum swinging from rage to disbelief.

"Still won't talk to me? Surely you're bored by now."

He was doing it again, the Reluwyn, he'd been saying things to her for the past hour. Teasing at first, then provocative, now he was starting all over again. Kiara rolled her eyes. A tapping on the bars of her prison cell caused her to rise. Apparently, this store room had been created to house prisoners before it stored food. She took the skin of water that was offered and the bread that came with it. When she did so her eyes caught sight of the tall thief across the way. He stood opposite to her, his hands hanging through the bars, watching. His eyes were dark and as they caught with hers a smile flickered onto his lips.

"I don't know how I didn't realise you were a woman before."

Kiara felt heat creeping up her neck, but it was quickly dashed by cold words.

"Must be your boyish attributes."

She wanted to throw the bread at him. His smile made her fingers itch around the potential missile.

"Tell me," Kiara knew what was coming. "If it wasn't someone else you were protecting from the Prince, was it yourself? Were you chosen for the Edict of Maidens?"

Clearly, he hadn't overheard anything that had passed in the other cell. He still didn't know she was Laowyn.

"From the colour rising in your cheeks I'd say you were a maiden."

The words set Kiara's cheeks fully ablaze and with a suddenness that surprised her she dropped to the floor out of sight of the Reluwyn. She exhaled, leaning back against the door, her head looking up at the ceiling once more. He had been at it for the last hour. She was losing patience.

"Afraid to spend a night with the Prince? With a man?" He was laughing now, the sound mocking, his hand slapping against the wood of the door. "Poor innocent. I bet you've never felt the touch of a man."

She breathed steadily, refraining from retort, the inaction taking all of her self-control.

"And what will the Resistance do with you now? Send you back to whichever poverty-stricken hole you crawled from? Who knows, maybe you'll be lucky enough to still be captured for a night with the Prince."

That was it! Kiara leapt up, swinging round and without thought launched the bread she held through the air, it was just shy of his head, knocking on the top of the doorframe and then plummeting to the floor in a scattering of crumbs.

"Woah!" The dark-haired man jumped backwards and then came back to the small cell window again, his smile full, his eyes satisfied. "Fiery for such a small woman. Did I frighten you?"

"I'd die before being touched by one of your race," Kiara spat, anger blazing from her eyes, her fingers twisted around the bars of the window so tight that her knuckles grew white.

"That's because you don't know how good it feels…" He looked at her provocatively. "To be touched…"

She spluttered, disgust marking her face. "You Reluwyn have no self-control. It's not enough to conquer other nations, you must seduce their women in your barbaric celebrations."

"Barbaric?" But his question wasn't answered. She had lost her temper and any rein she had on her mouth.

"And what does a filthy thief care for the business of a Prince he does not serve? Your disloyalty to your own race amazes me. Tell me, how much shame do you carry for being part of a race of savages?"

Something had changed in his eyes during her speech. There was a hardening in the dark depths. "Only one who does not understand the Reluwyn would talk so."

"Oh please, tell me of the orgies your race has, of the drunkenness they love to indulge in, of the pain they enjoy inflicting on others."

"And what of your race? You are Laowyn, no doubt..."

"Do you think I'd still be a prisoner if I was?" She cut him off, her words sharp and quick, drawn from anxiety – surprising her.

"Well, you still haven't told me where you come from. Do they not teach women proper respect? Do they not tell a woman how ridiculous it is to dress as a man?"

"They taught me how to fight. If you were in here I would show you," she challenged.

"If I were in there maybe I could show you what it feels like to have a man touch you. Ah, that delightful colour in your cheeks again, but don't flatter yourself," came the cutting reply, "I would kill you as soon as touch you for getting me caught in Grûl."

"If you hadn't have been so foolish, we would never have been in that jail cell."

"Imagine if they had found out..." he left off tellingly, there was cruelty in his voice.

Kiara closed her eyes against the sick feeling growing in her stomach. A resounding bang. Her eyes opened to the sight of Zeb at the door of the opposite cell, a cudgel in his hands.

"Shut up, Reluwyn."

The thief, who had jumped back in alarm, came back to the window, arms raised. "Touchy, touchy. I'm sorry, did I intrude upon a flowering love when I was thrown in the cell with you two?"

Zeb's eyes narrowed at him. The elf looked down and saw the bread on the floor and then came over to Kiara's window.

"Hungry?"

The look in his eyes was unreadable but he was already unlocking her door so she replied positively.

The Reluwyn looked on with mounting interest, but Zeb refused to catch his eye again. When Kiara left her cell to follow Zeb she glanced back only once at the other prisoner. His eyes were following her. A feeling dark and ominous grew inside her.

○○○

"Amazing."

"Indeed."

"She really is a woman, isn't she?"

"I would have noticed it when first I saw her, except that she was captured by the other scouting party."

Kalev elbowed Jaik. "Rubbish.

"I'll have you know I'm a first-class spy," Jaik snapped back.

"You realise I'm right here?" Kiara was sat across the table from them, her arms folded across her chest, her brows raised.

"It speaks," Kalev whispered loudly to his brother.

"*Sounds* like a woman."

"Pack it in." Zeb pulled another chunk of bread from the platter in the centre of the table. He gave the two a hard stare.

They were sat in one of the lair's kitchens. A fire blazed in the hearth and Kiara could not help wondering where the smoke was going. Vegetables of all kinds were hung up to dry or keep, just like in her make-shift cell.

There were various barrels too, stacked in an alcove further down the room. It was from one of these that Zeb had poured a jug of strawberry cordial.

"The elf is joining with her now. Both of them have such mad looks, brother."

"Indeed, brother, *indeed*."

Both mouths of the twin men jerked upwards in simultaneous grins. Zeb threw a chunk of bread at their heads, they ducked smoothly, allowing the food to sail past.

"Zeb! You're showing the prisoner bad manners."

Zeb frowned at the irony.

"And don't waste good food," said Jaik, picking up the bread from the floor and dipping it in his own bowl of stew before tearing off part of it with his teeth.

"So, why are you here, woman?" asked Jaik.

"What's your name?" his brother chirped up.

"Who am I to answer, you, or him?" asked Kiara, her arms still folded in judgment across her chest.

"Me," said Jaik simply.

"Him," accepted his brother, still chewing.

"I ran away," said Kiara simply. She didn't want to have to recount her story. All it did was remind her that she was sentenced to return home. That she had no hope.

"And made friends with that Reluwyn criminal did you?"

Kiara gave them a withering look.

"Or not friends." Jaik widened his eyes as if he'd stepped on something spikey.

"That man is like all the rest of them. His mind only works in two ways, killing and…" Kiara didn't finish. She couldn't. Besides, the other thing the man had been suggesting to her *had* scared her. The way he had looked at her was intense and unyielding but the anger he had shown her before had still been there. She had no doubt that had she still been in the same cell with him, woman or not, he would have made her suffer for the ills against him.

The twins had fallen silent for the first time, exchanging glances and looking slightly uncomfortable. Jaik tried to fill the silence.

"He seems to have escaped from the palace y'know. Fidel's going to interrogate him now to find out who he helped to escape with him, who could be important enough for Imperial Guards to be after them."

Zeb glanced across.

"The palace? He can't have, I encountered him in Grûl like I told you," said Kiara, a frown appearing on her face. A matching frown appeared on Zeb's but he said nothing.

"Why'd you run? Edict of Maidens?" asked Jaik, lifting a large hand to tug at his hair meaningfully.

Kiara flushed a little, her hands drawn unconsc[...] to her head. Her hair was touching her shoulders now, nowhere near as short as it had been yesterday, but still too short for a woman. Zeb possessed some kind of magic she was sure, but she had hardly had a moment to ask him about it. When she had checked her leg as he had bade her do on coming into the kitchen, she had unwrapped the bandage to find nothing there but a fine silver scar where the wound had been.

"Leave her alone you rascals." A woman came over to the table with another loaf of fresh bread. "I'm sorry for my brothers, I'm Ria." She held out a flour-covered hand.

Kiara, not having experienced such polite behaviour for days, took her hand with some hesitation.

"Come away from them, you can sit with me." Ria beckoned her to a second table, smaller than the long one at which they sat. Kiara moved her untouched food over to that surface and sat across from the brown-haired woman.

"They mean no harm, they just like to tease. It's always getting them into trouble around here."

As if in confirmation, a plate clattered against the wall. Kiara spun round to see an irritated Zeb glowering at the twins he had targeted.

Turning back she stared ahead thinking on her future. She and Ria sitting in amicable silence for a time.

"You should eat something," said Ria finally, mopping up the last of her stew with a piece of bread.

Kiara wished she could. Her stomach was churning, her heart unable to keep a steady rhythm. The thief's words had shaken her, and the Commander's words had determined her fate. She was to be sent back to face capture and possible execution. It would have been quicker to have been killed by the thief on the side of the road. He'd be happy. She wouldn't have anything left to fear.

All they needed was Kiara's name to track down her relatives, but she had no intention of telling them. She'd be dumped in the woods without protection, and if they were swarming with as many soldiers as the twins had said she'd be caught in no time.

Despite these thoughts, Kiara managed a few mouthfuls, if only to please Ria. The woman was nice, she chatted away merrily, not seeming to care if Kiara was listening or not. She laughed and joked, and when she smiled Kiara could see the resemblance she had to her brothers. They were all grown, their parents moved on to the next life, and they had been part of the Laowyn Resistance for several years. If Kiara were allowed to stay, she imagined her and Ria might be friends.

Kiara pushed the plate away. Ria took it up to wash it, leaving Kiara alone for a moment, but that moment did

not last long. The brothers came over to tease her more,
until Zeb shooed them away.

"Get back to the Commander, you have new orders
to receive, don't you?"

"Such a sour one Zeb." Kalev said in annoyance,
obeying nonetheless. Jaik followed him closely behind.

"There aren't many women here for them to see, and
those that are here have brought their families. A young
single woman has them drooling."

Kiara reddened. "I'm dressed as a boy!"

"Now your hair's growing, you're looking more
feminine," Zeb's mouth softened.

"Yes," said Kiara and planted her hands on the table.
"I wanted to talk to you about that..."

"We haven't time," Zeb interrupted, "While we're
alone I have much to tell you." He sat down beside her,
his voice dropping to a whisper. "The Commander will
not change her mind, despite my pleading on your
behalf."

Kiara was a little surprised that Zeb had done so.

"You said that returning would put your life in
danger- perhaps even that of your family." A shadow
passed over Zeb's face. "I will not let you do so."

Kiara's heart was beating faster. Her blue eyes
widened as she realised where the conversation was
headed.

"If I can get you a Resistance uniform, I may well be able to sneak you out the main entrance. Very few of the Laowyn Resistance have seen you, fewer with your long hair. I can say you're a new arrival."

"Once we're out, I'd have to leave you for a brief time. There are horses kept in caves near the entrance, and if I steal one you'll have a chance of evading both our scouting parties and the Imperial Guards. It's an almost impossible plan."

"Better almost impossible than certain death."

Zeb nodded grimly.

"Why are you helping me though? Won't you get into trouble with the Commander?"

"Yes, but I'm not unused to being in trouble. Besides, if I can help I will."

Kiara felt the admission had layered meaning, but she had no time to think upon his words.

"We must move. Ikara wishes to speak to you again soon, and Fidel is busy with the Reluwyn. This is the best time for escape."

Zeb laughed, as if they had just shared a joke. Kiara noted the action was unfamiliar to him.

"Come, I will show you over our base," he spoke loud enough for the kitchen workers to hear. Picking up his cudgel from a nearby surface, he guided her from the room.

They walked down various corridors, Kiara deciding not to question the plan - no matter how curious she was. She had no idea where they were but guessed they were winding their way slowly upwards so as not to attract suspicion. Zeb talked loudly, pointing out various features of the base, such as how they extracted their water from an underground stream, where the families slept, how these earth-caves had been excavated since the Laowyn had been conquered.

He drew her off into a smaller side room where uniforms were hung from wooden pegs. He left her for a few moments while she changed from her week-old clothes, thankful for the feel of clean material against her skin. She hadn't washed in days so despite the clean clothes the smell lingered.

They moved on from there and soon the entrance opened out before them. The doorway to the outside was covered by hanging vines, allowing thin slithers of daylight in.

"Your purpose?" queried the guard.

"Scouting."

"Who's this?"

Zeb stuck to the plan. "A new arrival – she needs to gather herbs for the kitchen"

The guard looked unconvinced for a moment, but a call from a man on duty distracted him and he waved Zeb and Kiara past without any more questioning.

"Easier than I thought," muttered Zeb.

Whatever took the guard's attention from them had worked a miracle and Zeb didn't intend to challenge it. He drew Kiara off to a small clearing, a short way away from the entrance.

Kiara breathed in the fresh air, looking about her at a forest bathed in afternoon sun. Beams draped themselves over the leaves and grasses, falling through the canopy above and hurting her eyes a little. There was a golden haze of light left in the air and insects navigated drowsily through it.

Kiara looked left and then right. She couldn't see or hear any movement.

"Stay off the roads for now." Zeb was dragging a pony towards her. "Imperial Guards are patrolling all the thoroughfares of the forest." Zeb grasped her leg and hoisted her into the saddle. "Though I prefer your hair longer, you'd better cut it again when you get the chance. You look less and less like a boy."

Kiara nodded.

"Use my dagger to do it when you pause for rest, but now you must ride hard."

"Thank you," Kiara bent down and put a hand upon Zeb's that was busily securing the packs and tying the dagger to her saddle. Her eyes looked into his. Something in his moved, the hardness of the mysterious elf dropped for a moment. "Thank you for this. I shall never forget it." Zeb gazed at her for a moment and then turned back to securing the packs without answering.

That was when Kiara saw something. A dark figure slipping between the trees.

"Zeb…" She dropped a reign to point but her warning was too late. The Reluwyn leapt from his covering, tackling the elf, causing the pony to rear.

Kiara leant forward, heart racing wildly, desperate to stay on. "Zeb!"

The elf was quick and agile. He fought nastily, scratching and kicking the Reluwyn who was almost double his size. He tried to dart out of the Reluwyn's grasp but the thief's large hands closed in around him.

"Run!" Zeb's command was cut-off as a fist impacted his face. Blood flew from his nose, spattering his opponent, his eyes closing as he fell.

When the thief turned upon her his eyes didn't contain the anger she expected. They were gleaming in a way that frightened her, the pony skittered sideways, branches scratched at her face. She needed to run. She knew she must. But the sight of Zeb's unconscious body stilled her. The Reluwyn was still crouched over him like a wildcat over a carcass.

He rose then, his shoulders broad, his height challenging, his mouth set in a sneer. A smile licked up the sides of his lips. "You had the same idea – except my escape was impeded, not helped, by my captors. Tell me woman - do you still not wish to meet your Prince?"

Kiara tried to still the pony who jumped and banged against shrubs and trunks. Even the animal could sense the menace of this man.

"Leave him," Kiara said, "Come and get me." The challenge raised the temperature of her blood, anger for Zeb overcoming the fleeting fear she'd felt.

She turned the pony quickly and began riding away. The hoof beats of her pony and the whipping of leaves was all that she heard. That was until she heard others, many others. When the trees thinned she saw Imperial Guards surrounding her. Then suddenly, one darted in front and she yanked her pony up, bring him to a sliding halt.

Her life was forfeit.

"Dismount." One of the guards circled his horse to face her.

She did as she was bade, grabbing the dagger secretly as she did so. Holding it hilt downwards, she hid the blade up the length of her arm. If they came to take her she'd kill them.

"Drop the blade."

She recognised the voice in shock, turning to see the thief striding towards her, his breathing heavy from running.

Her eyes switched between the troops and the lone Reluwyn.

All of them suddenly bowed their heads. What was going on? Had everyone gone mad?

"I said, drop the blade."

He was getting nearer. Too near. She didn't understand what was happening but if he was in league with the troops then she'd kill him first. She didn't think anymore, she just ran, flying into him, blade raised.

He was ready for her. His hand came up, clamping hard and fast to her wrist. The other came about her waist wrenching her towards him.

"I've never had a woman in the woods before."

Kiara's heart was racing wildly. Her blood ran cold. The look in his eyes ensured her he wasn't lying. She tried to move the arm that held the dagger. He twisted it painfully forcing her to drop the blade and causing a burning ache across her recently healed shoulder.

"But, being as my troops are already upon us and there is no escape for either of us, I have another idea for you." His top lip curled into a sneer.

"*Your* troops?" Kiara's voice sounded more faint-hearted than she could bear but she couldn't help it. Nothing made sense.

"Yes, mine, and now you're *my* prisoner."

"Wh…what?" Damn it! Why couldn't she pull herself together? Who was this man?

The question must have been clear in her eyes for he answered it without her needing to ask.

"I am Trevisian Alakvalto, Prince of the Empire of Emrilion, heir of King Emril."

Kiara's mouth fell open in disbelief. It couldn't be true. It couldn't be. She didn't want to wait and find out the truth. She twisted in his arms, writhing beneath his grip, desperate to get away from him.

"Kill me! Oh, kill me now," the prayer came out half-panted, half-whispered.

"Don't be so hasty." With a suddenness that surprised her, the Prince flung her away from him. A command was issued by the Prince, lost on Kiara whose vision spun about the forest.

Before she gained her balance, pain shot through her skull, she wavered, and then blackness descended, her body crumpling into the arms of a waiting soldier.

CHAPTER 10

K iara woke in a daze. Her eyes fluttered open catching sight of silk hanging in thick swathes above her, floating listlessly in a slow breeze. She turned her head to see where it came from, the movement sending lancing pains through her skull, forcing her to shut her eyes against them. Lovely scents filled her nostrils. The smell of spices and incense, and then of hot chicken and herbs cooking somewhere near. She could feel the softness of the fabric on her skin and the warmth of a fur covering her.

When she opened them again she saw the richly covered sheets on which she lay, and across from her an ornately carved cabinet and wash stand next to it. There was the hum of far-off voices.

She raised a hand instinctively to her neck, but finding nothing there to comfort her her brow puckered. Where was her necklace? Where was she? Her mind traced strands of memory. She had been captured once, no, twice now. As she focused on the rich furnishings, she realised that she had never been in a room like this. Her eyes traced the pattern of a tiled mural on the opposite wall. A man and a woman were suspended in it. They were engaging in… Her body convulsed as she flew upright, her hands clutching at the covers as she scanned the room in a panic.

She pushed her hair away from her face. Zeb. What had happened to Zeb? That's when she caught sight of someone else. He was sat in the far corner of the room beside a large wooden door with decorative gold handles.

His eyes were dark, almost black, watching her as a hawk would its prey. Her knuckles turned white as her fingers tightened around the fur covering.

"I was worried my guard had hit you so hard you'd never wake up." He didn't look worried. "You've been asleep for two days, but as you are awake now, perhaps I should rescind my orders to have the guard beaten." His fingers were drawn together at their tips, tapping together slowly. She didn't doubt his cruelty.

It was definitely the Reluwyn thief, but he looked different. His poor, dirty clothes were gone; he was arrayed in a black silk tunic, the collar and cuffs trimmed with gold. His black hair, which reached his shoulders, was washed and combed back from his face and his beard was trimmed back. He looked clean, in control, but that look of animal ferocity in his eyes was still there.

"Who are you? Where am I?" Kiara pulled the covers back towards herself, covering the dirty clothes she still wore.

"I told you who I am." He raised a hand and gestured to her. "I have already seen it, remember?" That same dark smile.

Kiara had been protesting his identity but his words made her break off. She looked about herself again. The furnishings, the Reluwyn décor, that mural.

"What? Don't you like Reluwyn art?" He had seen her recoil. "Too barbaric for your sensibilities?" he asked scornfully.

Her eyes filled with fear. Did he know? Was that an allusion to Laowyn culture?

"Murals of sexual pleasure lay throughout the harem. Get used to them - I intend for you to be here a long time."

He couldn't know. Kiara looked down at the tattered shirt she still wore bound around herself. No one had seen her mark yet. "You can't be him. You can't be."

He rose, coming towards the bed. She shrank back instinctively, looking around for anything that could be used as a weapon.

"Don't you recognise the Prince you hate? You proclaim to know me so well. Why don't you recognise this barbarian? Trust me, you shall see just how barbaric I can be in the coming days." He wasn't looking into her eyes. He was looking at her lips, his gaze rising and falling with their fullness.

She could smell the scent of rich spice and soap. She had counted herself dead the day she'd been chosen by the Edict of Maidens, so what did it matter how or where she died? But she would not be taken by him - nor any other man in this place. Her defiance lunged into consciousness. Let them try and take her. He would have to kill her first.

"Go ahead, barbarian, prove me right." Her heart beat wildly against her chest. She thought it would burst through her skin. She had baited him but her mind ran fearfully over what he might do. Silence! Why couldn't she ever be silent?

He chuckled, his breath sweet, white teeth gleaming against olive skin. He straightened, his height seeming more than it ever had, his body broader, stronger than she had seen it before.

"Get dressed." He nodded to material draped over the cabinet. She looked at it and then back at him.

"No."

He came at her then, his hand grabbing at her neck, his fingers tightening as he drew her face to within inches of his own. "You may have been able to rebel outside, but this is my Kingdom and within these walls I will be obeyed." His voice was forceful enough to cow any subject.

Her breath came out strangled and hissing. She spat at him.

He barely flinched. He released her to wipe his face.

"That's one way to taste you."

The words caused her skin to crawl. He was mad.

"Dress." He resumed his seat. Apparently, he was going to watch. Kiara looked at the Reluwyn dress in disgust.

"Wear it or leave this room naked." He looked at her as though he already saw her so. "Both choices are equally agreeable to me."

Kiara bit back a retort and instead asked the question she was burning to ask. "Why am I here?"

A smile spread across the Prince's lips. "Because I wish you to repay me for the trouble you have caused."

"Trouble?"

"I was caught, remember?"

"You did not wish to return to this?" Kiara's words seem to hit somewhere between his armour. His gaze faltered for a moment, something else shining between the rays of fury.

Kiara indicated the rich furnishings. "What hardship you suffer, *my Lord Prince*," she mocked.

The taunt brought back his anger. He ignored her and continued, "You have been chosen to participate in the Edict of Maidens, woman, and although I doubt you'll be chosen," he masked a smile. "I'll take my payment when I test your *abilities*."

The words made her feel sick. The feeling wrapped its way around her stomach. She threw off the covers, dropping her dirty feet to the floor.

"Perhaps you should bathe before you dress." Apparently, he was going to order the bath to the room, for he pulled upon a rope, Kiara assumed it would summon a servant. He was a Prince? How could he be the Prince?

She had to get out of here. The pain in her head was growing. Would he watch her bathe too? She felt her stomach contract.

"And where do you think you can go? Do you really believe you can hide from me in my own palace?" asked the Prince, a smile still playing over his lips. She stumbled towards the door, almost falling against the handles.

Everything was spinning. The Prince made no effort to stop her leaving, but followed instead. She came out into a corridor which encircled a courtyard. Pillars lined her left, and there was a wall with various doors in it to her right. She had to get out of this place.

She moved forward quickly, swallowing down the feeling of sickness, grasping at any pillar or wall near enough to balance herself. She moved along a mosaic floor, her dirty, travel-worn clothes seeming even more out of place. Her hair fell forward and she batted it away, trying to see where she was going. She barely noticed the people that surrounded her. Women and girls were sat in the gardens talking and laughing, and servants were handing around food. Conversations stalled as this strange creature passed, and faces were veiled in respect as the Prince came after her.

She could hear his footsteps behind her, relentless. She knew it was him. She fell against two large doors that led from the courtyard to another corridor, her breathing ragged. There were guards at the end but Kiara didn't notice them. Nothing was normal, nothing was real.

The Prince nodded to the guards who moved aside, allowing the woman passage. The floor turned to stone slabs that were cold under her feet and when she glanced upwards she could see tapestries hanging from brass poles the length of a hall filled with columns. This was not real. It could not be real.

There were people, hundreds of people, she couldn't escape, they parted and stared as she walked forwards. Dark Reluwyn eyes all turned upon her, haughty gazes took in her clothes, words passed behind her back.

A man, taller than the rest, standing on the raised dais caught eyes with her.

She drew in her remaining strength and cried out, "Release me!"

"What is this?" bellowed Garesh, his anger terrifying. But Kiara was dead anyway, she didn't care.

"One of the latest arrivals for the Edict of Maidens." She could hear the Prince's voice behind her. It was filled with that arrogant disdain. She could not see the smile he wore.

"Please, no! Please!" she cried as she turned to see the Prince striding towards her. But he did not relent. Her battle against nausea was finally lost and with a heave she vomited all over him.

The smell was acrid but the Prince chose not to heed it.

"You shall return to your quarters." The Prince took her arm but received a sharp slap in response, her hand leaving stinging red marks across his cheek. His fingers pinched her upper arm in response, and it was just as well his grip was strong for in the next moment her legs crumpled beneath her. He caught her firmly and swung her over his shoulder roughly. She would have beaten his back with her fists had she remained conscious.

When the Prince turned on his heel and retreated, chaos broke out in the hall. Sameedos and Mishka demanded revelation from Garesh, but the High Councillor remained silent, his furious eyes beholding the retreating form of what he could only describe as trouble for his carefully laid plans.

❂❂❂

Ikara was being given a massage by Ria. The woman had wonderful hands and a way of seeking out a knot in muscles as though she were a bird looking for berries. Her long fingered hands were strong and pushed and pulled the skin and muscle until it gave up to the unrelenting movements.

"You're in bad shape again. Have you been sleeping much?"

They were alone. Only those of the same sex could massage each other, an art in Laowyn culture that had survived the invasion of the Reluwyn. In a community dominated by men, it was one of the only times Ikara could be alone with another woman.

"No," Ikara muttered into the towel her head was buried in. Her short silver hair was sprayed out in all directions.

"Why?" Ria picked up a small terracotta vial of oil from a nearby table and was about to drop more of the fragranced liquid on the Commander's back when Ikara started up slightly, a sheet clinging to her half naked frame.

"Did you lock the door?"

"Yes!" said Ria in exasperated tones, pushing at Ikara's back to force her down again. "Three times I have checked and it was locked the first time! Now," Ria poured more of the oil onto Ikara's skin, her hands far more gentle now than her tone. She felt for the Commander. It was not easy being a woman within the Laowyn community, let alone their leader.

Ikara had been private ever since Ria had known her. She rarely gave away what emotions she was feeling, like a spy with a secret. As a result, her back was like a pile of knotted ropes and it had only been a week since her last massage.

"What's bothered you this week?"

"Everything." Ikara answered vaguely, groaning as Ria worked a knot in her left shoulder.

"There's no use evading me - you are much more tense today."

Ikara sighed and turned, her back giving way under Ria's hands. Imprints of the towel patterned her face and her hair projected at mad angles. It was the most human Ria had seen her in a long time.

"The Elders have met."

Ria took one of her arms and began working the oil into the skin.

"They have all agreed to wait and see what the Reluwyn intend to do." Ikara spat out the words.

"And you do not agree?" Open questions, it was the only way to get Ikara to talk. And when Ikara talked, her muscles relaxed.

"I know what the Reluwyn will do. They wish to kill us all. I can...I can feel it."

Ria nodded, moving on to Ikara's hand and working the flesh between her knuckles, finishing by pummelling her palm.

"Is that the only reason they wish to wait?"

Ikara's ice-coloured eyes flicked up to meet the warmth of Ria's. "You already know the answer."

"Other arm," commanded Ria.

"You ask questions but you already know the answers," Ikara sighed again, lying on her back now with the sheet pulled up over her body. "The Great Spirit. When was the last time the Great Spirit moved and showed us what to do using the Ensper?"

"When was the last time you thought about your own breathing?"

"Just now when you were causing me pain." Ikara's lip curled slightly.

"A smile! Well I never." Ria grinned, suddenly looking just like the twin brothers she laid claim to. She gave Ikara back her arm. "We are given the Ensper for a reason, Ikara. Losing people to enemies does not mean the Great Spirit is not sovereign. Do you think constantly about how you must breathe? No, because it's just happening all the time. The Great Spirit is here all the time."

"I don't wish to speak of this any longer."

"How is Zeb?" Ria knew her friend and leader well. She obeyed without any further pressing. The subject was changed and Ikara relaxed again immediately. She was sitting now, drawing the sheet about herself and looking for her clothes.

"He's doing better, just bruised."

"And the girl?"

"Gone."

"The Rcluwyn prisoner?"

"Him too…" Ikara paused halfway through pulling on a garment. "We missed a valuable opportunity for information there."

Ria hummed as she put away the oil and towels. "Do you think she ran off with the Reluywn?"

"If she did I think her a fool. But Zeb didn't seem to think so."

"And what do you think?"

Ikara finished dressing and folded the sheet. "Something is going on I don't know about."

"And what does Captain Fidel think?" Ria braced herself. At the mention of Fidel, Ikara always grew irritable.

"He agrees with Zeb."

"And is he well?"

Ikara continued to glare at Ria who simply answered by wiggling her brow. "Perhaps you should ask him yourself."

"Oh no," replied Ria, "I think he prefers talking to you."

Before Ikara could think of a biting retort, a banging sounded on the bolted door.

"Commander, I have news." Fidel shouted.

"Perhaps there will be light in the dark after all." Ria said cryptically. She obeyed Ikara's nod and unbolted the door.

CHAPTER 11

H e was bent over the edge of a blade when Kiara entered. She had been summoned to the Prince's chambers, a great honour – yet she had needed the persuasion of armed guards to obey the Prince's demand. On the way one of them had explained the favour she was being shown, that one who is not summoned entered on pain of death. A pity she didn't care.

Dressed in robes laid out for her, she stepped soundlessly over the threshold, light shining on her gold sandals. Her nausea had subsided and with its disappearance a numbness was taking over. She was the walking dead. The only thing which kept her from revealing her identity was a faint flicker of defiance. She would give up her life for a much better cause than a petulant Prince.

The robe was formed of twisted lengths of gold embroidery that clung to the curves of her body, designed to expose her stomach, chest and arms. Across her back, a golden panel covered her Ensper and the encircling tattoo. Strips of long fabric covered the front and back of her legs, but the sides exposed a silver scar across one thigh.

Coscian, as head of the Prince's harem, had been instructed to beautify all women brought in to the harem, and Kiara had been dragged to the top of his list when she arrived. She didn't have to guess who had commanded that to happen.

Yesterday, Coscian had forced her to stand in the flimsiest of muslin rags while he waxed the hair from her legs with quick, efficient motions. In fact, Kiara hadn't been that adverse to the Harem Master - he was brusque, but who wouldn't be when surrounded by hundreds of gossiping women all day. Kiara was sure he appreciated the silence she gave him. He even treated her skin more carefully after she winced. He'd asked about the scar on her thigh, and she'd told him it was inflicted by an Imperial Guard. He'd made no comment.

The Prince looked up from the blade as Kiara entered. After taking half a step forward, she halted, recognition flashing across her face. That was her father's blade. But she removed the look quickly. She could not let him know her desire for the sword.

The guards closed the large gilt panelled doors with a low thud behind her. The sound of isolation. She considered lunging for the sword but quickly discarded the plan.

Surprise was probably the only way she could win against a man twice her breadth and a head taller, but the Prince was looking at her. He didn't smile when he saw her, though he took his time taking in her appearance.

She stared back at him, her eyes hooded with derision and a coldness that she allowed to steal over her frame. She didn't care, she didn't care about him or what he intended for her. She still wasn't sure why he had brought her here, but she would not be a willing pawn in his game.

"Has the nausea subsided?"

Kiara didn't respond.

"I ordered your water to be laced with a concoction from one of my healers. I can't have you vomiting all over me again."

As he walked closer, Kiara saw his eyes drop to her body again. She looked past him and took in the sumptuously decorated apartments. Murals were painted across the walls, as they were in the harem, but these ones depicted great battle scenes. Swathes of fine muslin and silk were suspended tent-like across the ceiling, no doubt an allusion to the Reluwyn's once nomadic existence. Low couches layered with cushions were collected around a table, beyond them stood a desk, beyond that a door to what Kiara assumed was a bedroom.

"There is something I still cannot work out."

Her blue eyes retracted from the further extremities of the room and locked onto his. Perhaps he would now tell her what he would do with her. No doubt she would become a whore in his harem. Was now the time to reveal her race and save herself by forcing her own execution?

"When I first met you, we were taken by Imperial Guards to the Watchtower of Grûl. I left you in a locked cell. How did you escape and come to be captured by the Laowyn Resistance in the Great Forest instead?"

Her eyes hardened and then moved from his to look beyond his left shoulder refusing to make eye contact. She could still see the ends of his black hair which fell about his neck.

He came closer, now standing just before her, forcing her head further back to maintain her defiant attitude.

"Perhaps you decided to uncover your sex when you were stuck in the prison cell." A taunting smile appeared on his lips.

Kiara could feel the indignation rising but she held her temper. Let him think what he would, all she cared about at this moment was the blade in his hands.

"I expect the guard was more than compliant."

"If you say so it must be true." She was too focused on the blade to notice a look akin to vexation pass over his handsome face. All she could think about were his filthy Reluwyn hands holding her father's sword.

"For all your protests, you are now a whore in a harem. For someone who gives their body up for life out of a prison it's surprising you'd refuse me and lose the chance of gaining all this." He gestured about himself. "Whore," he said it again, his eyes challenging her to a fight.

"Upset I don't desire you, Prince?" she asked sarcastically, her temper finally flaring.

He laughed, harsh and grating. "It hardly matters. You already know I can take you any time of my pleasing."

Her eyes belied her fear but her body involuntarily trembled. "Give the blade to me," she said it abruptly, her face unmoving. She wanted to take it from him and cut those hands off.

"What, this?" He turned the blade over in his hand. "Yes, it is yours. As fine a blade as my armourer can produce. How a street-waif like you came by it..." he trailed off. "You want it?"

"Yes."

"No." He sneered. "Prisoners don't get weapons, especially not in the company of the Prince. Now, tell me how you escaped Grûl."

She wouldn't obey his commands. He may be the Prince, but she would never acknowledge him as such. She held out a slender hand.

"Like I said," he sighed, apparently disappointed she would not word-spar anymore. "Prisoners don't get weapons to play with." He sheathed the sword, his face unsmiling for a moment, the taunting looks covered by something far less amused. He walked back towards the double doors. Kiara moved with the blade, pausing on the threshold. She watched him hang the weapon across two golden hooks beside the large, plush bed.

"Though I'm sure," he continued, as he came back and locked eyes with her, "You wish to maim me for touching your precious sword." The amusement was back, the provoking curve to his lips. Whatever had made him check himself now gone.

Kiara felt her top lip twitch involuntarily.

"I can read your feelings from your face as easily as the words from a book in my hand."

He was close now, almost close enough to reach out and touch her. If she had the blade, now would be the time to remove those hands.

"Now," the Prince carried on, as though there was no animosity between them and violence had not been part of the conversation. "Tell me who you are." He took a seat by open doors that led onto the balcony at the opposite side of the room. Reclining on the silk cushions he looked every inch the Prince, arrogance emanating from him as though he could command anything he wished.

Kiara almost laughed. He could of course - he was the Prince - but she would surely die before becoming some puppet for his pleasure. Let his Reluwyn whores play along to his tune, she would keep marching to the war beat of hers.

"No wish to recount your story to me? Your name then?"

She glared at him. She would no sooner give him her name than she would willingly give him herself. It wasn't just about hiding her race. Somehow in this moment it felt as though telling him her name was too intimate. A gift she would not bestow.

"Very well, tell me neither," he sighed, "Though it's a shame. I have to admit, I'm slightly intrigued as to how a beautiful young woman could become a thief."

"And I a Prince," she shot back, she was getting tired of this posturing, and the way his eyes kept drifting over her body.

His brow clouded a little but he assumed a look of bored amusement, "Sometimes a little excitement is a nice change."

"From what? Ruling an Empire, yes, that would be boring. The lives of so many in your hands, how could that interest you?"

"Temper, temper, Little One." He spoke as if to a pet. It made Kiara's blood boil. "A fitting name. If you will not give me your name then that is what I shall call you. I must say, you are looking," his took in the strips of exposed skin, the smooth legs and the feminine curves of her body, "Different."

Kiara turned away, as if doing so would obscure her body from his view. She saw her opportunity and strode quickly towards the bed spread with silks and furs.

Her hand reached out to the leather scabbard, the ties inches from her fingers when she felt his hand clamp down on her arm, pulling it roughly down to her side and ramming her against the wall.

"That was not wise, Little One." He called her that again, but for a term containing words of such sweetness, it was uttered with undisguised contempt. He hated her. He must hate her.

He pushed against her but she wasn't struggling.

"You had better learn manners if you are to be here."

"Let me go." Kiara wasn't asking for his hands to release her. She was asking for freedom.

"Killing me is the only way you're leaving this palace. And you don't even have a sword." He started chuckling and then laughing loudly and Kiara just felt sick.

"That's enough for today. Leave."

She *was* his pet. She *was* his to command. Unless she left this place she would be his indefinitely. It was flight or death. The former seemed worth the risk.

❂❂❂

"Welcome Zephenesh, come, let us feed you after your long journey."

"I will not refuse." Smiling lines appeared at the side of the old man's mouth. He rested a hand on the Captain's shoulder as he walked down the main tunnel with him. "This is my companion Djeck."

"Ah yes, I remember." Fidel did not try and grasp the elf's hand in the traditional Laowyn greeting. He knew from their last encounter that the sullen elf held no truck with niceties. He was a strange and silent fellow. "How were your travels?" Fidel turned back to Zephenesh, knowing he would not cause offence.

"The Imperial Guards are out in force on the main roads."

"Did you run into trouble?"

"Me? An old man? What trouble could I cause that would encourage them to stop me? They were more interested in the young. I saw a family attacked, the husband arrested for trying to move them out of Miresh. Everywhere the Reluwyn are stopping migration of the

Laowyn, they have plans but I have yet to determine what."

"That is what the Commander has been saying, but the other Elders are intent on no action at present."

"I see, and Ikara, how is she faring?"

Fidel didn't answer immediately. He turned the old man down a passage towards the kitchen and dining hall. "She commands the respect of the men."

"You are ever the faithful friend." Zephenesh chuckled, patting Fidel's shoulder once again. "I shall not fight you for answers, I will see her myself soon enough. Tell me, how have the raiding parties fared since the Laowyn trading ban?"

They took a seat at one of the long wooden tables and Ria came to serve them cold meat and bread. Zephenesh took her hand and exchanged a few words of greeting to the woman he had met at the last few Elders' gatherings. He then turned back and gestured with a knife for Fidel to continue.

"They have taken more causalities but continue their mission to protect those persecuted. Though recently they did pick up a Reluywn in the forest." Fidel's brow furrowed and he stopped eating, looking off into the middle-distance for a moment.

"Who was he?"

Fidel drew himself back into the present. "You will not believe me. We should have taken decisive action, but does the Great Spirit condone the killing of an enemy who does not bear arms?"

"The scrolls advocate the fair trial of an enemy, you know that Fidel."

The Captain did not nod in agreement as he usually would have to the words of one of the most learned Elders in the Laowyn community. For once his feelings were conflicted.

"And if breaking that rule could avert a potential war? The deaths of hundreds if not thousands?"

"*'Those who evade the law, breaking the Great Spirit's commands, shall face repayment one hundred-fold, for the good-doer shall have the Spirit dwell within the heart of his hearts, just as the good-doer seeking protection shall draw the Spirit from his heart within hearts to protect him.'* The words of the Spirit as written down in the scrolls of Inarr."

Fidel took a mouthful of bread and meat, forgetting to chew and grimacing as a lump of deer-meat slowly made its way down to his stomach.

"Who was the Reluwyn prisoner? Do you speak of him in the past tense because the deed has already been done?"

"He escaped, the Prince escaped."

Zephenesh's hand stopped midway to his mouth, a piece of meat dropping from the bread he held and falling on the wooden table. He gave Fidel a measuring stare and then took the mouthful, processing what he had heard slowly, a cog turning with every chew.

"How can you be sure it was him?" He picked up the meat from the table.

"The forest was crawling with Imperial Guards searching for a palace runaway."

"It could have been a criminal."

"There were circumstances which led us to believe it was him, but only after he and the female prisoner we held escaped."

"Female? Another Reluwyn."

"No," Fidel countered Zephenesh's certain comment. "She was Laowyn, her mark was checked, but there was no love lost between the two, we can't quite figure out what happened. Our comrade, an elf by the name of Zeb, was knocked unconscious in a struggle of some kind which took place on the surface after the escape. He hasn't fully recovered yet. I am due to check on him."

"May I accompany you?"

"Yes, although it does not have much bearing on the Elders meeting later."

"On the contrary, if the Prince is abroad away from his palace, we must be in charge of as many of the facts as possible."

Fidel considered this but did not follow. The old man's thoughts drifted in all directions, forking like a river here and there, trying to understand the Prince's absence from his city.

"The Edict of Maidens is supposed to come to a conclusion in a few weeks' time. So why is he not at the palace?"

"He is."

Zephenesh frowned. This conversation was not yielding any expected answers. At his age he had a quick mind, but today it was not enough to piece all these facts together. He remained silent, awaiting enlightenment.

"We have received reports from our scouts that he has returned and, though we could not confirm they left together for lack of Zeb's account, we have since heard of a golden-haired woman at the palace."

"Golden-haired?" Djeck's first words were curt.

"Yes." Fidel answered Djeck's question, his green eyes resting upon the elf's stern countenance. "Matching the description of the woman we held here. Apparently, the Prince had a better offer for her than we did. The Commander would not offer her permanent sanctuary - she was to be sent back to her family." Fidel then turned to Zephenesh. "Palace gossip is usually no concern of ours, but the woman has caused quite a stir, and stories seep from the city walls."

"Why is that?"

Zephenesh had fallen silent. His eyes were wide and hard and his gaze was on Djeck who had already guessed what Zephenesh now feared.

"Some say she is the new concubine of the court, turning heads wherever she goes; some say she is one of the maidens; others say she is a prisoner of great beauty who defies the Prince even in his own court. The reports are mixed and confusing, but it is clear that her true race must remain concealed - her continued presence defies the Laowyn feeling at court."

"Did she give a name?" Zephenesh's voice came out in a strangled whisper, his knuckles were white on the spoon.

"She would not," Fidel eyed the Elder. Zephenesh was acting strangely, and the elf whose gaze usually did not linger on anyone was boring into him. "She said she had been picked by the Edict of Maidens and her family were willing to sacrifice her to protect themselves. Return meant death, that's why Zeb was so adamant she should be allowed to stay."

"Please take me to this Zeb now," Zephenesh's voice brooked no argument. He rose, placing his knife on the half-eaten platter of bread and meat and turning to the door before Fidel had even risen.

The Captain looked to the elf for explanation.

"The woman you described matches the appearance of Zephenesh's niece Kiara. She ran away not much over two weeks ago."

Fidel only hesitated a moment before following after Zephenesh who was rushing in the wrong direction.

"Your niece?!" he exclaimed as he caught up with the Elder.

"Take me to the elf."

Fidel was at a loss. He merely nodded and turned to lead the way to Zeb's quarters. The elf was up and dressed when they entered the room. Apparently even in his sickened state he had managed to mix one of his healing potions.

"Zeb, this is Zephenesh, Laowyn Elder, and Djeck, a Mcir Elf."

Zeb looked between the two men.

"The woman's uncle and servant?"

Fidel noted the surprise on both the visitors' faces. Zeb's uncanny intuition caught most people off guard and the longer Fidel knew him the more he suspected there was more to his unexplained knowledge.

"Kiara?"

"The Prince has taken her, but I have no idea whether she still lives."

"You let her escape?" Djeck's angry words were spat first at Fidel and then at Zeb.

"Do not look to me, Meir Elf!" snapped Zeb, his voice suddenly filled with cold authority. "I had no intention of letting her be captured by the Prince."

"You're Southern," muttered Djeck, taking a step back, his eyes clouded with suspicion.

"I don't appreciate my quarters being invaded, Fidel."

"I came to see if you were well again."

Zeb only scowled in response.

"The Commander ordered it." The tension increased with the ensuing silence. Fidel should have considered this more carefully.

"Zephenesh, no more can be done here. The Commander is awaiting you with the other elders."

Zephenesh looked for a moment as if he might take physical action, but the light in his old eyes slowly died. He drew away from the elf whose judgemental stare followed him and Djeck from the room.

"I urged you, master, to tell Kiara of your involvement in the Resistance." Djeck whispered as they followed Fidel to the meeting room.

"And expose her to the same fate as her parents?"

Fidel could hear the emotion thick in Zephenesh's voice.

"Were you not making that decision when you said she should obey the Edict?"

"She should not have been chosen and would not have been but for her stubbornness marking her out."

"Are you so oblivious to your own kin?" Djeck ventured to chastise his master but Fidel heard him hesitate. "Kiara is a great beauty."

Zephenesh did not respond. The three men continued down the hall in silence, each wondering if it was Kiara in the palace.

"I thought she would come back," Zephenesh finally whispered.

They walked in silence, but they'd all heard.

CHAPTER 12

J ohan and Trevisian stood at a balustrade overlooking one of the main palace entryways. Men and women milled below them like worker bees about one of the palace's largest honey pots of trade. Horses and mules passed each other closely, their tails swishing and ears flying back. Shouts were flung across the courtyard, and answers were hurled back. Some raised greetings, others were demands by Imperial Guards, and still others were tradesmen, selling their wares, desiring entry to the palace where they might secure a generous patron.

The stone that formed the ground had large nomadic letters in heavy indented script across it - the language of the old Reluwyn. When the streets cleared near dusk the snaky writing could be seen; right now it was covered by hundreds of rushing feet and deluged with waste that ran in the lettering's rivulets.

The sandstone walls of the city held writhing labyrinthine streets, and it was from these that Emril's citizens oozed past the system of circular palace walls, clamouring to gain access to the innermost area where only courtiers resided. Their bobbing heads were oblivious to their Prince who stood above them. Most were dark haired Reluwyn, but occasionally a fairer haired incomer would catch Trevisian's eye. He would follow them from the shadow of the Tower Gate as they threaded their way like gold through the tapestry of dark heaving silks. None of them had quite the same fair skin as her though, and it was to her that his thoughts always drifted back.

He had commanded a display of all the maidens who had finished their beauty treatment yesterday. The golden-haired thief had been there. She had spat in his eye when he had touched her. Unfortunately for her, he did not respond with anger but amusement. He was almost certain she was indeed a maiden. That was the only possible reason for her tense reaction whenever he came near. Her eyes had flashed brimstone at him when he'd chuckled in response to her action. He had demanded she give her name, just as he had all the other maidens present. She had not obeyed, but he was sure he could eventually break her.

"Did you see the way the other women looked at her?" Johan's thoughts echoed Trevisian's.

"How do you do that, Johan?"

The Radichi warrior ignored the question, leaning his thick forearms on the balustrade and watching the waves of people ebbing against the palace's shore.

"Your favour singles her out."

"Favour!" Trevisian spat. "She is in receipt of my wrath."

Johan ran his calloused fingers along a crack in the stone beneath his arms. "Is she?"

Trevisian clenched his jaw and pushed the hair out of his eyes. Today he had changed his courtly tunic for leather trousers, an open black shirt and spurred boots. He had spent the morning relaxing in the harem, and some of the tension which had bothered him since the High Council meeting at dawn had been worked away.

Garesh's constant complaining of the rebellious Laowyn had irritated Trevisian into doing his bidding. He'd signed an Edict to suppress the Laowyn and only then had he been freed from his duties. He had to trust the man who knew more about his Kingdom than he did, but still, the action had plagued his mind afterwards.

The feeling of uneasiness had sent him in search of carnal pleasures, but even that had left a bad taste. He had lain with two of the maidens now that the examinations had begun. Both were beautiful, both were satisfying. One, who had been bolder than the other, had touched his back, tracing the markings which coloured the length of it. She had asked about them. The two were now back in the harem, demarcated as concubines for the rest of their lives. Trevisian would not call upon them again.

The questions had resurrected thoughts of his mother, the marking linking him with her. Only one knew of the true meaning behind the marking on his back. His High Councillor had not mentioned it since the day he'd made Trevisian promise never to use his abilities. He had protected Trevisian from himself and a people who would not accept his true nature, and that was why the Prince trusted him. But recently that promise had been hard to keep. He had been at the palace for weeks now, and the last time he had run, truly run, was over a month ago.

Trevisian looked sideways at his companion and then back at the crowds. Johan had never asked about the marking, although Trevisian had caught him staring at it more than once over the years they'd known each other. There had always been a knowing look in his eye which made Trevisian wonder if such bloodlines existed within the Radichi clans who came from the same desert as the Reluwyn.

All of this had put Trevisian's mood on a distinctly dark path. Now Johan was pushing boundaries.

"She's a petty thief." Trevisian finally replied. "One who cost me my freedom."

At least if he was to be caged here he had the satisfaction of knowing another suffered the same fate.

"Yet she is treated as a harem favourite."

"Your point?" Trevisian could feel the heat of the midday sun touching his shoulders.

"I hear things. The harem's temperature is running high."

"It's hot everywhere," said Trevisian, passing a hand over his brow.

"The women are becoming competitive. Your thief could be targeted."

"Good."

Johan turned, leaning on one elbow so he could face his Prince, but said nothing. Trevisian had called him half an hour ago and since then they had been watching the comings and goings below, a guard standing behind them in the shadows.

"What would be your next move if you were her?"

Johan's sandy brows rose a little, but his eyes remained firmly on the Prince's sharp profile. "Escape," he answered.

"Precisely."

"She defies you."

"She will break."

"And when she does?"

Trevisian said nothing.

"Her ingenuity has saved her from two prisons. I like her."

Trevisian looked up sharply at this. "You admire the Prince's enemy?"

"Radichi admire courage."

"As do Reluwyn." Trevisian turned back to the crowds.

"We admire it, even in our enemies. Many would have relented, but she…"

"Remains unbroken," the Prince cut in abruptly. He pulled his friend away from the view and down some back steps, the guards parting for them to pass. "She is indeed escaping."

"How do you know?"

"The guards saw her slip out of the harem in the early morning. I have had watches stationed at the Tower Gate ever since."

At the bottom of the stairs was a street narrower than the one they had been watching. In it stood two rider-less horses and a group of mounted guards behind. Trevisian took the reins from a waiting servant and mounted Dainus who had been pawing the ground impatiently.

"Ride with me, friend, and we will catch our prey." A smile flashed across Trevisian's face, breaking his heavy mood. He had seen her, one of the only people below to have their head covered. He had seen her look back at the entrance and a strand of her golden hair had whipped out of the hood. She had been quick to tuck it in, lowering those bright eyes, hurrying between the people. Not quick enough.

Johan was up on his mount quickly, although he did not look nearly as pleased as the Prince. They rode into the current of the main crowd as guards began to shout for people to clear the road. Trevisian silenced them - he didn't want her to know he was coming.

They pushed forward, Dainus' wide chest and heavy hooves providing a deterrent for anyone getting in their way. Trevisian had seen her towards the south side, carefully skirting the market sellers. Although far shorter than others in the crowd, her head covering was too noticeable. He caught sight of her ducking between two horses laden with market goods.

Men and women scattered before him, Johan and the guards following as close behind as they could in the packed square. If he could make it past a group of silk traders ahead he would be able to cut her off. He pulled Dainus round, shifting his weight, making it past the traders. The guards and Johan falling in behind him as he swung towards his target. Several people collided with Dainus, not expecting the sudden wall of beast, and Trevisian took his chance, reaching down and snatching at the hood of the one he sought by his foot. Gold hair met sunlight and up flew those blue eyes. Trevisian was on the verge of smiling triumphantly when the head ducked away. He reached to grab her but before he could she shot beneath Dainus, flying between the two sets of legs and out the other side. Trevisian sat up, swinging around and yelling after her, his strangled words coming out with laughter.

"Johan – after her!" But she was too quick, slipping between the guards' horses before they even realised she was there, preparing to shoot beneath the legs of Johan's. Trevisian saw the beast's ears flick about nervously. The whites of its eyes showed and the stamping of its hooves became a clatter, lashing out. Before they could find their mark, Trevisian was off Dainus' back. He leapt into a run and was within reach of Kiara just as she began to dive beneath the horse's stomach. He yanked her back, grabbing her arms to pull her away from the hooves.

"You idiot! Do you want to get trampled to death?!" Trevisian shouted in Kiara's face. He saw her confusion, and instead of recoiling as he thought she would, she became still in his arms.

"My lord, the people." Johan didn't have to say anything more. The crowds, realising that their Prince was among them, the ultimate patron, had begun surging towards them.

The spell was broken, and his prisoner pulled away from him.

"When will you see that there is no escape? Come." Without waiting for an answer, he took hold of her waist and threw her up into the saddle. He didn't get up behind her but instead led his horse. Guards filed in next to them, escorting them into the palace before the zealous crowds could get near their ruler.

Silence cloaked the returning band. Trevisian did not even need to order his prisoner to dismount when they came to a stop. She walked up ahead of him and entered his chamber when the guards opened the door for her.

She stopped, the ragged peasant's cloak still about her, and Trevisian came to face her, arms folded across his chest. He studied her silently, unable to read her expression, just as he had been unable to understand what stopped her struggling in the busy courtyard.

"Who gave you this cloak?"

There was no answer. But before he could ask again, Johan entered.

"It was Coscian, my Lord Prince."

She flinched. "He did not know what I asked of him."

"That he was providing you with a disguise in order to escape?"

Trevisian raised his hand to give an order.

"He didn't know!" Kiara fell before him on her knees. He paused, too surprised to carry on. "I told him it was for..." she struggled with the words. "To...to entice the Prince – a game of sorts."

Trevisian saw Johan's lips twitch, struggling not to smile at the sexual preferences Kiara implied. After being silent for a few moments, his mind torn, he made a decision.

"Bring Coscian to the harem courtyard, he shall be beaten for his crime."

"No!" She repeated it over and over, following him to where the Harem Master would be punished. It was the most emotion she had displayed since coming to the palace, and the Prince found the sudden change intriguing.

As he walked out into the harem courtyard he realised that he had never had a servant beaten before, no matter what the crime. Imprisoned, yes - even executed if the crime had warranted it - but never beaten. The bruises that had patterned his body throughout childhood but were long since healed seemed to come alive again. The shadow of their memory bringing back every blow he had received.

The entrance of the palace jailer appeared to cause the bird-chirps and fountain song to fade away. The women too had scattered from the courtyard, covering themselves with shawls, fleeing into the shadows of the pillared edges. Coscian appeared shortly after the jailor. He looked about himself, slightly confused, and at the sight of the jailor full bewilderment took over.

"My Lord Prince," he said as he came near, spreading his hands out and bowing. Kiara's eyes darted between the two in fear.

"This prisoner," Trevisian cast a careless hand in the direction of his fair-haired thief who seemed frozen to the spot. "Was caught escaping the palace through the Tower Gate, wearing the robe you see upon her. A robe given to her by you, Coscian. What do you answer to the charge of conspiracy to help her flee my custody?"

Hundreds of eyes watched from between the pillars. A fine show, thought Trevisian. She would not be so quick to try and escape again after Coscian had seen the lash.

"My Lord Prince, I…" but Coscian had not words. He had no excuse. He seemed startled by the charge and his widened eyes took in the woman who stood silently, pleading for something.

"You shame me, Coscian. Loyalty is my highest requirement and to break your ruler's loyalty requires punishment according Reluwyn law," Trevisian continued, "Even in the case of a penitent subject." Johan was by his side now.

He nodded to the jailor, two guards moved with him, taking hold of Coscian's arms, turning him. One of the guards stamped a booted foot hard into the back of the Harem Master's legs causing him to grunt as his knees hit the tiled floor.

Whispers threaded between the pillars surrounding the courtyard. They were quelled with one sweeping look from the Prince. It may be shocking for men to invade the women's quarters, but he cared nothing for tradition in this moment.

He watched as the jailor came around to Coscian's back.

"For this crime you shall be lashed until the blood soaks the clothes upon your back." The jailor recited the Reluwyn law as he had done a thousand times before.

He pulled a pile of leather straps from his belt, gripping upon the handle, letting the long, plaited lengths fall. Even as Trevisian took it in he felt his blood run cold with the memories.

The guard planted his feet squarely and then with a large swing raised his implement of torture.

"Stop!" cried Kiara. Before anyone knew what was happening she had leapt forward between the punisher and Coscian. The jailor looked to the Prince for direction but it was not his ruler who spoke.

"You want blood? Let it be *mine*. Coscian knew no part of the crime I made him commit." Kiara practically spat at the Prince. "If you must lash someone, let it be your whoring thief."

Trevisian watched her face contort at the words. Still the jailor looked at him, happy to beat either subject as long as his job was done.

"My Lord Prince," Johan whispered so quietly that no one else could hear. "She could not withstand such a beating thin as she is."

Already Kiara was turning, kneeling before the jailor, baring her back. She would take a punishment destined for another? That woman didn't know what a good beating felt like. She didn't know that it could reduce a grown man to tears, how it would ruin you for days, that cleaning it with salt water was almost worse than the beating itself.

"Show fair judgment and you will not appear weak."

Trevisian raised a hand to his ear, silencing any more of Johan's council. He walked forward instead and took Kiara's by the jaw, forcing her to stand. "For the benefit of that smooth skin of yours I shall spare you and Coscian. If you had ever been beaten in your life you might not have been so eager to take another's place." Then, with a suddenness that seemed to frighten the woman, his face changed.

A thought had dropped, quite surprisingly, into his head. If she wished to receive a punishment, it did not necessarily mean that Trevisian had to deal it – after all, Johan had mentioned the atmosphere of the harem.

"Oh dear, my Little One, what a fuss you have caused." A light-hearted smile marked his dark features. "I shall forgive you, for you are my…" he dragged on the last word, looking about him until he caught eyes with Johan. "*Favourite.*" The words echoed off the walls of the courtyard. He released her. "I shall be calling for you soon."

He turned upon his booted heel and left the courtyard. Moments before the door closed, he heard the furore of woman's voices break out behind him.

CHAPTER 13

"Infighting in the harem. Your presence accompanied by a mere eight guards in the Tower Gate square. Your absence from the court of appeals. Need I go on?" Garesh remonstrated, pacing before his Prince who lay propped up on multiple silk cushions, crunching on an apple.

"Infighting?" Trevisian shot a look at Johan who lay opposite.

"The competition for your favour grows daily, my lord," answered Garesh wearily. "Coscian has had to deal with many accusations and some of the maidens are demanding to be sent home."

"Are they?" Trevisian was enjoying this. His smile had broadened and now he let forth a deep chuckle. "I don't doubt it."

Johan did not join his friend.

"They are making a mockery of your forthcoming nuptials. I am told that... that petty criminal of yours had to be physically pulled off another woman. Coscian defended the girl but a blade was involved. It is getting out of hand, to say nothing of your other actions. Do you not realise how detrimental this is to your standing? To *my* standing?"

Trevisian finished the apple and tossed the core into a golden bowl by his elbow, licking the juice that had trickled down his fingers. He'd take it down to Dainus in the palace stables later. "Your standing?"

"But of course, my Lord Prince," came the deferential tones, "Your standing is of the utmost importance, but I would be ignoring my duty if I was not to demand the imprisonment of that street-brat. Your..." the High Councillor searched for the right word, "... *association* with her does you no good." Garesh was a master of flattery, but his patience was wearing thin and the Prince's usefulness was reaching its limit. Once the Edict was proclaimed across the land it was merely a matter of time before the Laowyn were put down and the Prince's popularity waned.

Garesh continued. "Your safety is of the utmost importance." Was it? Or would Garesh have been happy to hear of some mishap befalling the Prince. "And your presence is always required at the court of appeals, in your absence it was necessary for me to take your place." Garesh had enjoyed it, the feel of the throne and all that power, but with the Prince so close to choosing a bride and taking up full Kingship there had been a restlessness in the crowd of courtiers.

"*Association?*"

He hadn't listened. Garesh glared about the room, striving to maintain control, but that was just it, he didn't have control.

"Your relationship."

"Relationship!" Trevisian shot up from the cushions.

For the first time Garesh saw how tall, how broad and how powerful, his protégé had become. He felt a cold and sharp fear pierce through his mind. His plan was being enacted, even Nisa had called on the dark spirits to sway the hearts of the court in his favour, but if things deteriorated faster than the Edict came about, nothing was guaranteed.

"I have no relationship with a petty thief!"

"Then send her to jail." Garesh rose up, inch for inch, to face his Prince. He must maintain control of him. Total power over the entire Kingdom was within reach and once Garesh had it there would be no obstacles. Emrilion could expand to the east, they could explore across the Western Sea, but until then he had to hold onto the reins of power. He changed to a pleading tone. "She has done more than others who have faced imprisonment for less. Her actions are causing problems and she must be punished. You know the importance of punishment." The allusion to the Prince's past was misplaced. He should have calculated better.

"I will determine what happens to the woman." The Prince's voice had turned from heated to cold, "You may leave us, Garesh."

The High Councillor made to speak again.

"I have no further need of you today." The Prince sat back down upon the cushions, his body retaining its tension and his eyes averted from his Regent when he dismissed him with a hand.

Stunned, Garesh bowed, retreating. Whatever control he had enjoyed over the Prince had just come to an abrupt end.

●●●

Kiara had been rubbing a honeyed balm into her cut lip when the Prince summoned her. She could still taste the sweetness in her mouth as her sandal-clad feet pattered a rhythm across the tiled floor. She almost felt normal walking the corridors of the great palace of Emril city now. It was several days since her attempted escape and she had now been at the palace for many weeks.

The last time she had seen the Prince he had acted bizarrely. At least that was what she had thought, until his words, his manipulations, had become clear. She now knew exactly what his *'favourite'* comment had meant - her lip was testament to it. Before, the women in the harem had warily kept their distance; now they treated her with undisguised contempt. She was the one who stood between them and life as Queen of Emrilion. Today, one of the women had cursed her, threatening to destroy the face that had the Prince so enraptured. She had intended to do it with a knife.

When Kiara and her guard reached the Prince's chambers, the doors were already open. The Prince had not looked her in the eye when she had arrived, instead walking past her out into the corridor.

"Come with me."

Kiara's fair brows had risen but she did as she was bid. Turning upon her heel she set off after him, followed by her handler. They finally stopped in front of two great doors on the south side of the palace, and entered the room alone.

The sight inside was enough to make Kiara gasp. Either side of her rose huge bookcases filled to the brim with books and papers; in front of her were volumes piled high on tables. The furniture in all different shapes and sizes drawn from a myriad of craftsmen across the empire.

Slung over the piles of books were leather maps and drawings, as if keeping the literary works warm within their blanketed embrace. It seemed as though all the creative minds of the Kingdom had drawn together their thoughts and thrown them out across this room.

Windows stretched from floor to ceiling, framing the southern view of the city. The suns lit up the sandstone dwellings of the city outside, pouring back into the hall and illuminating words across many pages.

"How many books are there?"

The Prince had been toying with a giant globe that stood at hip height its circumference the size of a doorway. In truth, Kiara had temporarily forgotten whom she was with. When her eyes dropped from the heady heights of the bookcases to him, she retracted them quickly, looking to the floor.

"Surprised that a race of barbarians care for literature?" he hissed.

So, he *was* angry. She studied a pattern in the carpet that resembled an onion. She heard him exhale heavily.

"I will trade a question for a question."

Her blue eyes caught up to his again as he finished speaking. She had paused within the threshold of the room, caught in awe, but now she walked further in, keeping to the edge, as far from where he stood at the centre as she could be. Was the game he wanted to play that simple? No doubt it was a ruse to find out who she was.

She brushed the spine of a book gingerly, immediately snatching her hand away, frightened the precious object might disintegrate beneath her touch. She turned back to dark eyes that flashed with brief amusement. "Must we answer every question put to us?"

"Yes."

She could always lie. Besides, what else were they to do? If she could keep him occupied, and learn a little whilst doing so, what harm could there be in it?

"My High Councillor wishes me to jail you for your escape and… anti-social behaviour."

"That is not a question."

His dark eyes rested upon her, and a small upturn of his lip appeared. Had she just made him smile?

"More than ten thousand." He spun the globe, his forefinger running across countless miles.

Kiara nodded, suitably impressed at the number of volumes. Now it was his turn.

"Why did you offer to take Coscian's beating?"

"Because I deserved the punishment." She shrugged.

"Do you know what a beating with the lash entails?"

"It's not your turn." Kiara was halfway to the window now. Even from here she could see over a hundred buildings. She glanced at the globe which now stood to her left. "What is on the globe?"

"The known world – and the worlds we believe exist."

She detoured, walking towards the globe, now suddenly interested. "Believe?" she queried.

"It's not your turn." He mimicked her voice. She saw he was wearing an open collared black shirt again, the wide opening slung back as he hunched over the globe, showing the colourful top of a marking on his back. "This is Emrilion." He jabbed a finger at a large oblong landmass on the right-hand side of the globe.

Kiara wanted to see, but she didn't want to get any nearer to the Prince than she had to. Even in his current, oddly amicable mood, she did not trust him. Beneath it all was tension. He could turn.

Surprisingly though, he stepped away from the globe, that she might get a closer look.

"How did you escape Grûl's jail?" he whispered it by her ear, having suddenly stepped in behind her. Kiara pulled back, stumbling away and sending a pile of books to the floor from a nearby table.

Instead of acting like a terrified deer in range of a hunter's bow however, she stooped to pick up the books. "Now look at what you've made me do," she chastised, making the Prince chuckle. It was a nice sound, deep and rich.

"Answer me," he then demanded.

"I fit between the bars of the window. They don't build cells to keep women in."

The Prince looked her over and nodded. "I shall make a note to tell my Councillors."

Kiara was happy that he did not probe further. She would never tell him she had escaped half-naked.

"What is that to the west of Emrilion? I've never heard of any land lying there."

One of the Prince's brows rose. "For a street-brat you do know a little." He turned back to the globe. "It is a land that my explorers believe exists. They are mapping the known world."

"That more races may be made subject to yours," she replied bitterly, continuing her journey to the window.

"How did you become a thief?"

Kiara measured this question. What was safe to give away? Realising that nothing but her race was dangerous to recount, she offered the truth.

"I was chosen for the Edict." There was a slight pause. "I held no desire to be presented for you to sample, as you would a hundred others, but my uncle urged me to go. That same night, I cut off my hair, dressed as a boy, and decided to live a life raiding royal caravans as I had already been doing at night for months."

She looked at the Prince, challenging him to say something, but he merely continued to stare.

"Robbing my tyrannical regime."

"Why…" She was almost at the window. There were questions that had been nagging at her mind some for days some for weeks. "Why did you leave the palace disguised as a common thief? Were you in some kind of special envoy?"

"Is it the first or the last question?"

"The first."

He exhaled again as he paced, eyes falling over the objects that littered his path, his hands picking up various metal implements which lay scattered across maps, before replacing them and moving on.

"I did not want to be here, at the palace. I…I like to be elsewhere. To be unknown. It's the only place I can be myself. Be free." The admission seemed intimate.

Suddenly the huge, hall-like room was small. His thoughts voicing themselves to her. He could have answered the last question with a simple no if he had not stopped to ask which one Kiara really wished to know the answer to.

Had he wanted to answer the first? He was the Prince of a scarred land, but in this instant, in this moment, he was simply a man. She wanted to know why. Why was she suddenly seeing more of him than before. Seeing his humanity. The sudden honesty.

She reached the window and looked out at the sandstone buildings a hundred feet below, warped by whirls in the glass. They rose and fell with the land, but all were below her. Suddenly, escape from the palace as she had planned just a few days ago, seemed so foolish in the face of the maze which lay before her. How many thousands dwelt in the capital of Emril city? She was one. One in a thousand, one in thousands more in this Kingdom, and here she stood in the company of the one who controlled it all. Why her?

His voice came from the other side of the room. "Have you lain with Coscian?"

The very accusation was ridiculous. Coscian was married, he was in love with his wife, and if the Prince knew anything about his subjects he would know that. Kiara had learned it in a little over a week. "Of course not!" She jumped, finding him directly behind her.

"Do you always stand so close to people?" she asked crossly.

"No." He reached up a hand and touched her face, his thumb resting on her full lip. She froze beneath his touch. He pulled it down, exposing the cut running down its centre. "How did you come by this?" He released her lip.

"My question didn't count."

"A question for a question, that was the deal."

Kiara sighed. "One of your women tried to cut the skin from my face." The defiance was suddenly back in her eyes. "Not even my face would stop her getting into your bed."

"First Coscian, now this - and didn't you have a knife in your leg before I met you? Don't answer that, it isn't my question."

"It's my turn anyway." She moved her head, but still his hand lingered. "You said to me in the courtyard that if I had known what a beating felt like I would not have volunteered, and just now, you asked me if I knew what a beating with a lash was like. It was as though...as though you did." She took a breath. "Were you beaten?"

She saw it happen, shutters dropping like armour over his eyes. Whatever had been happening since they had entered this library was at an end. He drew away from her, his hand dropping from her face. She had forgotten it was there, that it had been warm against her skin, that she could smell the spices he had bathed in. It had felt...good. What was wrong with her?

Then it came, anger boiling and spitting. "The Reluwyn, as you said, are a barbarous race." The embittered words were accompanied by a rapid stride back to the centre of the room.

Kiara leant against a pillar between two of the windows. Had he just admitted to it? He had. He *had*. She watched his back as he walked away, his shoulders tense beneath his shirt, all calmness evaporated. He had spoken angrily and she could almost feel the rage rolling off him.

"Why did you bring me here?" she said softly, not wishing to taunt an already angry bear.

It was too late.

"Because I can command anything! Because I am ruler here and you are nothing, nothing but a criminal, a thief turned whore."

Kiara's chin came up at that. "We had a deal, you said all questions must be answered. Is the deal at an end?" She pushed off the pillar and made her way down the side of the room, towards the door.

"Yes," he was hissing again. He met her by the door, his eyes darker than ever, his proximity too close. He took her chin but this time without gentleness. "Once again you have proved us barbaric but failed to tell me who you are."

Kiara's blood froze, her heart paused, this was it. He would demand to know her race.

"Or your name," he carried on, oblivious to her fear. "But now it's time you discarded your past, after all, you are part of this palace, as such you must become barbaric yourself."

"I didn't..." she wanted to defend herself - or apologise for asking a question which so clearly upset him. But he cut her off.

"Tonight." That was all he said. Then he released her, threw open the doors with both hands and called for the guard to escort her back to her room.

CHAPTER 14

"I am told you spent time in a cell with my niece while she was here?"

Zeb was busy packing herbs and small colourful bottles into his satchel. He had barely looked up at the entrance of the Elder and the elf, and even in answering he merely nodded. Fidel sat back in a corner observing the conversation.

The next words got his attention. It was not the words per se, though, it was the tone. "Did she…was she well?" There was a brokenness in it.

Zeb paused, his fingers lingering on the corks which plugged each of the bottles that poked out of his bag. His serious gaze found the Laowyn Elder. He only held it for a moment before continuing to pack.

"No," he said, speaking while he worked, "She had an infected wound, probably caused by a blade. She was unconscious for a while."

He could hear Zephenesh's breath quicken.

"And what did you do?" Djeck's voice was accusing, his look distrustful. He had accompanied Zephenesh promising silence.

Zeb did not bother looking the Northern Elf in the eye. "I treated her. Once we realised she was a woman, she was moved to a separate cell from the other prisoner."

"Once you found out she was a woman?"

"She was dressed as a boy, her hair was cut off."

Zephenesh nodded absently. They had not found any evidence of what she had done, nor where she had gone after she had disappeared. They had assumed she would come back after a few days of raiding Reluwyn carriages. They'd had no idea she had left them for good.

Zeb picked up a necklace and dropped it into his bag.

"That's Kiara's!" cried Djeck indignantly.

"She lost it when the Prince took her," Zeb replied without much care.

The command had been given at dusk the previous day, the Laowyn Resistance was moving out. The lair that had been their home for the past two years was to be abandoned to a few guards; the majority of the forces, which were swelling daily as the persecution increased, were moving out. Commander Ikara had not specified their objective, but Zeb was no fool, she was retreating to the broken stronghold of Ishtalia on the Western coast, the old Laowyn capital.

News of the latest Edict was not public knowledge among the tunnels of the Resistance, but it would be soon enough. The Reluwyn had commanded all peoples of the Emrilion Empire to rise up, in exactly a month's time, and eradicate the Laowyn. It was not just the Resistance who were being targeted now, it was all of them, even the women and children. Every Laowyn was to be executed. Neighbours would turn against neighbours, friends, against friends. In one month, Laowyn bodies would be scattered across the Empire, a race extinguished in the quest for supreme unity.

Zephenesh knew all this, and yet he was here. "She was taken by the Prince – but why?"

"They had encountered each other before. He was alone, and not dressed as the Prince. It seems your niece did not recognise him, for she spoke to him about the Prince."

"No doubt critically." A mirthless smile warped Djeck's face.

Zeb carried on, "I only heard scraps of information as I was knocked unconscious. I have tried to revive my memories and bring clarity with herbal remedies, but it remains fragmented. The forest was crawling with Imperial Guards and he thought she had brought them down upon him - I believe he took her as punishment. Knowing your niece as I did, if only for a few days, I do not believe any rumours of her complicity as a concubine."

The very thought sickened Zeb. He had seen the fear upon Kiara's face, he had seen the way the Reluywn had looked at her. Zeb had been formulating his own plan, it differed from Ikara's, and she would not know it until he was gone.

"If that is true, then she must be saved."

"You know the Commander's plan, you would be disobeying if you went to Emril city." Fidel spoke for the first time out of loyalty to his Commander.

Zephenesh rose abruptly, his chair clattering against the wall. "I will *not* leave her. You were right," he gestured at his elvin companion. "I should have told her about my part in the Resistance." He drew his hands up and rubbed them across his eyes, pressing upon the bridge of his nose.

Zeb had been folding clothes into the bag, taking up a small, delicate piece of armour and he placed it on top of the pack, but he halted at Zephenesh's words. "She didn't know about your involvement?"

"Her parents were part of the Resistance, and they died defending what was left of Ishtalia before the Edict of Unification. I lived, for I was in a watch-station some miles out. She became my responsibility, my child, and I was not going to expose her to this, to the danger. She is so much like my sister was." Tears were coming to

Zephenesh's eyes and slowly falling down the lines of his face, filtering through his beard, dropping onto his robe. "I thought that if she obeyed the Reluwyn laws she would be safe."

Zeb placed a hand lightly upon the Laowyn's shoulder. It only rested for a moment, "Take hope. She is stronger than you know." He hesitated, his eyes darting over to Fidel. Then, a decision made, he spoke, "I... I failed her too. If I had been more observant I might have stopped her capture. She needs to be rescued."

"We cannot leave the Commander now to go on some hare-brained rescue mission!" Fidel broke in. "Not when the Resistance is moving out and our race is about to be attacked." He folded his arms across his broad chest.

"Suit yourself," said Zeb brusquely, picking up his pack. "I know where my duty lies."

"Wait! Wait a moment!" Fidel held up a hand. "How are you intending on breaking into the most heavily guarded building in the Kingdom to steal a prisoner?"

Zeb halted by the door. "Two things. Firstly, you have heard the same reports that she is a Favourite of the Prince, so we can assume that she has some degree of freedom within the palace. Secondly, what makes you think I am going solely to help her escape?"

"Then what else are you going for?" asked Fidel.

"Have none of you thought of how incredible it is that one of your people has direct access to the ruler who sanctions your persecution?"

"You mean to sway the Prince?" Fidel asked.

"Your race is set to be wiped out in a matter of weeks and you've been waiting for the Great Spirit's providence. What can you lose?" All three men stood staring into Zeb's determined face. "I have a plan," he said simply.

◉◉◉

They were laid out across the room. A foot apart, arms by their sides, chests still. Each pair of eyes stared at the earthen ceiling, seeing nothing. Each body was covered in a thin swathe of forest green gauze, pulled down from hangings that had adorned the Elder's temporary meeting hall. Now the hangings kept the dead warm in their eternal sleep.

There were seven. Seven lost. Seven gone. Seven dead. She had sent them on a routine mission. Now they were dead. All they had asked for was food supplies from the small trading community that resided on the southern edge of the forest. A community who had received their copy of the Edict for the Suppression of the Laowyn. A community who had decided not to wait the three and a half weeks until the appointed day. They had slaughtered them, and Calev and Jaik had found their bodies, strung up against the gates of the town, parchments pinned to their chests. Laowyn dogs they had been called, worthy of death as such.

Teo was only seventeen - Ikara would have to inform his mother. At that moment she would be helping to pack up the kitchen, looking forward to the supplies her son was supposed to bring for the journey. He wasn't coming.

Ikara knelt there, between the bodies, surrounded by them, her eyes almost as unseeing as theirs. She had looked at each of them, directly in the eyes, then she had ripped the parchments from their chests. She had been the one to place their hands by their sides, to tilt their heads that their eyes could look heavenwards towards the Great Spirit. She had helped to bathe the blood from their faces, their necks where the blade had slit across.

She did not hear Fidel enter. There were two members of the Resistance standing at the entrance to the room, they backed away at a signal from Fidel, drawing the thick hessian curtain across the entrance. The Captain paused for a short while, surveying the bodies, but his eyes were caught upon the figure knelt between them. She was wearing her armour. Her hair unkempt, forgotten. She looked so still, Fidel could not even see her breathing. He came up behind her, dropping a heavy hand upon her shoulder.

"I'm sorry Ikara, I'm so sorry." His eyes filled with grief, his heart aching as much for her as for the dead.

He felt her shudder beneath his hand but she made no sound.

"Ikara, you must come away. You must eat. Everyone is preparing to leave, the families of the dead must be informed."

"They were killed as dogs."

Fidel was not sure she knew to whom she was speaking.

"They slit their throats, they allowed them to bleed out, choking upon their own lifeblood. They tore out their Enspers, now their family will not receive the jewels, their bodies will be carried to the sea with nothing left over. They are gone." The last words came out as a moan, a deep sound of pain. "They are gone."

"Ikara, you must come away. We..." Was this the time? What other time was there? Fidel knew that Ikara blamed herself, the responsibility of the Laowyn Resistance weighed heavy upon her. There was no longer any good time to address issues of planning. "I have been in conference with Zephenesh and Zeb. The Laowyn woman we held in captivity, who we believe was taken by the Prince..."

"Taken? She *left* with him." The words were in a tone Fidel did not recognise as Ikara's. There was much malice there.

"Whichever, Zeb believes that if they could get a message to her in the palace that she might be able to do something for our cause."

She said nothing.

"We have nothing to lose at this point, we must take any opportunity we can."

"Opportunity?" She looked up suddenly, locking sorrow-filled eyes with Fidel. "Zeb was beguiled by that woman the moment he saw her, he has no sense of judgment. And you," she stood up, her height level with Fidel's. "You would have us make a deal with the race that has done this?" She gestured to the men who lay lifeless in the room. "Blood can only be paid for by blood, Captain."

Fidel flinched at that, the title like a verbal blow. They were friends, but her sadness, her control, would not let her see it. He took a breath slowly.

"Ikara."

"Commander."

"As you wish." He inclined his head. "I am your friend, you know that, I... do not let your grief destroy your military judgment."

"You think I will let these *murders* go unpunished?" She thrust her palms hard against Fidel's chest, but even her considerable strength barely moved him.

"The Great Spirit does not ask for punishment to be dealt by us. You know that. He will stand in judgment of all one day. He calls us to make peace where we can."

"That may have been us until now, but we will soon be a military force." Ikara threw back. "Captain Hendra lies to the west in Ishtalia, his securing of the old capital has given us a place to grow our forces and train. We can defend ourselves from there and others can seek refuge with us. We will recruit more of the Laowyn and we will train them to fight."

"Ikara, the Great Spirit…"

"Where was the Great Spirit when these men died?" she screamed. "Where was he when Teo was taken from his mother? I don't know this God." Her long fingers clenched in white fists.

"Do you wish to strike me? If it will make you feel better, if it will right these wrongs," Fidel jerked his chin towards the dead. "Do it."

"Waste my strength on you when I could be killing the Reluwyn?" she sneered, making her face contort into one Fidel didn't recognise.

"Her name is Kiara, she is the niece of one of our Elders. Do you not think it's worth a shot?"

"A shot?" Ikara's anger crumbled into despair. She turned back to her task - the preparation of the dead.

Fidel grabbed her, the action stirring the storm within. She flew at him, her clenched fist raised, and struck him across the face. It drew blood as his teeth cut into the soft skin of his cheek. A drop of blood fell from the corner of his mouth, but he did not retaliate. His eyes were filled with frustration but beneath that was so much care, so much love, that Ikara couldn't bear to face him any longer. But he refused to release her, letting her struggle before drawing her close and wrapping both arms around her.

He felt her shudder as she wept for the dead, for the Laowyn who would die in this conflict, for the future which was tainted. What hope had they?

Ikara was no small woman, but she felt fragile within his arms. She was muscled and strong, but he had seen her skip meals, over the past few days. He held her tighter, his body transferring peace to hers. As leader of the Laowyn she bore the brunt of these circumstances and they were crushing her.

She pulled back, wiping away whatever remnants of tears remained and along with them any vestiges of weakness. She pushed her fingers through her short hair and looked about her.

"Where are the families, Captain?"

And just like that they were back to officialdom.

"I left instructions with Calev and Jaik to gather them whilst I came to collect you, but," he hesitated, "Commander, I understand your wishes. We will fight the Reluwyn, we will fight for the survival of our people, but Kiara - whether whore or prisoner - seems to have the Prince's ear for the moment. We have never had anyone inside the government before, someone who could fight for our cause. Let Zephenesh and Zeb go to her."

Ikara was silent for so long that Fidel was about to repeat his plea, but her eyes finally retracted from the faces of the dead. "They cannot go alone. Calev and Jaik can be spared while the Resistance journeys to Ishtalia, but only for two weeks, then they must catch up. They're excellent close-quarters fighters and I need them to pass on that knowledge before the time comes."

Fidel nodded. He would have said more, he would have said what lay in his mind, but Ikara had already moved on. If he said what was on his mind, in his heart, he might disrupt her newly found calm, and the Laowyn needed a leader who was calm in the face of this crisis.

CHAPTER 15

A woman called Nisa was dipping her graceful fingers in paste-like paint and drawing lines across Kiara's face. They had been at this for over an hour, but the job was not done until all of the Kiara's body was intersected by the terracotta stripes.

She had not been told much about tonight's events. All she knew was that it involved almost all the inhabitants of the palace. Servants had been running to and fro all day, preparing food, decorating and giggling amongst themselves in excitement. The women of the harem had been preparing themselves too. The concubines were evidently accustomed to whatever was going to take place and had been showing the new additions what the appropriate dress was.

The men on the other hand had totally disappeared – off hunting somewhere, preparing in their own way.

"The ceremony this evening will symbolise where our race came from. The Tao desert, where the Radichi warriors now reside, is where our people used to live. The men from our people were the hunters and they still honour that tradition. The Radichi took over the lands and we were driven north, but we have since re-conquered our lands and some of our people live alongside the Radichi."

Kiara was almost certain that when Nisa used the term, 'live alongside' it meant tribal wars were frequent occurrences. The Reluwyn were a bloodthirsty race. Her mind tripped back over the conversation she had enjoyed earlier with the Prince. He had behaved strangely, almost human, but then he had shut himself off so quickly, so completely when she had mentioned the beating. She wondered who had done it. Who had been outrageous enough to harm the Prince of the Kingdom of Emrilion. She had already excluded all of the courtiers, definitely the servants, and only two people remained. His mother and his father.

"We are the women..."

"Really?"

Nisa rolled her dark eyes at Kiara's tone and carried on, "When we were nothing but a tribe in the desert, the woman's role was to..."

"Keep tents for your master husband and breed him good babies?"

"That is the tradition in almost every tribe," countered Nisa. Kiara had only just met her, but as well as being the only concubine willing to help the Favourite to ready herself, she was not afraid of arguing with her either. "Reluwyn women are also in charge of teaching the young to fight, they are the reason that the warrior culture continued within the Reluwyn race, they created what we are today. Hand-to-hand combat has always been taught by mothers. The design of our dress started with the need for fighting moves and has evolved into the alluring one you see now. They would use daggers and other small weapons when preparing the kill for the table and would teach the skills to young children. Larger weapons are the domain of those who are older. Even then, the women are the teachers until the men take over the training of the adolescents. There have been many skilled female warriors in our history, and although traditionally women are put in charge of defending the camp or settlements during a time of war, and men take the offensive, women have fought too in the past.

"From the age of thirteen, male children are taken on by the men to be taught strategy and battle tactics. The females continue their weaponry study but learn about defensive techniques, guerrilla warfare - and cooking and babies." Nisa looked almost as if she smiled at that. Poking fun at the Favourite. "That is why we paint ourselves like warriors, to honour that part of our heritage."

"So, that's what this is tonight? Celebrating the Reluwyn heritage?"

Nisa hid another smile. "In part," she murmured. Her voice was as sensual as her appearance. The woman was dark, like many Reluwyn women, but she stood out from the majority by being incredibly beautiful. Her hair was long, raven black and moved in glossy curls. It was decorated with fine gold chains which wove in and out of the lengths in a careless yet artful way. Her strikingly dark eyes were framed with black lashes and emphasised with smoky kohl.

She was tall but her figure was lusciously curved, clung to by the thin strips of her Reluwyn dress. Across her arms were designs made with the same paste as Kiara's but Nisa's were finer. They ran in spirals in and out and on to the next part of the pattern, creeping down to the bases of her fingers and up across her shoulders, joining at the back.

Kiara hoped she would not suggest doing any such drawing on herself. Hiding her Ensper was becoming increasingly difficult. She'd had to fashion her own dress for this evening's event, combining a beautiful silk wrap with a low-backed aqua marine dress. She had checked, behind the locked door of her room earlier today, and the top of her Ensper tattoo showed above the dress back. The Prince had sent the dress to her with no other explanation than that she should wear it tonight. Now she had managed to cut the wrap and had sewn the new fabric across the back of the dress with a needle and thread procured from Coscian. The doubled over material would cover her markings.

She had not been paying attention to Nisa's ministrations, but was watching the comings and goings outside the door.

"Maybe it is that far-off look which captures the Prince so." Nisa teased.

"I appreciate your help." Kiara gestured to the markings, ignoring Nisa's inquisitive look.

"I thought it only fair, the other maidens have their helpers."

Kiara's lips pinched a little. Nisa's attempt at a kind comment was double edged. The other concubines and maidens hated her. Whatever it was that attracted the Prince's sole attention attracted double the amount of dislike.

Well, they could all go to the Spirit Realm! She did not wish for the Prince's attentions, for any of this, and she despised those who did. The look of anger must have showed on her face.

"They are only jealous," Nisa said it so matter-of-factly, as though it was something to be gotten over, even rejoiced in.

"Of what?!" Kiara threw up her hands in exasperation and winced. Her shoulder was mostly healed but occasionally sharp movements would make it twinge.

"Injury?" Nisa gave her an assessing look, taking in which arm had caused the pain.

"I'm fine." Kiara was not fine. If she had just submitted to the Edict she would never have been singled out by the Prince for punishment. If she had submitted to the Grûl guards she would already be dead; if she had done as the Resistance told her she would be back with Zephenesh. But her emotions could not be hidden nor controlled.

"I have been concubine to my Lord Prince for three years and I have never seen him so obsessed with a woman."

"Three years?" Kiara turned, sending a smudge of paste in an unseemly line across her nose.

Nisa huffed, picking up the damp cloth she had been forced to use several times already.

"And does he..." Kiara's forehead puckered. "Does he call you? That's how it works isn't it?"

"Yes, that's generally how the role of a concubine works... what am I supposed to call you?"

"Little One, that's what he calls me." Kiara grimaced.

Nisa's brows rose. The Prince had given a pet-name to this nobody? She truly had not seen him behave so in her three years inside the palace walls. He had called her a handful of times, she had come to his bed, left him satisfied, and returned to the harem. She had not been called for two years, yet still in the harem she stayed, as did all the others. Why else would she be helping Garesh?

Nisa was not about to use the Prince's pet-name for this fair-haired woman. She had seen the mood the Favourite had left him in, using a name which was clearly a marker of their relationship, whatever it was, and to risk being overheard was simply unwise.

"Favourite, can I call you that?"

"I don't really care."

"Very well, Favourite, the role of a royal concubine is prestigious. You are chosen at a young age by the Harem Master. Coscian's predecessor chose me, and my family were honoured. I was brought to the harem when I was only thirteen, the age I would have learned to take care of a family, instead I was prepared for the Prince."

"He... when you were thirteen?"

Nisa put the bowl down with a clunk. "No," she looked exasperated at Kiara's dim-wittedness. "I was brought here to be prepared, much like you and the other maidens, except that I was never destined to be a Queen. Now I have a place here for the rest of my life, excellent food, the best clothing, and access to everything I could possibly want."

"Apart from life outside these walls," Kiara retorted.

"To be disgusted by something you don't understand shows ignorance."

Kiara flinched. "I'm sorry, I didn't mean... I didn't mean to make you feel as though..."

"As though I'm a whore?" Nisa's dark eyes were suddenly enigmatic, she forced Kiara to hold her stare. "What you have yet to realise, Favourite, is the power that lies in the hands of a woman *because* of her sex." She licked her lips. "Has that not been your game? I am already a concubine, Favourite, I have no need for more. However, a whore who spends time alone with the Prince behind locked doors, that is a different matter."

The concubine let the words hang on the air.

"A whore am I?" Kiara thought of a thousand retorts, but the cold clarity with which the Reluwyn concubine had spoken stilled her tongue. If she was like all the others, if she truly believed Kiara a whore, then why was she even speaking to her?

"A woman with her eye on the Queenship."

Kiara scoffed at that, rising from the cushions.

"And do you feel you are more deserving? Your three years of service must count for something, mustn't they?"

Nisa's red mouth curved slightly. "Three years have taught me to know an imposter when I see one. Your harsh treatment is working, soon he'll dangle the crown just low enough for you to take it."

"You think that it's a game?"

"What else?"

Kiara's body stiffened. Is that why she had been sent here? Or had she come of her own accord? To find out why the Prince was in her thrall? Trevisian wouldn't have sent her, he knew she loathed him. Maybe he had questioned that earlier when they had talked, but she was sure she had left him more angry than ever.

So who was Nisa? She talked of Kiara's manipulations, but what about her own? Kiara had seen her before, mostly on her own or in the company of courtiers who frequently passed through the harem. She could never become Queen, she was no maiden, so what gain was she desiring?

"I dislike people guessing at my intentions," Kiara's safest choice was to remain ambiguous. If she lied and agreed, she could be inviting a future attack from any of the women in the harem, if she told the truth, she was publically denying the Prince's attentions. "Thank you for the warrior paint."

She left the room. Whatever Nisa wanted, Kiara would not give it to her - she could trust no one in this palace.

❂❂❂

Torchlight lit everything in the palace in a hot primal light and Kiara could hear the beat of drums in the distance. She followed the procession of women from the harem, their figures weaving in and out of the shadows. Conversation was hushed but excited. The women walked together whispering, laughing, each casting eyes at the others comparing themselves. Every woman had prepared all day for the night, each now at the height of their beauty.

The women had been given different garments but now they were together Kiara could see the similarities. All had their legs bared, their stomachs exposed, but each also had greaves on their legs and leather vambraces on their forearms. They looked beautiful, seductive, and deadly. It was all part of their heritage, Kiara now realised, their warrior past which was so important to the culture. Kiara wondered whether any of these women even knew how to hold a sword. More than that, she wondered how she would have turned out if she had been raised Reluwyn.

She was walking behind Nisa who stood almost a head taller than the rest of the women. She walked apart from them as well, exchanging greetings with the merest nod of her head but refraining from conversation. Kiara watched Nisa's skin fall in and out of the torchlight as she walked, the patterns coming alive. She cast an eye across her own arm. Her patterns were just as striking in this light, shimmering.

The drumbeat was getting louder, deep rumbles bouncing off the stone walls of the palace corridors. Kiara was learning her way around the palace and she now recognised several of the rooms they passed. They were headed to the jewelled courtyard. Were the women to be paraded in front of the men?

For all her guessing, however, Kiara could not have been more shocked. The troop of women was finally at the wider hallway that led to the courtyard. The women at the front paused on the threshold, but only for a moment, soon they were pouring out, filtering to the edge of the gathering and peering over shoulders to gain a better look.

Kiara had nearly a hundred women before her, and it took some time to get to a position where she could see. In the end, she climbed onto a small wall which hemmed in a man-made stream along the edge of the courtyard. Now she could see a huge fire which lay at the centre. The drummers were to the left, the animal skin instruments slung across their fronts, their arms thrashing out a constant beat. Kiara could now see why all the women had stopped. Before the fire was a line of young men moving together to the beat of the drum.

Kiara's eyes grew wider as she took in the bare chests of all the men. Around their waists was the leather of animal skins, draped carelessly across their thighs and jumping up and down as they danced. Across their abdomens were scarlet lines of paint, mirroring those of the women. Each man's hair was rough and damp, perspiration soaked the edges and ran down the planes of their muscles. They were all barefoot, their feet rising and falling upon the tiles of the brightly patterned courtyard.

Kiara, who had been utterly mesmerised for the past few minutes following the undulating moves of the men, started as she realised what she was seeing and dropped her stare to the floor. Half-dressed men, half-dressed women. She had never seen men dressed like this before - it was not the way of the Laowyn. A woman saw her husband's unclothed form and no one else's. Even Kiara, who liked to break the rules, felt heat warming the edges of her face. What was the purpose of tonight?

She tried to dismount from her wall and ended up stumbling forward. The women in front of her parted as her arms flayed them apart. Glares were directed towards her but she had not disrupted the main event. She turned, mumbling apologies, and tried to grope her way back to the main entrance. She didn't want to be here.

Behind her she could hear the voice of a man. It was Johan the Prince's personal guard who looked different to the other Reluwyn. His words found their way over the crowds, the drumming never ceasing.

"It is tradition in the Reluwyn culture for women to choose their mates. The life-mate of a Reluwyn warrior, by custom, warms his bed, pitches his tent and raises his young. But the woman must choose her mate, it is her choice whose bed she warms, whose tent she pitches, and whose young she bears and raises."

Kiara was at the entrance to the hallway but so were two guards. Their long staffs moved, motioning towards Kiara, forcing her to stop. She tried to move around them but they wouldn't let her. One gestured to her and said something about returning to the ceremony.

"Once a year, the young warriors of the clan don their war paint and perform an ancient dance ritual to show the women their prowess in fighting. The women can watch, and then they pick their mate, joining his dance as a symbol of her acceptance.

This year is different, many of you have been summoned according to the Edict of Maidens, and many of you will choose the Prince." A chorus of laughter broke out in the ranks of the men whilst the women looked suddenly coy.

Kiara, after shooting venomous looks at the guards, faced the melee. She moved back towards the position she had held at the side, leaning against the wall, pressing herself against the cold stone as if it might camouflage her or at least cool her flaming body.

"As such, the women may watch and admire," another bout of laughter rumbled through the ranks. "They may choose a dance partner, but dancing will be all the partner can provide for tonight."

Breath hissed from between Kiara's teeth. She wouldn't be dancing with anyone, but at least if she was forced to do anything, it would be to do no more than watch.

To her horror however, some kind of order was given and the concubines split off from the maidens and suddenly the crowd of women was thinned. Coscian was moving among them, moving them into different places, and it didn't take Kiara long to realise he was forcing the maidens into sight of the dancing men.

She pressed harder against the wall but the Harem Master spied her quickly and placed a gentle hand beneath her elbow to guide her to her place.

"Do as I say, unless you want to draw attention to yourself."

"Not the centre," she begged in a whisper.

"I have my orders." Coscian let go of her arm then, moving back and leaving her in a central position, the men only feet away.

The Prince no doubt had done this on purpose. He had clearly been paying more attention to Kiara than she would like to admit, if he knew that drawing her to the front would cause her such discomfort. This must have been what he'd planned.

In the emotion of the moment, Kiara had not even looked to see where the Prince was. She had seen the men moving, but they had all looked the same, bare-chested with war paint slathered across them. When she saw him, she realised that she could not be more wrong.

He was entirely different to the others. He had been to her right, but now he moved back across the floor, his thighs tensing with the impact of the moves. She saw his bare-chest, the patterns across it rising and falling with the lines of muscles, contracting and releasing with the movement. The pattern was as bright red on him as it was on the others, but it was less of a contrast against his olive skin. The pattern moved and swirled, and as he turned, she saw it weaving in and out of itself. Beneath the paint she could almost make out the rest of the tattoo she'd seen at the top of his neck in the library - only earlier today. Was this even the same day?

She could not fully see it through the paint, and he had turned again before she had more time to look. His long hair glistened with sweat, the flames of the great fire outlining him. A leather loincloth covered him, the strips of it doing little to hide his thighs. She fell into a trance-like state, taking in all that she had never seen before. Her eyes rose from abdomen, to chest, to neck, and then breaking the spell, the dark eyes looking back at her.

Heat, burning hot, flooded her body. Jarring from the shock of being caught so brazenly evaluating him, she flinched, moved backwards, hit someone. Hands pushed roughly back at her. She steadied herself. There was nowhere to run.

He came towards her then, moving in time with the drums.

"Come and dance with me, Little One," he said, the breath licking in and out between his lips, the light of amusement in his eyes. He knew exactly what she had been thinking - Kiara could see his satisfaction.

"No!"

"Why not?"

Kiara did not answer. Instead she looked to her left and right and saw the line of heads turned her way, the women and girls all judging her, each craning their necks that they might hear the conversation between the Prince and the Favourite.

"Are you afraid, Little One?"

Yes, she was. Here he was, parading himself and she... she had been admiring him. She had felt stirrings, deep within the pit of her stomach, as she had looked upon the barbarian Prince.

"I will not dance like a whore."

The Prince made a face which signified amusement rather than chagrin. He stopped dancing, moving over to where his confidant Johan stood. He whispered something into his ear and soon another announcement was made.

"The Prince is allowing the women to join the dance floor."

That was it, the only command. The other women, unlike Kiara, leapt at the chance, moving forward like one penetrating force. The concubines led the charge, swiftly finding admiring men to dance with, the patterns of their dance clearly marked, no doubt Reluwyn. The maidens followed suit, no less eagerly, mimicking the dancing of their more experienced peers.

The Prince was still in front of Kiara, and before any other woman could move in on him he stepped forwards, taking her firmly by the arm. Her reflexes had not diminished with her captivity, she lurched away. He went for her again, no doubt trying to gain the proximity that so many of the men were currently enjoying with the other women on the dance floor.

Kiara didn't trust herself to get that close, but before she knew it, his offensive and her defensive were forming some kind of dance of their own. Other dancers moved away from them, out of the line of the violent movements, and soon they had created their own circular space before the fire. It was like they were fighting again, on the dirt track, beside the carriage, as they had done all those nights ago, but the weaponry was unfamiliar to Kiara, and the danger more terrifying.

The drumbeat was quickening, reaching a crescendo, and just as it dropped out completely, the Prince made contact, his fingers wrapping themselves around her forearm. He pulled her towards him with a sharpness that shocked her, and without warning kissed her forcefully.

Feelings which Kiara had until now been unable to identify burst forward into bloom within her. It flooded her limbs and sent a shiver up her spine. His lips were warm and demanding upon her own. He retracted just as quickly, a wide smile breaking out upon his face.

Kiara was left breathless, the Prince's hold the only support keeping her upright for a few seconds. Her mouth felt hot and swollen, but it was nothing compared to the heat searing within her.

"You're right, Little One." The drumming had ceased, and the circle they had created for themselves now felt like a prison with hundreds of faces staring in at them. "You are no dancing whore, only a true maid could blush like that." The joke rang out loud and clear. The men present immediately erupted into laughter, as did many of the women.

Before Kiara was able to give any retort, the drumming had struck up again, and the majority returned to their partners.

The ceremony was supposed to continue all night. The men were to keep on dancing, gradually pairing off with the women who joined them, and feasting tables were set out for an evening of eating and drinking. Kiara did not stay for any of it. The heat still burning in her cheeks, she made her way rapidly back through the crowds, the Prince not stopping her.

She made it to the hallway before she knew where she was. This time the guards let her through, although Kiara was oblivious to the nod that signalled for them to do so. It came from Johan, who had watched the scene with rising sympathy, and who understood the maiden's need for escape.

CHAPTER 16

The next morning Kiara had mostly regained the composure that she had let drop so completely the night before. Gone were the feelings she was unsure of, she had banished them. But the feeling of humiliation still reverberated within her, accompanied by a violent anger.

She had played by his rules, been his prey, but today it would end. Yesterday she had been unsure of the strategy he used. After a night spent alone and brooding, she had drawn her own conclusions about how to fight back. Let the battle continue, it was her turn to inflict some damage.

She was making her way to a part of the palace that she had heard about but never seen. She was a woman, that was why she had not seen it, but thanks to the Prince's marked favour she was finding herself able to traverse the palace with increasing ease. Guards moved out of her way, allowing her passage, and even when she entered a wing of the palace reserved for the men she was allowed.

One of the guards raised an eyebrow and opened his mouth as if to say something, but the other gave him a look which quelled his protest. They moved away and Kiara continued. She wasn't sure what was motivating her, what was pushing her on, all she desired was revenge for the humiliation. If the Prince was bent on using sex as a weapon against Kiara, then she would use it against him.

She entered an antechamber inhabited by a young man who sat writing at a golden desk. He did not look up as Kiara drew near, she was touching the desk with her fingertips as he spoke.

"Family name and sparring level?"

Kiara's heart was racing a little but she didn't look away from the top of the fight-master's head.

"The Prince calls me his 'Little One'."

The head jerked sharply up at this, his mouth falling open when he saw who it was.

"And as for sparring level, I am competent with blades, but my footwork could do with some improvement." Kiara felt a surge of boldness. She fell into the attitude she had seen practiced and used in the harem. She leant forward toward the man, fluttered her hand over his that still held the quill, and changed the look in her eyes from wary to warm and inviting. "Will you teach me?"

"I…" the words died on the young man's lips. He looked past her to the door where guards were watching.

"They let me through," said Kiara carelessly, she withdrew her hand from his and sighed as if bored. "The Prince has allowed me to go wherever I may please in the palace." She dropped playful eyes on the young man's face again. "It pleases me to fight," then she gave the practiced laugh of the courtesans she had heard so often. "What's your name?" she asked before the man could utter a protest.

"It's, well, it's Mosian, I must check…"

"Mosian," said Kiara, as if rolling the name around in her mouth. She laughed again, "I like that name, but I prefer my name, the one the Prince gave to me, 'Little One'…" Her eyes were darting covertly back to the young man at the desk as she wandered around the room. She felt a surge of satisfaction seeing the transfixed look in his eyes. They were roving over her frame, over her markings from the night before. "I will need some more appropriate clothing." She traced a hand from her stomach to her thighs, the move suggestive. "I am sure the Prince will be along this morning and I wish to practice before he sees me. I would hate to disappoint him." She looked pained but her voice was still light and appealing. "May I go in now?"

She moved towards the door before waiting for an answer and the young man opened it. As she stepped over the threshold into the Fighting Hall she felt a thrill run through her. Let the Prince try to manipulate her all he wanted, she would not bend to his will.

The Fighting Hall, Kiara had learned, was a place reserved for the men of the court. Here they sparred, trained and learned the warrior ways of the Reluwyn. The very fact a woman was even in the same area of the palace, let alone crossing the threshold of this room ruptured the social rules. These women might be given more authority than Laowyn women, but they had the same social rules, and this was no place for women.

Rather than the men rising up to throw her out, however, they simply stopped their training and turned, watching her as she walked through. A few whispered, but the majority of the stares were not malicious, only intrigued.

Two men were sparring in the middle of a tiled circle on the floor. When one caught sight of Kiara, a blow from his opponent sent him reeling across the floor. Before he could steady himself, one foot had crossed the red line. A horn sounded and the man gestured to Kiara in frustration.

"An unfair victory."

The other man, young and handsome, had already taken Kiara in. "You can't keep your defensive parries up when a woman turns your head, Yulesh?"

"Shut up, Gorian." Yulesh took off the bandages that had encased his hands and threw them at a waiting servant. He stalked off to the side for refreshment, the only man in the room to ignore the woman in their midst.

"A bit far from home are you not, Favourite?"

"I prefer Little One," replied Kiara. The man had no idea how right he was.

An attractive smile spread across the clean-shaven face causing drips of perspiration to skirt around his mouth.

"Little One." He mock bowed, walking over to her, the other men watching. "Tell me," he said, looking down at her and appraising her form without shame. "Did you enjoy your kiss last night, maid?"

"Not as much as I will enjoy beating you in the ring." Kiara's eyes had hardened and a forced smile appeared upon her lips.

Gorian looked uncertain for a moment, intrigue battling a sense of danger.

"I wouldn't want to hurt a woman," he said finally, his face marked with arrogance. "Especially one who is the Prince's Favourite."

"Funny." Kiara bent slowly to pick up a cast-off tunic by the side of the ring. It probably belonged to this Gorian who was stripped to the waist. "I wouldn't want to hurt one of his courtiers." She didn't let her eyes drop below his neck when she spoke to him. Flesh was becoming familiar to her, but the discomfort she felt was still there. She slipped the tunic over her head and bound it at the waist by tying a large belt around herself.

Gorian's brow was raised. "Do you usually steal other people's clothes?"

Kiara allowed the smile onto her lips again. She could not wait for the Prince to see how many rules she had broken. She had noticed his protectiveness when she had tried to escape through the Tower Gate, and she sensed that her interest in others would irk him just as much.

"If I'm to fight you on your terms, as a man, then surely I must dress as one."

Gorian allowed a laugh to ripple from him. "True, your attire is perhaps a little sparse for rapid movements." He came closer to where she had moved into the fighting circle, his eyes dropping to the open neckline of the tunic. "Isn't it?"

Perfect, Kiara had the attention she had been wanting, but she needed to keep him at arm's length. She had no doubt the Prince would be here soon. Despite her manipulation of Mosian, she was sure that word of her antics would spread quickly to the Prince. Let it.

She leant in to Gorian, pushing herself up on her toes so that her face came within inches of his own. Then, with a suddenness that shocked him, she gave him an almighty shove backwards.

Her opponent regained his footing quickly, breaking out into laughter at her backhanded move. He began to dance on his feet, shaking his head and waggling a finger at her. "Sneaky, sneaky, Little One, not what I expected."

"Precisely," Kiara was moving her feet too, but her movements were inexpert compared to Gorian's. What she lacked in skill she made up for in speed however. She was small and her manoeuvrability was unique, a fact she had used to her advantage when raiding Reluwyn parties. She jumped forward, jabbing at her opponent, catching his side lightly as he ducked away.

Her eyes moving rapidly around the edge of the fighting circle, Kiara was satisfied to see all occupants of the hall had their eyes on her. The fight continued, she was on the offensive from the start, Gorian responding with effective parries. As she tried to strike again, she stumbled a little; regaining her balance, she saw a pitying look in Gorian's eyes. He had stopped his fighting dance, waiting for her to recover.

Kiara struck up her movements once again. "Afraid of hurting a woman?"

Gorian rubbed a bound hand over his brow, soaking up the sweat. "It's not a fair fight."

"Not fair?" Anger flashed into Kiara's eyes. This man didn't know who he was dealing with. The anger gave her a burst of energy, her movements became even faster and before long she had dealt three successive blows upon Gorian, the final hitting his jaw. He stepped backwards, rubbing it.

Kiara saw the warning light in the man's eyes and picked up her feet in anticipation of his response. He came at her harder this time, his blows quicker, with real weight behind them. If he struck her it would hurt.

"Tell me, how does a maiden come to learn to fight so effectively?" asked Gorian between pants.

"Aren't all Reluwyn women so trained?" Kiara danced to the left, keeping her arms up ready to block.

"You aren't Reluwyn." He jabbed again, this time catching her upper arm. The pain was sharp where his knuckle connected with bone. Her arm went numb.

As he became more confident, his stance slackened and his movements slowed. There was no sign of the Prince. Would Gorian stop before hurting her? A shot of fear ran through her, had she been relying on the Prince to save her? She had to change her tactics. She needed to swallow her pride.

Her expression softened. "I may have underestimated you."

"And I you," Gorian acknowledged the loss of her fighting stance, slowing his pace and circling her. "Perhaps I can see why the Prince is so enchanted with you, Little One." He reached out to where he had struck her, and smoothed his fingers over her arm. Kiara felt sick in the pit of her stomach.

They had both come to a halt and it was only now that Kiara noticed the deathly silence in the hall. She had thought it was on account of them, but when Gorian visibly paled on seeing someone behind her, she knew why.

Kiara turned towards the focus of his surprise with a false smile painted across her rosy face.

"My Lord Prince." Even after planning this, Kiara was not prepared for the fury on her captor's face. The burning eyes were not directed at her, however, but at Gorian.

Before she knew what was happening, Trevisian strode forwards, all his weight behind his fist as it connected with Gorian. The courtier fell backwards, blood flying from his nose. The man's hands groped across his face trying to quench the flow which was rapidly pouring down his chin and onto his chest. Johan, who had accompanied the Prince, picked up a towel and threw it at the injured man.

Trevisian, whose shoulders were visibly shaking, turned upon his Favourite. She could see he had been lately riding, mud spattered his boots and leather trousers, his whole stance one of tense anger. He snatched at her wrist, his fingers closing around it remorselessly, dragging her from the room.

He did not stop until they were out of the male wing of the palace entirely. He was still dragging Kiara when she suddenly yanked back.

"You're hurting me!" she cried, yanking her arm but unable to get freedom from Trevisian's grip.

He turned upon her then, his silence ending, "And what if I am? Why should I care over a street-brat like you?" he shouted, inches from her face.

"Don't act as though I have done something wrong," she yelled in response, dealing back what she was being dealt.

He laughed, the sound coming out as a strangled bark. Several courtiers rounded the corner, coming upon the couple in the alcove.

"Leave!" Trevisian threw at them, sending them scampering quickly away. Johan, who had been with the couple until now, left with the courtiers.

Trevisian then turned back to Kiara, pulling her closer to him. She yelped as burning laced through her shoulder socket.

"Trying to dislocate my arm again? Taking back any good you have done me in payment for my sins against you?" she spat at him, her tone venomous.

"I told you I would take payment for what you have done."

"Then kill me! I don't care."

The Prince checked himself. Kiara's eyes were as honest as her words.

He pulled her again, trying to move forwards.

"Don't drag me, I am not some animal of yours to do with as you will." She pulled away again. "Strike me if you intend to, hit me like you did Gorian."

"Gorian?" Trevisian's face looked confused for a moment, then the look of malice was back. "You mean that courtier who called you Little One? The one who hit you and then dared to touch you again?" The questions were asked as if he was reliving the sight again his voice heating with every syllable.

"Hit me! Isn't that what you've been wanting to do since you met me?" Again, she saw a look of confusion cross the Prince's face.

"Why do you think I hit that man?" He came towards her and she backed away as far as she could. "You think I enjoyed it?"

She didn't answer.

He looked to the hand which had struck Gorian, it was already swelling and the skin had split over his middle knuckle. "You think I enjoy causing you physical pain?" A sigh escaped him. "Damn this all."

His hand loosened on her arm. She could have pulled away if she had wanted to. But she didn't understand her own feelings in this moment, not when confronted by the conflict in the Prince's face.

"I don't understand you," she whispered.

"Come with me."

Kiara realised that this was the closest he was going to come to asking. She nodded and they walked on in silence to his chambers. It was not until the door was closed that he released her arm and spoke again.

"Take that off." He didn't even look at her, his hand gesture taking in Gorian's tunic that still covered her frame. She did as she was bid, pulling the fabric over her head. She threw her hair back over her shoulders and laid the tunic down on one of the cushions surrounding the table. A breeze coming through the open doors of the balcony caused a shiver to run through her.

She thought the Prince had not been looking at her, but she realised she was mistaken when he went into his bedchamber and returned with a black tunic of his own. He handed it to her without speaking.

Had the circumstances been different she would have refused, but for some reason it felt like a peace offering. She took the soft fabric and pulled it over her head, happy for both the covering and the warmth.

"Does your arm still hurt?" he raised a hand as if to touch it but stopped short.

"No." It did a little, but the look in his eyes made her want to reassure him. What was wrong with her? This morning she had been set on getting revenge for his actions last night, but now she didn't want to. One moment he was angry and vengeful, the next he was defending her, giving her a tunic to keep her warm, asking if she was in pain.

Satisfied with her answer, the Prince gestured for her to sit on the cushions surrounding the table. She did as she was bid, but rather than joining her the Prince continued to pace. When he finally sat opposite her he remained silent, staring into the middle distance and then at her. They sat like that for some time before he spoke.

"Why do you think I hit Gorian?"

Kiara shrugged, but seeing the intent look in his eyes she answered. "Because he touched your property."

He did not respond to her answer.

"Why were you in the Fighting Hall?"

"I was angry."

His head cocked to one side as he examined her. "I embarrassed you."

"You humiliated me," she corrected, unable to hold his gaze. She pulled the neckline of the tunic closed and pulled the hem lower on her legs.

"You are more comfortable in men's clothes."

"I don't like being stared at."

"I've noticed." his mouth tilted upwards but his eyes remained unamused. "You're very beautiful."

"Am I?" She wasn't doing well under the scrutiny. She had never been so brazenly called beautiful, as if it was some fact. "Is that why you..." she faltered, breaking off her line of thought before she could finish. She didn't want him to answer.

"I don't enjoy hurting people."

The abrupt admission asked for no reply. He said it as though under pressure, as though the admission was essential. She stared back at him but he was already rising. He walked into his bedchamber again. This time he returned with her father's blade.

"This is yours?"

"It was my father's." She didn't need to admit anything, but something told her that what she was seeing of the Prince was the truth. She stood up before him, her hands remaining by her sides rather than trying to snatch at the blade as she would have done before.

"Is your father dead?"

"Yes."

"And mine. Do you miss him?"

"I barely remember him." She turned away, looking at the trinkets that were spread over his desk. It was easy to talk when she forgot he was the Prince. "I think I do, sometimes. Do you miss yours?" An odd truce lay between them.

He turned the sheathed blade over in his hand and then held it out to her. "You may have it."

She hesitated.

"It will not be allowed in the harem, but it's yours."

Her fingers opened and he placed the weapon in them.

"I could kill you," she said, her tone surprised.

"Yes."

"I don't understand you."

"You said that before."

She turned the blade absently until she could clasp the hilt and then let it hang by her side.

"If you wish to fight so much, you can fight with me, I can teach you," he held up a hand, as if to stop her protest at his assumption of precedence over her skill.

"You're quick, but your skill was lacking with the blade when we fought outside Grûl."

"And you're willing to teach me?"

Trevisian shrugged. "I am unwilling to share your company with others."

Kiara felt her heart beat faster at the words and the allusion to the Fighting Hall.

The Prince's hand came up again towards her injured arm but this time he did touch her. He traced his fingers down the length of it, ending on her fingers. "No one else can call you Little One."

She nodded automatically. His hand came up again, and this time it travelled lightly up her neck and onto her chin.

"I kissed you last night."

Again, she nodded, barely realising what she was doing. She saw it again, the shadow of pain which showed when he allowed it. His touch was light, his eyes softer than they had ever been. This moment was so unlike last night. "I want to kiss you again."

Her breath became thick and shallow. In her anger she had buried the feelings he had stirred in her last night. Now they were back, filtering through every fibre of her being, bringing every part of her alive.

He had waited, watching the response in her face, now he leant down, his fingers threading through her hair, drawing her to him. His lips were soft and warm against hers. They didn't push immediately with passion as they had done last night, they asked and she responded. The sword hilt fell from her grasp, the weapon clattering on the tiled floor, her hand coming up and flitting shyly from his shoulder, to his neck, to his hair in unpractised but natural movements. The Prince pulled back gently for a few moments, studying her face briefly, and as if happy with what he saw there, bent to the task once more.

His arms became stronger, wrapping themselves around her frame and drawing her against him. His hands raked their fingers through the long golden curls, and his mouth became more urgent.

The moment was so distracting that neither of them heard the knock at the door. Neither did they hear it open, in fact, it wasn't until the Radichi warrior had walked in, shut the doors behind him to preserve their privacy, and coughed loudly, that they noticed his presence. Trevisian pulled away and looked over to his friend whilst Kiara, caught in such a position, raised her hands to cover her burning cheeks and turned away.

She escaped the Prince's arms, shyness forcing her to walk away from the visitor and the man who had been kissing her. She allowed her hair to fall forward about her face to cover it and pretended to be looking at the trinkets on the desk again.

"My Lord Prince, I am come with a summons from Garesh for your immediate presence."

The Prince was not looking at Johan, his eyes were captivated by the woman whose back was to him, her head bent as though in concentration. His eyes slipped over her frame, the black material which ended at her lower thigh revealed smooth legs below.

"I am busy, Johan."

"Yes, my Lord Prince, but the High Councillor said it is of the highest urgency."

The Prince sighed in frustration.

"I will not be left in peace unless I respond?"

"I fear not."

"Very well." The Prince withdrew his eyes from Kiara reluctantly. "Can you take my Favourite back to the harem?"

"Yes, my Lord Prince."

Just before he left, the Prince came alongside Kiara, his fingers touching her own in light movements. "I will see you again soon, my Little One," he whispered, and then he left her.

CHAPTER 17

"I don't know, Fidel." Ikara twitched, her words like the swish of a tail trying to shoo away the prying questions.

He said nothing in return but kept riding alongside her. They had made it to Ishtalia a few days ago. Today they were patrolling the city ramparts, watching members of their race who poured in daily to escape persecution. The Resistance was becoming simply the Laowyn people gathering together for protection.

Ikara's white mount shied at a group of travellers who held great bundles hung on their backs. The horse's hooves clattered, swinging sideways and its flank hit Fidel's horse. As one of the biggest men among the Resistance, the Captain was on one of the biggest mounts that they had. The horse was solid and didn't pay much heed to the jostling of Ikara's more sensitive mount. Pushing his horse forwards prevented Fidel from asking her again how she felt.

He had been doing so every morning, and every morning she failed to reply. Today she was reaching the end of her patience. Through the cracks of her temper came truth - she had no idea how she felt. How should she feel when her race was under an extinction threat from the reigning powers? When their fate lay in her hands? One moment she was angry, the feeling burning so brightly within her she felt it might consume her. Then, just as if someone dashed water over it, she would feel a wave of grief over their circumstances. When the grief came so did a feeling of weakness, of powerlessness. The cruelty of this life seemed insurmountable, why bother to attempt the climb? Those feelings, in the nights since they had been here, had almost destroyed what she had left. Her reserves, the last parts of her which were left, were eroding away. Now as she rode with her Captain, she really did have no answer for him. She did not know how she was feeling. How could she? There was nothing keeping her going. A faint hope in the Great Spirit which had lingered at the beginning of her leadership had been extinguished with the death of Teo and the other Laowyn scouts whose lives had been forfeit.

Ikara was reluctantly drawn out of her maudlin reverie with the arrival of Hendra. The older Captain came alongside Fidel on a large hairy beast that was not quite the rival of Fidel's own.

"A thousand more have poured into the city walls just today. We must make a decision, Commander, the city is indefensible after the Reluwyn armies slighted the walls. We cannot stay here."

"What are our options? We will be a slow cavalcade now we have so many Laowyn in tow, wherever we go we must measure the decision carefully," replied Fidel thoughtfully.

"The Elders are meeting as we speak, that's why I have come to fetch you both." Hendra scratched his short grey beard. "They are meeting in the ancient hall, I had a hard time making sure the civilians stayed out, our race is so damned respectful they are forever clamouring at the Elders. I have taken the liberty of stationing some of my troops around the building to keep their privacy."

"Privately deciding their fates. It's no wonder they are scrambling at the walls," Ikara replied grimly.

"We will come shortly," said Fidel, inclining his head to the older Captain.

Hendra nodded happily enough. He had re-joined them six months ago when the threat from the Reluwyn government had strengthened. His mission to the provinces to find support for the Resistance had been useful but a time of war was coming and he had been reassigned to gather all Resistance supporters to the shell of their old capital.

Fidel had seen the knowing look Hendra gave him and the Commander when he was around them, and it was the same one that was on his face now as he rode away.

Hendra turned his mount, peeling off from the other two, returning to the patrolling of the Elder's meeting. Behind him, Ikara and Fidel continued on their perimeter walk around the city. Ikara's horse picked its way nimbly between the rubble and fallen masonry which was scattered across the white paved path. Either side of them were derelict buildings which had once housed shops, meeting places and homes, their doors hanging slack and ajar, while creeping vines anchored themselves in the crevices of the white plaster.

In stark contrast, the bright sun was giving the white stone city a feeling of life even after its tragic death more than twenty years ago. This was only emphasised by the myriad of incomers who were commandeering old buildings for shelter while swelling the Resistance's ranks.

"I can't see a way out of this." Ikara watched a small girl and boy build their own miniature city out of rubble in the street.

"Nor I," Fidel had his reins in one hand, the other resting lightly on his thigh as they rode. "The Great Spirit can, Ikara."

She didn't speak for a few moments, not until they had turned off the main street and picked their way through one of the city's broken walls. Now they were outside the settlement, the rising white wall with the city and sea behind it to their left, the open hill country of eastern Emrilion to their right.

"Commander."

Fidel felt a rising frustration at the correction.

"You never know, Commander," he said, forcing himself to use the title. "Zeb, Djeck, Zephenesh and the twins may yet be successful."

Ikara made no response. Fidel knew from experience that her silences indicated scepticism.

"Have faith, Ik...Commander," he corrected himself, seeing tension flicker across her profile. They were still continuing along the city's perimeter, their journey turning downward towards the abandoned docks of the western shore.

"The Great Spirit can work in incredible ways."

"Can he?" The blasphemous question came before she could stop herself. Fidel could tell she didn't mean it. Her faith had been wading through rocky shallows every day since the massacre.

He turned his horse to follow Ikara's down the slope, into the face of the two setting suns that were soaking the landscape in blood-red rays.

He inhaled deeply. In one moment Ikara was intent upon reinforcing the rigid gap of formality between them. In the next she was uttering things that she would not say to anyone else. She was voicing the doubts that haunted her decisions. Her words, her question, would be condemned by the Elders of the Laowyn, yet were they not fair to say and ask?

As if tracing his thoughts, she spoke again, a small fracture in her emotional armour letting the truth seep through.

"I cannot understand this faith. When our race was consigned to defeat twenty years ago, where was the Great Spirit? Now we face annihilation, and where is He? Were we ever His race at all? The scrolls say He is jealous of his people, and yet he lets others murder them? It makes no sense Fidel, it never has."

He didn't reply at once. The use of his name did not go unheeded either, though Ikara seemed oblivious of it. That was when he received the true woman, when she did not realise she was giving of herself.

"You don't know his plans, Commander. Faith is trusting in the scrolls regardless of outward appearances." Fidel's right hand, free from the reins, drifted over to Ikara who was now riding beside him, and rested a moment on her own.

The touch sent a shockwave through her body. No one was allowed that close to her, not without her consent. She had to maintain control, but that desire was becoming all consuming.

"The outward appearance is death, Captain," she snapped back at him, withdrawing into herself once again and pulling her horse away. "And if the Great Spirit cannot share His plans then I will make them. I already have."

"Oh?"

"We will face this enemy and we will kill or be killed. I wait upon no spirit for deliverance whilst my people die."

"They believed."

"And for what?! More fool them!" The bitter words caused the Commander to flinch, sending her horse into Fidel's path.

"Damn it, Captain!"

They had found their way back into the city walls and reached the end of the dock path, before them lay calm waters between wooden jetties naked of boats. They would have to turn back if they wished to continue on the perimeter path.

"Ikara." Fidel took advantage of a moment in which they were totally alone, "This attitude – this need for blood – is wrong."

Her eyes flashed at him, her mouth tight and angry.

"I am your Commander, Fidel, remember that! And as your superior I expect absolute obedience."

Fidel's face broke at the words. He dismounted and, leaving his horse, started towards the water's edge.

"Captain! Fidel!" Ikara's voice was raised, the usual control she had over it broken. She leapt down and strode after him, her long legs catching up to him quickly enough.

"Fidel!" There was an urgency in the voice, a fear lying under the angered tones. She reached out trying to pull him back.

"Captain," corrected Fidel. "Isn't that my name to you?"

He had no choice, he needed to speak, and there was only way he could do so before his superior officer. He drew the sword from his belt, looking between the blade in his hands and Ikara's ice-coloured eyes. "I cannot follow you on a path of destruction. Take my sword."

But she would not.

He dug the weapon blade-first into the ground between them. "I will speak to you as one Laowyn to another. Ikara you are lost, and I would find you again, but you will not be found. I cannot watch you... I cannot stand by and see you take this path, not when..." Fidel's hand reached out and then dropped to his side again. He turned to look over the waters, the breeze pushing back the hair from his face, showing the lines of his compassionate brow. He had waited so long to tell her, and now that it seemed that this might be the end, perhaps the time was right.

He turned to her, taking her hand from her side before she could flinch away. He drew it up, pressing his mouth against the smooth skin and held it there. When he rose he saw the mist of tears in her eyes.

"I will always be yours, but to watch what you are doing is to watch a part of myself destroyed. I will not do it."

He released her hand. "I will make my way to Emril City and see what use I can be to Zephenesh." He took in a breath. "Goodbye Ikara."

CHAPTER 18

"He hasn't called for me," hissed Nisa, defending herself against Garesh's rage.

He had been in a foul mood ever since his disagreement with the Prince over his pet prisoner – Garesh had come away seething and the Favourite had stayed. But Nisa would be damned before she allowed herself to become his verbal punching bag, she had done her job, she had enticed the Prince with her wiles and befriended the fair-haired woman.

Nisa knew her job well and had been playing the courtesan ever since she'd become a woman, she had learned that people worked off the basic motivations of sex, power, and fear. But these two weren't responding to the best of her tricks. Simply put, there was something different about them and she didn't trust that.

"Judging from your performance last night I'm not surprised."

Nisa would have spat venom if her mouth opened. She remained silent trying to block out images of

Garesh's old sinewy frame laid on its back throughout last night's session.

"Why is it a problem? You have his signed name on the massacre Edict, do you not?"

"Much good it will do me if I cannot rule after its enacting, whore."

Nisa's eyes narrowed like one of the stray cats of the city. Now was not the time to unveil her claws however.

"We have discussed this, my lord, either you will continue ruling over the Prince, or if there is a rebellion you will have the Prince to blame."

"He's causing problems now, I may not be able to wait until the Laowyn are destroyed."

Nisa skirted around a table and traced a hand over Garesh's shoulder before moving away teasingly. "There are ways to have people silenced, my lord." Her eyes flashed back at him momentarily. "I am surprised you have not used them before now."

"Our race revere their rulers."

"Yes, and they will revere you, when the Prince is sadly assassinated. It would not be surprising in the current political climate, my lord. Just think about it, you'd be using the climate to your advantage rather than having your actions dictated by it."

Garesh, whose mind had been sceptical, suddenly felt sparks of excitement ignite in his imagination. The whore was right, it would be easy to blame the Laowyn, and the Prince would be gone, leaving Garesh as ruler of Emrilion.

"I have served for many years upon the High Council, and I have exceeded every expectation of my office."

"Yes, my lord," murmured Nisa, allowing him his arrogant ramblings. What did it matter to her that she despised the man when he could be her way to security? Without ever being called by the Prince she was as good as a prisoner, just as his Favourite had implied. That was not how Nisa Kardeeshi would end her days.

"The rule of this Kingdom is something I have undertaken since the minority. Do I not deserve recognition?" His tone was agitated and harsh, his mouth pulled into a distorted smile and his tongue darting in and out between his lips. "Ruler of Emrilion. Who knew a whore could have such wise ideas?"

"The dark spirits tell me things," she replied, enticing the power-hungry man. "And my security will be assured?"

"Of course," said Garesh, coming to her and ravaging her mouth for several minutes. Once he was finished he pushed her away. "You shall be my premier concubine." He registered the fleeting look on her face. "What? You thought I would make a concubine my Queen? I think not, woman."

Nisa struggled to control her desire to scratch out his dark, sadistic eyes.

"Now, now." He patted her backside. "Premier concubine will see your power increased throughout the court."

That was true, and even if Garesh tired of her and failed to call her as the Prince did, the premier concubine did not lose her position, she maintained control over the majority of the harem under only the Harem Master Coscian. He would have to be replaced of course. After all, he had favoured the Prince's prisoner.

"Very well, my lord, and the girl?"

"She will have to be silenced too – your dark arts can take care of it?"

"Only if you want the blame laid at a Reluwyn's door – none of the Laowyn practice Spirit Conjuring – no, poisoned food would be better."

"Yes," Garesh began to laugh, the sound high-pitched and maniacal. "Yes, it would be better!" After he had laughed his fill he spoke again, "You know men who could get this job done?"

"I do."

"Discreet men?"

"But of course, my lord."

Nisa watched the High Councillor considering for barely a moment before he nodded abruptly.

"Get it done."

⊙⊙⊙

It had taken five days for Fidel to catch up with Zephenesh and the others, and a further two to reach the city. When they had entered the outskirts both Zeb and Djeck had recommended disguises for all of them. The best option was to hire a pack donkey whilst they were in the city to appear as traders. The elves could have worn some kind of turban to hide their ears, and the Laowyn could have bought Reluwyn clothes. All suggestions however, were rejected by Zephenesh.

"I will not hide my heritage, I do not fear these people." It was all the answer that the Elder would give to the entreaties of the Elves, and after the seventh time they realised that the stubborn man had no notion of relenting.

Thus, they entered the city as themselves. They drew much attention once they made it past the suburbs and into the centre of the city's thriving streets. Vendors and street-sellers all watched them pass by, conversations dropping and whispers picking up.

"We shall be lucky if we reach Tower Gate square alive," muttered Djeck irritably. He, Zeb and Zephenesh had been here before. They knew the best place to try and make contact with the palace's inhabitants. The Tower

Gate was the entrance for traders into the palace precincts and, although Zephenesh had refused to disguise his heritage, he had acquiesced to the use of donkeys and products as a pretence for entry, and the elves being the leaders of their party due to the Laowyn trade embargo.

The twins were each pulling a donkey and neither had visited the bustling metropolis before. They walked side-by-side and made the same awe-filled noises as they took in the height of the sandstone buildings, the grand architecture, the myriad of products sold on the streets and the thousands of people that heaved along the belly of the city.

"Stop trying to beat me with that mule of yours," Calev light-heartedly tugged on the opposing donkey's bridle so that he slowed. "It's not a race."

"Oh yes? Well, then why are you practically dragging that donkey of yours to make it faster than mine?"

"Pack it in, the pair of you," Fidel warned in undertones. They didn't need any more attention than they were already getting. Fidel was aware of all the eyes that followed them, especially him, he was taller than the others and his hair the fairest. His broad shoulders and muscular frame would be seen as a threat to these people. They had travelled through at least ten settlements with Edicts for the destruction of the Laowyn hammered to the central buildings. Fidel wondered if the looks were appraising, wondering how difficult it would be to slay him? How many moves it would take to get him into a position where his throat could be slit?

He ignored the looks and focused on the road ahead. If it was possible the crowds had increased, the heat was becoming almost unbearable and the dust being kicked up was sticking to their skin. Right at the point that Fidel thought they would be crushed, the narrow street let out into a vast courtyard.

People surged with them into the open area, pushing the small party forwards. Zephenesh tripped on a ridge in the tiled floor, Fidel catching his elbow and steadying him before he could fall and be trampled. Once they were in the courtyard, Zeb, who had been heedless of the others progress for the entirety of their journey, turned east towards the main gateway that led off the courtyard. The great entryway was the first of many leading to the various inner circles of the palace. Looking up Fidel saw the reason for the entrance's name Tower Gate.

The entryway was an elaborate arch, covered in gold and engraved around the edges. Above the apex, the sandstone blocks carried on, forming a tower which housed several large oval balconies before it was topped by one of the highest domes Fidel had ever seen. The entrance was aptly named and this was only the first of many. He wondered what the Laowyn woman Kiara had thought when she had first seen this place. He had never witnessed a Reluwyn settlement, let alone their capital city.

As they passed beneath the arch, Fidel saw that its width stretched several cart-lengths and off to the sides ran alleyways threading the lengths of the walls. The shade was a welcome relief from the heat. Several booths were erected on either side of the entryway, Imperial Guards stood in clusters around them to vet each visitor to the palace.

When it was their turn, the twins remained remarkably silent. Fidel glanced at Zeb, but the elf was already moving forward.

"Good morning, sir," he inclined his head respectfully but received no such reply. The young guard looked down his nose at the elf, taking in his old-clothing and the tell-tale Laowyn symbols on his companion's brooches. Lines appeared on either side of the man's nose in distaste.

"State your business at the palace."

Fidel was quick to realise that any misspoken words would be used as a means to bar them entry. He felt his stomach tense as he watched the interchange.

"We have spices and perfumes to sell in the harem quarter if you will allow us."

Fidel exhaled, realising the reason for spending extra on the donkey's cargo. It had been Zeb's idea, even though the twins had protested. They had wanted edible cargo if they needed to bring something into the city. Still, he wouldn't have minded being told the plan before they had been faced by armed guards. The elf was as recalcitrant as ever.

Fidel eyed the scimitars of the armoured men. The blades looked deadly, complementing the red paint which aggressively marked each man's cheekbones.

A commotion on the other side of the street drew his attention. He heard a scuffle and then shouting, catching sight of a man being hauled away from his cart. He was clubbed with the handle of a guard's scimitar, his form falling limp between the two men who dragged him down an alley.

"Weapon smuggling," the young guard filled in pointedly, drawing Fidel's attention back to their present situation.

The guard was looking directly at him, or rather up at him to be more accurate. His inconspicuous height was proving problematic.

"The unrest is growing and we take no chances, it'll be a year in the Watchtower for that offence. I don't suppose you have any weapons to declare?" He seemed hopeful, but Zeb had made them leave their weapons hidden in a grove on the outskirts of the city. Clearly, he had known that this would happen.

"We carry no weapons, sir, we are happy to be searched."

"Good." The guard jerked his chin at two subordinates who immediately began to ransack the goods on the donkey's backs causing the beasts to paw at the ground irritably. In the time it took for the search, three Reluwyn parties had made it through the checkpoint on the other side of the street. Zephenesh, Fidel, Djeck and the twins waited silently whilst Zeb answered the questions.

"You have until dusk to complete your transactions." They were scrabbling about on the floor picking up each of the spice and perfume parcels which had been thrown out by the guards. When they had re-packed their animals, they went to move away from the booth.

Before they could leave the young guard leaned towards them, evidently displeased with having to give them passage. "Anyone found within the palace boundaries when the gates are closed will be thrown into the Watchtower until first light," he spat on the floor by Zephenesh's feet. "Or longer if I feel like it."

The disrespect to Zephenesh's status beggared belief, but none of the party even batted an eyelid. They moved off into the less densely populated courtyard on the other side of the gate. Fidel saw that this was one of the four circles which surrounded the palace; he could see the wide arc of the street stretch out on either side of them.

"The entrance to the harem courtyard is two more circles in," Zeb said, not looking any of them in the eye. "This way." He led them to the right.

"How does he know where he's going?" asked Jaik, one comical eye brow raised his mouth curving mischievously.

"What a question to ask," replied his twin, looking over his shoulder to Fidel, "Let's ask Fidel."

"I have no answers for you." Fidel felt their humorous attitudes chafing at him. This was their last hope as a race; there was no part of him that could relax. Since he had left Ikara, he had been plagued by doubts every day. Had he made the right decision in leaving her? "That elf is a mystery to everyone but himself."

"Maybe even to himself," Jaik said, his brother instantly chuckling.

"I was about to say that."

"I know, now move that mule of yours."

They kept up the conversation until the next checkpoint when the entire party fell silent once again.

The guard at this checkpoint seemed less bothered about his job. There was no checking of the cargo, just a flippant hand waving them through. The gateway was smaller but no less elaborate.

"The emerald arch," muttered Zeb as he walked next to Fidel.

They walked at the front of their party. Fidel ignored a grumbled remark from Djeck about Zeb finally speaking of something other than the plan. Those two clearly didn't get on.

The Laowyn ex-Captain looked up at the pointed arch covered in tiles the colour of the forest leaves. The more he looked the more he realised the colour was moving in slow swirls.

"The material comes from Castir, a gift from the child-Queen before she was deposed." The elf was talking absently as if to himself.

Fidel felt the impulse to comfort him. He reached out a hand and touched the smaller man's shoulder, just for a moment, and then took it away again. Zeb seemed finally to come into the present. He didn't look at Fidel, but the Laowyn saw the lines on his face lessen for a few seconds. The elf nodded sharply, and then carried on as he was before.

Fidel knew he still carried the guilt of letting the Laowyn woman be taken. That was what he had recounted when he had regained consciousness, not that Ikara had believed him. Fidel thought with a certain degree of anxiety that soon the elf's faith in Kiara would either be proved or else her alliance with the enemy race would be exposed.

The final checkpoint was manned by men with the same disregard for incomers. Of the two booths, theirs was manned by three guards huddled together talking in hushed tones. There must be so many intrigues going on in a place of this size, thought Fidel, eyeing the men who were throwing occasional furtive glances across the entryway.

The party continued and finally they were approaching the entryway to the harem marketplace. The crowds were far less here, the majority of the palace visitors heading to the courtiers' domains where they might obtain patronage or sell far more valuable gifts. The group found a space among the sellers easily enough, Zeb getting the twins to unload their cargo just as if they were ordinary traders. Zephenesh and Fidel stood together behind the blanket on which their goods were being laid.

"Do you think she's really here?"

"I have never doubted it," Zephenesh smiled a little, "I felt the Great Spirit confirming it as soon as I heard of it, this cannot be a coincidence, Fidel. She has been placed here for a purpose, for such a time as this. It's exactly as the elf has said."

The courtyard was lined with a colonnade towards the east end. A door opened and several women entered the covered area, walking beside the columns and entering the courtyard. Fidel's breath caught in his throat - no Laowyn women would ever dress like that.

He heard laughing from across the courtyard.

"I think you're in the wrong place, giant!" called one of the guards who stood at the entryway to the marketplace. He elbowed the other guard in the ribs and pointed to Fidel whose heightened colour could be seen from a mile away.

The women who were browsing at the stalls looked over to the fair-haired giant, giggling and whispering amongst themselves.

"Their culture is different from yours, is it not Fidel?" Zeb said, his face clear of embarrassed colour and his eyes meeting both the women's and the guards' gazes with steadiness.

"If Ria dressed like this I'd skin any man who looked at her," Jaik said darkly, his eyes entranced.

"I can't..." Calev stuttered.

"It will become easier," replied Zeb.

"Look at their faces," Zephenesh advised, his face hard and calm.

"You sternly judge a nation you have chosen not to understand," Zeb responded to Zephenesh's harsh tone.

"Do you understand them?" asked Fidel, sitting beside the twins and Zeb who were now ready to receive patrons of their goods.

"I do not dislike a race based on cultural differences which are preferences, preferences that do not sit against my own beliefs, against the spirits which guide us all, just against my tastes. I refuse to wilfully misunderstand others."

"Sometimes people's tastes are right," Djeck replied, the only one unimpressed by the Southern Elf's speech.

"You realise your niece may no longer agree," Zeb said, looking past Djeck to Zephenesh.

"There are more women coming out, she may be among them."

They stayed there for the rest of the day, managing to sell some of their stock, but unable to see Kiara. She did not venture into the courtyard, and when the Harem Master finally came through to usher the rest of the women back inside they knew that they would not see her that day.

They were packing up, Fidel wondering whether they had been wrong all along, when Zeb intercepted the Harem Master.

"My lord," he bowed his head, his hand touching the elbow of the bald man. He clearly carried much authority in this section of the palace.

Fidel saw a look pass over Zeb's face as he touched him, as if understanding something, and then the elf spoke.

"The fair-haired one, the Prince's Favourite, we have come to see her."

The Harem Master made to turn away, clearly bothered one too many times by people interested in the court gossip.

"I entreat you, her uncle is here." Zeb gestured to Zephenesh who stood beside Fidel, watching with the others the conversation taking place. "We mean to cause no trouble, I only ask that you tell her we are here, that we will come back tomorrow, her uncle wishes to see her, if only once."

The man's eyes softened at the mention of a relative of the Favourite. He looked over to Zephenesh, and Fidel saw the uncertainty in his eyes. He looked back to Zeb, his face still undecided, and then without saying anything in reply he left, herding the last of the women through the door and shutting it behind him.

Zeb watched after him and then turned back to the party.

"We will come back tomorrow."

CHAPTER 19

When Johan entered the favourite's room, he saw Coscian talking to the fair-haired woman. He was explaining that a trip to the harem market could be beneficial because of all the excellent perfumes on offer. He was rather firm with her, explaining the approval she would receive from the Prince if she were to wear perfumes brought from the provinces of Castir. Johan wondered how much more approval was needed - he knew his friend had kissed the woman, and that he was planning to bed her too.

She seemed less than interested however. As Johan stood in the doorway he saw the fingers she was tracing over her lips and the far-off look in her blue eyes. Trevisian didn't know he was here, no doubt he might comment upon it when he heard of it later, but Johan felt a need to speak to the woman his friend clearly felt deeply for. He wanted to know he could trust her.

He knocked on the doorframe. "I'd be more than happy to accompany you, my lady." He bowed, the lengths of his Tao-style hair falling either side of his muscular neck. He threw the lengths of knotted curls back over his shoulders. Kiara looked a little startled. "We have not been formally introduced. My name is Johan, bodyguard to my Lord Prince."

"I… er…" Her blue eyes flicked over to Coscian whose implacable countenance remained unperturbed by the interference.

"I am sure she would appreciate your company, Johan." In the Harem Master's hand was a bloodied towel. "Perhaps you could escort her back here afterwards too?"

Johan's quick eyes took in the cut which had freshly sealed itself on the woman's forearm. "I will."

Coscian moved towards the door. "I shall see you later then, my lady." He slid from the room silently as though he had never been present.

Johan turned back to find her watching him cautiously. Her frame was rigid, the injured arm now tucked protectively behind her body.

"My lady," he bowed again, sweeping an arm towards the door to allow her passage.

She took the opportunity immediately, breathing easier as soon as she was out of the confines of the room.

"You are not Reluwyn."

He caught a furtive glance cast sideways at him. A chuckle rumbled up his chest. "Direct. The Prince said you were."

His step paused a moment so that he could turn and display his back to her. Whilst he wore a leather skirted loincloth, his upper half was covered only by a sash of animal skin, the fur yellow and dotted with dark black spots. A desert wild cat, a vicious creature whose fur could take on the colour of its surroundings. Johan had killed it beneath the shade of a waterfruit tree.

Either side of the sash, the Radichi's pale tattoos could be seen covering his torso. Reluwyn men tended to be swathed in billowing silk tunics, and Johan was the only man of court who remained in tribal attire at all times.

"I am a Radichi warrior from the Tao desert in the south."

A line had appeared between Kiara's brows, and she looked as though she was working out a sum. She began to speak and then stopped, refocusing upon her surroundings. Johan filled in the blanks.

"What is a Southern warrior doing in Emril Palace?"

She nodded.

"I was taken captive during the re-conquering wars of the Reluwyn and kept at the palace as a kind of exhibit of the Southern Nomads." He noted the curl of her lip. "I grew up with the Prince, became his bodyguard, his friend."

Her fine brow rose.

"Is the…" she hesitated.

"Generally, people call him my Lord Prince," another rich chuckle rumbled out. "Though I know you've had choice names for him before." He looked down at this woman who barely came up to his shoulder. "I am not come to fetch you to him. He has not called for you yet." He saw a look akin to disappointment fleetingly cross her face.

"You know you're not like any other." His voice had dropped low. "That cut proves it, and the others know it."

"I don't understand why."

Johan's mouth curled upwards, a gentle smile taking over. "Put your hand upon my arm. No one will harm you when you are with me." He saw reassurance rush over her face.

"I can see why the Prince likes you." She smiled then, her eyes sparkling with humour.

"Because I hold his hand too you mean?" Johan laughed, stepping out into the sun and guiding her toward the first of the market-sellers.

She looked at each of the stalls but was not convinced by any of the wares to part with the purse of coins Coscian had given her. When she came upon a stall in the corner, a blanket laid on the ground spread with bottles of perfume and piles of spices, she paused once again.

Until now she had not interacted with any of the market sellers. Johan had greeted each one, exchanging a few pleasantries, particularly with those he already knew from other markets that took place within the palace walls.

"Good morning." He greeted the small gathering of men.

A few sat back against the wall but the elder among them remained just behind the blanket with another man. The second man was as tall as a tree and broad, rivalling Johan in stature. He was fair too, responding in a steady voice to the greeting. He bid the Radichi good morning but his eyes were on the woman on Johan's arm.

At the sound of the man's voice Johan felt her hand grip tightly. The older man offered a greeting, and the grip became tighter still. She stepped back and then sideways, all the time holding onto Johan.

"Are you well, my lady?" Johan looked down at her, seeing the shock etched into every feature of her face. She couldn't reply.

Johan looked back to the merchant party and saw that every pair of eyes was upon her, though none of the men had moved. The tension was finally broken by an elf, who now stepped towards them.

"My lady, a bottle of perfume for you? Only 10 reels? It is from the heart of Castir, the provinces with the best Occia trees." He picked up a purple bottle from the blanket and thrust it forwards.

The woman took it, looking dumbly at the perfume and then back at the seller. Johan's heavy brow was furrowing slowly. Was that recognition he had seen? His measuring gaze was cast back over the traders. Their dress was that of the Great Forest and he glimpsed a few Laowyn badges in the folds of their cloaks. Then there was the elf who'd come forward, his dress more akin to a Southerner near Johan's home.

Johan looked back down at the Favourite. His words carefully chosen, "My lady? You do not have to buy it, are you wishful to return to your quarters?"

"I…"

"Your lip," Johan jutted his chin in a gesture towards the blood on her lower lip.

"My lady, please take this silk for no extra charge." It was the older man who stepped forward now, coming out of the trance that the rest still seemed stuck in. He offered the silk and she took it. In doing so she dropped the perfume bottle, the delicate object shattering on the tiled floor. A heavy floral smell rose up, the liquid dripping into the cracks of the floor. The whole courtyard stopped and turned to look at the upset.

The Favourite wiped her lip carelessly, the blood smearing. The sounds of the courtyard slowly filtered back into place. As they did so, she looked away with great effort, muttering something Johan did not catch. Suddenly her voice raised,

"Coscian!"

"My lady?" He frowned. His eyes switched several times between the blue eyes of the old man and those of the woman.

She tried to hand back the silk.

"A gift, my lady," the old man affirmed, his hands remaining by his side.

She turned to Johan, a look of anguish on her face which she rapidly forced into a smile. "Please, Johan," she said in a voice lighter than her body language would suggest. "Will you take me to Coscian? I have just remembered something I forgot to speak to him about this morning."

Johan looked between her and the traders. Both remained silent under his scrutiny and he doubted very much he would obtain an answer from the woman in this public place. "Very well. My Lord Prince will see to it that you are reimbursed." Johan nodded to the broken shards of bottle that still lay at the Favourite's feet.

"Of course, my lord. Perhaps we may see you again, my lady."

She made no answer, turning away with Johan and retreating to the shade of the colonnade. It was not until they re-entered the harem that Johan felt the small hand finally relax upon his arm. It turned out that the Favourite had a past after all, and Johan guessed that it had just found her.

●●●

Kiara was so agitated that she barely looked at the silk that her uncle had pushed into her hand. Once Johan had left, she had paced her room for some time. Her fingers now touched her lip, not to remember the Prince's kiss, but to feel where she had bitten down on it in the market. If she had given anything away, everything would change.

Did she not want it to? Was she happy that Zephenesh was here? That Zeb had come for her? Zeb was alive! She had thought him dead, but there he had been, handing her a bottle of perfume as though he was any normal market seller.

Why were they here? Zephenesh's look had not been one of joy she was sure. Relief had been in his eyes, but those eyes had also taken in her Reluwyn dress, her exposed skin, her hand on the arm of a man equally half-dressed. What had he thought?

Her pacing distracted her, hiding the sound of the door opening and shutting. She turned to retrace her steps for the hundredth time almost colliding with Coscian who was holding a tray of fruit. He placed it on the table before facing her again.

"I…" she looked into his eyes. He had encouraged her to go to the market, yet usually he encouraged her to keep secluded, to keep protected. "Coscian…" How did she address this?

"Yes."

"Why did you…" She continued to pace. "Why did you encourage me to go to the market? What was the purpose?"

She saw it! The flicker of guilt that manifested itself in the pursing of his lips.

"For perfumes, my lady, to entice the Prince. Do you care for some fruit?" He picked at some dates, chewing them without pleasure.

"You've never called me 'my lady'." Her blue eyes were like fire, her shoulders shaking. "Tell me the truth Coscian."

He looked conflicted.

"I know nothing of the goings on in the market place. Except that one party requested to speak to you yesterday. They seemed determined… are they who I think they are?"

She began pacing again.

"You must be careful, rumours are quick to ignite the court's forest."

"Johan saw them, I... I tried not to be shocked, no thanks to you," she shot it at him and the barb hit its mark. "Oh!" She cast her hands up. "I do not mean to... it's just... it's all so complicated now."

"He told me."

So Johan had guessed, for her uncle had been wearing the symbol of the Laowyn. Damn his pride! And yet with such bitter sweetness she had looked upon him – after all, she had never thought she'd see him again.

"Johan's no fool."

"No."

"If he tells the Prince I..." she drifted off again.

"He won't. Not yet. I am told the Prince favours you highly."

"Everyone said that from the beginning."

"True, but has there not been a change in his attentions?"

She coloured then.

"Johan?" she asked a little helplessly.

Coscian nodded. He moved towards her now stilled figure. His hand lay on hers for a moment.

"You have to tell him on your own terms."

"Why do you protect me?"

Coscian removed his hand, smiling wanly. "Johan seems to think you two suit."

"Suit!?" But Kiara had no arguments left. She had nothing left after arguing for so long, battling every feeling, trying to escape every attention. Something in her had changed, as if something had grown, and it would never be the same again.

"But you must be the one to tell him. No one else must hear of this until he knows, Laowyn prejudice it running high in the court and..." His colour was heightened. He grasped for the next words but they failed to come.

Kiara waited for the rest, but he simply kept opening his mouth silently. An odd tinge of purple ran across his lips. His hands flailed pointlessly at his throat.

Kiara suddenly leapt forward, her hands trying to pull his collar open. He was suffocating, she could see the colour deepen.

A coughing rasping sound suddenly emitted from his throat. He stumbled forward into her.

"Help! Someone help!" she screamed, trying to support the man's weight as he began to cough, blood splattering across her face and hair. "Coscian, you'll be alright, Coscian!"

The man continued to rasp as Kiara managed to lay him down without hitting him against anything. As soon as he was on the floor his body contracted violently, taken over by uncontrollable spasms.

She screamed again, louder, longer. The doors to her room flew open. She didn't see the women in the corridor gathering between the columns to peer in. Guards flooded the room, standing around the prostrate man and the woman covered in his blood. None knew what to do.

Then all of a sudden it all stopped - the rasping, the thrashing, the coughing. Coscian was rigid, his face contorted, his lips deep violet, the remainder of the blood dripping slowly from his silent mouth. He was dead.

CHAPTER 20

Trevisian shouldered guards aside, running into the room. He stopped short when he saw her. She was kneeling beside the body, her hand stroking the dead man's back without regard for the lack of movement beneath. Her eyes uncomprehending, her body slowly rocking.

Johan had fetched him. News of the death was still spreading around the palace but Trevisian had not waited for further reports. Was she dead too? Or dying? He had left his chambers at a dead run, bellowing at servants and courtiers alike to move out the way. Now he was here and she was alive, but beside her lay a dead man.

She didn't seem aware of anyone around her.

"What happened?" Trevisian cast back at one of the guards who stood uselessly by, watching the woman.

He started sheepishly to attention. "My Lord Prince, we are unsure, she won't speak."

Trevisian made a guttural sound of frustration, not wasting another moment on the guard. Coming to his Favourite, he knelt beside her.

"Little One." His hand gently pushed away the blood-speckled hair from her face. The intimate gesture provoked no response, neither did the words. She just kept staring. He leaned forward and took her hand from Coscian's back, holding it tightly between his own. "What happened?"

"My Lord Prince, it is not advisable…"

"Go to the dogs!" Trevisian barked back, the guard cowering in response. Johan, who had accompanied the Prince back to the harem, muttered instructions to the guards.

Trevisian cupped a hand to his Favourite's face, gently turning her from the Harem Master's open eyes to his instead. She gazed straight through him, as though he were not there, he could feel her hand trembling in his own. She had never seen death, not like this.

"Little One, you must tell me what happened." His dark eyes were gentle but demanding.

She shrugged helplessly, clearly in shock.

"Tell me," his voice was low and hoarse.

"We were talking," her lips twisted and trembled and then, a low mournful sob escaped her.

Trevisian's hand tightened around her own, his brows drawing closer together as he watched her distress. Her eyes clouded over again, and without a second thought Trevisian pulled her firmly into his arms.

Johan stepped forward after conversing with a physician who had just arrived on the scene. "Poison." he murmured low in his ear.

Trevisian nodded once jerkily. "Little One?" He drew his head away to look at her. How could he still not know her name? "Did you see him eat or drink anything? You must tell me."

Kiara's blurry vision focused for a moment on the fruit platter, sat where Coscian had left it on the table just a few moments before.

"The fruit."

Johan went immediately to work. He gave orders to the guards who moved quickly, taking the platter away to the physician's quarters to be inspected while the body was covered and removed. In the midst of all the activity, Trevisian slipped his free arm under Kiara's legs and picked her up. There was no protest.

When they reached his chamber he ignored the guards, taking her straight to his bed, placing her on the soft covers.

"I am going to get you a drink." He didn't bother telling her to stay there. Ducking out of the bedroom he came back into the main chamber.

"Trevisian, are you thinking the same thing as me?" said Johan as he entered.

"She was the target." The grim line of his mouth might have been mistaken for quiet sadness. Johan knew better.

"She was attacked again this morning by one of the women. Coscian was treating a cut on her arm when I went to see her."

"Get out!" The guards scattered. "You were with her?" asked Trevisian after the door was closed.

"I wanted to get to know the woman you love, Trevisian." The light eyes held his friend's stare, not bowing to the dark look.

"I'll have whoever is responsible hanged! They'll wish they had taken their own poison!" Trevisian was hissing like a snake. The scene he had walked into was replaying in his mind. Except the figures were switched. It was his Favourite who lay dead on the floor, blood pouring from her mouth, lips purple with suffocation.

"She will stay here." Trevisian turned to pour water from a decanter. "Johan can you…"

They both stopped talking and turned to the sobbing noise. Trevisian's Favourite standing in the doorway. She looked confused, and in her outstretched hand was a silk handkerchief.

Trevisian was beside her in seconds but she wouldn't let him comfort her, she just pushed the silk towards Johan. There was a faint pattern on it and small patches of blood from Kiara's lip, but there, in the pattern were words.

Prince and you in danger. Guards at third gate plotting.
Assassination imminent.

"So it was not some rival in the harem." Johan spoke.

"Get rid of it." Trevisian ordered.

Johan was already moving to the door.

"Take this fruit to the physician too." The guards came in, removing an identical platter of fruit from the dining table.

Trevisian shuddered and then turned back to the woman who was still relying on the door frame to hold her up. "Where did you get this?"

"I should have read it," she replied. "I should have read it."

"Woman, answer me!" Trevisian's voice was no longer gentle.

"A trader gave it to her in the market place for a cut lip, Trevisian. She had nothing to do with this, can't you see it?" Johan gestured towards the woman who was a clear wreck.

The Prince's shoulders relaxed somewhat.

"Have all guards on the third gate imprisoned and order some warm water and towels to my room. Then you may go, Johan."

"Are you sure?"

"Look at her," Trevisian gestured fiercely, "she needs to be cleaned and she's hardly in a state to do it herself."

"Someone could…"

"I'm not letting her out of my sight."

Trevisian watched acceptance dawn in his friend's eyes.

"Watch the door." Trevisian knew the request would see them left alone.

Johan nodded once and was gone.

Trevisian led Kiara back to sit on the bed, only leaving her briefly when the servant came to the door holding a golden bowl of steaming water and a selection of towels. He allowed them to be set down on a bedside table before dismissing the servant. She had not moved. Her eyes still staring through him.

"I'm going to wash your face." Trevisian sat beside her, picking up a small towel and dipping it in the water. He lifted it to her face and, after hesitating a moment, pushed it against her skin, cleaning away the blood. He rinsed the towel and then did the same again on her forehead. Her eyes closed as he cleaned her neck, and strands of her hair. He cleansed her skin gently and her breathing lengthened, her muscles slowly relaxing in response.

He left her with her eyes still closed, but when he came back with a cup of water her eyes were open and searching for him. When they alighted on him the puckered brow undid itself, spreading smooth across her forehead once more.

He sat beside her again, handing her the cup and moving the towels off the bed and onto the side table.

"No one should have to watch anyone die."

She nodded.

"You will stay here until the danger has passed."

She nodded again. Then, without speaking, she leant into him. His arm came up in response, his face surprised but his body acting automatically. He drew her towards him, her head laying against his chest, her hair touching his chin.

"No one can harm you here, no one can take you from me, do you understand?" He felt the shudder of her shoulders beneath his arm. "You're mine."

She drew away enough to look him full in the face, her eyes locking with his. A timid hand came up and ran along his jaw, falling to his neck. He saw a look in her eyes he had not seen before. An open and inviting look.

"I *want* to be yours."

The words sent a shockwave through him. Feelings heated him to the core. He caught her hand upon his neck, holding it there, and then pulling her closer with his arm around her waist he kissed her.

316 ● P. J. KEYWORTH

The action seemed to answer everything that had happened in a way that transcended words. It wasn't like last time, her mouth was hungry, her hands clinging to him, permission finally, excruciatingly, given. He pushed her gently back onto the bed, shifting his body, his hands pinning one of hers to the bed, the other still wrapped around her, pressing them closer together.

He reached up and pushed the hair from her face, pausing, looking at her. "I've wanted you for a long time."

A flicker of fear passed over her eyes, but she reached up, her fingers threading through his hair, pulling his head towards her again, her mouth open. Her willing sent a shiver through him, waking him up. He ran his hands over her, over the body, the head, the face, defiant. Now she was here, in his bed, all his, entirely.

She pulled at the hem of his shirt. He knelt up, pulling the clothing off, revealing his chest and back. He turned to throw it on the floor but before he could turn back he felt fingers tracing the line of the phoenix feathers tattooed on his skin. His whole body tensed at the feeling but when he turned back she didn't say anything. She didn't comment. She didn't ask questions. She just held his neck, asking him to come back to her.

The woman who had denied him. The woman who had incensed him. The woman who had captivated him. Here she was. He picked her up to sitting, gently pulling at the straps of her dress. The desire within him burned for release but he took his time. She was beautiful. When she finally lay naked before him, she blushed under his gaze but he would not answer her embarrassment with words, but kissed her again, running his hands over her body, drawing the covers over both of them. She sighed against his cheek, the sound sweet and light.

They lay face to face, stilling for a moment, their eyes searching each other's. He did not wait long but lay his arm around her back, drawing her to him again. The indented pattern he felt made him stop.

She looked suddenly fearful, turning to escape his hold.

That's when he saw the blue Ensper, recognising the black tattoo that laced her back.

He sat up, the covers rumpling around his waist.

"You're Laowyn."

He didn't say anything else for some time.

"My name is Kiara." Her shoulders trembled with the whispered admission. Whether it was a gesture of peace, a truce, he didn't care, she had given herself to him.

He reached a hand out to touch the Ensper. His hand ran up, laying gently on her shoulder. "Come back to me," his voice brushed warm against her skin. He pulled at her, drawing her back to him, under the covers, and into pleasure.

⊙⊙⊙

"Do you think it worked?"

"Yes, if she read it." Zeb was tired of aimless chit-chat. This was why he ordinarily worked alone. He was the one who had heard the guards who were planning on killing the Prince and his Favourite this morning. Kiara's cut lip had provided the perfect excuse for passing the message they had hastily written to her. But the elf wouldn't be surprised if she was too shocked to notice any writing on a piece of material.

Zephenesh had been praying since they had delivered the message that she would read it. He and Fidel had been discussing what to tell Kiara when next they saw her, hoping she would be alone in the market place. The look on her face when she had seen them all had not just been shock, it had been fear. Perhaps Ikara was right and she was in some kind of relationship with the Prince. Maybe she didn't want to come back. Even if that was the case, Zeb knew she would not turn her back on her people. Now they weren't just waiting for an opportunity to speak to her, they were waiting to see whether she was alive.

As those thoughts ran through his mind, Jaik began overtly coughing. Calev slapped his back hard, almost causing an argument to break out, but the signal was given. Zeb turned with the others to see Kiara entering the market place. She looked paler than the other day, but no less beautiful.

She wore a dress similar to the gold one she had worn yesterday, but today she covered it with a thin cloak. The finely woven material was in a deep hue that set off her long blond hair, the hair that Zeb had regrown for her. Her blue eyes traced over each of the parties in the courtyard until they fell upon the Laowyn party.

Her step slowed as she came closer. All the men were there, watching her intently, just as they had the day before. Zeb saw her falter, but she steadied herself, coming directly to him.

"I thought you were dead."

"We thought *you* might be dead by now," Zeb didn't try to touch her in greeting. Neither did he smile. "I'm pleased to see that you're not." He bent down, picking up a bottle of perfume and holding it out to her. She took it without looking. "Are you well?"

Zephenesh came to stand beside Zeb. The others hung back so as not to draw attention, though they followed the conversation as closely as the participants.

"Kiara," his hand came out, but she didn't move closer.

"Uncle."

"I never thought to see you again, but by the Great Spirit's power."

Zeb noticed one fine brow rise involuntarily.

"Yet here I am." She held out the blood-soaked silk. "What is this?"

"You received it in time."

Her words were cold. "I did, the Prince did, others did not."

"Thank the Great Spirit you are safe!" Zephenesh's whisper came out on a sigh of relief.

"My friend is dead."

"I am sorry Kiara." Zeb had never used her name before. It felt strange on his tongue, but his sincerity won from her a fleeting smile. "We overheard the guards on the gates when we were passing through yesterday, we tried to get the word to you as quickly as possible."

Her expression softened for a moment. "I am so glad you're alive Zeb." Her eyes misted slightly.

"Have they hurt you?"

"No." She turned from Zeb and cast accusing eyes at her uncle. "If you only heard of the assassination plot after you arrived, I want to know what you are doing here in the first place?"

Fidel came forward.

"We are here to speak to you – to ask you to speak to the Prince on our race's behalf. There are rumours that you have his... his favour. Kiara, we need your help."

She looked as though she had been struck across the face.

"Help? And where was yours when I sought sanctuary? It's only thanks to this elf that I am alive today."

"Kiara lower your voice."

She shot a venomous look at her uncle, but it was lost on the older man who was watching the guards at the gate.

"Kiara your uncle's right," Zeb warned, noting the guards' heightened interest.

Kiara turned, raising a hand of reassurance. They returned immediately back to a neutral state either side of the gate.

Zeb was impressed. He wasn't sure the others saw it but he had. It was not just the obedience that was telling, it was the slight bow of their heads. He looked back to Kiara. She was no prisoner, nor was she a mere concubine. She was highly favoured.

"So I'm not even worthy of your rescue, uncle? Have I fallen so far from your graces?"

"Kiara." Zephenesh looked suddenly confused. "Have you not heard of the Edict which has been passed?"

Her silence was answer enough.

"Kiara, our whole people, they are to be destroyed."

The anger and frustration in her face vanished all at once. Zeb watched her turn over in her mind what all of them had been attempting to grasp for weeks.

"The Prince is the only one with the power to help."

"He has not spoken of this."

"Kiara." Her uncle stepped forward and grasped her hand. "The Prince's seal was on the document."

"No," her voice was faint. She yanked her hand from Zephenesh's grasp. "No, he wouldn't have allowed that, he…"

"Kiara, you must help your people, you must plead with him."

"Please Kiara," echoed Fidel.

"But he…"

"Will he listen?" Zeb asked the most sensible question.

"I don't know."

"Try. If it goes wrong we are here. The twins are working on an escape plan. We can get you out of here Kiara."

The look on her face was unreadable to most but Zeb who saw conflict there. He watched her closely during the rest of the conversation but she said little. They went over practicalities, meeting places, escape possibilities. She nodded absently when it was needed but other than that she looked through each of them, her thoughts elsewhere. Zeb watched her return to the harem, the weight of her condemned race lying upon her shoulders. She would petition the Prince tonight, and they would rescue her at dawn.

CHAPTER 21

"I have no idea who would wish to harm you, my Lord Prince. The woman is a different matter."

"The woman is my wife," replied Trevisian, staring down his High Councillor. "Any attempt on her life is considered an attempt on mine."

Garesh's face was contorted as though by a foul stench. His dark eyes were sharp and angry, his mouth a twisted line. This shock was real, unlike that which he displayed when he was told of the poisoning.

"Wife?" He had lashed Nisa himself for her failure. Her cronies' incompetence had cost Garesh any element of surprise or deniability where the assassination was concerned.

"Yes."

That street brat had become Trevisian's wife the moment he had spoken it. Damn him! The declaration was binding.

"But, I…" Garesh's knuckles were turning white upon the chair back he leant against. "She is not a wise choice."

"You dare question me? I am the King now Garesh!"

Garesh's eyes flashed and then narrowed. His tongue ran along his bottom lip. "Do you not think that at a time of anxiety in the Kingdom, when the Laowyn are gathering at their old capital Ishtalia, making ready to fight, that taking a wife you know nothing about is foolish?"

"I know everything about her."

Garesh scoffed. "Do you? Are you sure it was not her who attempted to poison you? Have you not thought of that? Convenient that she ate none of the food presented to her, but instead offered it to the Harem Master who would die from it."

"Enough!" Trevisian raised his voice in warning. "She would do no such thing."

Garesh stopped pushing. He had planted the seed, let it take root. "All I am saying, my Lord Prince, I mean, my Lord King, is why not wait until the situation is resolved before you make the declaration." Garesh took advantage of the Prince being on the back foot. "You have a race rising up against you - the Laowyn amassing is no coincidence, they will rebel."

Trevisian didn't answer him. His thoughts were already back on Kiara, the woman he had left in his bed, the woman he loved. He didn't believe she had poisoned Coscian, or that she had tried to poison him, but he felt unsettled. He knew she was Laowyn. No one else did. No one else could. He would hide it, he would keep her safe.

"Are you sure that is what they intend? Are they not amassing because of their persecution?"

Garesh's ears pricked up at this. "You have no knowledge of such matters, my Lord King."

"I am not sure you are qualified to tell me what I have knowledge of Garesh. You are no longer my Regent."

Garesh's voice hardened. "This Edict is necessary for the control of your kingdom."

"Precisely, *my* Kingdom. And now I'm married, is not your role in all this at an end?"

"At an end is it?" Garesh mocked. "I should think that any youthful would-be King - whom I practically raised - would be happy for my council."

Trevisian strode forwards his shoulders broadening. "You go too far Garesh!"

"Do I?" The High Councillor's eyes took on the light of cruel amusement. "You doubt my knowledge of *you*, King. Do you think I have forgotten what you truly are? Everyone averts their eyes from the markings on your back because nothing has been confirmed. It would take one word from me to see you branded as one of the Shifters, just like your mother." His tongue licked in and out of his mouth like a snake as he hissed the threatening words. "One word and you'd be sentenced to death."

Trevisian was only motionless for a moment before he launched himself at Garesh, pinning him against the wall by the throat.

"How dare you." Trevisian's teeth were an inch from Garesh's face.

"Are you sure," rasped the official, his fingers scrabbling at the wall, scraping at the tiles. "You wish this to be your end?" He coughed and spluttered against Trevisian's arm. "One call is all it will take. Do you not think I have had control from the beginning?"

Images flashed through Trevisian's mind. "You took power from my father," he hesitated. "You killed him."

Garesh laughed, but the airless sound came out like scratching against a wooden door. "You were as happy as I was that the King was dead. No more beatings for you."

Trevisian pressed mercilessly harder. The Councillor's face was deepening in colour, and his hands were becoming less insistent on the tiles as he rasped. "Would you...would you like to be executed...just as your father executed your mother? I have... always held the reins of power... boy."

Trevisian pulled away from him, letting him drop to the floor. Garesh rubbed at his neck, his mouth still twisted in a half sneer. He had won.

"We will have to meet the Laowyn forces with our own." Garesh gripped onto the wall to hoist himself back up. He spoke as if he were the Regent again. Pushing home the control he had over Trevisian. "We cannot leave it up to rural populations to suppress the rebels."

Trevisian didn't reply. He was already walking out of the door.

⬤⬤⬤

Kiara did not wait to knock on the door, to ask for admittance, to be accepted and announced. She couldn't risk being turned away. She pushed open the doors to his chamber and neither of the guards stopped her. They couldn't now she was their Queen. It had been announced. The women who had been gathered by the Edict were pouring out of the harem, released just as Kiara had returned to the palace from the market.

She hoped, she beseeched the Great Spirit, that she would be blessed by good fortune, that Trevisian might grant her wish. Her race depended upon her.

He was pacing when she entered and the doors shut before she could retreat. This was not a good sign. Had he seen her talking to her uncle? Was he angry?

"Do you know the punishment for entering without a summons?" His eyes were wild and he came towards her as a predator upon prey. The man she had known last night was vaporised in a flash of angry heat.

"I am your wife," she offered.

"Where have you been? I left you here. Do you not know the dangers outside this place?"

So now he wanted her here. Confusion enveloped Kiara's face.

"Those guards killed Coscian but we don't know the depth of the conspiracy. There may be more involved."

He picked up a porcelain horse figurine from the desk and threw it against the far wall. It hit with such force the tiles cracked and the horse was shattered into countless pieces.

Kiara jumped at the sound, her back slamming against the door to which she had retreated.

"You think I... I had something to do with Coscian's death?" She hesitated, her eyes searching. "You think I tried to kill you?"

"The Laowyn are rising up in Ishtalia." He came towards her. "Were you sent by them? I don't want to believe it." His fist slammed against the door above her head. His eyes closed. "I don't want to believe it."

"Then don't! Do you not think I would have done it already? Do you think I would have..." Damn her for wavering. She dashed a hand across her face to push away the tears. "You said you loved me," she said accusingly. "You know I love you. I would never have given myself if I hadn't. And now..." she gestured at the meaninglessness of their argument. "Was that all a lie? To bed me?" Her chin came up. Had this been his plan all along.

He raked a hand savagely through his hair.

"Did you lie to me?" Kiara asked, her voice steadier. "Did you lie to me?!" she asked again, pain fracturing her voice as she looked upon him.

"No!" He grabbed her, kissing her urgently at first, and then all at once, as if something broke, he slowed. His hand was soft in her hair, his lips were soft on hers. "I love you," he murmured against her cheek before he pulled back.

"Garesh believes you are a spy sent to kill me. He is gone to amass the Reluwyn forces to put down the rebellion."

"You must stop them! The Laowyn are not rebelling," Kiara wanted him to look at her. "They are coming together because they face death." She touched his arm, turning him towards her, but he would not look at her. "Trevisian," she said softly, seeing the answering gentleness in his eyes as she used his name. "You must do something."

The look in his eyes faded away. "Do what?"

"You must save them. You must save me."

"They cannot touch the Queen." A shadow passed over his eyes as he said the words but his voice gained confidence. "I will not allow it."

"I will be safe while my people are slaughtered? Trevisian you are the Prince – now a King – are you not? You can revoke the Edict."

"You don't understand."

"Why will you not stop Garesh?" She bit her lip. What she was about to say could lose him. Perhaps forever. She took in breath. "Are you the Prince I thought you were, or are you the King I know?"

He sighed, his shoulders slumping. "Kiara, if I could do anything for your people I would, but I cannot. The law is passed" He came to her, holding steady her protesting hands. This was the end. She could feel it. She had failed. "I cannot save them, only you." She let him kiss her cheek, the action sending shivers through her.

She would not let them die alone. She had been blind to them locked in the palace for too long, it had to end. He kissed her mouth, his hands following the lines of her body, remembering the night before, hungry for more. A tear fell unseen from the corner of her eye, running the length of her cheek. They would be married one more night, then she would leave.

⚫⚫⚫

Kiara slipped from the bed, her bare feet padding across the tiled floor until she came to her pile of clothes. She dressed as quickly and quietly as she could. Zeb had told her she could not wake him even if she smacked him across the face after he had drunk the powder, but every pause in breathing, every minute movement, made her pause and look over to where her husband lay. Her husband. That was what he was and she was leaving him.

She paused at the door looking back at him. He was laying so still, and in sleep he looked peaceful. He had taken the wine from her without question. He had trusted her. He wouldn't anymore, not after this.

She came back to him. How could she leave? Her heart had two forces pulling it in opposite directions. Looking down at Trevisian, knowing she was leaving him, she already felt she had lost. She wouldn't survive this. Tears welled in her eyes and dripped steadily on the covers. She needed to go. She needed to leave. In the half light of the room she bent and kissed him on the mouth, her hand brushing at his dark tousled hair. The pucker of his brow faded away for a moment before drawing back together as he kept on dreaming. He would never forgive her for this. She bit her lip to keep from sobbing.

"Goodbye." She drew away from him then, walking straight to the door, unable to look back. Knowing that if she did she would never leave.

She moved quickly through the night-time palace, and if she had been asked to recount her trail when she met with Calev and Jaik she could not have. It blurred with memories and the thoughts that haunted her down the passageways.

"Did anyone follow?"

She shook her head. The few guard patrols she had seen on her way here had paid her no heed. The palace was preparing for a mass movement of troops. A veiled woman, probably a concubine hiding in the shadows, was of no concern to the guards.

"It's good to see you girl. Any news on the Edict?"

She shook her head again. Despite their best efforts, even the cheery expressions of the half-shadowed twins looked disheartened.

"Well, at least we can get you out of here. Come!" Calev took her hand, Jaik following them closely behind. They left the ghostly market place, following the third circle of the palace until they came to one of several taverns which were housed within the walls. Kiara remained outside with Jaik and the donkey while Calev went to fetch the others.

Zephenesh hugged Kiara when he made her out in the shadows, but she didn't respond. He pulled back and if she had looked at him she would have seen a hurt, searching look in his eyes. Other greetings would have to wait until they found safety.

Zeb came forward. "You must lie over the donkey. We'll cover you with the blankets so that you'll look like cargo, and I've already bribed the guards to give us passage after dusk."

"The last of our money," muttered Djeck.

"We're lucky they took it at all."

Kiara climbed onto the donkey. Lying across the beast on her front she was then bound up with blankets until none of her was visible. They wrapped packs of perfume and spices across her back and hung them over her head and legs. If the guards decided to dig around hopefully, they would only find the cargo. That was unless they dug a little deeper.

The guard who had accepted the bribe opened the smaller inner gate without question at the sound of Zeb's knock. He did not say a word while they passed through. Once they were on the other side the guard closed the door behind them and walked straight back to his watch position.

The second gate was opened to Zeb's knock, but on the other side, before they were through, their bribed guard was hailed by another.

Everyone in the party halted, holding their breaths. Kiara wondered what Trevisian would do with her if she was recaptured. Her escape was a betrayal. She shifted slightly on the donkey, blood running to her head and the pommel of the beast's harness digging into her stomach. She'd faint if she stayed like this much longer. Zeb had told her they would be through in under half an hour.

"Don't move." The words were whispered near her head but she couldn't tell who spoke. She did as she was bid the pommel continuing to dig into her abdomen.

"What's this then?"

She could hear the voice of the second guard more clearly now. He must be looking through the gate. She was suspended in a sea of black with voices sounding from different directions.

None of the party answered.

"A double deal." The guard laughed, she could hear him slapping something. "Grease my hands and we'll say no more about it."

"My lord," It was Zeb's voice. "We have no more money."

"Do you not?" The guard's voice was turning hard. "But I have no doubt you had money for my friend here." She heard a man yelp. "No passage without a fee."

"We have spices and perfumes, my lord."

Kiara felt a package removed from her head and shoulders. She heard shuffling.

"What's this? Whore's perfume?"

She heard something shoved hard against something else. The sound of wood knocking made its way through the material to Kiara's ears.

Then there was the sound of wheezing, quick movements that she couldn't define, and finally two heavy objects fell to the floor.

There was no more talking. The donkey moved off again, the swaying motion making the harness dig further into her stomach. They made it through the third gate without any problems and after a few more minutes they were running, their footsteps echoing against the sandstone buildings, the donkey's small hooves clattering. The pommel made a few hard jabs at her stomach before she hoisted her hands up, pushing herself away from the harness. It still bruised her but at least she wasn't about to throw up. She held herself like that until her muscles burned and she was about to collapse. That was when they stopped.

She was lifted off the donkey, and the blankets were stripped from her. Fidel held her steady as her legs, which had been bound together by the material, were released.

She looked around her. They were still in the city, but when she turned she saw the streets angling downwards, and beyond the rooftops lay open country. It was the country she must have been brought through unconscious months ago. Now she was fully aware of where she was travelling, she had woken up, and the world was a different place.

CHAPTER 22

"If she has left for the Laowyn Resistance, she will be killed with the rest of them unless I do something."

Trevisian and Johan were on their way to the Hall of Banners as they spoke.

"She has honour."

"She's a fool!" Trevisian snapped, not breaking his stride. "I promised her safety and she goes to die with her people."

"Maybe she considers her life the same as others, not of more value."

Trevisian drew both hands back through his messy locks. "It's of more value to me."

Johan didn't respond to that remark. Kiara had been discovered missing this morning. Trevisian had tried to raise a search party, but preparations for the Edict were all-consuming for the Reluwyn troops.

"Garesh has turned against me."

"What?" Johan's face turned grim. They were only a short walk from the Hall of Banners now, the same stretch of passageway down which Kiara had stumbled on her first day at the palace. Things had been different then. He had been different. Trevisian pushed the image of her from his mind - he needed a clear head to think properly.

"You know what I am, Johan." Trevisian jerked his head backwards, a gesture barely indicating his back and the markings there.

"I have seen you watch me, looking at my tattoo, have you not guessed?" He must have, he came from the same lands Trevisian's ancestors had walked. Legends remained no matter the people who dwelt there.

"There is talk of a marked race among those who carry the bloodlines of old. Shifters." The Radichi warrior's pale eyes took on concern. "Trevisian, if he knows too, then what you are about to do could be your end. He will turn the people against you and you will be executed."

"I know." He stopped outside the door to the hall. Putting a heavy hand on Johan's shoulders. "You have been a good friend to me, a loyal servant, you do not have to follow me any longer. I release you from your service to my crown."

"You release me?" The usually calm Radichi looked stunned.

Trevisian nodded with an effort. Johan was his friend, perhaps his only one, the closest thing he had to a brother or family. There were those who thought Trevisian truly his father's son, but he would not be dictated to by the memory of a cruel ruler. It was time he shaped his own actions, his own future, however short it ended up being.

"I release you," he said again when Johan didn't move.

"So I am free?"

"Yes."

"Then I follow you, Trevisian. I no longer follow you as a King but as a friend. As such you cannot command me otherwise."

"Johan," his voice became tense. "I am probably going to my death."

"I have a good feel for the men who loyally serve your crown, I know some to call on for support."

"Why?" Trevisian felt a hard lump in his throat.

"I knew this day would come." Johan's face broke into a smile, one lit by the anticipation of fighting in the future. "When you would wish to lead - and I have waited to follow you. When this deed is done, I will return to my homeland, but not before.

Trevisian watched him a moment, the open strength in his friend's face inspiring awe. Then he grasped his forearm warmly. "Thank you, my friend."

"If you feel the tide turning against you, keep them talking for as long as you can. I will rally those who still support you over Garesh. We will have to be ready to leave. If Garesh chooses to use your heritage against you, we will have to flee before he can capture you."

Trevisian nodded, trusting the friend who had helped him escape the palace numerous times before.

"You look the King you were born to be." The Radichi smiled, stepping back and taking in the official silk robes of the royal wardrobe. Trevisian had never needed to wear them, but today he needed all the authority he could muster. "May the blessings of the spirits be with you." Johan set off at a dead run.

Trevisian was thoughtful. He didn't want to remember the two council meetings he had attended recently but still they came to mind. The second had been to sign the Edict suppressing the Laowyn according to Garesh's wishes. The first had been the brief visit he'd made with Kiara on her first day here. He put her from his mind again.

Garesh had provided him with reports and given him documents to sign, but he hadn't been involved in the workings of government directly for a long time. Drawing his shoulders back, he took a deep breath, pushed the doors open and strode through.

There was a small amount of murmuring amongst the crowd who were gathered in an oval between the pillars. One man was speaking above the rest. Garesh.

"They have made a stronghold of their ancient capital and are amassing. I propose adding our own troops to the local collectives to put down the rebellion. We did not anticipate such behaviour from the Laowyn when the Edict was first issued."

"You are not asking permission, High Councillor, I have already seen the troops you have deployed from the city." Trevisian's voice cut through the murmur, the sound causing every head to turn in his direction. He watched each man's eyes fall upon him and widen. He watched mouths open in disbelief. They came back to themselves as he came closer, each bowing as he came past.

They parted like a river before him until he reached the centre of the oval. The rich red of his tunic was broken by the line of a black fur-trimmed cloak. On his head sat the twisted gold that marked him as their sovereign. At his waist was the sword that every ruler of the Reluwyn since their nomadic days had carried. His hand rested lightly on its ruby hilt. He turned in a large swoop, allowing each of the councillors to gain a good view of him. If this situation had not been so dire, he would have laughed at what Kiara would have thought of this drama. Instead his mouth remained in a firm line, his dark eyes looking down on those around him, his head held high. A true ruler. He came to stand opposite Garesh.

The High Councillor was glaring across at him, his eyes like white fire, cutting the air between them. Trevisian allowed a lilting smile onto his lips - Garesh had not expected this. Why would he? Had Trevisian ever disobeyed him in such a manner before? No. But now he knew her, he loved her, and she would die if he did nothing.

"In fact, the reports of rebellion are from your lips alone, are they not Garesh?" Trevisian's heart was beating hard in his chest. He never spoke publically like this. He wasn't used to it. But thoughts of Kiara that refused to go away came back and with them a renewed sense of urgency. "The Laowyn are merely amassing in fear of their impending slaughter, a slaughter unjustly called for. How do we expect to unite a Kingdom if you are bent on dividing it with suffering?"

Each eye was transfixed by the King.

"I? Have I not prevented any such disunity in my thirty years of service? I have been loyal to the Kingdom of Emrilion since its inception." Garesh was turning and speaking to the crowd, not to Trevisian. He knew what to do, he had thirty years of practice and it showed.

Trevisian couldn't just attack the High Councillor, he had no trust here, not like Garesh. "All I ask is for a detailed reconnaissance of the Laowyn - to be sure of their actions before any Edict is fulfilled. Until this is done, I command that the Edict for the Suppression of the Laowyn be suspended."

If he could buy time, maybe he could dismantle the law before it was put into practice. Trevisian saw the High Councillor attempt to hide a smile. What had he figured out? The uncertainty which arrested the features of Trevisian's face seemed like the confirmation Garesh was waiting for.

"My Lord Prince," Trevisian could see Garesh was determined not to acknowledge his King. "Surely you know that once passage is given to Reluwyn law, the law cannot be revoked or suspended. I know you were aware of this when *you* signed the Edict." The syrup dripped from Garesh's words. He carried on and Trevisian could see the room was with him. "I understand your sudden sympathy for the Laowyn rebels, but we cannot be seen to be weak -and nor can we disobey the laws our ancestors made. Edicts signed by the ruler of the Reluwyn are irrevocable."

There was a call of agreement from one of the crowd, then another, and another.

"We must protect our people!" Garesh's voice rose with the emotion in the room. "We are Reluwyn! Surely, my Lord Prince, as the son of a Reluwyn King and Queen, you understand the need for this action. My gathering of troops is just a sign of my loyalty to the cause, to our people."

The mention of his mother was a warning shot. Garesh wasn't afraid to expose to the Reluwyn people their Shapeshifting King. Suddenly the High Councillor's fascination with power was so clear. Trevisian had let this happen with his lack of interest. He had not taken responsibility so Garesh had, and with it he'd taken all the power he'd wanted.

He looked about and saw the feeling in the room rise. Councillors were beginning to cry out Reluwyn chants. Garesh was doing this on purpose. Trevisian saw a gleam as the Councillor caught eyes with him. He was waiting until the crowd was wild for blood. Then he would sacrifice their Prince upon the altar of their racial loyalty.

A man came up and whispered something into Garesh's ear. The dark smile on the High Councillor's face turned impossibly darker.

He raised his hands to quiet the crowd. "My Lord Prince, I have heard disturbing reports that you are gathering troops in the palace through your dog-blooded Radichi warrior. What are we to think?" He raised his hands, beckoning the shouting to rise again and then again dropping his hands so that he might be heard. He was drinking in the power, his intoxication evident. "Are you planning to break our ways, our ancestor's laws, by force?"

A cry like a pack of dogs came out of the crowd who looked to their Prince for his answer. He was losing them.

"Your massacre of the Laowyn includes the murder of my wife." He could not let Kiara meet with the same fate as his mother.

The statement caused a break in the shouts. Many faces changed to a look of fear.

"I ask for the suspension of the Edict as the full King of Emrilion."

His second call might have fallen on fertile ground. But now he was threatened, Garesh let loose the missile.

"A rebel Laowyn woman who would be *our* Queen?" His voice was despising. "And reports circulate of you, King," he omitted the correct address of *Lord King*, an outrageous sign of disrespect. "That you have the same blood as your mother. I have held my tongue thus far under duress from our sovereign, but I can no longer protect one unprotected by the laws of King Emril, Conqueror, King of the Emrilion Empire." Garesh's hands rose with the voices and he pointed a menacing finger, all eyes following the line it made. "I must confirm what I know to be true," his eyes took on an inhuman fury as he hissed. "*Shapeshifter!*"

Chaos erupted in the hall. Trevisian knew he would be taken in minutes - and he'd be lucky to reach the prison in one piece. It was then that Johan arrived.

A barrage of Imperial Guards threw open the doors to the Hall of Banners, the sound of wood on stone cracking throughout the hall. Horses clattered into a place they should not be, and soldiers dropped lances in councillors' faces.

"To the King! Protect the King!" Johan bellowed, his heavy horse barging several more zealous councillors out of the way before swinging its quarters and cantering towards Trevisian.

Imperial Guards pierced the crowd surrounding their sovereign, Dainus was brought forward and Trevisian mounted quickly into the saddle. He took the reins in a firm grip and looked around him; the Councillors were scattered but Garesh remained on the dais spitting curses.

"Silence!" Trevisian's voice rang out across the din. "Yes, I carry the mark of the Shapeshifters as your High Councillor says, yes I am of Alakvalto blood - but I am also your sovereign. My mother's execution was unlawful and so King Emril made it lawful - our ancestors never condemned Shifters, so consider that among your accusations. And consider this, your future Queen is in danger, she lies with the rest of the Laowyn in Ishtalia at the mercy of those who would obey an Edict which should never have been signed. Rally with me, save your Queen, save the unity of the Kingdom. Or else stay with this dog whose lust for power would see us forsake our ancestors' ways, forsake peace, even to death."

With that Trevisian turned Dainus towards the great double doors and pushed him forward into a clattering gallop. The loyal troops that Johan had gathered followed soon after, turning in unison and departing. They left the councillors to their own decisions.

A call was raised by the loyal troops to gather those still allied to the King throughout the city as they left. News spread fast and families were torn between the old Regent and this new King.

Those who were loyal could not stay any longer.

Before long, the cavalcade left the last dwellings of the city behind. It would take time for Garesh to gather his forces, and by then they would be halfway across the Great Forest. Behind lay a fractured Kingdom, ahead the unknown - and somewhere was his wife.

⊙⊙⊙

Her blond curls were pushed over one shoulder, exposing her neck to the sun's warmth. She watched sunlight dance and jump on the water threading between her toes and over the arches of her feet. They were numb but she kept them in the water anyway, feeling the cold water slicing at her ankles. A breeze that tumbled over the surface of the stream swept up, pushing the hair from her face in a caress that drew on the wells of her memory. The shadowy figure in her mind drew in and out of focus pushing for recognition. She battled against the intruder but her attempts faltered. Dark eyes watched her through her memories - they had since the night she had left him a week ago.

She had not spoken much. No one had asked questions. They daren't. Laowyn modesty made them fear to ask and she knew it by the way they looked at her. Zephenesh had been watching her on their journey as he was now during their break by the stream.

Calev and Jaik were off snaring rabbits for dinner, bickering as they always did, and Zeb was grinding herbs, crouching by the horses they had bartered their trading cargo for on the outskirts of Emril City. Djeck tried to talk with Zephenesh, but the Elder remained stonily silent.

Fidel was on the bank of the stream a few paces away. He hadn't really spoken to her, and perhaps he was wondering as the others did, if she had become a Reluwyn whore. She picked a foot out of the water and smashed it through the liquid surface. Diamond drops showered the long tunic she wore.

She bit back a curse as the water seeped through to her legs. If she had been wearing her Reluwyn clothing, she would have been able to let it dry on her bare skin. She stood up in the water, the loose cloth falling into the depths of the stream. The riverbed was hard and rocky under her feet and she felt the water on her clothes pulling at her. She stood there, feeling the rhythmic movement, then suddenly bent down and yanked the bottom of her dress from the stream, the water pouring from the fabric in great rivulets. She turned, one bare foot reaching the dusty bank and then the other. Dirt stuck to her skin and the trail of her tunic turned brown before she reached the horses. She ignored the others who stared at her as she wrestled with the saddle bags.

The leather strap was tough, and by the time it gave way there were unwanted tears rimming her eyes. She yanked at it, throwing back the canvas lid and automatically moved out of the way of the beast's side as it fidgeted at the disturbance.

"Kiara, what is it you want? I'm sure Djeck can find it for you."

She ignored her uncle but when he said her name again she looked at him, her eyes cold and unreadable.

"What is it you want?"

He didn't know what he was asking. She didn't know what she would say if she answered truthfully.

She took the dress and cloak she had escaped the palace in, and walked away from the travellers to find some kind of shielding. It didn't take her long to change, and when she had, she felt free. She wrapped the cloak about her shoulders. At least it would provide a little modesty for them, but in truth, she was past caring. When she came back she threw the tunic back in the saddlebag and closed the lid, her hands steadier, her breathing calmer.

"Kiara, what's wrong with your tunic?" Zephenesh was by her side again. She felt her lungs constrict. She couldn't breathe while he was around. He didn't understand. He couldn't.

She ignored him again but this time his hand took hold of her arm stopping her escape.

"Kiara, why must you wear that? It's inappropriate."

Her eyes were ice. "According to you."

"According to our people, Kiara."

"I must hide myself for the men's sake? I must wear clothes that will not let me move, or fight, or defend myself? Are we not going into battle uncle? I may wear armour, but underneath it I will wear this. You can't stop me."

"Kiara," the first ray of bright anger broke through his passive front. "You are like a daughter to me." His voice became gentle. "Please redress."

Kiara looked around her. Fidel was watching from the river bank, although he tried to hide it; Zeb was staring openly at them; Djeck peered from behind a horse. They were all looking at her.

She freed her arm from her uncle's grasp. "I'm not your child any longer uncle. You would not protect me when I needed it," her voice cracked.

Zephenesh coloured deeply, his face crumbling at her words. He tried to come closer but she only stepped back in reply. The twins, who were approaching them, stopped. Their usually quick tongues held captive at this moment.

"You can't tell me what to do any more." She turned to hide the tears welling up again.

CHAPTER 23

"For what it's worth, I like the dress." Zeb's face was deadpan while he crunched on his apple.

Kiara couldn't help giving him a sideways look as they rode through the eastern end of the Great Forest. They'd fallen behind the rest of the group some time ago. Kiara finally able to relax a little.

He shrugged, acknowledging her look but not meeting her eyes. "The Laowyn grasp of the Great Spirit and Spirit Realm is exceptional, but their cultural rules encourage ignorance of other races." He huffed a little. "For a peaceful race they spend very little time trying to create relationships with others. It would go far in unifying this land."

"Are you saying dressing like this promotes peace?" She fell into talking to him without thinking about it. It was easy with Zeb - there was no judgment.

"Well that's a rather crude translation, perhaps."

She pulled the cloak she was wearing further around her legs and tucked it in. The air had become cooler over the past few hours.

Zeb drew a piece of jewellery from a pocket and held it out to her wordlessly.

"My necklace!" she exclaimed, reaching a hand out towards the dangling gold.

"It dropped when the Prince took you in the woods."

She nodded, her thoughts clouding with memories. The man who had taken her was a King now. "You know I thought you might be dead."

"Death wouldn't suit me."

The frown on her brow was broken for a moment before reforming.

"What happened in the forest?"

"I was knocked unconscious."

She nodded and they carried on in silence for a time before she spoke again.

"You haven't asked me what happened in the forest."

"No." Zeb turned his eyes upon her. The lines on his face were deeper than she remembered. His long hair was loosely tied at the nape of his neck and his clothes looked dirty and travel-worn. "I haven't."

Kiara sighed. "What happened after I left?" She avoided the question he still didn't ask.

He turned his eyes back to the wide forest road. "Your uncle arrived. We decided to set off for Emril city to see what persuasion you could use upon the Prince."

"Persuasion?"

"Ikara didn't want us to go," Zeb ignored the defensive tone in her voice. "But Fidel insisted. Your uncle wanted to come – to save you." He would have carried on but she interrupted him by snorting. "I'm only answering your question." The reprimand was softly spoken and gently meant.

"And he's the one who cannot even look at me in this clothing."

"The problem with the history of this Kingdom, is that different races are afraid of integrating with each other"

"My people have forbidden it."

"Your people are afraid. The Spirit promotes good, He promotes peace - not evil. There is a difference between mixing the good between races and mixing the evil."

"You know a lot of this?"

Zeb shrugged, his face solemn.

"There won't be a peaceful resolution."

"You think you failed, but you have not said what happened."

"It doesn't matter." But it did. The weight of what happened rested heavily upon her, tugging at her chest, a deep, unforgiving ache within her. If she gave voice to it, if she acknowledged the whole truth, it might fracture her in two. "The Prince refused his help. That is all anyone needs to know."

The conversation was at an end then. They rode on, but silence reigned between them. They had been following the stream westwards for some time when it meandered across their paths turning south bringing the group together again. Zeb explained in his off-hand manner, to no one in particular, that it would be tracking south to join the other tributaries of Lake Radial at Emrilion's heart.

Kiara liked the sound of Zeb's voice - it was quiet and steady. He was clearly more knowledgeable than he let on, but he allowed small pieces of information to trickle through from time to time. If she hadn't been so preoccupied she would have asked him about Lake Radial, about the Chieftain Lands and the Southern Forest.

At the edge of the stream, they crossed two at a time through the least rocky part, the horses protesting as they splashed through the cold water. Zeb had gone first with the others, leaving Kiara to cross beside Fidel. They were the last to cross and Kiara's horse, a sturdy little brown gelding, tripped on a loose stone on the streambed.

Lurching forward, the horse's forelegs scrambled to gain purchase. Kiara was taken by surprise, slipping sideways.

A large, heavy hand caught her ankle just before she would have fallen off completely. It held her steady long enough for her to right herself, her little gelding swinging back up and stepping out of the stream with zeal.

"Thank you." She reached the bank, catching her breath back. She saw her rescuer avert his eyes. Her smile disappeared.

"Have no fear, Fidel, it is not the leg of a whore you've touched."

He looked up suddenly, startled by her bitter words. The others had already disappeared behind the trees. He looked back to her, his soft brown eyes falling on hard ice.

"I had no such fear."

"Did you not?" He saw the shadows darkening beneath her tired eyes. "For I am sure that's why you all look at me like that – wondering if I'm the Rcluwyn harlot you all fear I have become."

Fidel relaxed visibly. The furrow in his brow smoothed and the set of his large jaw firmed.

"I would not assume anything about you - I have no idea what you have been through since you were taken." He pushed his horse on until they rode abreast around the trees and on to the track again The others remained just out of earshot. "I can see that whatever it was gnaws at you."

She shot a sharp look at him but he just shrugged in response.

"Maybe you should talk to someone about it."

Her jaw clenched. "It won't be understood."

Fidel did not argue - he had grown used to this behaviour from women.

"Why did you insist on coming to find me?" Her mind ran over what would have happened if they had not come. Would she have heard about the Edict condemning her race? Would she have known before it had happened? What if she hadn't, what if she had been kept safe by Trevisian as he promised? Would she ever have forgiven herself for being blinded by her feelings for him? It didn't matter. Her sight had been restored. "Did you hold that much faith in me?" She wouldn't have, not if she could have read her own heart as someone else. She had made a decision but the breadth between that choice and another had been as fine as a strand of silk.

"My faith is in the Great Spirit. Your presence at the palace was His doing."

A pained smile twisted her mouth. Afterall, what good had it done? The curse upon her people had not been broken. The only object that had been broken lay within her chest, and it still lay there, in sharp jagged pieces that dug in as she moved, as she carried on, as she continued to live. She shifted in the saddle, her legs and backside aching from the journey. She did not want to talk about the Great Spirit anymore. Before Fidel could speak again, as she was sure he intended, she cut in.

"You disobeyed your Commander. Will you be in trouble?"

She watched a shadow pass over his face.

"I am no longer a Captain in the Resistance."

Kiara felt the stirring of feelings in her numb depths as she registered his words. "Why?"

"Perhaps." Fidel turned his head towards her, his eyes catching hers and surprising her with the pain they so clearly held. "You will not understand either." His open, handsome face broke into a forced smile. "Maybe we shall have to not understand each other together."

She turned back to the forest road ahead, her eyes tracing the pattern of a falling leaf.

"Autumn is coming," said Fidel, following the same leaf's descent and then casting his eyes upwards through the thick canopy above them. "We'll see the first of the rains today."

She saw for the first time the heavy thunderheads that had rolled in over the forest canopy, and heard a light pattering on the canopy above. A heavy drop of rain fell on her hand, the next on her head. She pulled up the hood of her cloak. The leaves dipped with the increasing weight, water spilling to the forest floor. Emrilion's seasons were changing: the weather had already turned.

ooo

"I've been watching her. She grieves you know."

Fidel turned to Zeb, a little surprised by the honour of the monosyllabic elf starting a conversation with him.

"She has not told me what about."

"Do not panic yourself." Zeb almost smiled. "She tells me she thinks of her friend who died. It is not the whole story."

Zeb picked up the spoon that rested in the cooking pot and stirred the bubbling mixture of vegetables and rabbit. He pulled a dagger from his boot and stabbed a piece of meat watching the steam rise from it in the night air before eating.

They were enjoying a brief respite from the rain, enough time to get warm food in their stomachs. They had passed by a small community as they had come out of the forest. Zeb had spoken to the owner of a small, run-down inn, and the bearded man had told him that previous travellers knew of a Reluwyn force moving west. They were a day, maybe two, behind Zeb and the others. They couldn't afford any long breaks.

"Do you think the Prince and his councillors have sent out the army to aid the Edict?"

Zeb chewed for a while before answering, his eyes never stirring from the restless form of Kiara. In sleep she was haunted as in wakefulness, her body twitched and small murmurs escaped her. Zeb swallowed, the warm meat tracking heat down his chest to his stomach, he looked at Fidel, the firelight making his eyes seem bright, almost feverish.

"I think the Prince has sent his troops out to find *her.*"

They both stopped talking when Zephenesh and Djeck came over to fill their bowls with stew. When they were safely over the other side of the fire again, Zeb resumed the conversation.

"Kiara does not blush when she sees the bare chest of a man," he said it simply, as though it wasn't abnormal to discuss such things. Fidel and the twins had removed their shirts and coats to dry them by the fire after they had been soaked. Zephenesh and Djeck had changed discreetly elsewhere. Only Zeb had continued wearing his wet clothes - and no one questioned the elf's choice. "And she wears the same look on her face as you do on yours. The look of someone who's love is out of reach."

"Zeb!" Fidel's harsh whisper was not enough to attract the attention of the others. "You shouldn't spread such rumours. Do not compound what we have no evidence for."

Zeb's eyes suddenly turned cold, his face implacable. "I did not call her a whore." His teeth ground together and a muscle in his jaw jerked. When he saw a widening of Fidel's eyes he relented. "And I do not spread rumours. Do you not think I tell you because I trust you?"

Fidel leant back on a tree stump in exasperation.

"I have no idea what you *think* Zeb."

The corners of the elf's eyes creased. It was the closest he came to smiling. Fidel knew that after spending the last few years with him.

"I think you love Ikara. I think that woman," he nodded to Kiara, "loves someone at the palace, I think she loves the Prince. Do you not see? If she does we may still have a chance to avoid this war? If he is coming after her, there is hope."

"We don't know that."

The elf shrugged and then lay down beside the fire as if that ended the conversation. He closed his eyes, his clothes steaming beside the heat, and fell asleep in seconds.

Fidel rested his head on the top of the tree-trunk, ignoring the hardness against his skull. He caught sight of a lone star throwing its icy light rebelliously down through a tiny gap in the still heavy clouds.

He thought of Ikara then. He had failed in his mission - a mission he had believed in enough to give over his sword. What would she say when he returned? She would not say anything. Anyway, he was not going to go back to claim his sword - the Spirit must have a plan, some way to lessen the blood that would be spilled, a way to save His people.

He turned his head and watched the restless sleep of Kiara. Maybe she *was* in love. Was that why she did not believe that anyone would understand? If it was true, she was in love with a Reluwyn —no Laowyn would accept that easily. Zeb's words, *she grieves you know*, circled in Fidel's mind. He had thought she had suffered abuse at the hands of the Reluwyn, that she carried shame for something she could not have controlled - but perhaps that shame was because of something else.

"I'll take first watch, Fidel." Calev rested a hand on the ex-Captain's shoulder making him jump a little.

"I didn't even realise you weren't here with us."

Calev grinned "I'd make a good spy I reckon." He winked. "We've been out scouting. Jaik's still at it. Sleep." He rested a hand on the low bow of a tree and swung himself nimbly up into the branches. "I'll wake you all in half an hour."

"Not an hour?"

Calev shook his head, his face solemn. "Jaik's positioned himself further east. He'll alert us when we need to move off. We passed a band of Meir Elves on one of the forest roads north of here, they've heard talk of an army moving our way."

Fidel nodded and closed his eyes against that lone star that continued to glare down at them. The Meir Elves had also been persecuted and it was no wonder they were moving away from the advancing Reluwyn army. His mind became drowsy but it still travelled slowly over his thoughts.

What if Zeb was right about Kiara? What if the army was coming for her? More importantly, it was only three days until the rest of the nation would rise up against the Laowyn and suppress them on behalf of their Reluwyn ruler. They needed to get back.

●●●

This was the first Kiara had seen of Ishtalia. She knew her parents had died here, but Zephenesh had never seen fit to bring her. The travellers left the forest behind yesterday evening and camped out on the plain which would lead to the final hills of the western coastline.

She couldn't even see the sea yet. Ishtalia was built upon a large outcrop of rocks and rose up high above the way they had been travelling for the last day and a half. She had watched the city grow as they drew closer, and now the tall white turrets soared above them into the heavens, high enough to spear the clouds. She knew from stories that Ishtalia had a large port on its western side. That was how the Reluwyn had won, by surrounding them land and sea. The Laowyn had been in control of the Western Sea for decades and the Reluwyn had allied with the peoples of the Western Isle, which lay off the coast to the west of the Tao desert in the south, to surround the final Laowyn stronghold. Perhaps it was those same sailors who were sailing across the globe to the supposed lands across the Western Sea, the ones Trevisian had told her about in the library. She shook her head, the hood of her cloak falling down to her shoulders.

The rain that had dogged their every step since that day in the forest had only let up for the last hour. Down on the plain there was a gathering warmth, oppressive and sticky. Kiara undid the clasp of her cloak and bundled the material into a saddle-bag. She heard Zephenesh making a disapproving noise and looked across, catching his eyes just before he averted them.

"The heat will abate when we climb into Ishtalia. The wind coming off the sea runs through the streets."

"Good," Kiara said. She noticed that Fidel could look at her without turning away now. "You've been here before then? I thought the others left from the forest base."

"They did, I joined them later."

A fine brow rose. She allowed her horse more rein as it negotiated the uneven tufted grass of the plains.

"You decided later."

"I wasn't sure it was the right decision at first."

She pushed a strand of hair off her face, drops of perspiration bordering her hairline. "But you did eventually. Did that right decision cost you your Captainship?"

"Yes."

She watched a muscle contract in his square jaw.

"Do you blame me for failing you?"

He turned to look at her, his eyes gentle.

"You don't know you've failed yet."

She laughed bitterly. "I overheard the report you tried to hide from me at the inn. The Reluwyn army have marched out of Emril City. I don't know why you all assume I am too fragile for the truth."

"Are you not?"

Her expression became earnest. "Not anymore." She turned her eyes back to the track. She had come to a decision last night, she would not allow her blindness to stop her from helping her people again. Isn't that why she had protected those children from the Reluwyn patrol who would have taken them as slaves? Isn't that why she had started to attack the Imperial coaches that carried Reluwyn Edicts? She decided to change the subject. "Aren't you worried about what the Commander will say when you return?"

"What makes you say that?"

"You were close. I saw it when I was at the base in the forest. Are you?" It was easy to talk about someone other than herself. Since he had saved her from her fall in the forest she had talked to him more than the others. He didn't have the same darkness about him that Zeb did.

"Not worried." His shoulders were broad and his height considerable, even on that huge beast he was riding. "It's just I didn't leave...on the best of terms."

"We need to push on if we are to get there before nightfall!" Zeb called, cantering a circle around the other two, making their horses throw their heads up in protest.

"I think the elf wants to race!" shouted Jaik, his little pony snorting as he gathered his reins. "Don't you Calev?"

"I think that's exactly what he's after."

"Are you crazy? On this terrain?" Fidel cautioned, reining his huge horse back a little, checking the energy that was building up in the creature.

"The track over there looks flat enough – haven't you seen the sure foot of a Laowyn pony before?"

Not many Laowyn in the forest had ponies or horses. Kiara had only learned to ride because Zephenesh had taken her to the edge of the plains when she was young. She had never been far enough in to see Ishtalia, but she had learned to ride on this ground.

"I never said anything about a race."

"Ah, Zeb," Jaik, his grin twice the size of his brother's, circled next to the elf and punched Zeb's arm playfully. "Forgetting what you've said in your old age?"

The elf's grey eyes narrowed. "You want a race?"

"Oh, by the Great Spirit!" Fidel rolled his eyes.

"The first home gets Ria's stew!" Jaik called.

"That'll be me then!" Calev tore after his brother, whose smaller pony had already bounded over the tufts and onto the dirt track which threaded its way through the grassland.

The others followed at their own pace once they reached the track, and before long, the party was cantering past the outer markers of the old city, the shadow of the broken towers welcoming them home.

CHAPTER 24

She was refusing to look at him although they had been in the same vicinity for some minutes waiting for food.

"Smells delicious," Fidel said, his face breaking into a broad smile as he saw Ria. Her warm rosy face had been bent over a second pot which she was stirring and smelling when she looked up. Her eyes lit the minute she saw him.

"Fidel!" She cried, dropping the spoon and splashing the stew over her apron. She threw her arms open and disappeared into him as he hugged her. He caught sight of the ice-white eyes that had begun to watch them.

"Oh, you scoundrel! I have missed you and you left without so much as a word." She swatted him in rebuke. As she did so she took in the lack of uniform. His forest garb - the Laowyn Resistance camouflage - was replaced by leather breeches, a jerkin, and a worn beige shirt. He had picked them up near Emril City and now they were his only clothes. The only part of his former clothing he had kept was the Laowyn sigil, which was fastened to the breast of his jerkin.

"I see you have become a civilian," Ria's soft brown eyes drifted over to where Ikara stood conversing with Hendra.

"A civilian who will still fights with the rest in two days' time."

Ria nodded, her face thoughtful for a few moments before she smiled again, breaking the spell. "Well, you must eat then! It has been a full-time job cooking for this many people - have you heard? Many of the Meir elves are on their way to us."

As she spoke, the sound of a horn echoed across the crowds in the old square. Fidel saw Ikara and Hendra look up and immediately make their way up a ruined stairway to the ramparts of the city wall. He had seen that the slighted walls had been patched up while he was gone. Rubble from the streets and other parts of the city had been put in to plug the gaps, and although the wall would lack strength it was at least defensible. Perhaps Ikara was planning to defend the people from here.

"Maybe it's them," said Ria hopefully. She turned to her helpers and asked for another large cooking pot. "They'll be hungry after travelling."

"Something's wrong," Fidel replied, watching Ikara and Hendra on the wall. They had glanced over, but their expressions were anxious. Rapid words were being fired between them. The troops who stood on the wall were looking over and then at each other, their faces marked with disbelief.

"What do you mean?"

But Fidel was gone, even as Ria spoke the words. He bounded through the crowds and up the stairs two at a time. The Laowyn in the courtyard below were whispering amongst themselves, but they carried on their meal, welcoming others into the courtyard to claim their share. Children and parents sat in small circles while single men sat together and the women largely worked with the cooks in between spooning mouthfuls of stew.

Fidel turned his back on the peaceful domestic scene. He looked down from the parapets, his hands on the stones ready to steady himself as he leant over. In the distance there was a force moving in the direction of the old city. There had been something about it which had sent Ikara and Hendra into panic. He squinted at the small moving swarm and then he saw it - the glint from the light of two setting suns on armour. It disappeared for a short time, and there it was again.

"An army." He turned to Ikara who was arguing with Hendra.

"Fidel, you have no right to be up here. Get back with the civilians."

He ignored her orders, turning to Hendra. "Reluwyn?"

The old Captain nodded, "We are still amassing those able to fight, and fitting them with whatever armour and weapons we have; the repairs on the city are not yet completed. We're not ready for them, Fidel."

"This doesn't concern him." Ikara's long arms were folded across her chest and she had drawn herself up to her full height, almost equivalent to Fidel's.

"You should direct all your forces to repairs while they are still on route. We may have time to prepare the soldiers whilst they are trying to break our defences."

"I agree," replied Hendra. "But the Commander wants us to round the rest of the people up."

"It will start a panic Ikara."

"Isn't that my decision?"

"What do the Elders say?"

Hendra made a face which only Fidel could see and turned towards the wall leaving Fidel and Ikara to each other.

"What happened?" Fidel asked Ikara. It was as if a mine was set between them and both in danger of setting it off.

"I will see to the repairs." Hendra came away from the wall and began to walk past Fidel towards the stairs. He evidently held no desire to become collateral damage.

"I haven't agreed, Captain Hendra, come back here!" She tried to push past Fidel but he caught her. His hands dropped the moment he stopped her. She turned angry eyes upon him.

"Don't do that! You undermine me."

"Then let's talk over there." Fidel gestured to one of the turret guardhouses that once appeared every fifteen foot before the walls were slighted. She relented and marched towards the turret, Fidel behind her.

The inside of the turret was a bare, small circular room with arches leading out to each length of wall. On the outside and inside walls of the room were arrow loops that allowed the evening suns to penetrate the white stone with a warm glow. She rounded on him as soon as they were inside.

"You left me!" She pointed accusingly.

"Yes."

"And now? You wish to fight with me?"

"I don't know about that Ikara."

"Well," her usually steady voice was undulating in an odd rhythm. "Hendra will tell you that the Elders agree with your insanity, they refuse to act without a sign from the Great Spirit." She turned towards the plains and looked out of one of the arrow loops. Her long-fingered hands were spread out on the wall either side of the window, the muscles in her sinewy arms raised with her tension. She wore a tunic beneath her armour, and draped around her shoulders was an emerald cloak. Fidel knew it to be her father's.

"We have to know if it's His will for us to fight, that He wishes us to battle in His name."

"A Spirit who does not even talk to his people anymore?"

Fidel shrugged. "Maybe we have lost our way. Kiara feels much as you do, but she has also seen the other side. I don't know what she's been through, but her insight into our neighbours in this land makes me think we have done wrong to always view them as our enemy."

She stalked towards the other arrow loops that looked out onto the courtyard, her shoulder barging into Fidel's. "So you brought her back with you did you? The one who betrayed us for a Prince?" She already knew the answer. "I've yet to see her, but I've heard how she dresses herself these days. She has turned her back on her own people!"

Fidel's voice became firm, "You have no idea who she is or what she has done for us."

"Clearly she has brought the Reluwyn to our door before we are even prepared to defend ourselves, let alone go on the offensive. Tell me," her voice became a hiss and her eyes searched Fidel's. "Does that Reluwyn dress rule you as it does my troops?"

Fidel flinched. "I can't talk to you when you're like this."

"Then why talk to me at all?" The defensive words were immediately thrown back at him.

Why had he come up here? Because he'd wanted to know what was wrong. Because he wanted to protect his people. The decision he had made to give up his sword seemed both foolish and wise. He didn't want to fight for what was not right - but he did want to protect his people, all those women and children in the courtyard eating Ria's stew. The Elders had refused to allow offensive action unless the Great Spirit sanctioned it. Had he been right to leave his Captainship behind?

He turned to leave.

"Fidel?"

But the horns on the parapets overrode her voice.

Fidel shot back out of the guardhouse and onto the wall; Ikara was by his side now, thoughts of their argument forgotten.

"I don't believe it."

"I don't see it." She craned her neck next to Fidel's.

"They're carrying a flag of surrender."

❂❂❂

Johan's horse moved in a wide arc around the last of the cavalcade that was at the gates of Ishtalia. The small contingent of Imperial Guards, who had followed their King from the palace, had been joined by groups in Emril City and people in the lands through which they had journeyed. Now they had amassed a rag-tag gathering of Meir Elves, those Laowyn who had not yet left for the safety of Ishtalia, and a few others from elsewhere in the Kingdom. After their first night on the road to Ishtalia, Trevisian joined Johan's effort to rally people to their cause. The Kingdom was at stake, and those who lived in it were under his protection.

Now he hoped that the Laowyn had seen their flag - red, the sign of blood, of sacrifice. They would have seen the Reluwyn armour in the distance a short time ago; now all that was between them was one listless piece of fabric barely moving in the humid breeze.

As if in answer to his thoughts, the heavy gates of the old capital were drawn back and a single rider left the fortress. He looked back and saw Johan circling back around to him. The Radichi warrior reined his horse in next to Trevisian's.

"An emissary?" asked the King.

"Let's hope a peaceful one."

Trevisian's heart was racing - not just because of what he had done. His heart had soared after they had broken free of the palace with a sense of freedom he had not felt since he had been on the road alone, but now he was close to her. His dark eyes drifted up to the parapets where he saw soldiers dotted along the lengths. Was she up there?

Trevisian looked back across the crowd behind him. Reluwyn soldiers, whose names he now knew, rode behind him. Other infantry walked behind, and then the clothing lost its uniformity among the Meir Elves, Laowyn and other citizens from parts of his Kingdom he had never been - *his* Kingdom. He had never thought it before.

He looked back to the emissary. They were drawing close, the horse at a slow loping canter, the man riding holding a matching blood-red flag. In that moment, he thanked whatever spirits watched over them - those waiting behind his guards held no weapons in their hands.

The man drew up his short Laowyn pony a little way before them to prevent himself being dwarfed next to Dainus and Johan's mount. He was a stocky man, close to fifty judging from his greying beard. He wore a forest green uniform of sorts, with a Laowyn sigil on his chest. He drew the flag up, over his pony's neck and then dropped it down the other side until the tip touched the floor, bowing as he did so.

"My name is Captain Hendra of the Laowyn Resistance. We acknowledge your flag of surrender."

Johan turned to Trevisian, a slight nod passing from him to the King.

Trevisian cleared his throat. "I greet you Captain Hendra of the Laowyn." Trevisian inclined his head. "I am King Trevisian of Emrilion. I am here to fight with you against the Edict which has been wrongly cast on your people." He took the flag from the guard next to him and performed the same ceremonial gesture as the Laowyn Captain, though his bow was restricted to his head inclining.

"And you bring with you this force?" said a surprised voice.

Trevisian nodded. "There are others too, wanting protection." Trevisian handed the flag to Johan.

"My Lord King." The Laowyn Captain looked across the crowd before him, catching sight of the rag-tag mob behind. "We are indebted to you for securing a number of our people."

"And the others," Trevisian added, his eyes almost imperceptibly hardening.

"Yes, my Lord King, but forgive me for asking who we are now fighting against if you are here to lend us aid?"

Trevisian took back his reins and straightened in the saddle. "That is a conversation best held within your encampment, do you not think Captain?" The authority which rang clear from his own voice surprised him. "May I speak with those who lead you?"

"I think you're right," replied the Captain. "Leave your people here and return with me. You may bring another for council." Captain Hendra turned his pony on the spot and raised his flag again, signalling those on the parapets. A trumpet sounded and the huge gates of the city began to open.

"Follow me!" he called, setting off across the last of the plains and up the high road towards Ishtalia.

● ● ●

"Kiara!"

She tossed on the makeshift bed, beaded sweat on her brow.

"Kiara!" he called again. He was in the doorway of the small dwelling she and her uncle had claimed on the crest of the city's hill.

She mumbled, groaned and then started crying out. Her hands thrashed at the thin blanket covering her until her fingers were clawing at the dirt beneath.

Zeb's hands were clamped hard down by his side. He called her again, a last vain attempt, there was no one else here to wake her and she needed to be woken. He looked around, there were only a few stragglers on this street, the rest were gone to watch the refugees brought by the King pouring into the city. Even now the King was in the midst of a meeting with the Elders.

"Cos… Cos…" He heard her mumble. Then it became louder until she almost screamed the name. He ran to her side then, grabbing hold of her arms and holding them still.

"Kiara! Wake up!" he shouted it at her and her eyelids fluttered against the clutches of sleep.

"Coscian!"

He released one arm which had ceased thrashing and ran a hand down the side of her cheek.

"Kiara," his voice was soft, softer than it had ever been. His brow was puckered and his eyes traced the lines of her face, the arched brows, the finely tipped nose, that smooth mouth. Her eyes fluttered open then, but he didn't stop staring for a few moments.

"Zeb?" she asked, half whisper, half breathless. "Zeb?"

"Who's Coscian?" He kept his hand on her cheek, knowing this moment would only last so long.

She sat up, and his hand fell away from her face. She looked away, pulling the blanket up around herself.

"You screamed his name just now."

"It doesn't matter anymore."

He shrugged in the way he always did. Then he withdrew his eyes from her. He rose and walked back to the door, leaning against the frame, crossing his arms over his front.

"The King is here," he said it so matter-of-factly that she clearly didn't comprehend his words at first. Then her sleepy blue eyes widened and her mouth dropped open.

"Wh… what?!" her whisper was almost strangled as though those memories that had held her captive in her dreams were now wrapped around her throat.

"He waved the crimson flag of surrender. He has arrived with a contingent of Imperial Guards. They are waiting outside the walls until his true motives can be ascertained, but a band of refugees he brought with him have already entered the city walls, he negotiated their shelter half an hour ago."

She had begun shaking her head. "No, no, no…" she whispered. She stood up dizzily, but Zeb didn't go to help her. He couldn't touch her again. She started wringing her hands. "He can't be… He can't be…"

"He is." Zeb unfolded his arms. "He's meeting with the Elders as we speak; I came to fetch you."

"No!" There were tears in her eyes, tears that had never appeared over the last week as they had journeyed here. Zeb watched the first of them fall from the perfect rim of her right eye. If it were possible, she looked more beautiful when she cried.

"I doubt he will hurt you, he is here to help, but I also doubt that it's his hurting you that scares you so much."

"He's my…" She choked on the tears which were now pouring freely. "He's my husband." The words poured out of her, bursting the damns of secrecy that had left her so isolated.

Zeb felt the stab of something sharp within his chest. He grimaced against the pain and refolded his arms again. "You must come with me. He has requested your presence from the Elders. They know that you were at the palace, but they don't know more than that. I had been listening to the whole meeting from a… safe place…" Zeb avoided her eyes when he said it. It had been accepted among the Resistance that Zeb listened to most meetings and decisions that were made, but this time the Elders probably wouldn't take as kindly to his actions. "This is your chance to go before your people and explain what happened at the palace."

She shook her head.

"Kiara." Zeb ran a hand through his shoulder-length fair hair. It had come undone from the leather string that usually held it back. He felt the grease in it as he did so. He badly needed to wash but when had there been time? "In this moment, whatever happened at the palace…

between you and the King... seems like the most important thing, but you must think. Kiara, you are married, and if you love him as I think you do," the words stuck in his throat. "You need to come with me. Kiara, your people face... they face annihilation in two days."

"I know." She leant against the wall and Zeb could see the profile of her face, the gentle upturn of her nose and the deep line of shadow under her eyes. She looked as though she hadn't slept since they'd taken her from the palace. "Everyone will know."

"Whatever his reasons for allowing those refugees to join him and find sanctuary here," Zeb swallowed. "You are the reason that he set out from the palace. Whatever you said to him mattered. You matter to him."

"They'll never accept us, if there even is an 'us'."

"Maybe this is the start of something. Come on, he was already in conference with the Elders when I left."

They left the dwelling and walked toward the main courtyard of the old city, back over the spine which ran under its centre, separating the drop of the docks from the drop onto the plains to the east. Zeb stopped once to steady Kiara. Her footsteps were so erratic on the cobbled street that she was in danger of tripping at any moment. When she almost did Zeb caught up her arm, steadying her with a surprising amount of strength for his size.

"Be calm, Kiara."

The fear didn't leave her eyes but the command was something she needed to hear. She nodded and immediately slowed her walk.

When they reached the large square, there was the rumble of voices. If it had been anywhere else in the world there would have been uproar, thought Zeb, but here among the Laowyn, even their surprise was reasoned. They were surrounding the refugees who stood at the centre of the square, exactly where the King had left them. Zeb saw Ria pointing to the group and sending off volunteers with bowls of stew four at a time.

"Cutlery!" she shouted, grabbing a bunch of wooden spoons from the table and thrusting them at the nearest helper.

The newcomers accepted the bowls with murmurs of thanks, but it didn't take long for Zeb to see that the helpers were only providing food for the Laowyn newcomers and no others in the crowd. Without thinking of Kiara, he pushed through the ring of spectators to where Ria was directing operations.

"Are these ready?" he asked, gesturing at three bowls of stew that stood steaming on the side of the makeshift table.

"Oh, Zeb! Thank you, yes, take them please, here." She handed him spoons.

With one bowl resting on his forearm and the others in his hands he made his way over to the crowd. A Laowyn stretched out their hand for the bowl but he moved over to where a female Meir Elf stood half-turned away from the stares of the old city's inhabitants.

"My lady." Zeb nodded at the bowl in his right hand. "Please eat."

She didn't look up at first, but when she realised he was addressing her, a tentative hope flooded her face. Her hands came up hesitantly and then she grabbed the bowl quickly.

"Spoons are in my pocket." Zeb turned sideways so she could reach one.

She snatched one out, scooping the warm food gratefully into her mouth. She paused only once in her rapid consumption to jerk a nod of thanks at Zeb but he was already turned to the next elf, and then a trader from the mountains of Lothian.

When he turned every eye on his side of the courtyard was watching him. He looked back at them each in turn, defiantly, a fire lit in his cool, calm eyes. "Shame on a race who faces destruction that they would turn away those who face a similar fate at the hands of tyrants. What have your peaceful race become if you turn away from those who live by your side in this land? Your ignorance towards those who differ from yourselves is disgusting."

He halted his monologue and strode over to Ria again, thrusting his hand in his pocket to grab out the left-over spoons and throwing them clattering onto the table. He marched to Kiara's side and took her arm, the crowd at the northern end of the square breaking apart to make way for them.

"Are you okay Zeb?"

No, he wasn't. The hackles which had risen on the back of his neck were slow to go back down. He was sick of the in-fighting in these races. Couldn't they understand what was at stake here? It wasn't just about their own individual race, why couldn't they see that?

Laowyn were still lining the streets, but these were troops from the Resistance. They formed lines on either side of the street, reaching up to steps at the far end. The meeting hall was behind the doors at the top of the steps. From this side the façade was still intact, though without a roof, and some of the graceful beauty of the old city could be reimagined.

"Excuse me," Zeb spoke to the soldiers on the left. They would be stopped if they carried on but they needed to know what was going on in the meeting hall. More importantly he had to get Kiara to the King. If she didn't realise what her marriage meant, he certainly did.

"Aye, aye, Zeb!" One of the Laowyn Resistance called out, a cheeky tone in his voice.

Both of them turned. It was Calev. "You're a bit out of your area, aren't you?"

"Can we get to the meeting hall?"

"I think that's the point of me standing here, Zeb." Calev was stood to attention against the wall, but not even that official stance of his could stop his half grin. "I'm supposed to stop people crowding into the meeting hall. The King is in there, negotiating."

"Let's just go." Kiara pulled on Zeb's arm lightly, but now he knew the King was in there his heart was racing faster, his mind more determined.

"He's requested Kiara come. Calev you have to get us in there."

"Do I now? The Elders haven't sent any orders."

"I'll give you my portion of your sister's famous stew at dinner."

Zeb watched Calev think about it, moving his mouth and tongue as though imagining what that extra portion of food would taste like. He finally looked back at the elf.

"Done." He moved out from the line in a strict march pausing only once. "This is important, right? The Commander has not been best pleased with me and Jaik since coming back from Emril City."

"Believe me," Zeb said, guiding Kiara firmly forward. "This will change everything."

CHAPTER 25

"Before we speak of the defence of your people in two days' time, I have to first ask if someone resides within your refuge." Trevisian was stood before a makeshift table which stretched out in a crescent moon, a collection of angled pieces of wood and struts.

Some of the Elders looked to each other. The woman with white eyes, who had refused to sit at the request of the Elders, was watching him with obvious mistrust. A broad-shouldered man, almost as big as Johan, stood by her side but was not in armour. In fact, he looked as though he had just come out of a cattle shed somewhere. Trevisian wondered why he was attending this meeting - and why there was something familiar about him.

"There are no Reluwyn here." One of the Elders spoke, a man with grey streaked hair.

"I seek a Laowyn."

Johan turned towards his King, and Trevisian inclined his head.

"The man stood beside the white-eyed woman," whispered the Radichi. "He was at the palace. He was part of the group of traders who wrote the assassination warning."

"A Laowyn?" An older man, with a grey beard and shoulder-length grey hair spoke. Others turned to him as he did so. Trevisian saw looks pass between them around the table.

"Him too," whispered Johan. "If they're here, it's safe to guess that she escaped the palace with them."

"What are you saying?" The white-eyed woman stepped forward aggressively.

Trevisian doubted he had ever seen such a tall woman. Her armour was all-covering and well-made, she must be part of their military force. "Why is there any need to whisper when you are come to broker a truce with us?"

Trevisian turned dark, sardonic eyes upon her, "My friend was telling me that I owe the debt of my life to several in this room – but not to you."

She looked a little surprised by his abrupt answer but it didn't last for long. Her hard, distrustful gaze came back. "I am Ikara, daughter of Zenex, Commander of the Laowyn Resistance." A woman in charge of their forces? Surprising.

"Commander," Trevisian gave her a slight nod. "The man who stands to your right." Trevisian nodded to the fair-haired man in the jerkin. "Your name is?"

"Fidel, my Lord King."

"Don't address him as such!" The white-eyed woman hissed. "He's no King to us."

"And you." He turned to the grey-haired man who had addressed him a moment ago. "What is your name, Elder?" Trevisian used the correct address. He would show deference even if these high and mighty Laowyn would not.

"Zephenesh, my Lord King." The Elder rose slightly from the table and bowed.

He inclined his head to both the Laowyn men - Fidel first, then Zephenesh. "I am told I owe you a debt, that of my life. As does another   the woman I seek."

"Who is it that he seeks?" the Elder with grey-streaked hair spoke again, but this time to Zephenesh.

"So the offer of your arms is simply a pretext..." Zephenesh was cut short.

"It is not a pretext," Trevisian replied curtly, his patience fraying. That old man didn't deny it - she was here. His heart beat became more persistent, faster, and his patience drew thin. "But it is dependent upon her safety."

The Commander whispered to the man named Fidel.

"Now it is your turn for whispering?"

Johan put a tempering hand upon Trevisian's arm, but it would not calm the King's spirit. She was within reach

and these old fools would not let him near her. What did
they think he intended?

"Who is she to you?" It was Fidel who spoke.
Trevisian could see the Laowyn's eyes measuring him. His
face was open, waiting for an honest response. It was in
that moment that Trevisian remembered who he was. The
one Trevisian had shot in the arm back in the forest. The
one who had captured him. Now he wanted to be an ally
with Trevisian.

"The woman who you took from my palace is the
rightful Queen of Emrilion."

Whispers immediately erupted in the ruined hall. The
white-eyed woman looked to Fidel, but he was still staring
at the King in silence. Other Elders at the table were
murmuring amongst each other, a few cast their eyes in
the direction of the door, no doubt wondering who the
Queen of Emrilion was among their people. Kiara's return
from the Palace had caused a stir but no explanations had
been given by Zephenesh or the others. They wouldn't
have known what to explain. Definitely not this.

"You took her unlawfully from me, even under your
own marital laws, and I demand she be brought before
me." Trevisian's voice was fierce. "I married her in full
knowledge of her Laowyn blood. It is Garesh, my High
Councillor, who constructed the Edict against your
people, and I, in my ignorance of your position - and

thinking your people were rebelling against me - signed it. Kiara has since told me of the persecution you have suffered at Garesh's hand. For too long have I allowed my Kingdom to be ruled by another, and now is the time I wish to take it back. For the protection of my wife, I will grant permission for any Laowyn under attack in two days' time to defend themselves with equal force, and I will stand in defence of them."

"Can you not stop Garesh?" The Commander ignored the mention of the Queen.

"I cannot."

Johan stepped forward, his deep voice booming off the crumbling walls, "In standing for your people's protection before the Council, my Lord King kindled the wrath of Garesh. The High Councillor now leads an uprising against the King. This has forced us to take up arms to defend the King and the Laowyn he stood for."

"An uprising?" questioned the first Elder.

"Well I'm hardly shocked." The white-eyed woman folded her arms, a smug smile spreading across her face.

"Yes." Trevisian was not proud, but Johan had just saved him from admitting his Shapeshifting nature. It was so clear to him now that Garesh had been working against him for a long time. Ever since the High Councillor had forged his father's hand on the Regency document his sights had been consumed by power. Had Garesh always planned to turn against him? "My army and my government has been fractured. The troops outside your gates are the last loyal to my crown."

The Commander scoffed.

"You would do well to realise that I am not your enemy," Trevisian's eyes hardened. This was a waste of time if they didn't understand the urgency. "And that your gloating should wait until the Edict has run its course and we have defended ourselves against my rebellious troops and the usurper Garesh."

The Commander looked uneasy at this, turning to Fidel behind her. He touched her arm briefly and whispered something to her. She seemed irritated by whatever he said and shook her head as if to ignore it.

"Are you helping us to defend ourselves, or are we helping you regain your crown?"

"Both." There was no point in lying to these people. "But in doing so I will be indebted to your race. More than that, I will be a part of it because of my marriage, and I wish to rule for the future prosperity of the Kingdom. Our Kingdom."

"Inspiring words." It was Fidel who spoke. When Trevisian looked at him he saw no derision there, only honesty.

"And this Kiara," said the old man. "What if she was forced to marry you? Are we still to return her to you if she does not wish to be?"

Trevisian suddenly strode forward, fire ripping through his body and mind. It was only Johan's heavy hand on his arm that halted him.

"It's not the way." Johan whispered.

"She consented." Trevisian's voice was controlled but his eyes blazed. "Our truce depends on her safety - and on her return to me."

"She is not property," Fidel spoke again, those honest eyes and that deep but soft voice.

Trevisian turned on his heel and made to exit the hall. He would not be made to discuss her publically, it was between them. A deep thudding ache had settled in his chest since she had gone, and now he knew she was so close it was heavier, more painful.

He lay a hand on each of the meeting hall doors and threw his whole weight against them, sending them soaring open. He could hear Johan's steady step behind him, but his eyes barely saw anything. Until he saw her.

He stopped short and blinked, focusing on her. She was standing there, next to someone else that Trevisian barely noticed. All he saw then was her.

Her thin frame was in the same Reluwyn gown she had worn in his court; her hair was the same tangled mess of golden curls, but dark smudges shadowed her blue eyes. She had gotten as little sleep as him since they'd been apart, and now she was looking at him with those same blue eyes. She was here.

He caught the look of uncertainty in her eyes, as if she didn't know what he would do, and resolved to wipe it clean. He strode forward, suddenly certain for them both, wrapped both arms around her and pulled her forward until their lips connected. He wouldn't be letting her go again.

OOO

Ikara stood open mouthed several paces from the table. They had all seen it, just outside the doors of the meeting hall, the King and Kiara embracing. They could still see them through the open doorway, clinging to each other as if every breath depended on it. No one had expected that, least of all Ikara - this King who had seemed so fierce now buried his face in Kiara's hair, his body pressed against hers.

Before anyone could register what was going on, the King was walking down the steps outside the hall with Kiara. Ikara stepped forward. What if he had gotten everything he'd come for?

She felt a large hand enclose her forearm, but before she could turn to face Fidel, the Radichi warrior had moved into the doorway before her.

His light eyes took in their shocked faces before he spoke. "The King has laid his offer before you, and he has been reunited with his wife as he requested. He is now returning to his troops outside your walls and will await the Laowyn response there." He raised a fist over his heart and bowed his head. Ikara didn't recognise the gesture, but she understood it as a sign of respect.

The Radichi then followed after his King. Ikara could hear the Elders debating the truce, questioning the new alliance and the sanctity of the Laowyn race. Their voices descended on the hall like the buzz of swarming bees.

Fidel caught Ikara looking at him. "You knew," she said, a whisper in the midst of the storm.

"I only suspected." He drew a hand over his stubble - he'd been clean shaven when he'd left for Emril City. "It was Zeb who first guessed." Ikara took in Zeb's advancing figure.

Of course *he* knew - he was always trouble and he'd probably put Kiara up to all this. That story of him being knocked out in the woods was probably as false as Ikara had always deemed it to be. She didn't trust him at all, and yet he had helped the Resistance for a long time now. When he had turned up just over a year ago, he had treated her for an arrow wound - now she carried a silver scar on her arm just like the one Kiara bore on her thigh. But that kind of charity didn't make the questions surrounding Zeb disappear. She knew he had a past, and somewhere in that past was a woman he had loved, a woman who was dead.

"Zeb." She turned, folding her arms across her breastplate and looking down at the elf.

"Commander," he inclined his head. "Fidel." There was the shadow of a smile on his face when he spoke to Fidel. They had never been close, but that movement was the closest Zeb would get to proclaiming friendship. When had that happened?

"It seems that we can look forward to a marriage truce between your people and the Reluwyn?"

Ikara snorted. "Do you seriously believe that?"

Zeb raised an eyebrow questioningly, and she felt a check in her mind at that look.

"Are you *seriously* going to let your prejudice prevent your people from forming a lasting, equal peace with the Reluwyn?"

She didn't have anything to say to that.

"Is it possible?" asked Fidel.

"It depends." Zeb waved a lazy hand over at the Elders who were still immersed in discussion. "Will your Elders allow the reconciliation?"

"Reconciliation? Do you even think Kiara wants that?"

"She looked pretty happy to me." The corners of Fidel's mouth curled up slightly, and Ikara watched those lips for a second. She shook herself.

"Can't you see love when it's in front of you, Commander?" Ikara saw an almost imperceptible slump take over his shoulders. "Did Kiara speak to you?" Fidel turned to Zeb.

"Yes." The elf sighed. "Kiara just made an incredibly brave decision that will lift her up to derision on every front, but her act of courage will be of no value if the Elders don't make their minds up soon. We have to prepare for an attack."

Ikara felt an irritating chaffing at the statement. Maybe Kiara was brave, but she was also stupid. She had just put herself completely in the power of another.

"She has given everything of herself away all at the same time."

"You don't know her." Zeb shot back with a hiss. "She has sacrificed everything for her people, and it's time they stopped judging her for supposed crimes and started thanking her for single-handedly bringing about the best ally the Laowyn Resistance could have ever asked for." He left the words hanging as he stalked away.

Fidel was scratching his beard again. "Falling in love is not something to be controlled Ikara, you know that."

The words hung between them for a moment like fuel above a fire. Ikara felt the heat sweep through her body. She was always in control — there were responsibilities.

"I want to say one more thing before I leave you. You asked me what the Great Spirit had done to save His people, didn't you?" He continued without waiting for her answer. "Do you not think that the King falling in love with one of our people is some kind of miracle?" He gave a slight shake of his head as if throwing off a spell and went towards the door.

Ikara watched him speak to Zeb who had paused in the doorway. When Zeb responded with his usual deadpan expression, Fidel gave a broad smile. She couldn't remember the last time she had seen that smile. He shouldered against the elf, and then they fell in step beside each other leaving the hall.

"She's gone," Zephenesh was behind her. "We must take the truce - perhaps the Great Spirit did not want us to fight before, until this could happen, now he has provided an army. We must ally with the King."

Ikara glanced between Zephenesh's anxious eyes and the Elders.

"Yes," she nodded slowly, hardly believing she was saying the words. "We must ally with the King."

CHAPTER 26

"There's something you should know."

They had been sat in silence for some time, Trevisian reclining on an old abandoned bed, Kiara resting against him. Both of them were looking out of the wide broken window over the western slope of Ishtalia down to the docks and over the sea. They had spoken already the few words that explained everything, only the words that mattered. Outside, the two suns were setting over the sea.

Kiara and Trevisian had been afforded these apartments when the alliance had been accepted. It wasn't much, but it was the best the Laowyn could offer for the King and future Queen. Would she reign as Queen? If they didn't make it through tomorrow when the Edict was enacted she never would and Trevisian would die a young King barely having reigned.

She could feel the strong and steady rise of his chest beneath her, one hand was twisted in her hair, the other resting on her stomach.

"What is it?"

"Garesh didn't just use the Laowyn's supposed rebellion to turn the court against me."

The fingers she had been lightly tracing over his hand on her stomach stilled.

"Do you know anything about my mother?" he asked.

They had already talked about her parents. Kiara knew they had died here in Ishtalia, and that from this city her parents bodies had been sent to sea, Zephenesh had told her that long ago. It was not until Zephenesh had requested to see her earlier today that they had spoken of it, although he hadn't known quite what to say.

They had spoken quietly, sitting on the docks, running over the past months and years. He had described her mother for the first time, of how like her Kiara was in her boldness, and how much that had scared Zephenesh when she was growing up. He had not condoned her behaviour, and she doubted that he ever would, but had felt a change in the Great Spirit since she had been united with the King. Something was different now the Elders had met and decided in favour of battle. The Great Spirit would be with them, and if he was, perhaps there would be a sign as in the days of old, when the Enspers had shown the Spirit's favour. When Zephenesh spoke this way, Kiara listened, but the underlying pain of his betrayal had not yet been abated.

After they had left each other, silence no longer separating them but nothing really resolved, Kiara had returned to Trevisian. She told him briefly about her mother and father, showing him the necklace. She explained to him that the sword he had taken from her at the palace was her father's. He had given it to her then. Now it was Trevisian's turn.

"She was Queen of Emrilion." The steady rise of Trevisian's chest became unpredictable beneath her. "Her crime was Shapeshifting. She was executed when I was very young and I remember very little of her. She told me…" Trevisian trailed off, shifting his weight on the bed.

Kiara put a hand gently over one of his, the tense knuckles hard beneath her palm. He took a breath, ready to start again.

"My mother told me that Shapeshifting is an ability that can be passed on to another."

Kiara's mind was working twice as fast to catch up with what he was saying to her.

"I've heard stories but…" she trailed off.

"The Reluwyn do not speak of it, and my father…" again he paused before continuing. "He was infatuated with power. Power over his race, over others, over his family. You argue for Reluwyn barbarity, and that is what my father was, barbaric."

Barbaric. That *is* what she had argued about with Trevisian since she had met him, before she had known who he really was. King Emril was barbaric. Kiara's mind skipped like a stone over the waters of her memories, back to the palace, back to the library, back to the game they had played of questions and answers. His words had been *the Reluwyn are a barbaric race*. The question had been, *have you ever been beaten?*

Her hand tightened over his, clasping the long fingers and wide palm.

"He hated anyone who threatened his power, and my mother was from an ancient line of Reluwyn known for magic. When your race speak of the Great Spirit, our race speaks of magic, and my mother could shift into animal form. The Reluwyn used to fear and revere those who were gifted, but my mother's influence surpassed my father's as she mastered her gift."

He paused, his hand turning under hers and his fingers tracing over her palm.

"I saw her once, shifted, into the form of a horse. I don't remember much of what happened, only that afterwards things changed in the palace. My father would no longer see my mother, and whenever I was with her there were always eyes watching us. One day she was gone, and I was told later that for the crimes of shifting, a practice now outlawed by my father, she had been executed."

"You inherited this ability?"

"The phoenix tattoo on my back is the tribal mark of my mother's line. I was given it a few months before her death to show the gift that runs in my blood."

"Have you ever shifted?"

"Yes," again he said it so simply, as if it were nothing, nothing to discuss, nothing to think about. "I believed that Garesh saved my life when he made me promise never to use my ability within the palace walls."

Kiara remembered the times he had escaped the palace.

"I used to run away just so I could be…" he struggled for the right words. "Myself. I never wanted to be King, but if the reins of power are to be left in the hands of evil, I cannot be content."

Kiara slipped from the bed and padded barefoot to the window. A fresh sea breeze pushed up from the docks, through the window and ruffled her hair. "Would you have let my people die if it had meant your safety?"

"Maybe."

His honesty sent a chill through her. She shivered, hugging herself against the night air.

"But you wouldn't have let me die?"

She could hear him rise from the bed. A few

moments later his hands came to rest on her arms and he drew her back against himself. "I didn't come for them, Kiara, I came for you and I'm staying for you."

"What's it like – changing?" She could feel his breath against her hair, feel his heart beating against her back.

"It's like... freedom. In every fibre of your being."

Kiara wanted to see him change. It all seemed too incredible, too unbelievable. She had heard the stories, as everyone had, of Shifters, those who shifted between human and animal forms.

"Alakvalto, that's the name of my mother's family."

"Alakvalto." Kiara rolled the Reluwyn name round in her mouth. "Alakvalto."

"I like it better when you say it." Trevisian turn her around in his arms, laying his lips on hers, drawing her close.

She drew away from him. "So I am Kiara Alakvalto?"

"If you wish." He kissed her again. "If..." he looked almost shy for a moment, all fierceness fallen from his face. "If you'll still take me, Shapeshifter that I am?"

She wondered at him. The King who had ruled an entire Empire up until a few days ago. A man who had legions to fight for him. A fierce fighter himself. A Shapeshifter who could take any animal form. It was all brought to naught with one question.

"Yes." She reached up, threading her fingers in his

hair.

He pushed against her until her back was pressing on the wall. He leant into her, his hands becoming forceful on her arms, his mouth hungry, his eyes possessed by her. He pulled away from her for a second. "You've enchanted me."

She chuckled against his mouth as he kissed her again. He moved to her neck when her mouth continued to be rebellious.

"Do you know what I was thinking?" he said between kisses.

"What?" Her breath was catching in her throat as she felt each fluttering of lips lightly against her skin.

"That those Edicts we sent out with the riders are just like those you sabotaged months ago." Another kiss. "I would have stopped them for money, you for the paperwork, and now I am the one sending them." The new Edicts, hastily drafted on what paper they could find within Ishtalia, were proclamations allowing the Laowyn to defend themselves against aggressors. It was the best that Trevisian could do without the ability to revoke the previous Edict. The Laowyn could legally defend themselves.

Kiara's laugh was husky against his neck.

"I love the way your laugh sounds." Another kiss.

"When we go out and fight together, I hope Fidel gets

reinstated as Captain. The Commander was refusing to do it."

"Who told you that?" Trevisian came away a little, his amorous efforts apparently unable to deter his wife from her unromantic line of thought.

"Zeb."

"I don't like that elf."

"You don't like most people." It was true, he had been grumbling about almost all of the people he had met and those within his own troops all day.

"He looks at you, you know."

Kiara did know. She knew exactly what he meant. If another woman looked at the King in the same way she might be jealous.

"We have been through a lot together. He helped me escape my fate when the Laowyn captured me. It was more than my uncle did."

Trevisian shrugged off her words, becoming more distant.

"I do not like the Commander."

"I know, you told me."

His shot a challenging look at her.

"The tall one, Fidel, is a good shot. He should fight tomorrow." There was a sardonic smile that appeared across his mouth. Kiara wondered what was triggering it. "You should not." The words brought her up short.

"What do you mean?"

"You know what I mean." The stubborness was suddenly back in his face like a wildfire spreading rapidly over his features. "You shall not fight."

"Do not think that because I am some kind of royal woman that I shall not fight. I know as well as you that the Reluwyn respect female fighters."

The knowing comment saw a gentler look war with the angry one on his face. Apparently unable to decide on a response he gave none.

"I shall fight alongside my people and yours."

He sighed. "I wish you would not."

"I cannot sit and wait."

"I cannot have you fight. If they break into the city, you must run to the docks - they have been making rafts all day for escape. You will have your father's sword, and this," he pulled back his sleeve and began untying the leather straps of a small sheath. She could see a small horn-handled dagger encased within it.

"Give me your arm."

She obeyed his demand, raising her left arm for him to tie the sheath to.

He tugged her gently towards him, as if in compromise to his earlier zeal. "I don't wish to spend tonight talking of serious things." He pulled her into his arms.

"Neither do I," she answered with a kiss.

CHAPTER 27

Sheets of rain fell across the plain, the pale layers obscuring Garesh's forces from usual visibility. Calev and Jaik had been sent out with several Reluwyn scouts. They had spied the hostile army in the early hours of the morning; now they were halfway across the valley and were halted, holding their line.

The battlefield was eerily still and silent as Ikara's piercing eyes swept across the opposing army. They outnumbered the loyal forces three to one, but the Resistance force which had left Ishtalia's walls to meet the enemy was only half of the whole, the rest remaining within the city. They would be faced by a sea of enemies, a sea which was only paused between advancing waves, a sea which she would be commanding her troops to hold back.

She rode forward to meet the enemy commanders with the King and his Radichi warrior to her right, and the Laowyn Elders on her left. Fine droplets of rain collected in the angular plains of her face and ran in rivulets making her shiver.

She couldn't help glancing back at her troops. The Laowyn and Reluwyn warriors stood in perfect unity through the ranks, just as if they had always fought alongside each other. The green of the Laowyn tunics was visible around breastplates on all the soldiers. When Ikara turned back she saw lines of crimson before her, stained much darker by the rain. As they drew near, and the rain became heavier, the droplets made tiny singing sounds as they fell on the armour of the motionless enemy soldiers. All looked ahead, mouths firmly shut, eyes wide open.

The centre of the field was quickly gained and the Laowyn party halted, standing silently, eyes ahead. Hendra's horn had sent the leaders of the Laowyn forward to meet the enemy in one last attempt at peace. In the past perhaps this had worked, but everyone on the field knew that today it would do no such thing.

A section of riders broke away and advanced. Ikara guessed that they were led by the High Councillor - even in his battle garb he still wore the blue and silver robes of state – and in this moment she wanted nothing more than to pull the dagger from her boot and hurl it directly into his fleshy neck. But her aim was not sure, and besides, she had reluctantly agreed to an honourable discharge of the Laowyn people today. The Laowyn faced death, but the Great Spirit had brought them a King and a small army. The odds had gone up significantly since two days ago.

She might have a chance to stab her dagger in that man's neck herself, but it would have to wait until war was declared.

By his side rode two other officials, but neither seemed competent horseman. They looked nervously about themselves, the fat one's neck rolls becoming more grotesque the more his head fidgeted from left to right; the other had thin sinewy legs that were far too long for his horse.

Before they had even reached the Laowyn party, Garesh called out unceremoniously. "I see you've taken in our cast out King!"

They were face to face with them now, Garesh's horse squelching to a standstill in the mud.

Ikara made to retort, but Trevisian spoke. "I am their King, and they are my people, Garesh. It is *you* who have been cast out as a rebel in the Kingdom of Emrilion; it is you who dishonours the Reluwyn. Desist from the violent action you plan to take, and I will have mercy upon the men who follow you in ignorance."

"Captain Aktabad, Captain Lira, your King demands your loyalty as he has always done," Johan called.

"Silence!" roared Garesh.

Ikara watched the face of the High Councillor change colour, his countenance darkening into a look so full of malice that it shocked even her.

"I am Regent by proclamation of the document King Emril signed on his deathbed."

"You were, until I married. That proclamation is now null and void. But you know that, do you not Garesh?" The King was taunting the High Councillor. "For you are the one who took my dead father's hand to sign it falsely all those years ago."

Ikara saw the opposing party look fearfully between themselves. The thin man, who had been looking at Garesh, now eyed Trevisian. The nervousness of the opposing party was clearly seen in the fidgeting of their mounts.

"An outrageous accusation - the sign of a desperate man! My Regency is all that has saved this Kingdom from your reckless apathy and evil nature. Do you not know," Garesh looked to the Elders, his gaze falling briefly on Ikara. She felt a sickness creep into her stomach. "You have a devilish creature, a *Shapeshifter* among you?"

They had all known that the accusation was coming. That the King was a Shapeshifter was something which Ikara had only ever known as legend. Even tales of the Emrilion Queen who had been executed had been silenced by the Reluwyn. Now, in the space of two days, it had not just been the King who had been discovered as a Shapeshifter. There were others among the loyal troops who had since come forward and admitted their true nature. It had changed everything - now the Reluwyn were fighting for their lives as much as the Laowyn were.

"Enough!" It was Zephenesh who raised his voice in authority. "High Councillor Garesh, have you not come to enact an Edict against my people - and the King to whom your allegiance is owed? We came in peace but it is evident you have no such sentiments."

Garesh's grip was vice-like on the reins, making the creature fret and stamp on the slippery ground. Ikara could not tell whether it was because of being addressed by a Laowyn, or because of the truth that Zephenesh calmly spoke.

"As you are aware, the King has issued a second Edict which allows us to take up arms to defend ourselves. You see us before you." Zephenesh gestured to the ranks behind him. "If you are unwilling to renounce your Regency claim to the crown of Emrilion, or to reconsider the tyrannical Edict against the Laowyn of the Kingdom, are we not done here?"

Garesh's thin lips quivered, baring fangs like a dog. He jerked his head once towards the fat man next to him, who immediately pulled out a scroll and unravelled it. The only other sound was the whipping of the Reluwyn banner in the wind picking up from the sea.

"The Laowyn Edict," came the squeaky voice of the terrified courtier. "Was presented to your people four months ago. It proclaimed a command for the people of Emrilion to rise up against the rebellious Laowyn and destroy them for the protection of the whole Kingdom of Emrilion. The gathering in the old capital of Ishalia... talia," he corrected himself, darting fearful eyes at Garesh, "is seen as the final rebellious act against the authority of the Reluwyn Empire. Our presence here is only in response to this continued rebellion."

"Very well." Zephenesh's voice seemed dispirited. He looked to Ikara. "Commander?"

She nodded and turned her cold eyes on each one of the opposing party in turn. "In response to the legalisation of the slaughter of the Laowyn, and your rebellion against our rightful ruler," she couldn't believe she meant the words. "We have no choice but to meet you in the battle you seek. If we die," her voice was rising, the call going out from the small party to the edges of the defenders ranks. "We die at the calling of the Great Spirit in freedom!"

A great roar went up from the defender's ranks. The Reluwyn defenders clanged curved scimitars against their shields, the Laowyn stamped their feet in the mud until a rumble ran throughout the ranks.

"So be it!" growled Garesh, turning his horse on its haunches and casting one last malevolent look at Trevisian. His party followed after him.

"You have made his troops question him, Trevisian. It's a good start for us," said Johan.

"It will be a good start when I'm rid of that man." The fierceness on the King's face made Ikara wonder if he too had been thinking of stabbing Garesh in the neck with a dagger. He certainly seemed capable of it.

As the defender's party turned back, Johan's horse fell in step with Ikara's.

"And so, we are at war."

"They have no idea who they are facing," she said it with some kind of excitement. By the end of this fight their fate would be decided, no more uncertainty.

"Garesh is the head of the snake, Commander."

"Yes," she replied, considering how much in this moment Johan seemed like Fidel. His calmness, the way he was thinking. Where was Fidel? She pushed the thought away. He was a civilian, and as such he would be within the city walls helping with the barricades and the missiles. "We must stamp on the head of the snake."

"If you will let me, Commander, I have a plan."

⦿⦿⦿

Kiara had never been in a battle before. Time seemed to suspend itself while she waited for the Reluwyn troops to charge at them. Their ranks were moving forwards, their jogging quickly becoming a run. The defenders held their line while the Commander cantered along its length, sword raised, crying out for their position to be held.

Then she saw the King and averted her eyes immediately, forgetting that her helmet protected her from recognition. Her heart was beating fast and her hands tingled with nervous energy.

Zeb stood by her side wearing his traditional elven armour. Its design was beautifully ornate in an unusual emerald hue. Strapped to his waist was a sword, its ivy-carved handle crafted to fit his hand alone.

He had scavenged a set of armour for Kiara so that she could stand unnoticed amongst the ranks. She could not be left inside to wait for her husband to die for her, or her uncle, or her friends. She had to be here.

Kiara saw the King pull his mount Dainus around to face the enemy and raise his sword. "Alakvalto advance!" He moved the sword in a fluid arc towards the advancing forces, his voice bellowing over the din. Kiara watched men on the front line leave their fellow soldiers to form their own contingent, none of them with weapons.

The Reluwyn broke into a run as one of them issued a loud cry and the others replied, their voices sounding far more animal than human. The transformation happened so fast it was hard to know what had happened at all. Skin became fur, ears grew, arms dropped to the floor becoming forelegs with paws. Tails sprouted, and that was now the only part visible from the defender's line. They bounded as wildcats with such massive strides that they overtook Trevisian who was galloping alongside them. The wildcats met the Reluwyn with so much ferocity that Kiara had to look away. Even from this distance she could see the blood and hear great howling cries filling the air. Before the enemy forces could collect themselves, the creatures had already slashed their way through hundreds.

"And so the Shifters have returned," murmured Zeb, but Kiara didn't hear.

Trevisian still sat astride Dainus, unchanged, the mighty black stallion sliding to a halt before a mass of pikes which were thrown across his path. With cat-like agility, the horse sprang into a jump from standstill, making it over the majority of the pikes, his hard hooves landing on the poles of those still beneath him, the sound of splitting wood cracking through the air. Kiara watched again, she saw the mighty swings of Trevisian's sword. It was all happening so quickly, and the first charge was over in a few minutes. Hendra's horn sounded and the Alakvalto retreated.

The opposing Reluwyn were left shaking and uncertain, pulling their injured and dead back through the halted ranks.

"You stay beside me all the way." Zeb's hand clapped heavily onto Kiara's armoured shoulder. All troops were readying themselves, preparing for the next advance. Kiara turned away from the wildcats and looked into Zeb's face.

"You hear me?" he asked, his voice filled with urgency.

Kiara swallowed, her neck rubbing against the coarse green tunic beneath her armour.

"You look for my armour if you lose me, understand?"

She nodded.

"Ready yourself."

She drew the silvery blue sword which had belonged to her father from her belt. She felt its weight, recalling her fighting skills, hoping they would now be enough.

At Hendra's horn, they set off as one at a dead run. All that was ahead of her were the moving shoulders of hundreds of Laowyn and Reluwyn soldiers. Zeb had brought her in at the back; even so she didn't think there'd be enough time to steady herself. Her lungs were beginning to burn with the weight of the armour, her hands and arms shaking.

When she heard the first clash of metal up ahead, the sounds of the other fighters running beside her faded. All she could hear was her own breathing, the beat of her heart, the rapid stamping of her feet in the mud that fifty other men had already run through. And before her, as she looked ahead, in the space left open on the Laowyn's right shoulders, hundreds of Enspers stared back at her. She saw them glowing, each Ensper brightening like moving lights.

"The Spirit is on our side!" cried Zeb, raising his sword and letting out a battle cry.

It was as Zephenesh had said: the men ahead were darting left and right, their swords and axes swinging. Between their shoulders, the enemy that managed to avoid the blades crashed through. They were coming at her, and she wasn't ready for this.

She felt a hand pushing her through. It was Zeb, he was with her, shoulder-to-shoulder, ready to fight.

The first weapon she connected her sword with sent a hard shock through her arm, but the pain did something to awaken her. She threw herself forward, ducking under another blow, swinging around, slicing through the air, connecting with something.

A Reluwyn came at her from the side, easily a foot taller than her, bringing a savage scimitar slice down upon her head. She deflected it with her shield, allowing the scimitar to slide off it as she stepped in the opposite direction. She brought her sword up and round but the man blocked the blow and leapt back, reassessing her. He wouldn't recognise her, as Zeb had smeared mud across her cheekbones and nose.

He tried to strike a blow as she jumped nimbly out the way; she jabbed left, right, left again, but he came at her with force, sending her back on one knee. He wrested the sword from her grip, lying the scimitar across the padding protecting her throat.   He leant forward to whisper in her ear.

"Laowyn scum."

The pressure increased. The sound of the fighting was all around them. She could smell the sweat and blood on him. Other people's blood. She slipped the dagger from the holder on her arm beneath her vambrace, plunging it with all her strength into the side of his neck. Flesh parted. Veins opened. Warm blood welled over her hand, running down her arm.

Before she could throw him off, two hands grabbed her roughly up. The dead soldier fell forward and her knife fell from his neck.

"Your sword!" bellowed Zeb, thrusting the hilt into her hand and turning to fend off another attack.

"Keep on your feet," Zeb commanded, jabbing unrelentingly at the men who now surrounded them.

She picked up the dagger and they carried on, fighting until her arms burned in their sockets, her muscles were spent and her feet felt heavy. But she wouldn't stop, none of them would; every time she began to tire, a sword blow too close sent adrenaline rushing through her body.

They had broken the line of the Reluwyn but the enemy kept coming. Wildcats could occasionally be seen bounding at the enemy. Zeb and Kiara came across one lying on the field, a pike thrust through its ribcage, the human eyes dulled in death, the carcass covered in blood. They didn't look at it for long, another was running towards its fallen comrade, ready to seek vengeance. It cast a sanguine circle of death around the fallen Shifter, taking down several soldiers. A dagger came whistling through the air, burying itself in the creature's hind leg.

"Zeb!" Kiara called, but the elf was already moving over to the animal. They took up their positions at the creature's back, fighting off the advancing soldiers. The Shifters were attracting more than their share of enemy soldiers, eager to take down the wildcats that were causing so much carnage among the ranks.

"Too many." Zeb called, his breath coming in gasps as his body tried to catch up with his rapid movements. He was tiring - they all were.

That was when they heard Hendra's horn sound three short blasts. The retreat they had been waiting for. It sounded long and loud. Now they had to fight their way back. They joined together as more and more of them turned back to Ishtalia and suddenly they were more effective again.

She saw a dark horse moving through the ranks, it was Trevisian riding across, rounding up the last troops.

"Retreat! Retreat!" he bellowed, taking down a brave enemy troop who hounded the escaping soldiers.

Kiara could see the Commander further up the line doing the same, fending off the enemy who was intent on routing them, and seeing her troops safely back. All they had to do now was get close enough to the city walls. Kiara and Zeb moved together, the wildcat they had saved limping beside them, its large head constantly moving to assess new threats.

"The markers!" cried Zeb, thrusting his sword in the direction of a pile of stones to their right just visible beyond the crowd of fleeing soldiers. It was twenty paces forward. Just a little more. Kiara almost gave up, the burning in her lungs was acute and lights flashed in the corners of her vision. She slowed but Zeb's hand was on her immediately, dragging her forward so forcefully she almost fell.

"Ten paces!" he cried.

Ten, nine, eight.

They were almost there. The flashes became brighter.

Seven, six, five. She couldn't catch another breath, there wasn't enough air.

Four, three, two. She stumbled left into the wildcat the creature hefting towards her, setting her back on her feet.

One.

"Fire! Fire!" called voices from the parapets.

Zeb's hand released her. "Breathe, Kiara, breathe." He came round to face her.

"It's all your body needs. Just air."

She barely nodded, dragging in breath, the air raking at her lungs, forcing them to open again. She slowed to a walk, each deep breath burning. The flashing became less bright, less frequent.

She became aware of the volleys from above. Missiles whistled and screamed from the city's walls. Masonry and makeshift arrows flew in grey streaks above, falling beyond the stone markers and striking enemy soldiers.

Kiara saw a stone take out a horseman, the creature screaming as the rock broke its forelegs sending it sprawling to the floor, the rider thrown headlong into the stone. She looked down at her hands, red with blood. Whose was it?

"Move," commanded Zeb.

She did as she was told, as did every other troop. They ran again, knowing it was the last leg, the last part of this section of the battle plan. They passed through the gates of Ishtalia. When the heavy doors boomed shut and wooden beams were slid across them, the first half of the battle was over. Now it was time to defend their city.

CHAPTER 28

"My lord, we've lost the right flank to the missiles. We must regather the troops." Captain Aktabad's guttural voice carried above the distant sound of the dying.

Garesh had been watching from his vantage point while the rebel force fractured his army. The Shifters had been a surprise he had not accounted for - their charge had sent fear throughout the Reluwyn ranks, the untrained rebels breaking their line without effort. When he had finally thought the tide was turning, he had watched his right flank run straight into a trap, the enemy missiles smashing men and horse alike to death.

"Regather them," Garesh rode towards the tent which had been set up after their arrival. Dismounting and casting the horse's reins to a servant, he entered the dwelling and called for his captains to follow.

Discussion was loud and inconclusive. Aktabad argued for immediate action, and Lira for the necessity of gathering weapons first.

Garesh's mood was deteriorating rapidly. Today was supposed to have been easy, the Laowyn blood finally running back into the soil, eliminating the disunity of the Kingdom and solidifying his position as the ruling Regent.

Sameedos and Mishka were there too. Their contribution to the fight had been as minimal as Garesh's and now they argued siege tactic semantics with the Captains whose bloodied and mud-spattered faces spoke volumes.

"Am I the only one capable of intelligent thought?" snarled Garesh, his voice full of venom. He rose from the chair he had been sat in for only a few moments. Nisa had been offering him wine which now spilled across the desert furs on the floor - furs that were from the same creatures as those that had just decimated the ranks.

"You speak of a siege upon a city that was slighted. Have you not noticed the damage to the southern parapet? They only have a flimsy patchwork of makeshift rubble blocking the slighted walls.

"It could be breached," agreed Aktabad.

"Then why are you still here?" hissed Garesh, sending Captains and advisors scurrying like rats from his tent.

He could hear the cries of his Captains as they rounded up the army outside. In that first attack the rebels may have levelled the playing field somewhat, but now they mistakenly thought they were safe within their walls.

He could almost taste the power that would all be his if he could crush this rebellion - and their King along with it.

The Reluwyn were a warrior race. What spoke to them most was victory in battle, and if Garesh let those Shifters live they would become a symbol of power the Reluwyn people could not ignore. They had to die. *The King* had to die.

"Whore!" He moved away from the opening of the tent, through which he could see hundreds of soldiers reforming lines and ranks.

"Yes, master." Nisa had become his personal concubine publically since the King's departure, and had since witnessed the true character of Garesh.

He grabbed hold of her by the neck.

"You realise that this is all your fault? You promised me power and the sole ability to wield it, and you could not take care of one rebellious King? Barely a man, and you could not deal with him. You owe me a dead King, woman."

He threw her to the floor, her back hitting a chair and drawing from her a small cry.

He leant forwards, a cruel smile licking up his lips at her pain. "When they breach the wall," he said, his breath acrid upon her face, "you will go in as my assassin, find the King and his wife, and kill them with this." He took a dagger from the table and placed the blade across her open palm. "You boast to me of Spirit Conjuring – conjure all the darkness you can and put it in this blade. I want them to suffer."

Nisa had told Garesh what cursed weapons could do, the pain they could inflict, the torment of the dark spirits.

"I want them to suffer, and if you fail..."

Taking her hand in his, he folded her fingers around the blade and held them tightly there, forcing the sharp edge into her skin, and causing a trickle of blood to fall from the edge of her hand across her legs and onto the floor.

"I will draw more than a few drops of blood from you."

He bent closer, forcing his lips on hers, biting at her bottom lip to make it bleed. "Get dressed." He gestured to the soldier's clothing on the chair behind her.

"Aktabad!" he almost screamed the name. The Captain came in a few moments later.

"Nisa will be accompanying the contingent who breaches the wall first. Keep her well within the ranks, but when she is in the heart of the city, set her loose."

"My lord High Councillor, I have plenty of trained scouts if that is what you need."

Garesh couldn't explain his actions to the Captain. Even if the King was seen as a renegade, no assassination of him would be tolerated. "Did I ask for your opinion?"

again he screeched, like a bird who's prey was about to be feasted on by another.

The Captain maintained control of his face and voice. "My lord High Councillor, I shall see it done."

He left the tent and Garesh sat down to watch Nisa dress. Maybe she would die on this mission. The thought left Garesh with a small thrill. Payment for her failures. Still, if she succeeded he would have to kill her anyway.

⊙⊙⊙

The enemy forces took all night to breach the walls after they had regathered. Everyone had taken it in turns to sleep and launch whatever missiles they had left. By dawn, short of dismantling the walls themselves to create missiles, the rebels could do nothing but wait.

Ikara had ordered them to do nothing. Let the Reluwyn waste their energy taking apart the south wall - her troops would be well rested when they breached it. They had other tasks within the walls, building small barricades from the courtyard back towards the meeting hall at the heart of the city. Old doors, dock debris and loose masonry had been thrown in piles to make the enemy advance all the more difficult. More than that, this generation of soldiers had not been inside Ishtalia, and the King and Commander had agreed to take advantage of that fact: the barricades had been placed to encourage the enemy into the narrow, tightly winding streets and alleys that were etched into the hillside.

Ikara split her army into small contingents of five to ten men and spread them throughout the city. It would be attack and hide warfare, allowing the army to gain ground in the small streets before picking them off.

They had lost a few hundred men and twelve of the Alakvalto contingent in the plain battle, but nothing compared to the near thousand lost by the Reluwyn under Garesh. The element of surprise had paid off well.

Fidel could hear the Reluwyn gathering outside the broken section of the wall. Ikara had refused his re-commissioning in her army but inside these walls every man could fight, even the untrained women sat in upstairs rooms, ready to hurl whatever they had collected from upper windows.

The roar outside the walls swelled. Without the advantage of surprise, Fidel knew they would face the true might of the Reluwyn army. The enemy's battering ram thudded against the piled up debris again and again, making the white stones of the city floor shake.

Another few hits and the wall would give in. Rubble from the top of the makeshift structure loosened and tumbled down into the courtyard. No one needed to avoid the falling pieces, the courtyard was empty, the contingents placed around the edges behind barricades, waiting for the enemy army to pour in. There was not much talking now as everyone listened to the steady pounding, the battle cries of thousands. They had made good headway in the first battle, but surely this would decide their fate.

"Where is she?" The King's question rang across the courtyard.

Fidel could see fear in those dark eyes, though the tone of his voice was as fierce as ever.

"I don't know Trevisian, she was with you just yesterday."

"I know that!" The King reached up a hand and pulled off the helmet he had been wearing. His black hair was slick with sweat, and yesterday's blood and grime covered his face. "I've been with the Commander and when I returned to our quarters she was gone."

Did that mean the King had not slept since yesterday? Evidently not. And the Commander? Fidel looked up to a building near the inner side of the courtyard to where he knew Ikara was standing on the roof with Hendra. They had been up there some time assessing the Reluwyn forces over the wall, and she looked as aloof and distant as ever.

"We can go and find her," Johan offered.

"They are about to breach the wall," warned Fidel as another shudder went through the ground. Great chunks of rubble rolled into the courtyard and Dainus picked up his hooves nervously. Trevisian reined him away from the centre, coming around to the inside of Fidel and Johan's barricade.

"We must take up our positions," Johan urged.

"What if she's…" The King looked away over the wall to where their fallen comrades lay.

Johan grabbed a hold of Trevisian by the arm, his height making it easy despite the horse. "You must go, I promise we will find her." The King looked ready to say something more, but a final blow on the wall sent him cantering towards the building on which Ikara and Hendra had been stood.

Sections of the wall were falling freely now, rumbling down to the floor. Fidel saw the King join Ikara - they had both taken a leading position before, but this time they would be coordinating the small contingents from behind. Standing at the frontline, Fidel realised that this may well be his last battle. He felt a lancing pain as he thought of the things he still wished to say, which might now never be uttered.

"Cheer-up!" Calev and Jaik came out from a building behind Johan and Fidel's barricade.

"What?"

"Looking all pale like, you can't lose heart now, not when we're going to have a jolly time running this lot around the city and picking them off like flies."

"Or any other insect like creature."

"Yep, exactly, Jaik."

They both faced Johan, their small wiry frames dwarfed by the warrior. Unintimidated, they stuck out a hand each.

"Johan the Radichi – we've been assigned to your contingent."

Fidel watched Johan's eyes flick between the identical twins. It had taken him long enough to know them apart and he had lived with them for the past few years.

"Is this a joke?" Did Ikara doubt his battle skills this much that she had sent these two to watch him like a child?

"Probably," answered Calev.

"We wanted the frontline position. It's kind of our expertise."

He was right, thought Fidel, this is what they had done in the forest for the last few years only this time they exchanged living columns and canopies for stone buildings and streets.

"It's going to be so much…"

There wasn't time for the rest of that sentence. The wall which had been threatening to give way finally crashed down in a tremendous crescendo. A huge 'v' appeared in the centre, as the majority of the rubble disintegrated before the battering ram. There was a brief lull while the enemy drew back their battering ram, and then they poured in like water bursting a dam.

Soldiers came thick and fast, scimitars raised, eyes feverish with blood lust and screams of death coming from their mouths.

"Ready brother," Calev put a hand on Jaik's forearm.

"Ready," returned his brother, grasping his arm briefly before both of them drew out pairs of long daggers.

Jaik looked mischievously round to Fidel and Johan. "First wave's ours."

And before anyone could object, the twins had leapt over the barricade with the same agility they'd displayed in the forest and set to work.

Fidel and Johan watched as if they were viewing some kind of death dance. Calev and Jaik moved as one, daggers sweeping in elegant arcs, the only sign of battle being the streaks of blood as soldiers fell around them.

Calev ducked away from a lethal scimitar strike, allowing Jaik to lunge forwards and stab the sword arm of one of their attackers. Jaik then ran backwards with as much grace and speed as he would have done forwards, his brother signalling when to lean, before springing up behind him and throwing one of his daggers at another soldier's throat. Calev finished off the wounded soldier with a sharp, quick stab through the armhole of his armour and into his chest. Jaik retrieved the dagger and they set to work again, swiping and leaping and turning all in one long macabre pirouette of death.

"Break!" Calev shouted after a good twenty minutes of fighting, and with as much speed as they had exited the barricade they returned, Fidel and Johan running out to take their place.

They wielded their heavy swords, fighting back to back, taking out men on either side until the horn would signal when they were to pull the enemy forces into the narrow winding streets of the city and press the rebel's advantage.

It was not long in coming, the ram's horn sounded over the fighting again. This time however, the enemy troops were less inclined to follow.

"They've learnt from before," said Johan.

"Look!" cried one of the twins, Fidel saw the enemy climbing the broken wall, grouped close together.

"They're protecting someone!" shouted Fidel. He jumped to the side, showing his nimbleness despite his stature, just as an enemy blade caught his non-sword arm. He ground his teeth against the pain, feeling the blood rush from the wound and drip from his fingertips. "Retreat!" he called.

He caught sight of Calev eyeing his wound.

"I'm fine — and whoever it is in that crowd will come out quicker if we lead them in."

Behind them another wave of enemy troops swarmed down the broken wall. There was no time to argue. The four ran for the streets and alleys.

CHAPTER 29

F idel pulled hard upwards, his teeth clamped on the piece of cloth Johan had cut from a dead soldier's uniform. The wound burned, but the makeshift bandage would at least stop the bleeding for now. They were crouched in the ground floor of a small building. The enemy had not come this far yet, and both he and Johan had taken advantage of the break whilst the twins carried on. But they soon heard the clinking of chainmail and breastplates behind them.

"They're coming up behind us. They're quick."

"My sword."

"Shhh! Wait until they're upon us."

The rapid conversation that had just taken place was not between Johan and Fidel. It came from across the street. One of the voices was unmistakably female.

Johan locked eyes with Fidel at the same time, recognition dawning on both faces. They were up and out of the door before a minute had passed, just in time to see Zeb's green armour disappear beyond a barricade a little further down the street. Both Johan and Fidel ran after him, ducking down before the enemy soldiers were upon them.

Zeb and Kiara were shocked for the first few moments before they recognized the colour of the uniforms and the men who wore them.

"Trevisian is looking for you," Johan said, accusation in his voice.

Kiara's unmistakable hair was tied back in a tight plait, just visible below her helmet. Fidel saw her chin come up at Johan's words, "I fight with the rest of my people." There was dried blood and mud on her face. She had been fighting before today.

"Stubborn."

"She does what she knows is right," Zeb looked as irritated as Johan.

"At least we've found her, the King can finally be calm," said Fidel, ever the pacifier.

Johan didn't answer, his mouth set in a grimmer line than usual. His powerful thighs launched him up over the barricade before any more conversation could be made. He went for the first soldier while Fidel took on another, laying him out dead after a few minutes. They both turned on the biggest one at the same time, plunging their swords into his neck, almost severing the head from the body. Together they were a terrifying force.

Others were coming and soon Zeb and Kiara were fighting too. Fidel and Johan quickly went to Kiara's side but it was evident after a very short time that she needed no protection. She lunged forwards, out of their protective area and took on a small wiry Reluwyn. Her sword moves were not as powerful but they were twice as quick, taking her enemy by surprise as she wounded him and sent her blade through flesh and bone at his neck.

"Well fought." Fidel clapped a hand on her armoured shoulder.

Zeb was at her other side.

"It's not over yet," said Johan.

"We're ready," replied the elf.

They took on ten more, slowly retreating along the narrow streets, hiding in buildings and ambushing their advances. When one of them was tired, they hid in one of the buildings while the others fought. If they continued like this it would go on for hours.

They had just finished off the last of the recent soldiers, Zeb sustaining a small slash to his leg, when something different happened. A group of soldiers, shielding a hooded figure, moved down the street.

Fidel looked to Johan. "A trap."

The rebels closed ranks, shoulder to shoulder. The soldiers came towards the party. Fidel saw the eyes of the hooded figure, looking over the shoulders of the advancing enemy troops. He saw the figure flash a dagger and lower their shoulders. Whatever the person had seen they were now ready to fight.

The soldiers suddenly fanned out, taking one of the rebels each. Johan and Fidel were drawn off to the left, Zeb had two soldiers in the centre and Kiara was off to the right.

"Something's not right." Fidel looked over to her.

The fighting was short and sharp. These soldiers were not tired - unlike the others who had been fighting for several hours now. The rebels were fighting for their lives against an enemy with more energy, more power, more numbers than them.

Fidel saw Kiara take down a soldier in close quarters with a dagger. As soon as he fell, the hooded person came forward. The menacing figure moved quickly to Kiara who waited for her next opponent. Fidel managed to send his sword through the leg of his purser giving him time to move over to where the Queen stood.

As he ran he heard the clatter of hooves. Up ahead the King appeared in the street, his massive beast taking up the width of it as he swung Dainus' quarters round in a rapid halt. The King's eyes connected with those of his wife and that was all the distraction the hooded figure needed.

The attacker lunged forward. Kiara parried, but it was too late to prevent being knocked off balance. She had lost her sword in the last fight and all she had was her dagger, the same weapon as her assailant. The difference was, Kiara was on her knees. Kiara's arms moved as rapidly as they could, slicing from side to side, fending off the vicious attack.

Even as the realisation of a targeted attack dawned in Fidel's mind, he was at Kiara's side. But the assailant knew exactly where to hit her. She had repeatedly struck the Queen on one side, making Kiara defend herself with that arm and from her lower position her strength faltered. She groaned with pain. This wasn't an attack of war, this was an assassination.

The King only had to look once for the fire of urgency to set itself alight within him. He pushed his horse forward, taking down two soldiers with the weight of the beast's hooves. His eyes were wild, his face desperate, his actions reckless. If it were not for Johan he would have had a sword in the back; the appearance of Calev and Jaik saw the enemy finished off completely.

But it wasn't over. Kiara's assailant paused over her, and spoke. Fidel couldn't hear the words, but he knew it was a woman. With a savage upward stab the woman plunged her dagger up under Kiara's breastplate making her scream. She fell backward, her shoulder forgotten, her hands clutching the blood which bubbled up from her abdomen.

Before Fidel could take her down the woman turned, saw the King and ran towards him regardless of the flailing hooves. She grabbed a piece of mane and swung upwards, the dagger, covered in Kiara's blood, now aimed straight at the King's throat. But before it reached him, he vanished. At least that's what Fidel thought.

The black horse bucked, twisting, sending the woman hurtling to the floor. Where was the King?

Then Fidel saw the dark, sleek fur appear around the side of the horse's legs. The horse stood beside the creature, stamping his hooves and snorting at the injured woman on the floor. Like a streak of lightning, the wildcat shot forwards, vicious claws out, fanged mouth open, tearing at the weak body. Screams rent the air, the animal in a frenzy as blood sprayed across one of the street walls. The woman was dead long before the wildcat-King was finished. When he was done he howled, and with an incomprehensible shimmering changed back into human form.

He was covered in blood, hot and sticky across his face, his clothing somehow covered too. He ran forward to where Zeb knelt beside Kiara. All of the colour had drained from her face, the blood collecting in a pool around her.

"Do something!" Trevisian bellowed at the elf.

Zeb remained unshaken. "My healing satchel, it's in the meeting hall."

He didn't need to say anything more. Trevisian was already shifting into a horse and galloping down the street.

"We need to move her. Support her everywhere you can." Johan pulled off his Laowyn shirt, bundled it up and handed it to Zeb who pressed it against Kiara's wound. She convulsed, crying out.

"Take her into the building, we may be safe there."

Everyone surrounded her, raising her and moving her as gently and quickly as they could.

"Who was she?" Fidel didn't look back at the bloodied heap that had been the assassin. He didn't ever want to see that again.

"A concubine from the harem. She was Garesh's Favourite." Johan replied, trying to squeeze his massive bulk through a door without pushing into Kiara. "He must have sent her here to kill them both."

"He's afraid of losing," Calev said defiantly.

"I can't believe she was fighting." Jaik looked down at Kiara's pale face.

They had reached the top floor and pulled together what they could to make a wooden surface on which to lay her. Blood was still oozing from the wound, though

Johan's shirt had slowed it. Zeb kept it pressed against her abdomen as they lowered her.

"Everyone out." Zeb ordered.

No one moved.

"We're not going anywhere," Jaik responded.

"I have to undress her to treat the wound. Out." Zeb repeated, turning back to his patient.

No one argued after that, Calev and Jaik left to wait at the entrance to the house to direct the King when he came back. Fidel lingered. "Johan said that the woman was known for her dark arts."

Zeb's hand was over the wound holding the shirt. "I can feel it," he replied, the line of his mouth sharpening. "I'm not sure I can save her." The acknowledgement was only between them, a moment of vulnerability.

Fidel put a hand on the elf's back. "Don't tell the King." If he felt half the love that Fidel felt for Ikara, it would destroy him.

"I've killed her."

Fidel took him by the shoulders. "She's not dead yet, Zeb." He turned to leave. "You protected her as best you could."

"It wasn't enough."

"It's not your fault," repeated Fidel.

Fidel left him there, staunching the flow of lifeblood from Kiara's body.

✪✪✪

Trevisian kicked the door for the third time to no avail. He finally shifted back, knowing he was without a weapon if any enemies were to approach. He hammered his fists in the grooves on the door that his hooves had just made.

"Open up, in the name of the King!" he shouted at the wood. His voice frayed as he repeated himself, but after a few moments a head appeared somewhere above him.

"It's barricaded, my Lord King, we cannot."

It was Zephenesh.

"Zeb's healing satchel," Trevisian cried. "Kiara's dying, quickly!"

After the colour had drained from Zephenesh's face he disappeared.

A few moments later a call was given and the satchel was thrown down. Trevisian caught it in his teeth, in horse form once again.

He worked his way quickly back through the streets, jumping any obstacles and trampling soldiers underfoot. All the while he pushed furthest from his mind the possibility of what had happened since he'd gone. She wouldn't die, Zeb was with her. He didn't much like the elf but he had seen him heal. She couldn't die. He couldn't lose her. Sweat coated his flanks, white saliva foaming and dropping from the corners of his mouth and flecking his chest as he charged on.

He had left the Commander in a fighting party to the south of the city, hoping to find Kiara. They had been holding up well when he had left. The rebels were losing far less troops than the enemy forces but Ikara had noted a contingent Garesh was holding back. The troops had not yet reached the meeting hall where the vulnerable rebels were hidden. As thoughts of the battle that raged around him, of the friends who fought for their lives and the lives of others right now, it all seemed pointless. She couldn't die.

He reached the house, shifting and running up the stairs, ignoring the twins at the door. Zeb just held out his free hand. They had played these roles before, but this time the stakes were higher. She was paler than Trevisian had ever seen her, but she was awake. He went straight to her, looking into her open blue eyes.

"She can't see you."

Trevisian looked to him and then back at Kiara.

"What do you mean?"

"I mean she can't see you." Zeb was pulling herbs and bandages from his bag. He drew out a book, opening the pages which were scrawled in a language Trevisian had never seen before. The elf's eyes were rapidly scanning the words but, as if feeling a sudden wave of compassion, he spoke as he read. "The dagger was cursed with dark spirits. She was chosen by the Great Spirit long ago, but the evil spirits with which the dagger was cursed are fighting for her body. If I heal the physical wound, there is a chance she can fight the spiritual battle."

"And if she can't?"

Zeb ground leaves in a mortar, peeling back Johan's bloodied shirt and showering the contents over the wound. "Don't ask me questions I can't answer." He closed his eyes and took a deep breath, raising his hands palm downwards over the wound. Trevisian could hear him muttering something, his lips making almost imperceptible movements.

He looked back to his wife's eyes. The blue seemed veiled by darkness, something she couldn't see through. As Zeb continued, her movements became more distressed and soon she was thrashing on the wooden surface.

"Hold her," commanded Zeb.

Trevisian was already taking hold of her arms. He didn't want to hurt her but the power she was exerting was immense, far more than she should have in her current state. He pinned her down, the back of his eyes pricking as he saw the pain in her face. What if he lost her?

It went on, her struggling and Zeb whispering. As Trevisian grew tired, Kiara seemed to increase in strength. Then just as suddenly, she stopped. Zeb's hands jerked away and he lowered his cheek to just above her mouth. No breath.

"Get away from her," Trevisian thrust his heavy arm against the elf, sending him reeling backwards. He turned back to Kiara, pinching her nose, his mouth descending on hers. He pushed his breath into her lungs.

"Don't die."

He breathed another lungful into her, watching her chest rise.

"Don't you dare die!" he shouted, he pushed another breath into her. Still nothing. He looked in her eyes. They were dead. Her body wasn't moving. Her chest wasn't rising. Her skin was too pale.

"No, no, no…" he began, his voice raising in an urgency that paid no heed to enemy soldiers or the battle outside. "No!" he shouted, his voice cracking and hoarse, the cry coming from a place so deep within him he thought he broke with the sound. He raised his fist and dropped it in one hard pound upon her chest, the sound followed by a cracking.

"Wake up," the cries became softer, heavy tears filled his dark eyes as he looked on to the bloodied and muddied face. "Breathe and wake up, my love." He cupped her cheek.

All of a sudden her body violently contracted and then, rolling sideways, raising the wound from the table, she sucked in air, emitting a deep groan.

"Zeb," he called to the one he had thrown against a wall just a few moments ago. "Zeb."

"I must clean and bind the wound," said the elf, as if she hadn't just died and come back to life.

Trevisian stepped back in submission.

"They almost won for a moment," said the elf in response to the unasked question. "But she's fighting."

"What does that mean for her?"

"We won't know until later. Calm her."

Trevisian did as he was bid, returning his hand to her cheek, kneeling beside the makeshift table until his face was level with hers. He kissed her cheek.

"You're alive," he murmured.

She didn't reply, she just looked at him, her eyes clearer than they were, but something still lurking there. She made to speak but he stopped her, wiping the tears of pain from the tracks they made across her nose and cheek.

"Wait until Zeb has dressed your wound."

"Trevisian," Johan was at the door. "The enemy forces have advanced, it's only a matter of time until they reach the meeting hall."

"I'm staying here. Take Fidel and the twins and go."

"There's nothing more you can do here. Go."

Trevisian's eyes were dark when they turned on the elf. "I'm staying."

Zeb shrugged without bothering to return the glare. He carried on his ministrations and Trevisian carried on murmuring to his wife. Johan didn't wait. There was another battle to be won.

CHAPTER 30

"We've lost the southern section of the city."

Ikara received Captain Hendra's news in an abandoned market square in the midst of the city's winding streets. Several bands of rebel contingents had converged here ready to meet the enemy again.

"We're not far from the meeting hall. The King should be back by now." Hendra looked in vain for the missing ruler.

"He went to find his wife. We can't rely on him." She wondered where Fidel was. Was he dead? She had not admitted it out loud, but she had not recommissioned him for this very reason, and he'd disobeyed and fought anyway. He could be wounded somewhere and she wouldn't know. "How many other contingents are still fighting?"

"Without the twins, we're relying on relay runners to reconnoitre the streets. They say at least fifteen contingents are still active and mostly whole."

"We're still losing men, even if it's not as quickly as Garesh." The enemy Reluwyn had superior numbers. It was how they'd win. They could keep throwing men at the rebels until the rebels were killed, no matter the cost to their forces.

"We can't let them get to the meeting hall. Use the relay runners to pull back the contingents to the street before the hall. We must amass and meet them together if we're to have any chance. They can't be allowed to get to the meeting hall and soon they'll be slipping through no matter how well we know these streets."

Hendra nodded and passed on instructions to several men behind him who were covered in sweat and panting. The Laowyn Captain looked no better Ikara noticed. Her look was enough to provoke a response.

"I'm not as young as I once was, Commander, but I've no intention of lying down just yet."

She replied with a grim smile and then hefted her sword back into her hand. "Move out!" she gave the order.

They met no enemy forces on their retreat to the meeting hall - a good sign.

"Form lines. Square!" yelled Hendra, his sword raised to signal the command.

Ikara faced downhill to where the enemy would appear. The street had high walls on either side forming the heart of the city, the hardest area for an enemy to penetrate. Along with the other contingents filtering into the street came Fidel.

He ran alongside Johan, the twins up ahead of them. They took up their stations in the space she had meant to leave between herself at the front and her soldiers.

Fidel was alive.

"Good to see you, Commander." Calev drew one of his long daggers up in a mock salute against his head. She didn't react.

"Aye! Always nice to see you survived without our expertise – a miracle!" Jaik grinned.

"Insubordination in these extremes would earn you a flogging within the Radichi forces, boy."

"The giant speaks." Jaik stared up at Johan mockingly.

"Shhh! You'll make him mad."

"He's already mad," replied Johan, the corners of his mouth twitching. He was beginning to like these identical warriors.

"Like little boys. How can you fight with such grace and talk with such crudity?" asked Fidel.

The sound of his voice sent shivers down Ikara's back.

"This may be our last stand, little boys," said Johan.

"I'm twenty-seven," replied one of them

"As am I."

The twins puffed their chests out and found their formation line again.

Ikara could hear Hendra barking orders to each section of men as he came down the line to join her. He stopped before the final contingent. "You were the last to arrive. How long do we have?"

"They were minutes behind us." Fidel answered.

"Where's the King?"

"Kiara fell. There was an assassin."

Ikara's ears were attentive to every word.

"Zeb and the King are attempting to heal her."

"Will they be found?"

"It depends. Garesh is sure of a victory, he's trying to make it straight to the heart of the city so there's a chance they will go undetected."

Hendra returned to his position beside Ikara. She straightened her shoulders. This was it.

It made her jump, the hand that was suddenly placed on her arm, but she knew it was him. She didn't shake it off, but let it rest there. Everything they had argued about seemed so inconsequential in the face of death. The fingers tightened for a brief moment and then the hand was gone.

She took in a breath.

"For the Laowyn! For the loyal Reluwyn! For the King!" As she shouted, she raised her sword, its point piercing the air above her and the remaining Shifters made their transformations. She heard a clattering of hooves, much closer than the footsteps of the enemy. Garesh?

Then they saw him, the black horse without rider or saddle who moved rapidly up the street. A cheer broke out from those in hiding as they looked over the meeting hall doors, yelling and crying, waving their arms. Ikara watched the horse suddenly shrink and become upright, its face drawing in.

"My Lord King," she inclined her head.

"Commander."

He walked past her and placed a hand on the Radichi's shoulder.

"My place is with my people."

Johan nodded.

The King then turned and stood shoulder-to-shoulder with the Commander.

"I don't suppose you have a sword free?"

She couldn't help but let the corner of her mouth curve upwards. "My Lord King." She handed him her second sword. "Be careful with her."

He nodded, drawing himself up fully.

"Let us send them all to the Spirit Realm."

"Let us," she agreed.

They were all tired, but the sight of their King rallied them as nothing else could. A great war cry was rising among the ranks as the enemy appeared in front of them.

Garesh was behind the first three lines, his eyes flashing over his enemies with something akin to insane greed. Whatever he was shouting was drowned out by the rebels' yells.

"On second thought." The King pushed the sword back into Ikara's free hand.

All she could do was watch. This time his fur was sleek, his form more compact, the head square - and the yowl he let out was pure wildcat. He sprang forwards into the enemy's front line, ignoring the blades that caught at his flanks.

Ikara was mesmerised for only a moment, and then raised her sword.

"Forwards!"

"He's going for Garesh!" called Johan from behind her.

"To the King!" shouted Fidel.

The front line converged around the back of the King as he slashed and clawed his way through the two enemy front lines - just a little way further and he would have clear access to the head of the enemy army.

Garesh saw it too. Ikara twisted to avoid a blow, moving forwards with a couple of elegant slashes which sent two soldiers to their deaths. She looked up, seeing the High Councillor desperately trying to turn his horse, regardless of his own troops beneath his hooves.

"Stop him!" she shouted, hearing the crack of metal on metal so close it made her ears ring. She turned and saw Fidel deflecting a sword from where her head had just been.

She smiled quickly. He put a hand to her arm and she grasped it with her hand, then turned to strike out at another line of advancing troops. The King was almost upon Garesh and the rebel lines were advancing behind her. Fidel parried an attack from the left. Cries from the wildcat rent the air.

"Ikara!"

Fidel ran past her, taking the full force of a blow in her blind spot that would have met with her exposed side. He fell forwards with a grunt, the enemy's blade rammed between the bottom of his breastplate and the top of his armoured belt.

She screamed, lunging forwards and slicing indiscriminately.

"To the Commander!" Hendra's command sounded far away. She was already turning away from the battle line to where her saviour knelt in a slump.

"Fidel!" She threw her sword down, oblivious to the rebel soldiers who closed ranks around them. Her long-fingered hands reached out, trying to hold him up as his heavy form fell back on the street. Blood ran from his mouth. She reached across his armour, pulling futilely at the straps, trying to release him as she shook with great racking sobs.

Everything around her faded. She heard no sound of the wildcat King as he took down the leader of the enemy; she didn't see the King shift back; she heard nothing of the surrender, as the enemy raised their swords in horizontal lines to be taken by the rebels; she was deaf to the cries of joy that filled the streets. It was all as nothing.

"Commander." Hendra's call was far away.

"Get off! Get off!" Ikara screamed, frenzied. "I loved you Fidel." She reached forwards again, her arms slinging themselves over his still shoulders, burying her head next to the one who no longer looked up, touching his hair, stroking his cheek. "I love you, you can't leave me, I love you. I said it, I love you. You have to come back to me, I told you I love you." Her face tightened, pulling together in painful creases. The ache in her chest rose to her throat, her eyes filling with more tears, tears of loss, tears of grief. No, this can't have happened. He can't be gone. He was always there. "You can't leave me." She collapsed, her body broken with the loss.

Hendra's hands came around her shoulder. "Let him be laid out, Commander."

"Ikara. He called me Ikara." She obeyed the hands that pulled her backwards. She watched the Radichi take Fidel's shoulders and pull until he lay on the street with the other fallen. His legs were pulled straight and they drew the sword from his abdomen.

Johan's face was heavy with grief, though Ikara did not see it, she saw nothing but Fidel. She felt the heavy hand of the Radichi upon her shoulder. "He was a great warrior." He walked away.

"He isn't gone." She rocked on her knees. "He isn't gone." She scrambled towards him, and Hendra let her. She laid herself down beside him, resting her head on his shoulder, remaining there for a long time.

✪✪✪

"You've done an excellent job, Johan of the Radichi," said Zephenesh, his hand coming out from his sleeve and stretching out to take in the encampment of the surrendered Reluwyn soldiers.

"Thank you, Elder Zephenesh." He bowed, the long strands of knotted hair falling over his shoulders.

"The King tells me that you will not be with us for much longer?"

"I will help him to stabilise Emril city, and then my path lies south."

"To your homeland?"

Johan nodded, a small smile creeping across his face.

Zephenesh smiled too. "We have averted a crisis."

"Zephenesh," Hendra came up to them from the direction of Ishtalia's open gates. "You are needed by the Elders."

"Are the people already causing trouble?" asked Zephenesh, a rueful look taking over his face. "They are saved by the Great Spirit from death just yesterday and already they complain."

Hendra shrugged, his old shoulders weary in their armour, but his face seemed more relaxed than it had in days. "Some wish to stay, some wish to go."

It wasn't surprising - the Laowyn were in their old capital again, and many would not want to leave. The elves and rebel Reluwyn, along with the Alakvalto, were unlikely to want to stay.

Zephenesh sighed, tucking his hands in the opposite sleeves of his tunic and following Hendra out. "What does the King say on the matter?"

"He has not left your niece since the defeat. I daren't take him from her side."

Zephenesh nodded and they carried on talking as they entered the city. Everywhere the mood was light. Children were playing together, mothers laughed with each other and even the troops, who had seen the bloodshed first-hand, were enjoying themselves in the day after battle. Grief had yet to fall over the ecstasy of survival.

Zephenesh knew that Hendra had taken on much of Ikara's responsibility since the death of Fidel. She had stayed with the body through the night, preparing it for burial with all the formal customs of the Laowyn. His funeral was to be today, and he was to be given the full honours of a Laowyn Captain. He would be sent to sea, just as tradition had dictated when the Laowyn had occupied this great city before, just as Kiara's parents had been buried at sea.

Hendra had given Johan the responsibility of performing a census on the defeated Reluwyn troops and charging the rebellion leaders. When those who were now loyal to the King could be counted they would march back to Emril city and take back the King's rightful crown. Zephenesh's thoughts moved to Kiara who was still recovering from the stab wound. The King had been with her since, and Zephenesh had come to sit with her for some time during the night. He knew his role as protector was no longer - she had another now, and he was fierce.

They reached the hall which had been a refuge but stood once again as a place for the Laowyn Eldership to meet. The meeting was inconclusive, and Zephenesh drew it swiftly to a close. There was little point in continuing when equal weight was given to those who wished to make Ishtalia their permanent home, and those who wished to return home. The King must be consulted.

Zephenesh left Hendra in the southern market square, turning northwards towards Kiara's tower. He was waved through by Alakvalto guards who had been assigned to Royal's protection. Nothing was certain, and even though the Shifters were now known it did not guarantee safety.

As he climbed the steps, a heavy-footed weariness overtook him. He had not slept since the night before last, and it was taking its toll. He was not as young as he used to be, and at a time when there had been loss as well as victory, the grief was as exhausting as the battle.

He pushed the door of the room open after knocking briefly. He hadn't received an answer on his last two visits and he was sure he would not receive one now. An oil lamp flickered on the bedside table. The King was sat next to Kiara on the bed, one of his hands clasping hers.

As Zephenesh came closer he saw to his delight that Kiara was sat up, her eyes open, looking at Trevisian. Those clear blue pools turned upon her uncle soon enough and recognition dawned there.

She tried to speak but the sound did not come immediately. Trevisian picked up a flask from the floor and held it to her lips. She drank without argument and then smiled at her visitor.

"Uncle."

"My child." He came towards the opposite side of the bed to the King, perching gently upon its edge and reaching a hand towards her. "It is good to see you awake. How do you feel?"

"Alive."

Zephenesh heard the whisper of a chuckle from her husband.

"And the wound?"

She pulled weakly at the covers. There was no strength left to her and the King took over her actions without request, moving the material away to reveal a perfect silver line on her stomach, no longer than a thumb.

"Where is your saviour?"

"You mean the one who almost got her killed?"

"Trevisian." She placed a weary hand over that of her husband's. He did not calm immediately but relented on the line of conversation.

"We have not seen him since she woke. He said he had things to do."

Kiara's mouth took on a wan smile.

"I'm glad for his knowledge," Trevisian conceded.

"His magic," Kiara corrected.

The King rolled his eyes causing a rasping chuckle from his wife.

"You change to the form of an animal and you laugh at healing magic?"

"I think the events of the past few days show us just how little we know of the world." Zephenesh remarked gently.

"I don't care about the world," Trevisian replied.

"Your actions saved all of us."

"What actions?" asked Kiara softly.

"Your husband came back into the fray, after he knew of your safety, to lead the final charge. He killed Garesh himself. Once the head of their army was taken down the rebels surrendered."

"A great warrior." She smiled but then her hand suddenly twitched drawing Trevisian's attention immediately back to her. Zephenesh looked too, seeing her eyes suddenly take on the haunted look that the King had seen several times through the night.

"I can see them," she whispered, "I can see them."

"It's okay." The King moved in towards her, his hand coming around the back of her head and drawing it into his shoulder, quieting her anxiety. He stroked the thick hair, rubbing a hand across her back, waiting until the crying stopped.

"I'm sorry," she said, drawing away from him after a few moments, rubbing at her eyes. "When I see them they're so real."

They didn't know what she saw, or who she saw, not even she understood. The visions had started with the stab of that dagger. Zeb had listened to her description last night but had not ventured to express his thoughts aloud though they had all seen the knowing in his eyes. Zephenesh had watched the King pin the elf against the wall and command him to talk but the steely eyed elfin man had refused and Kiara's pleas had freed him.

None of them knew what it meant, or if it would stop, but for the moment, the fact that she was alive and safe was enough.

"I know you do not wish to leave her," said Zephenesh, turning to the King. "But some of the Laowyn are talking of settling here, while others wish to return."

"Let them."

"You do not understand; your Kingdom needs balancing."

"No, *you* don't understand! I shall not leave her again."

He had risen from the bed and Zephenesh knew argument was futile. He must go. He rose himself, squeezing Kiara's hand and smiling at her before turning to leave.

CHAPTER 31

"You must go."

"Do not tease me!" Trevisian was pacing, his hands raking back through his dark hair. He hadn't slept in days and it was showing. His patience was fraying.

"Come here." She patted the bed beside her and he came to her reluctantly. She made him lay next to her, his head upon her stomach, all thoughts of the stab wound gone.

"I thought I lost you."

She stroked the lengths of black hair back from his face. Her breathing was steady and his soon slowed.

"Don't do that to me again."

She continued to stroke him, as if that was all the reply he needed.

"What if the visions never go away?"

"They will," he replied with confidence.

She sighed.

"Fidel's funeral is soon and I wish to go," she said, her hands stilling upon his hair, then they picked up their rhythm again. "But you should sleep first."

"You should be the one sleeping, you barely slept last night."

She did not wish to. The visions came more easily in her dreams.

"Sleep," she said again, continuing to stroke his hair. He did not take any more persuading, his weariness weighed on him like a heavy blanket and he was asleep and dreaming after a few minutes.

When they rose to go to Fidel's funeral, Trevisian bore most of Kiara's weight. She wore one of his tunics, tied in at the waist with a silk sash, respectful both in its modesty towards the Laowyn and in its origin towards her husband's people. Although her wound was healed she felt a spiritual weight dragging at her. She was weary in mind and body and it was making her vision and thought hazy.

Many were the gathered, and many were the dead. Pieces of wood had been scavenged from all over the city to make funeral rafts. Oil lamps burned on each head, lighting the faces of those as they floated. Mourners stood in the waters holding them steady, waiting for the goodbyes to be spoken before they let go.

In front of the shadows of those gathered in the dusk of the docks, Hendra's horn was raised. Kiara could see his silhouette down by the water. He let out a low note, far different from that which had announced the battle yesterday. Was it only yesterday? It seemed so far away already.

A breeze picked up from the mouth of the harbour, flowing in towards the bystanders. Kiara shivered, Trevisian's arm around her instinctively tightening, her body pressed back against his chest.

"We have seen great victory and we have seen great loss." Ikara's voice, oddly hollow, echoed out. All her fervour and silent determination had evaporated like the dew with the dawn. "The Great Spirit has watched over our nation and taken back those he wished to call home. We commend our loved ones to him - let these lights lead them to peace in the Spirit Realm."

Kiara watched her move towards the water. She wasn't wearing armour but had exchanged it for a long flowing robe, looking more feminine than she ever had before. The soft, fine material trailed on the floor at her feet, clinging to her statuesque figure. The great rebel leader looked suddenly vulnerable, human. She bent to the nearest of the rafts. Kiara moved one step forward, Trevisian with her. She could see the outline of the one who lay on the raft. Fidel. In the light of the lamp she made out the fair hair which lay around his clean face. She could see the strong line of his chin, the handsome nose, his eyes closed in peaceful sleep. Ikara bent to him, the oil lamp behind her head, throwing her and Fidel's faces into shadow. There was the outline of her lips touching his, resting upon them a kiss. Her lips withdrew half an inch. She was saying something to him. Then she lay a hand over his heart and though her face was in shadow, the droplets of water which fell from her eyes onto Fidel's tunic caught the light like crystals.

She rose then, pushing at the raft as she did so, and all along the dockside others did the same, pushing the dead towards the vast expanse of water which was rapidly becoming black oblivion in the night beyond the harbour walls.

"Goodbye," whispered Kiara, her eyes still fixed on the silhouetted figure of Ikara on the shoreline.

"I must pay my respects." Trevisian released her but she was not alone for long, Johan taking up her husband's place as her support.

She watched Trevisian as he made his way down to the water's edge. Bearers of new rafts, those carrying the bodies of wildcats and other animals were brought down after him.

"Our kind will no longer live in secrecy. The Alakvalto and the Reluwyn are one people, and today we mourn those who fought for the protection of the innocent, for the unity of our Kingdom. From this day forward, I will appoint emissaries from every race within my Kingdom and equality will be part of our new unity. Tonight we mourn the loss of those who will never see this new future." He took a flaming torch from a soldier beside him and touched it to the first of the rafts.

It was then that Kiara realised they were pyres. The Laowyn saw this as barbarous, even now whispers were passing between people like diseases, but there was something heroic casting those to the flames who died in battle. If there was to be a future for this Kingdom and all of its races, the first dangerous step had been taken.

CHAPTER 32

"You're going!?" Kiara was shocked. Only last night they had burned or sent their dead into the sea. Today she was setting out with her husband for the capital, not knowing what they were to find when they got there. There was a fractured Kingdom which needed to be bound back together.

Zeb shrugged. "Your uncle is to be the Laowyn emissary to the Reluwyn court – a high honour."

"Don't change the subject." She narrowed her eyes at him. She had been watching him load a small pony for the past half an hour, just after she had heard from Johan that he and the elf would be leaving.

"I am being called elsewhere. Have no fear," he looked sideways at her and winked. "I have no doubt we will meet again."

"Called somewhere? What do you mean called?"

"There you are." Trevisian came upon them, his hand immediately going to her waist as if marking his territory. He eyed the elf with the same dislike he always had.

"Zeb's just up and leaving!" She threw her hands up, expecting the same reaction from her husband. "He says he's called elsewhere."

"Called?"

"That's exactly what I said."

Zeb sighed, turning away from his pony and slinging his hands on his hips while he looked at the future King and Queen of Emrilion. "I have been called," he said frankly. "Besides, you and Trevisian have much work to do to stabilise this Kingdom. I will leave with Johan and travel south with him. Then I'll go across the Western Sea."

Kiara hesitated, looking to Trevisian, remembering their conversation in the palace library, debating the existence of land to the west. Zeb had just confirmed it, but he didn't give her time to ask questions.

"I will see you again. I will need your help in the future." And he left it like that, as cryptic as he always was.

"Very well." Apparently Trevisian understood it better than she did. She looked between the two, a feeling of exasperation building within her.

"This is ridiculous - your place is here."

"My place has never been here."

Kiara couldn't argue with it. It felt irritatingly true.

"Who has called you?"

"Those I work with. The Spirit Realm is out of balance. I was called here to help avert the genocide of your race, Kiara."

Her capacity for shock was being tested.

"Your Great Spirit aided me, he directed me to you, even when we were in the cell in the Laowyn Resistance I knew you would be used. The Great Spirit has marked you out – both of you. The battle here has averted the genocide the dark spirits wanted. And now your marriage," Zeb swallowed, "will cement the equilibrium that has been created. But there are other places that it is not so. For now I am being called onwards." He looked straight into Kiara's eyes in that penetrating way he always did when he chose to really see someone.

"Kiara, what has happened to you will have its effects. You must believe that there is a greater purpose. Now I must go." He paused like that, standing there, for a moment and Kiara took the opportunity to hug him without his permission. His sinewy frame was hard and she held him only briefly until she heard him breath again. Then she released him and smiled.

"I shall never be able to thank you enough for my hair." She smiled, attempting to lighten the mood. She would never be able to thank him enough for saving her life, and she knew it was down to his knowledge, the knowledge that he had never fully explained the origin of, that she had been rescued.

"I shall miss you." She moved back towards Trevisian, his hand finding her waist once again.

Zeb swung himself up onto the small pony, and looked back down at her. With a frankness that denied all pretence he spoke, "I love you Kiara." He said it simply, as if it meant nothing and everything all at the same time.

And in that moment, knowing she loved Trevisian, knowing that nothing could ever change that, she stared back at him and replied, "I know."

Trevisian said nothing but Zeb nodded, as if something which had been needing to be done had been done, and then he left without uttering another word. Kiara knew she would see him again – he had said so himself, he would call upon them for the battle of the spirits. She was sure now that what they had just gone through was only the beginning.

About The Author

P. J. Keyworth, also known as Philippa Jane Keyworth, and known to her friends as Pip, has been writing since she was twelve in every notebook she could find. Originally trained as a horse-riding instructor, Philippa went on to become a copywriter before beginning a degree in History and graduating with First Class Honours. She now works in Digital Marketing and part-time as an author.

Philippa has always written stories and believes that, since it is one of her loves and passions, she always will.

She has dabbled in a variety of genres, and has settled for the time being in both fantasy and historical romance. An interesting combination of research and imagination Philippa believes it is important to escape into a world you want to be in. This is why she writes stories that will draw you into the characters' joys and heartaches in a world apart from our own. Philippa has three historical romance novels out, each a standalone with indomitable heroines and lovable heroes. Her third novel, Fool Me Twice (Madison Street Publishing, 2016), follows the exploits of a notorious female gamester whose carefully orchestrated life is turned upside down by the arrival of a most ineligible gentleman...

The Edict marks her first fantasy novel and is the first in a trilogy. Following the stories of strong yet markedly different heroines, the world of The She Trilogy will see the ultimate struggle between good and evil played out in a fantasy world, bringing it to the brink of destruction.

AUTHOR'S NOTE

I hope you've enjoyed reading *The Edict*. I must confess I love this story, but I think I'm allowed to confess it because the backbone of this story is true. The plot of *The Edict* is based on the book of Esther in the bible.

Esther is one of my favourite bible characters (along with Ruth, who forms the basis of my debut novel *The Widow's Redeemer*). Esther is a young and beautiful Jewish woman who starts life as no one particularly important and ends up saving a whole people. During the time Esther lived, the Jews were living under the rule of the Persians. The Persian King, Xerxes, was married to a woman called Vashti who treated him with contempt and as such he decided to find a new wife. In order to find another Queen, his government sent out a proclamation to gather all the eligible and beautiful maidens of the empire to come and partake in twelve months of beauty treatments and then spend a night with the King. If he wasn't too fussed, you'd end up relegated to the harem as a concubine, potentially never to be called again. One woman would be chosen to be the new Queen. It all seems quite patriarchal and yes, it was, this was thousands of years ago. It was onto this scene that Esther came. She was beautiful, her Jewish name was Hadassah, and she lived with her cousin Mordecai as her parents had died. When the maidens were chosen, Mordecai urged Esther to not tell anyone she was Jewish, so she didn't. She hid her race and she was chosen. Now, here's where our stories differ, my story doesn't follow that of Esther's absolutely, so it's worth remembering that, as Esther actually went to the palace without running away dressed as a boy and being captured first! You'll also notice that Xerxes was already King, unlike Trevisian. I guess after reading the book of Esther quite a lot (it's only short if you want to give it a go), I was struck by how the individual people must have felt in the midst of this great empire with all its tumultuous events.

So, Esther ends up at the palace and the eunuch, who looks after the concubines and is in charge of beautifying the maidens, favours her because she is beautiful in character and looks. He spends time telling her what the King likes and doesn't like. Eventually it's her turn to be called. She goes in and she finds favour with the King. She ends up becoming the Queen of all of Persia. How about that? Seems like a fairy-tale doesn't it? Well, hang on a minute. Right after Esther becomes Queen, her cousin Mordecai, who sits at the gates of the palace regularly, hears two of the King's officers conspiring to assassinate the King. Mordecai goes and warns Esther who in turn tells the King, the men are dealt with and this event gets recorded in the King's record book. Remember that because it comes up later. In the meantime, let me tell you about this guy called Haman. Haman was one of Xerxes officials and he hated the Jews. He wanted power and when Xerxes orders everyone to kneel before him, and Mordecai doesn't, Haman becomes furious and decides he wants to destroy all the Jews. Haman goes to Xerxes and explains that the Jewish people are different to the Persians, they don't obey the King's laws and it's not in the King's best interest to tolerate them. Can you guess who Haman is in *The Edict*? He convinces the King to put his seal to an edict which tells all the people of the country to destroy, kill and annihilate the Jews, young and old, women and children. Mordecai learned of this and he goes to Esther. He asks her to go to the King on her people's behalf. Esther explains that she has not been summoned by the King in thirty days and if you go to the King without being summoned the King can have you executed. Mordecai challenges Esther, telling her that she won't escape even though her race is kept a secret and says,

> *"...And who knows but that you have come to your royal position for such a time as this?"*
> ### Esther 4 v 14

Esther then asks Mordecai and all the Jews he can gather to pray and fast for her saying this courageous thing,

> *"...I will go to the king, even though it is against the law. And if I perish, I perish."*
> ### Esther 4 v 16

Esther goes to the King and he agrees to see her. She asks him and Haman to a banquet. They come for a meal several times and Haman thinks he's really in favour with the royals. In the meantime, with his plan to annihilate the Jews in full swing, Haman decides to plot the murder of Mordecai himself. That night, the King can't sleep and orders the chronicles to his room so he can read. There he finds the record of Mordecai saving him from an assassination and the next day he gets Haman to give Mordecai lavish clothes and has him ride a horse so the people can see him exalted for what he did. Haman, needless to say, is not best pleased. And all this time, the Jews' lives hang in the balance. The King and Haman come to a final banquet with Queen Esther where she steels herself to ask the King to save her people. She does it, admitting her race and putting herself in a position of complete vulnerability and calling out Haman at the same time. The King, who loves Esther, orders Haman be executed and, as he cannot repeal the edict which is already underway for the Jewish people's demise, he issues another which legalises their ability to fight for their lives against those who try to kill them.

It's the most amazing story. It's got it all, love, royalty, family, assassinations, courage and bravery! God had a way of saving an entire nation through one woman, and that one woman had to step up, risk her life and be courageous. What a woman!

NEXT READ

WORKS BY P. J. KEYWORTH

HISTORICAL ROMANCE NOVELS
The Widow's Redeemer
The Unexpected Earl
Fool Me Twice

HISTORICAL ANTHOLOGY
Castle, Customs, and Kings: True Tales by English Historical Fiction Authors

CONNECT WITH P. J. KEYWORTH

www. philippajanekeyworth.com
Twitter: @PJKeyworth
Facebook: /philippajane.keyworth

CPSIA information can be obtained
at www.ICGtesting.com
Printed in the USA
LVOW11s1721161117
556556LV00003B/617/P